BEHIND THE BACK OF THE NORTH WIND

Edited by John Pennington & Roderick McGillis

Illustration by Arthur Hughes (1869)

Behind the Back of the North Wind:
Critical Essays on George MacDonald's Classic Children's Book

Copyright © 2011 Winged Lion Press

Winged Lion Press
Hamden, CT

All rights reserved. Except in the case of quotations embodied in critical articles or reviews, no part of this book may be reproduced or transmitted in any form or by any means, electronic or mechanical, including photocopying, recording, or by any information storage or retrieval system, without written permission of the publisher.
For information, contact Winged Lion Press www.WingedLionPress.com

Winged Lion Press titles may be purchased for business or promotional use or special sales.

Cover illustration: "The Wind and the Swallows" by Frank Papé from *At The Back of the North Wind* (Blackie & Sons, 1911).

10-9-8-7-6-5-4-3-2-1

WINGED LION PRESS

ISBN-13 978-1-935688-41-9

Dedications

I (John Pennington) would like to dedicate this book to my partner and colleague Karlyn Crowley, who was always enthusiastic and supportive of the project, and to our daughter, Ada Mae, who can look forward to reading *At the Back of the North Wind*.

And I (Rod McGillis) offer dedication to Stephen Prickett, David Robb, and to two colleagues no longer with us, William Raeper and John Docherty, friends and friends in MacDonald Studies.

Permissions

Coleman O. Parsons, "The Progenitors of *Black Beauty* in Humanitarian Literature." *Notes and Queries* (19 April 1947): 156-58. Excerpt used by permission of Oxford University Press.

Robert Lee Wolff. *The Golden Key: A Study of the Fiction of George MacDonald.* New Haven: Yale UP, 1961: 148-60. Excerpt reprinted by permission of Yale University Press.

Richard H. Reis, *George MacDonald's Fiction: A Twentieth-Century View* (Eureka, CA: Sunrise Books, 1989): 82-84. Reprinted by permission of Sunrise Books.

Rolland Hein. *The Harmony Within: The Spiritual Vision of George MacDonald.* Grand Rapids: Eerdmans, 1982: 44-53. Excerpt reprinted by permission of the author.

David S. Robb. *George MacDonald.* Edinburgh: Scottish Academic Press, 1987: 110-28. Excerpt reprinted by permission of the Scottish Academic Press.

Lesley Smith, "Old Wine in New Bottles: Aspects of Prophecy in George MacDonald's *At the Back of the North Wind.*" *For the Childlike.* Ed. Roderick McGillis. Metuchen, NJ: Scarecrow Press, 1992: 161-68. Reprinted by permission of Roderick McGillis and Scarecrow Press.

William Raeper, "Diamond and Kilmeny: MacDonald, Hogg, and the Scottish Folk Tradition." *For the Childlike.* Ed. Roderick McGillis. Methuen, NJ: Scarecrow, 1992: 133-44. Reprinted by permission of Roderick McGillis and Scarecrow Press.

John Pennington. "Alice at the Back of the North Wind, Or the Metafictions of Lewis Carroll and George MacDonald." *Extrapolation* 33.1 (1992): 59-72. Excerpt reprinted by permission of Kent State University Press.

Naomi J. Wood. "Suffer the Children: The Problem of the Loving Father in *At the Back of the North Wind.*" *Children's Literature Association Quarterly* 18.3 (1993): 112-19. Reprinted by permission of the Children's Literature Association.

Roderick McGillis. "Outworn Liberal Humanism: George MacDonald and "The Right Relation to the Whole." *North Wind: A Journal of George MacDonald Studies* 16 (1997): 5-13. Reprinted by permission of the George MacDonald Society and the author.

Alison Milbank, *Dante and the Victorians*. Manchester: Manchester UP, 1998: 179-82. Excerpt reprinted by permission of Manchester University Press and the author.

U. C. Knoepflmacher, *Ventures into Childland: Victorians, Fairy Tales, and Femininity*. Chicago: U of Chicago P, 1998: 228-68. Excerpt used by permission of the University of Chicago Press and the author.

Lisa Hermine Makman, "Child's Work Is Child's Play: The Value of George MacDonald's Diamond." *Children's Literature Association Quarterly* 24.3 (1999): 119-29. Excerpt reprinted by permission of the Children's Literature Association.

Fernando J. Soto. "The Two-World Consciousness of *North Wind*: Unity and Dichotomy in MacDonald's Fairy Tale." *Studies in Scottish Literature* 33-34 (2004): 150-68. Reprinted by permission of *Studies in Scottish Literature* and the author.

Colin Manlove, "A Reading of *At the Back of the North Wind*." *North Wind: A Journal of George MacDonald Studies* 27 (2008): 51-78. Reprinted by permission of the George MacDonald Society and the author.

Jean Webb, "Realism, Fantasy and a Critique of Nineteenth Century Society in George MacDonald's *At the Back of the North Wind*." *A Noble Unrest: Contemporary Essays on George MacDonald*. Newcastle: Cambridge Scholars, 2007. 15-32. Reprinted by permission of the author.

Lauren A. Mills, illustrator for *At the Back of the North Wind*, Boston: David R. Godine, 1988. Five illustrations reprinted by permission of the artist.

Contributors

Rolland Hein is Emeritus Professor of English at Wheaton College, Wheaton, IL. He teaches classes on the works of the Wade authors at the Wade Center and is the author of several books on George MacDonald, including *The Harmony Within* (revised 1999) and *George MacDonald: Victorian Mythmaker* (1999).

U. C. Knoepflmacher is the Paton Foundation Professor Emeritus of Ancient and Modern Literature at Princeton University. He has authored, edited, or co-edited a dozen books in 19th Century British literature and in children's literature, and has written over a hundred articles in these two fields. His children's book, *Franny, Randy, and the Over-the-Edge Cat Person*, appeared in 2009 and his edition of *Victorian Hybridities: Cultural Anxiety and Formal Innovation* in 2010.

Lisa Hermine Makman has published essays in such journals as *The Lion and the Unicorn* and *The Children's Literature Association Quarterly*, and has authored the Introduction and Notes to Kipling's *The Jungle Books* (Barnes & Noble, 2004) . She is visiting professor of English and Education at the University of Michigan.

Colin Manlove is a literary critic with an interest in fantasy. His *Modern Fantasy: Five Studies* (1975) is a seminal exploration of fantasy literature. Since then, many books have followed including, *The Impulse of Fantasy Literature* (1983), *Christian Fantasy: From 1200 to the Present* (1992), *The Fantasy Literature of England* (1999), and *The Order of Harry Potter: Literary Skill in the Hogwart's Epic* (2010).

Roderick McGillis taught English and Film at the University of Calgary. He has edited two collections of essays on George MacDonald, *For the Childlike* (1992) and *George MacDonald: Literary Heritage and Heirs* (2007). With John Pennington, he edited a scholarly edition of *At the Back of the North Wind* (2011).

Alison Milbank is a professor at the University of Nottingham in the theology and religious studies department. Her research and teaching focus on the relation of religion to culture in the post-Enlightenment period, with particular literary interest in non-realist literary and artistic expression, such as the Gothic, the fantastic, horror, and fantasy. She is the author of *Dante and the Victorians* (1998).

Coleman O. Parsons (1905-1991) was a scholar, author and professor of literature, last as Professor Emeritus of English at CUNY's City College. He was the author of an important book on Sir Walter Scott, *Witchcraft and Demonology in Scott's Fiction* (1964), and he wrote extensively for academic journals in the United States, Scotland, England, and Germany.

John Pennington teaches English Literature at St. Norbert College, WI. He is co-editor of the George MacDonald journal, *North Wind: A Journal of George MacDonald Studies*. He has published essays on George MacDonald, Lewis

Carroll, J. K. Rowling, Ursula LeGuin, Peter Beagle, and others in such journals as *Journal of the Fantastic in the Arts*, *Extrapolation*, *The Lion and the Unicorn*, and *North Wind*.

William Raeper (1959-1992) was born in Kirkcaldy in Fife. His most significant work is his biography of George MacDonald (1987). He won a scholarship to Hertford College, Oxford, where he read English and had the rare distinction of being twice elected President of the Junior Common Room. He is the editor of the collection of essays on MacDonald, *The Gold Thread* (1990).

Richard H. Reis received his Ph.D. from Brown University. He is the author of *George MacDonald* (Twayne English Author Series, 1972). He was Chair of the English Department at the University of Massachusetts, Dartmouth.

David S. Robb teaches at the University of Dundee. His publications include studies of George MacDonald, Sydney Goodsir Smith, Hugh Miller, and Muriel Spark. Recently, he has completed a book on Alexander Scott (1920-89) and is editor of Scott's *Collected Poems*. Robb has also served as Joint General Editor of the Scottish Writers series and General Editor of the Scottish Classics series.

Lesley Smith was at one time teaching at the University of Guelph.

Fernando Soto holds a Ph.D. from The University of Glasgow with a thesis devoted to the works of George MacDonald and Lewis Carroll, and he is co-editor of *North Wind: A Journal of George MacDonald Studies*. Fernando is interested in MacDonald's and Carroll's use of Greek, Roman, and Hebrew mythology. His latest work (on Carroll's use of Aeschylus' *The Furies*) will be published in an upcoming issue of *The Lion and the Unicorn*.

Jean Webb is Professor of International Children's Literature at the University of Worcester, UK, where she is Director of the International Forum for Research in Children's Literature. Her publications include: *Introducing Children's Literature: Romanticism to Postmodernism* (2002) with Deborah Cogan Thacker, and *'A Noble Unrest': Contemporary Essays on the Work of George MacDonald*, editor (2007).

Robert Lee Wolff was a Professor of History at Harvard University. He was the author of *The Golden Key* (1961), the first major study of MacDonald's fiction. His other works include, *Strange Stories and other Explorations in Victorian Fiction* (1971), *Gains and Losses: Novels of Faith and Doubt in Victorian England* (1977), and *Sensational Victorian: The Life and Fiction of Mary Elizabeth Braddon* (1979).

Naomi Wood is an associate professor at Kansas State University where she teaches undergraduate and graduate classes in children's literature, young adult literature, and the Victorian novel. In addition to her work on MacDonald, she has published on other Victorian writers, Charles Kingsley, and Robert Louis Stevenson, and on twentieth-century and contemporary writers of fantasy.

Contents

Introduction — v
John Pennington and Roderick McGillis

The Progenitors of *Black Beauty* in Humanitarian Literature — 1
Coleman O. Parsons

Fancy and Imagination — 6
Robert Lee Wolff

The Imaginative Fiction — 15
Richard H. Reis

Outward Signs of Inward Grace — 20
Rolland Hein

Fiction for the Child — 26
David S. Robb

Old Wine in New Bottles: — 33
Aspects of Prophecy in George MacDonald's *At the Back of the North Wind*
Lesley Smith

Diamond and Kilmeny: — 41
MacDonald, Hogg, and the Scottish Folk Tradition
William Raeper

Alice at the Back of the North Wind, — 52
Or the Metafictions of Lewis Carroll and George MacDonald
John Pennington

Suffer the Children: — 63
The Problem of the Loving Father in *At the Back of the North Wind*
Naomi J. Wood

Outworn Liberal Humanism: 82
George MacDonald and "The Right Relation to the Whole"
Roderick McGillis

Imagining the Afterlife: 90
The Fantasies of Charles Kingsley and George MacDonald
Alison Milbank

Erasing Borders: MacDonald's *At the Back of the North Wind* 92
U. C. Knoepflmacher

Child's Work Is Child's Play: 109
The Value of George MacDonald's Diamond
Lisa Hermine Makman

The Two-World Consciousness of *North Wind*: 128
Unity and Dichotomy in MacDonald's Fairy Tale
Fernando J. Soto

A Reading of *At the Back of the North Wind* 148
Colin Manlove

Realism, Fantasy and a Critique of Nineteenth Century 175
Society in George MacDonald's *At the Back of the North Wind*
Jean Webb

Selected Bibliography 193

Index 199

Acknowledgements

A special thanks goes to the following students from St. Norbert College, who were diligent in their researching and copyediting of the manuscript: Kristen Susienka, Paige Caulum, Christopher Connors, Sarah Titus, and, in particular, Gretchen Panzer. A particular thanks goes to Gretchen and Sarah for creating the index for this book. The St. Norbert College English faculty members need mention, for they graciously and generously allocated funds to cover permission costs.

We would also like to thank U. C. Knoepflmacher and Robert Trexler for agreeing with us that publishing a volume of critical essays dedicated to *At the Back of the North Wind* was a worthy project.

A Note on the Texts

The articles in *Behind the Back of the North Wind* come from a variety of sources—books, articles, and other collections of critical essays. For consistency, we use endnotes for the articles, even when the original used footnotes. When we provide an excerpt of an article or book chapter, we took the liberty of reordering endnotes. Any obvious editorial or factual errors in the selections have been silently corrected.

Introduction

"I have been asked to tell you about the back of the North Wind." So begins George MacDonald's *At the Back of the North Wind*, a novel serialized in the magazine *Good Words for the Young* from 1868-1870 (MacDonald took over as editor late in 1869) and published as a single-edition novel by Strahan in 1871. Let's follow MacDonald's lead: it seems appropriate in this introduction that we tell you about the creation of *Behind the Back of the North Wind: Critical Essays on George MacDonald's Classic Children's Book*, the name of the collected essays that you are now holding in your hands. The creation of this volume follows from our preparation of a critical and scholarly edition of *At the Back of the North Wind*, published by Broadview Press (2011). While working on this edition of the novel, we realized the richness of the critical commentary on MacDonald's book, and we felt a collection of the major commentary on *North Wind* would prove to be a useful complement to the scholarly edition. We hope that this double focus on a classic Victorian children's book will generate further conversation.

Behind the Back of the North Wind is the first collection of critical essays devoted solely to MacDonald's *At the Back of the North Wind*. There are excellent volumes of collected essays on MacDonald—*For the Childlike*, *The Gold Thread*, *A Noble Unrest*, *George MacDonald: Literary Heritage and Heirs*—but none of these collections focuses on this seminal work. Only the recent collection, *Lilith in a New Light*, concentrates on one particular work by MacDonald. Our collection follows in *Lilith's* light. But why a volume devoted to *At the Back of the North Wind*? A flippant reply might be, "Why not?" But there is a compelling case to be made for the literary centrality of this fantasy novel.

Michael Patrick Hearn, who has edited *The Annotated* Wizard of Oz, *The Annotated* Christmas Carol, *The Annotated* Huckleberry Finn, as well as the important *The Victorian Fairy Tale Book*, agrees. He argues that "*At the Back of the North Wind* is one of the most remarkable children's books in the English language." This is certainly high praise. "Curiously," continues Hearn, "although it is said to be the best-selling of George MacDonald's many works, it can hardly be called popular" (303), especially if we compare it to two other works of fantasy—Lewis Carroll's *Alice's Adventures in Wonderland* (1865) and *Through the Looking-Glass* (1872). Or as Alice might say about *North Wind's* lack of popularity, "Curiouser and curiouser!" The comparison to the Alice books is not, however, entirely fair. Carroll's books have proved to be best sellers in the rare sense of books that have become an integral part of Anglo-American culture. They have spread beyond the confines of the book: Tim Burton's 3-D movie updating of *Alice* was a smash hit, as is the interactive e-book for Apple's immensely popular iPad. *At the Back of the North Wind*, for its part, has rarely been out of print since its first appearance, and this fact suggests staying power, if not best-seller popularity. It is popular in the sense of a book that has found a niche, and also in the sense of a book that appeals to a popular audience, that is an audience of children.

At the Back of the North Wind, in many ways, is as strange as the wonderland that Alice tumbles into—and as important a literary work. On the one hand, the novel is part social realism as practiced by Charles Dickens, exposing the harsh working conditions of the poor and the tenuous safety of children who are often required to act like adults: Diamond, the male hero of *North Wind*, befriends Nanny, a young street-sweeper who is neglected at home; Diamond becomes a moral touchstone to a drunken cabman, who promises to change his ways; Diamond takes on breadwinner responsibilities after his father's sickness by driving his father's horse-drawn cab throughout the often-dangerous streets of London. On the other hand, the book is an otherworldly fantasy that takes Diamond on a journey to a mystical land at the back of the north wind. Behind North Wind's back is an enticing place, yet it is the land of death. In addition, the book toys with narrative cohesion: it has an interpolated fairy tale—"Little Daylight"—nonsense poems that rival Edward Lear and Carroll, and sequences where characters relate their dreams in narrative form.

Yes, *At the Back of the North Wind* rivals the *Alice* books. *Behind the Back of the North Wind* positions MacDonald's novel in the center of Victorian literature generally and children's literature specifically. The essays gathered here argue for the importance of the book in generic, thematic, and historical terms. As we noted above, this volume complements the critical edition of *North Wind* that we have edited for Broadview Press. Now teachers and scholars will have a definitive scholarly edition of the novel and a dedicated collection of critical essays that can be used in the classroom and beyond.

North Wind, with its fusion of the real and the fantastic, is a touchstone for MacDonald's writing career, for he was torn between his fairy writing and the need to produce realistic novels that were more marketable. C. S. Lewis, the most important popularizer of MacDonald we have, claims in *The Allegory of Love* that MacDonald, a "mystic and natural symbolist," was "seduced into writing novels" (232). With *North Wind*, however, MacDonald is able to

Introduction

appease the call of the realistic narrative and the desire to promote fairyland. *Phantastes* (1858) and *Lilith* (1895) are MacDonald's adult fantasies; these play with fairy-tale structures and use "portals" that bring the protagonists from the real world to fairyland. But in *North Wind* MacDonald is more sensitive to the interchange between these two worlds, which becomes central to the novel's larger themes. We might say that in this book MacDonald found a way to satisfy his poetic ambitions by creating a world in which the noumenal and phenomenal interpenetrate.

North Wind is MacDonald's attempt to satiate his desire for faery and the public's desire for the more mundane found in the realistic novel. The novel hinges on the interrelation between the fantastic and the real. We see a preview of this approach in an odd early novel, *Adela Cathcart* (1864). Adela, like Miss Coleman in *North Wind*, suffers from some spiritual malady and one method of healing is to subject Adela to stories, particularly fairy stories—"The Light Princess," "The Shadows," and "The Giant's Heart" appear in the first edition of the novel. This therapeutic quality of literature reflects Matthew Arnold's and John Stuart Mill's claims about the power of Wordsworth's poetry. In *The Prelude*, Wordsworth confesses that "there are in our existence spots of time" (XI, 258) where "our minds / Are nourish'd, and invisibly repaired . . ." (263-65). MacDonald's fairy tales and fantasies are such spots of time for Adela and the reader. Mark Twain writes in a letter to MacDonald that he would like another copy of *North Wind*, "for our children's sake; they have read and re-read their own copy so many times that it looks as if it had been through the war." And Twain writes to William Dean Howells: "But how desperately more I have been moved to-night by the thought of a little old copy in the nursery of *At the Back of the North Wind*. Oh, what happy days they were when that book was read, and how Susy [died in 1896] loved it! ... Death is so kind, benignant, to whom he loves, but he goes by us others and will not look our way" (qtd. in Greville MacDonald 458). While *North Wind* is primarily about Diamond's preparation for death, or more life as MacDonald would argue, the novel has a homeopathic quality that nourishes the reader. We cannot necessarily say *that* about the Alice books.

North Wind is MacDonald's longest sustained fantasy narrative for younger readers, and the only one that focuses on the dual worlds. *The Princess and the Goblin* (1872), also published in *Good Words* while MacDonald was editor, *The Princess and Curdie* (1883), and *The Wise Woman, or The Lost Princess: A Double Story* (1874) round out MacDonald's full-length fairy tales/fantasies for children, but these tales are set in a Grimm-influenced world that is not directly connected to the real world. *At the Back of the North Wind*, in other words, is unique in MacDonald's canon.

MacDonald continued to write shorter fairy tales modeled after those from *Adela Cathcart*, and these are set in a distinct fairyland out-of-time from the real. "Cross Purposes" and "The Golden Key" (certainly a precursor to *North Wind*) appeared in *Dealings with the Fairies* (1867). H. A. Page, writing a review of *Dealings* for the *Contemporary Review* in 1869, claimed that MacDonald, "more than any other in our country, has raised child-literature to the level of high art. He has a pure, graceful phantasy. There is in his book a soft, gradual dawning of beauty and delight, like the clear light of a northern morning, as bracing as it is clear, he lifts and lightens and inspires" (23), thus signaling the importance of MacDonald to the evolving field of children's literature. In a glowing review in 1871 of *At the Back of the North Wind*, *The Athenaeum* claims that it "is a poet's own book. Whether children will understand the whole of it or not, they will be sure to love it for the sake of the lovely spirit by which it is animated, and for the charming sights and sounds from Fairyland and Dreamland, which come and go like the colours of the sky at sunset." The reviewer ends with this comment: "The whole work is woven into a lovely tissue, partly dream, partly vision, and partly a story which will be charming for readers of all classes and all ages" (303). *The Athenaeum's* contention about *North Wind* mirrors comments that MacDonald will make in "The Fantastic Imagination" (1893):

> "Everyone ... who feels the story, will read its meaning after his own nature and development: one man will read one meaning in it, another will read another." (7)

> "For my part, I do not write for children, but for the childlike, whether of five, or fifty, or seventy five." (7)

> "The greatest forces lie in the region of the uncomprehended." (9)

At the Back of the North Wind does indeed appeal to "readers of all classes and all ages" and challenges readers—whether of five, or fifty, or seventy five—to decipher the narrative complexity. All this mirrors MacDonald's self-reflective intent in "The Fantastic Imagination." In critical parlance, *North Wind* is an example of cross-writing—that which appeals to both the child and the adult. Some might call it fiction for all ages.

What does it mean, however, to write for both the child and the adult? As Jacqueline Rose points out, "children's fiction rests on the idea that there is a child who is simply there to be addressed and that speaking to it might be simple." But that assumption is problematic, Rose argues. She posits that such children's fiction is not possible, reflecting "the impossible relation between adult and child" (1). U. C. Knoepflmacher, in turn, argues that Victorian fantasies, in particular, require a delicate "balancing act" between child and adult, for "by the last third of the nineteenth century, when fantasies

Introduction

for children flourished in England, authors went one step further by self-consciously admitting their own role as mediators between the states of childhood and maturity" (498). At the end of *North Wind*, the adult narrator tells us that, "I saw at once how it was. They thought he was dead. I knew that he had gone to the back of the north wind" (378). The reader understands that the entire novel has been the narrator's (shall we say MacDonald's) attempt to prepare us for Diamond's death, for his continued journey to—and beyond—the back of the north wind. Death may not be the most comfortable theme for a children's book, but it is a recurring theme, not only in Victorian children's books, but also in children's books today.

Certainly Dickens relished in his ability to mine death melodramatically and sentimentally to reinforce his social outrage—think of Little Nell in *The Old Curiosity Shop* (1840-41), or Paul in *Dombey and Son* (1846-48), or the street-sweeper Jo in *Bleak House* (1851-53). These books, like Charlotte Brontë's *Jane Eyre* and George Eliot's *The Mill on the Floss* and *Silas Marner*, were embraced by children and adults, but these writers, one is tempted to argue, had an adult reader in mind. MacDonald seems more intent on addressing the child reader. Diamond is akin to Oliver Twist. Oliver's fate, interestingly, mirrors the traditional fairy-tale ending: he lives happily-ever-after. Diamond's death should reassure us of eternal life that is found in the fairy tale, but he must leave the known world for the unknown, thus complicating our reaction. When Robert Lee Wolff writes that *At the Back of the North Wind* may give "children the shivers" as it continues "delighting and disturbing generation after generation of children" (148), he enters the central debate. What constitutes children's literature? What precisely is cross-writing? How, exactly, should we approach a text like *North Wind*?

And that is the goal of *Behind the Back of the North Wind*: to focus on the critical interpretations of such an enigmatic work. The essays in this volume grapple with the fundamental tensions between the adult and child that are at the forefront of MacDonald's novel, as he explores the ways to present death to the child and adult reader. You will find essays that run the gamut from those situating MacDonald's Christian world-view in *North Wind*, to those examining the tension between fantasy and reality, to those grappling with *North Wind* as children's literature. In every case, the essays illuminate a complex book.

The organization of *Behind the Back of the North Wind* is straightforward: the essays are arranged chronologically, which provides an intriguing look into the evolution of criticism on *North Wind* and gives the reader a holistic sense of criticism on MacDonald's novel. In *Toward an Aesthetic of Reception*, Hans Robert Jauss claims that "the historical life of a literary work is unthinkable without the active participation of its addressees. For it is only through the process of its mediation that the work enters into the changing horizon-of-experience of a continuity in which the perpetual inversion occurs from simple reception to critical understanding, from passive to active reception, from recognized aesthetic norms to a new production that surpasses them" (19). Jauss's "aesthetics of reception" (19) situates a writer's critical reputation over time as readers' needs and expectations change. "The coherence of literature as an event," writes Jauss, "is primarily mediated in the horizon of expectations of the literary experience of contemporary and later readers, critics, and authors" (22). Jauss's "literary evolution" (34) suggests that a work's aesthetic response transforms—positively or negatively—according to the readers' views over time. Current MacDonald scholarship, consequently, is directly related to past criticism, and contemporary attitudes toward MacDonald will influence MacDonald studies for the future. *Behind the Back of the North Wind* traces the horizon of expectations that has defined MacDonald scholarship on *North Wind* historically, and may suggest to readers the future direction or directions for MacDonald studies.

The earliest essay (1947) by Coleman Parsons instigates the critical road for contemporary literary critics of MacDonald. Parsons argues that "MacDonald's greatest originality" in the novel is his "chronicle of the horse," thus connecting MacDonald to Anna Sewell and *Black Beauty* (1877) and demonstrating the centrality of MacDonald to the nineteenth century. Robert Lee Wolff's excerpt on *North Wind* from *The Golden Key: A Study of the Fiction of George MacDonald* is vital to the development of MacDonald criticism, for Wolff's work is the first full-length critical examination of MacDonald, primarily a Freudian interpretation of MacDonald and his work. Wolff highlights the tension between the real and the fantastic in *North Wind* and argues that this tension allows MacDonald to construct his key "mythology": "Evil is only the shape that good takes if we but knew it."

Richard Reis argues that "perhaps the most remarkable thing about *At the Back of the North Wind* is that MacDonald is trying, in fact, to justify death, that most inscrutable of the ways of God, to children," and Rolland Hein examines the sacramental nature of the novel and suggests that MacDonald subverts traditional Christianity to highlight "his belief in the essential goodness of man's primary feelings and passions to produce a view of human experience quite different from that of much historic Christianity. It opposes the ascetic tradition and solidly challenges the essentially Platonic assumptions upon which that tradition is based." Reis and Hein are foundational critics on MacDonald, as central to the development of MacDonald criticism as Wolff. So far, however, modern criticism of MacDonald and *At the Back of the North Wind* does not consider in any sustained manner children or their literature.

With David Robb we see a turn to the issue of MacDonald as a writer

Introduction

for children. Robb argues that children's fantasy literature "was a ready-made medium for the imaginative freedom [that MacDonald] so often needed," but, for Robb, MacDonald used children's fiction to explore personal issues "in order to contemplate difficulties and to reassure himself, one again, that it would be all right in the end." Lesley Smith examines how MacDonald reimagines the prophetic spirit of Old Testament prophecy that leads to Diamond's sacrifice that is demanded by such prophecy. William Raeper locates MacDonald in the Scottish folk-tale tradition by examining the connections between Diamond and James Hogg's Kilmeny, who also travelled to the back of the north wind, while John Pennington analyzes the metafictional aspects of *North Wind* (and the *Alice* books by Lewis Carroll), contending that the self-reflective qualities of the novel "redefine fantasy and fairy-tale discourse by dislocating structure through metafictional means." Naomi Wood engages gender and, by implication, Lacanian theory as she challenges MacDonald's "fundamentally conflicted ideology of fatherhood" that is depicted in the novel: "*At the Back of the North Wind* contains both masochistic and sadistic paradigms; this division attempts to resolve the problem of submission to a god who both loves and punishes." Roderick McGillis focuses on one chapter—Chapter 8: The East Window—to argue that MacDonald is subversive in *North Wind*, presenting "the reader with a radical critique of totalizing systems—whether these systems be political, economic, or religious—and an understanding of the self as a function of desire."

Dante plays a crucial role in *North Wind*, and Alison Milbank in an excerpt from *Dante and the Victorians* demonstrates how the author of *The Divine Comedy* informs MacDonald's novel: "Like Kingsley, MacDonald turns to Dante for an educative model of development in the afterlife, and similarly includes an element of the erotic in leading the soul to a fuller understanding of the divine." Milbank calls Diamond (the boy) "a junior Dante." U. C. Knoepflmacher's excerpted chapter on *North Wind* from *Ventures into Childland: Victorians, Fairy Tales, and Femininity* provides a gender analysis of MacDonald, arguing that the novel "dramatizes the same yearning for incorporation with a female Other that so powerfully fuels MacDonald's imagination." Whereas most studies of *North Wind* concentrate on the human hero, Diamond, Knoepflmacher spends equal time examining the importance of Nanny in the novel.

Lisa Hermine Makman's cultural reading of *North Wind* analyzes the novel in relationship to the evolving attitudes the Victorians had toward children and play. She argues that as children ceased to have "concrete economic value" as workers, their value transformed as their play made them a kind of useful moral toy: "As such, play in the novel comes to contribute to the reform of moral corruption in adults, thus bettering society for all." Fernando J. Soto provides an illuminating catalog of allusions to Greek mythology that inform *North Wind*. Soto suggests that these allusions to Greek myth complement the Christian readings of the text, for myth creates "darker and earthier aspects ... which counterbalance the sweet, safe, and perhaps childlike Christian readings of the book." Colin Manlove examines the incarnational sprit of the novel that "work[s] on us ... by using the frustrations of intellectual uncertainty to drive us towards simply testing the water through a relationship with God." The novel achieves this by "putting doubt at its core beside faith" and depicting "how both ordinary human life and the wild elemental forces of this world are joined in God." Finally, Jean Webb situates MacDonald squarely in the "realist social problem novel" tradition of Elizabeth Gaskell and the fantasy tradition of Charles Kingsley and Lewis Carroll. Webb demonstrates how the fantasy elements of *North Wind* allow MacDonald to engage "in a philosophical and moral discussion and critique of the contemporary Victorian English society" that is unique to the social problem novel.

The criticism of *At the Back of the North Wind* that comes after David Robb's work is instructive in its consideration of the social, philosophical, and theological aspects of the book. What we might notice is that the approaches to this Victorian children's book transcend a specific readership and preconceptions concerning the kind of literature a child is capable of understanding. More often than not, readings of this novel assume that *North Wind* contains complexities and ambiguities beyond the comprehension of most (or many) child readers. MacDonald himself imbeds such a view of child readership in his depiction of the relationship between North Wind and Diamond. North Wind is well aware that some of the things she is compelled to say will flummox Diamond, but that he will come to understand these lessons intuitively. The novel thus empowers the child reader. We might also notice another implied aspect of these essays: the respect these critics bring to MacDonald's novel is testimony to the power of his writing, writing that C. S. Lewis famously undervalued for its supposedly prolix prose. As Lewis claims about MacDonald: "If we define Literature as an art whose medium is words, then certainly MacDonald has no place in its first rank—perhaps not even in its second" (xxvi). This volume challenges Lewis's contention.

Behind the Back of the North Wind allows us to see the evolution of criticism on one of the most provocative Victorian children's books. Our hope is that the collection will spur further discussion about the novel: the transatlantic connections of *At the Back of the North Wind*; a more focused examination of gender and sexuality; the importance of law, justice, and legal theory to the text; the notion of Empire as related to post-colonial studies; or the significance of geographical mapping and the city in *North Wind*. The novel also offers opportunity to examine the relationship between verbal and visual texts since

INTRODUCTION

many illustrators, beginning with Arthur Hughes, have illustrated it. May the critical journey into *Behind the Back of the North Wind* be as exciting as Diamond's travels to the back of the north wind.

John Pennington
Roderick McGillis
November 2011

Works Cited

Harriman, Lucas H. Lilith *in a New Light: Essays on the George MacDonald Fantasy Novel.* Jefferson, NC: McFarland, 2008. Print.

Hearn, Michael Patrick. Afterword. *At the Back of the North Wind.* By George MacDonald. New York: Signet, 1986. 303-14. Print.

Jauss, Hans Robert. *Toward an Aesthetic of Reception.* Minneapolis: U of Minnesota P, 1982. Print.

Lewis, C. S. *The Allegory of Love.* London: Oxford UP, 1936. Print.

—, ed. Preface. *George MacDonald: 365 Readings.* New York: Collier, 1947. Print.

MacDonald, George. "The Fantastic Imagination." *The Complete Fairy Tales.* Ed. U. C. Knoepflmacher. New York: Penguin, 1999. 5-10. Print.

MacDonald, Greville. *George MacDonald and His Wife.* 1924. Whitehorn, CA: Johannesen, 1998. Print.

McGillis, Roderick, ed. *For the Childlike: George MacDonald's Fantasies for Children.* Metuchen: Children's Literature Association and Scarecrow Press, 1992. Print.

—. *George MacDonald: Literary Heritage and Heirs.* Wayne, PA: Zossima Press, 2008. Print.

Page, H. A. Rev. of *Dealings with the Fairies. Contemporary Review* 11 (1869): 187-94. Print.

Raeper, William, ed. *The Gold Thread: Essays on George MacDonald.* Edinburgh: Edinburgh UP, 1990. Print.

Rev. of *At the Back of the North Wind. The Athenaeum* (Mar. 1871): 303. Print.

Wordsworth, William. *The Prelude. The Romantics and Their Contemporaries.* Eds. Susan Wolfson and Peter Manning. *The Longman Anthology of British Literature* Vol. 2A, 4th ed. New York: Longman, 2010. 439-502. Print.

INTRODUCTION

HE LOOKED UP TO SEE HER FACE, AND SAW THAT SHE WAS NO LONGER A BEAUTIFUL GIANTESS, BUT THE TALL GRACIOUS LADY HE LIKED BEST TO SEE. SHE TOOK HIS HAND... AND LED HIM DOWN A GOOD WAY...

ILLUSTRATION BY LAUREN A. MILLS (© 1988)

SHE SAW HIM ALOFT ON THE GREAT HORSE.

ILLUSTRATION BY F.D. BEDFORD (MACMILLAN COMPANY, 1924)

The Progenitors of *Black Beauty* in Humanitarian Literature

From *Notes and Queries*

Coleman O. Parsons

Nearly two centuries of humanitarian arguments, narratives, pleas, laws and organised work created the atmosphere which sustained Anna Sewell in the writing and dictating of *Black Beauty* between 1871 and 1877. But the most distinct single influence on her work was, I believe, George MacDonald's *At the Back of the North Wind*. It has been the twentieth-century fate of MacDonald to be better known at second than at first hand. Thus more readers enjoy Sir James Barrie's *The Little White Bird* and *Peter and Wendy* than MacDonald's *Phantastes* and *Lilith*, which Professor Lionel Stevenson points out as sources. More attention is now paid to C. S. Lewis than to his "master," George MacDonald, and more children have a fondness for Black Beauty than for old Diamond.

MacDonald's story of a boy and a horse was serialized in twenty issues of the juvenile magazine *Good Words for the Young*, between 1 Nov. 1868 and 1 Oct. 1870, and was published as a book in 1871... . The plot may be reduced to a simple form: Mr. Coleman of The Wilderness, Chiswick, London, had a coachman, Joseph, who named his son Diamond, after a favourite horse, old Diamond. "God's baby" slept in the stable hayloft, where the North Wind visited him in the figure of a lady and bore him faraway to the back of the North Wind, where he found peace and calm insight. When Mr. Coleman failed because of dishonesty, he sold old Diamond and discharged Joseph. After being out of work for some time, Joseph bought old Diamond off cab-master John Stonecrop and began hacking in London. Driving for a fortnight when his father was sick, young Diamond reunited Mr. Evans and Miss Coleman and was a wingless baby angel to a drunken cabman. The juvenile cabby picked up good Mr. Raymond, who later helped the boy's crossing-sweeper friend, Nanny. After testing Joseph's integrity by leaving a horse, Ruby, in his charge, Mr. Raymond took Joseph and his wife Martha, their three children, and Nanny and her lame friend Jim to his Kentish home, The Mound. There the author met little Diamond, who died peacefully one night, and went to the back of the North Wind.

In the equine part of the story, we have the pattern of willing service, decline in status, pathetically hard work, and rehabilitation of a horse whose name, Diamond, was suggested by "a white lozenge on his forehead." Although MacDonald, as far as I remember, does not mention old Diamond's colour, the first illustrator, Arthur Hughes, makes him black in *Good Words for the Young*, 1 Aug. 1870. Black Beauty's self-portrait is: "My coat ... was bright black. I had one white foot, and a pretty white star on my forehead." Old Diamond's progress through life—that of a good job followed by adversity nobly borne and a return to clover—constitutes MacDonald's greatest originality in the chronicle of the horse. In literature, once a horse has started on the downward path, he goes from bad to worse, as in Sir John J. Hort's *The White Charger* (1850), a cavalry horse which is last seen "shorn of his flowing mane and tail, labouring along the slippery pavement performing the pleasant duty of offside wheeler in a Bank omnibus." So it is too with the lamenter in the anonymous and undated poem, "Poor Old Horse," which Walter de la Mare included in "Come Hither." Once sleek and snugly stabled, the horse loses his beauty, feeds on chance green niblets, is cursed as unfit for service, and is left out in bad weather: "I would rather die than live."

Old Diamond started on a similar descent, growing "very thin and bony and long-legged," with head drooping and bones showing through his skin. Then Joseph again became old Diamond's driver and worked lovingly with him. Although "it had been by no fault either of his or of the horse's that they had come down in the world together," the "better days" did not return immediately. As a cab-horse, old Diamond was in harness "all day and every day" and was well fed and cared for by his master. With the advent of Ruby to spell old Diamond, things seemed to look up, but Ruby went lame and Joseph's own beast, regretfully overworked, grew "as thin as a clothes-horse," gaunt, grim, and weary. It was only after Mr. Raymond made his offer that old Diamond got "respectably stout" for country carriage work with Ruby.

The parallels between *At the Back of the North Wind* and *Black Beauty* are fairly abundant. The horses think and speak. Whereas MacDonald is not absolutely certain of Diamond's mental processes, "for it is very difficult to find out what, any old horse is thinking," Anna Sewell shows no such diffidence. Yet even the cautious George MacDonald has young Diamond, perhaps walking in his sleep, overhear a conversation between old Diamond and Ruby, "in a strange language, which yet, somehow or other, he could understand, and turn over in his mind in English."

The general plot-development is the same. Both old Diamond and Black Beauty were thrust from their particular paradises of good treatment and moderate work through no fault of their own, the latter through the invalidism of Mrs. Gordon. Coachman and cabman are the same person in MacDonald;

The Progenttors of Black Beauty

John Manly and Jerry Barker are different persons in Sewell, who points out their resemblances in more than one comparison. Both Joseph and Jerry fell sick from over-work and exposure. A benevolent patron rescued Joseph and old Diamond from their London bondage and made little Diamond his page. The Barkers were employed at last by Mrs. Fowler, Polly Barker's former mistress and one of Jerry's London fares; their son Harry became the good lady's page boy. As for Black Beauty, his salvation from killing toil had to be deferred in order that Miss Sewell might round out her narrative sermon on the proper and improper management of horses. When he had repeatedly proved himself a good-and faithful, though much abused, servant, Black Beauty was sold by a kindly farmer to three maiden ladies, none other than the Blomefields, former playmates of the Gordon sisters. Their groom was Joe Green, whom Squire Gordon had employed as a boy. Thus known friends saved both horses from the final degradation portrayed by other writers and suggested by the title of Miss Sewell's twenty-seventh chapter, "Ruined, and Going Down-Hill."

Both authors moralize on the harm done to grooms and cabmen by drink. MacDonald presents only one ill-treater of horses, "the drunken cabman," who "put a stinging lash on his whip" and let his uncomplaining nag dwindle to "skin and bone." Here the blame rests on beer and a weak will, rather than on natural viciousness. Joseph recommended cold water, tea and coffee against the "thirsty devil" who induced the drunken cabman to strike his wife and almost starve his baby. Fortunately, young Diamond started a reformation in the drunkard's character. In *Black Beauty*, Seedy Sam, the Governor, and other cabmen are subjects of the "drink devil." Jerry Barker was freed from the craving ten years earlier by good food, coffee, peppermint, and regard for his wife Polly. Black Beauty's friend, the ex-cavalry horse, Captain, was shot after being run down by a drunken drayman who had lost control of his horses. And most disastrously of all, the Earl of W—'s drunken groom, Reuben Smith, galloped Black Beauty over a dark, stony road when the animal had a loose shoe. The inevitable fall cost Reuben his life; his wife Susan and their six children went to the Union House; and Black Beauty, blemished for life by cut knees, was sold to the owner of livery stables in Bath ... .

But to return to MacDonald's influence on Anna Sewell. Old Diamond's cab labours, with the London adventures of his name sake, fill up half of the narrative, "At the Back of the North Wind," and Black Beauty's career as a cab horse makes up nearly a third of the later book. The genesis of "Black Beauty," as well as the importance of that particular third part, is suggested by Miss Sewell's comment:

> I have ... been writing ... a little book, its special aim being to induce kindness, sympathy, and an understanding treatment of horses. In thinking of cab-horses, I have been led to think of cabmen, and I am

anxious, if I can, to present their true condition, and their great difficulties, in a correct and telling manner.

MacDonald's protest against the 6d. a mile legally fixed fare to which Joseph was held and his humane understanding that both cabmen and horses were victims of an economic wrong reappear in Anna Sewell's pages. In the chapters of "Black Beauty" that do not deal with cabbing, the authoress finds men and boys either good or bad in their treatment of horses. The exception, good Joe Green, through boyish ignorance gave Black Beauty cold water to drink when overheated and did not put a blanket on his back. A more complex and mature interpretation of injustice and final responsibility appears in the London passages. Seedy Sam had to pay Nicholas Skinner 18s. a day rental for a cab and two horses. He himself worked fourteen to sixteen hours a day at a pinching 6d. a mile, hardly ever got a Sunday off, and died at the age of 45, leaving a wife and children penniless. As Seedy Sam remarked, "It is hard lines for man, and it is hard lines for beast, and who's to mend it I don't know." Both MacDonald and Anna Sewell used the horse as a touchstone of human worth; coincidentally, in 1877, the year *Black Beauty* was published, the Scotch author introduced the demonic black mare, Kelpie, in *The Marquis of Lossie* as a test of integrity or duplicity.

Parallels, however, should not make a reader lose sight of differences. MacDonald emphasised good treatment of horses and concentrated chiefly on his human characters and his fantasy; Anna Sewell stressed ill-treatment, while introducing much material on sensible handling as exemplary instruction to bad grooms and owners, and she ranged much more widely in her special humanitarian field. Beyond the fact that old Diamond's somewhat mystical companion, Ruby, is a chestnut in colour, he bears no resemblance to Black Beauty's friend, Ginger, who performs a very special function in the novel. Whereas Black Beauty shows the effects on disposition of a gentle breaking-in and kind management, Ginger illustrates the proposition that horses are not born bad but are tragically made so by man: "I never had any one, horse or man, that was kind to me, or that I cared to please." No wonder that Ginger developed the vices of biting and snapping! After tempestuous protest against the bearing-rein, Ginger was turned over to the Earl of W—'s son, Lord George, whose hard riding touched her wind and strained her back. Sold and resold, poor Ginger died a cab horse and was carted off—probably to the London knacker's yard, where some four to five hundred horses were being reduced to commercial hides, hoofs for glue, and dogs' meat every week.

Besides her attack on the bearing-rein (to be discussed later), Miss Sewell exceeded MacDonald's scope in her objections to damp bedding, a cause of thrush; to inadequate lighting of stables, a cause of blindness; to docking of tails; to the use of blinkers, painful bits, and tight harness; to the theft of oats

The Progenttors of Black Beauty

by grooms, the flogging of cart-horses, and the clumsy driving of job or hired horses; to ploughboys' throwing stones at colts and boys' playing recklessly with ponies; to hunters' spoiling horses by hard riding and dangerous jumping; to cabmen's speeding for extra fares and driving seven days a week; and to many other abuses. Similar crusading, without the-enlivening narrative touch, may be encountered in treatises on horses published long before *Black Beauty*. To these and works of the imagination it would be well to turn …

Fancy and Imagination

From *The Golden Key: A Study of the Fiction of George MacDonald*

Robert Lee Wolff

Of all MacDonald's works, *At the Back of the North Wind* has remained the best-known, delighting and disturbing generation after generation of children. It takes place in two worlds, the real world of everyday Victorian London, and the dream-world of the imagination of Diamond, the coachman's son, named after his master's beautiful white horse. With equal matter-of-factness, and no change of pace, MacDonald narrates the events that take place in both worlds; so that the dream world seems a natural extension of the real world. He does not tell us that Diamond is dreaming whenever he sees North Wind, whether by night or by day. We are here not dealing with an explicit transfer from the world of reality to the world of dreams, as in *Phantastes* or the *Alice* books, which are purely dream narratives. For adults, *At the Back of the North Wind* is like Hoffmann's *Golden Pot*: as if falling asleep, almost without warning, we pass from one world to the other, and at times the two worlds are fused. No doubt this is one of the reasons why the book gives children the shivers.

In the real world, Diamond sleeps in a loft over the stable in the grounds of his father's master, Mr. Coleman, a kind man with a kind daughter. Diamond meets a miserable waif of a crossing-sweeper, a little girl named Nanny, and does what he can to help her. He goes for a visit to the seaside, visits a toy shop, goes to the beach with his mother, and has a severe illness. The Colemans are ruined through speculation, and Miss Coleman's fiancé is lost at sea in a wreck of one of their merchant ships that also shatters the family fortunes. Out of work, Diamond's father buys a four-wheeler cab and manages to acquire Old Diamond, the horse. The family has to live in a mews. Diamond rescues the baby next door; its father is a drunkard and beats his wife, but Diamond's gentle kindness launches him on the road to repentance. When Nanny is ill, Diamond makes a dangerous excursion into a desperate slum, where he is nearly stripped of his clothes by the predatory women who live there. He meets a kind man, an author named Mr. Raymond, who helps him get Nanny into a hospital.

Fancy and Imagination

When Diamond's father is sick and cannot work, Diamond himself drives the cab. He becomes a general favorite of the stablemen and cabdrivers of London. Miss Coleman's lover has survived the shipwreck after all; he comes home, and it is Diamond, as cabdriver, who brings him to the humble house where the Colemans now live. A baby girl is born to Diamond's parents. Diamond, who has always enjoyed making poems and singing songs to his little brother, welcomes her with the famous sentimental verses, "Where did you come from, baby dear?" Mr. Raymond offers Diamond's father the use of another horse while he travels abroad. Nanny too comes to live with them; this is very expensive. But when Mr. Raymond returns, he has married a charming woman, and offers Diamond's father a post as his own coachman. They all move to Kent, and Diamond becomes a page in the household, and a friend of the narrator, a tutor who lives nearby. Diamond has a nest in a beech tree. Diamond dies.

In the dream world, at the very beginning of the story North Wind makes a window into Diamond's bed by blowing through a knothole. She is a beautiful woman, who warns him at once that she will vary in size. Though she asks him to accompany her, she has vanished by the time he gets downstairs, and he wanders onto the lawn of the Coleman's house, and is eventually rescued. Everybody thinks he has been walking in his sleep. On her second visit, North Wind takes Diamond for a walk along the river and carries him behind her in a nest made of her hair while she "sweeps" out London. He gets a splendid aerial view of the city; and it is then he sees Nanny for the first time, and asks North Wind to put him down to help her. So the two worlds fuse; Diamond escorts Nanny through London for the rest of the night, and she will not believe what he tells her about North Wind.

In mid-summer, North Wind appears to him in the garden, during the day, very tiny, and tells Diamond that she has to sink a ship that night. She takes him along, but while she sinks the ship (Mr. Coleman's ship), she leaves Diamond in a cathedral on a high ledge, where he learns to walk alone, goes to sleep, and hears the Apostles in the stained-glass windows talking, and wakes up in his own bed. There has been a severe windstorm in the night. At the toy shop, North Wind appears to him blowing a tiny windmill. He tells her that he wants to go to the country at her back; she answers that this is very difficult to do; since the country is at her back, she cannot get there herself, but must sit on the doorstep, facing out, and listen to the voices inside.

This is the moment of Diamond's illness. That night North Wind blows him aboard a little northbound yacht, arranges his transfer to a German vessel, sets him down on a northward-moving iceberg, and joins him there, only to leave as the south wind, blowing the berg north, makes her faint. He is on the way to North Wind's house, and finds her on the doorstep, sitting as if dead on an icy ridge, waiting until she is wanted. To get to the country at her back, he must walk right through her … .

The narrator now intervenes to declare how hard this part of the story is to tell, because by the time Diamond got back from the country at the back of the north wind, he had forgotten much about it, and he found it hard to tell what he could remember. Other people have been there, an Italian named Durante (Dante), and a Scotch peasant girl, Kilmeny, who came back from it for a visit to her friends … . It is not hot, or cold; nobody talks; nothing is wrong or right; there is beautiful music.

So the land where Diamond is, at the back of the north wind, is a kind of limbo. It is clearly not paradise, but one of the way stations. When you want to know about anybody there, you climb a tree and wait to see what happens. Diamond looks for his mother, and sees her crying; then the land shrinks as if it were a map, and he steps across the whole country, and finds North Wind again. She flies him southward and home. His absence seems to him to have lasted for years, but only seven days have passed: here is another of MacDonald's dream-like distortions of time. When Diamond comes to himself, his mother is there; he has been very ill, and she had thought him dead. He has, an adult reader can see, been to death's door and come back again. In an earlier story, "The Shadows,"[1] MacDonald had told of an artist, sick almost to death, and of the way the shadows in his room, flickering in the firelight, become personages. and take him with them on two long night journeys flying over England and Scotland and the sea, to Iceland, where they hold a kind of conventicle and report on what they have been doing. "The Shadows" is a kind of preliminary sketch for what later became a major theme of *At the Back of the North Wind.*

After this episode, North Wind reappears three times more. Once she takes Diamond to the stable to hear a dialogue between Mr. Raymond's lazy horse, Ruby, and the good horse, Old Diamond. A second time, near the very end of the story, she dances with Diamond in an attic, and talks to him again … . She … explains that the country he had visited had been only a picture of the country at the back of the north wind, and that the real one is much more beautiful, and that he may see it very soon. On her last visit, she takes him out at night, and he sings a comforting song to a lady who is sorrowing at an open window. North Wind takes Diamond back to revisit his old stable and the Coleman's old house; but although he anticipates this with great pleasure, he finds it a letdown: the spirit has left it with the people. A few days later, everybody thinks that Diamond is dead. But the narrator knows that he has gone to the back of the north wind.

Whatever her size, North Wind has beautiful eyes, long deliciously fragrant hair, and a splendid bosom, to which she often clasps Diamond. She is usually tender and affectionate with him; on one occasion, she settles with him into the nest at the top of the beech tree, and "placed him on her lap, and began to hush him as if he were her own baby, and Diamond was so entirely happy that he did not care to speak a word." He loves her dearly, and in this capacity she has the motherly qualities of MacDonald's mythic grandmother or earth-mother. (The location of Diamond's nest in a beech tree is also no accident.)

But North Wind also has her "work" that she must do. Once she transforms herself into a grim wolf and terrifies an incompetent nursemaid who has been drinking and frightening the baby in her charge; the next day the nurse's employers will discharge her... . Sometimes North Wind takes care of a bee caught in a blossom. Sometimes she sinks great ships, and people think her cruel; but

> "I can do nothing cruel, although I often do what looks cruel to those who do not know what I am really doing. The people they say I drown, I only carry away to—to—to—well, the back of the North Wind."

She does not know how she gets her assignments; she just does what she must do. East Wind has told her that "it is all managed by a baby," but North Wind does not know whether or not to believe it.

By now we feel ourselves at home in the MacDonald mythology. Evil is only the shape that good takes if we but knew it. And a baby is in charge: this is the divine child who was the Old Man of the Fire in "The Golden Key," the Christ-symbol.

> "People," [says North Wind at another time,] "call me by dreadful names, and think they know all about me. But they don't. Sometimes they call me Bad Fortune, sometimes Evil Chance, sometimes Ruin; and they have another name for me which they think the most dreadful of all."
>
> "What is that?" asked Diamond, smiling up in her face.
>
> "I won't tell you that name. Do you remember having to go through me to get into the country at my back? ... You were very near knowing what they call me then."

North Wind does not tell Diamond what it is, but the reader will of course know that it is Death. But just as she is not any of the other things they call her, North Wind is not precisely Death either: she is a divine motherly messenger, with a wind's work to do. But the death of which she sometimes does the work, is the good, the welcome death of *Phantastes* and "The Golden Key," the death that is a reunion with the cosmos and mother earth, the death that is not to be feared but sought.

Diamond is preternaturally good: he loves everybody, and is always eager to help, simple, and kind. It comes as a surprise to the reader when Nanny, the realistic little crossing-sweeper, "tapped her forehead in a significant manner," when talking to Mr. Raymond, and

"the cabbies call him God's baby," she whispered.

"He's not right in the head you know. A tile loose."

Diamond is a Christ-like child, then, God's baby (his father's name is Joseph, his mother's name is Martha) whom people think silly—not Mr. Raymond who thinks him a genius, but those of coarser clay like Nanny and the cabmen— a model of divine simplicity, who does not care what people say of him, who lives only for others, who is indeed too good for this real world, which he must leave... .

The real world, in *At the Back of the North Wind*, is a tough place indeed. When North Wind first talks to Diamond, through the knothole before he has ever seen her, he asks her "'Why don't you make a window into Mr. Dyves's bed? ... he must have a nicer bed than I have, though mine is *very* nice, so nice that I couldn't wish a better.'" And North Wind answers "'Nobody makes a window into an ash-pit... . It's not the bed I care about; it's what is in it.'" Mr. Dyves (who is not a character in the book and is never mentioned again) is clearly *Dives*, the rich man, and MacDonald has nothing good to say of the rich, except for Mr. Raymond. North Wind tells Diamond that "'every man ought to be a gentleman and your father is one,'" and when Nanny has been ill in this hospital she is like a lady: "she might have had a lady and a gentleman for a father and mother"—radical doctrine indeed for the late 1860's in England.

Nanny's guardian, Old Sal, is a drunken wretch, who forces the child to turn over all her earnings as a crossing-sweeper, and will not get out of bed late at night to let her in to their squallid cellar, but keeps her out in the cold wind. Policemen are always moving Nanny on, just as they had done with her literary ancestor, little Jo, the crossing-sweeper in *Bleak House*: her cry is the same as his, "'They're always at it.'" She and Diamond have to take a nap in a barrel, huddled together for warmth. Nanny explains to Diamond why she does not commit suicide.

"When I think of it, I always want to see what's coming next, and so I always wait until next is over. Well! I suppose there's somebody happy somewheres. But it ain't in them carriages. Oh my! *how* they *do* look sometimes—fit to bite your head off!"

The drunken cabman, shamed by Diamond's kindness to his baby, stays away from pubs for a week, "hard as it was to avoid it, seeing a certain rich brewer had built one, like a trap to catch souls and bodies in, at almost every corner he had to pass on his way home."[2] The roughness of the slum-dwellers is matched by the bullies among the cabmen who do not know Diamond, and by the street toughs who beat up crossing-sweepers. Diamond, we are told, remains pure, despite the foul language of the stablemen. One wonders how many of the Victorian parents who made *At the Back of the North Wind* such a success by giving it to their children knew what incendiary material was in it. Novels of social indignation were by no means rare in the late 1860's, but they were seldom, like *At the Back of the North Wind*, books ostensibly for children, tricked out in lavishly gilt-stamped cloth, with a little girl on the front cover looking out of a window in the moon.

There are three interpolated fairy-tales in *At the Back of the North Wind*: Diamond and Nanny each has a dream, and Mr. Raymond tells the story of "Little Daylight," often afterwards reprinted separately. Diamond dreams of falling asleep in a rose garden, and being summoned to the sky by children's voices calling from behind the surface of the stars. The way up (as so often) proves to be a way down: via a staircase leading into the earth: of turf and moss, "a nice stair, so cool and soft—all the sides as well as the steps grown with moss and grass and ferns." At the foot he emerges onto a hillside, where the naked little boy-angels greet him. They dig for stars in the hillside; when they dig them up, they look through the star-holes down to earth again: this is how they had called Diamond in the first place. When one finds a color he likes, he throws himself through the star-hole into space. There are no little girl-angels, but the captain of the little boys tells Diamond that he believes the little girls come around later and polish the stars they have dug up. This cloying little fantasy reintroduces the familiar theme of a passage through mother earth providing the way to heaven, forewarns us that Diamond is to die, and illustrates once more the futility of trying to make life in heaven seem amusing even for a child.

Nanny dreams that the moon descends to her while she is in a summerhouse in a garden, and that a little old man steps out of a door in the side of it and summons her in. Inside, the moon is a charming little house with blue windows and white curtains and the mistress of the place looking out of one of them; it takes off from the grounds, and Nanny and the old man look back at the earth through the windows. Her work is to keep the windows polished. The moon is full of passages, and at the end of one Nanny listens at a door, and hears a hum: "my lady's bees, that collect honey from the stars." While cleaning the windows on the outside of the moon, Nanny climbs into the room where the bees are kept and accidentally lets them out, contrary to orders. The lady of the moon is angry, and says that Nanny won't do, that she is only fit for the mud; and she wakes up pulling at a ring she has been loaned by a kind visiting lady at the hospital; the moon-lady says she has stolen it. This dream, with its cruel touches of orders disobeyed and frustration, suggests that Nanny herself fears that she is not ready for the peaceful motherly interior of the moon, with its attendant lady, and that she has the guilt feelings of the poor: she is fit only for mud, she has stolen the ring

Mr. Raymond's story of "Little Daylight" tells of the princess at whose christening the wicked fairy requires that she sleep all day; the good one balances it by allowing her to be awake all night; the wicked one condemns her to wax and wane with the moon; the good one provides that when a prince shall kiss her, not knowing the truth, she will be released from the enchantment. When the prince does kiss her, in her wretched waning phase, he murmurs "Mother, mother! Poor mother!"; her lips are withered. After the kiss she is young and beautiful at once. To an ordinary fairy-tale of the enchantment-at-the-christening and the loathly-lady type, MacDonald has added two elements: the nature-myth that has the princess waxing and waning and the prince's kissing her out of filial pity, which turns into something quite different. Very similar to "Little Daylight" in some respects, though much longer and more developed, is the last fairy-tale MacDonald wrote, "The History of Photogen and Nycteris, a day and night Mährchen," in which there is not only a night-blooming princess but a day-blooming prince.[3]

Although *At the Back of the North Wind* has strikingly original features, it is much too long: MacDonald, one feels, did not quite know how to bring it to an end—a serious fault in his fiction generally—and there are many dull moments and oversentimentalities that prevent its reaching the level of his very best work. Yet it is unique among his stories for its combination of realism and fantasy. After completing it, he wrote purely in one vein or the other, but never in both within the framework of the same tale.

Illustration by Arthur Hiughes (1868)

Fancy and Imagination

Endnotes

1. "The Shadow," *Adela Cathcart*, II, 80-149. According to Bulloch (719), "The germinal idea of this fairy story occurs in a collection of manuscripts written by the Powell family for their father on his seventy-first birthday, describing, in Mrs. MacDonald's handwriting, the first Christmas spent at Huntly Cottage, Hastings, 1857.
2. *At the Back of the North Wind*, 359-60, 358, 59, 364, 186-87, 8, 32, 254, 51, 184.
3. "The History of Photogen and Nycteris; a day and night Mährchen," first published in the *Graphic*, 20 (Christmas, 1879), 4-5, 8-9; in book form in *The Gifts of the Child Christ and Other Tales*, 2 volumes (London: Sampson, Low, Marston, Rivington, & Searle, 1882); often re-issued; I have used an American reprint (New York: Routledge, no date).

Works Cited

Bulloch, J. M. "A Bibliography of George MacDonald." *Aberdeen University Bulletin* 5.30 (Feb. 1925): 679-747.

MacDonald, George. *At the Back of the North Wind*. London: Strahan, 1871.

ALL THE APOSTLES WERE STANDING ROUND AND LOOKING DOWN ON HIM.

ILLUSTRATION BY F. D. BEDFORD (MACMILLAN, 1924)

The Imaginative Fiction

From *George MacDonald's Fiction*

Richard H. Reis

I have already mentioned in the Preface to this study the rather anomalous nature of *At the Back of the North Wind,* one of MacDonald's most impressive works for children, and one which I am in the minority in somewhat preferring even to *The Princess and the Goblin,* excellent as the latter is. Unlike the other full-length children's stories, this one has a very real setting, though the events are not "realistic" in the ordinary sense of the word. The setting is London sometime during the middle of the nineteenth century, and the characters are mostly poor people.

Little Diamond, the child-hero, is so very good and innocent that most worldly folk think him absent-minded or even feebleminded. In this respect, he is like some of the saintly children of the novels, such as *Sir Gibbie* or the children in *Guild Court.* Little Diamond's parents are a London cab-driver and his wife; his best friend is Old Diamond, the cab-horse after whom he was named. Among Diamond's London friends is a little girl who sweeps crossings for the gentry, and whose earnings are stolen by Old Sal to buy gin. (The crossing sweeper is one of the most outrageous social institutions of the nineteenth century's brutal perversion of laissez-faire economics and "survival of the fittest": the sweepers were waifs, usually orphans, cast into the city streets to earn pittances by sweeping horse-droppings from the paths of gentry who wanted to cross at street corners without soiling their precious trouser-cuffs and hems.) The setting in general is comparable to the first part of Charles Kingsley's *Water Babies,* which was published eight years earlier and which may have suggested the idea to MacDonald; but, whereas Kingsley's chimney sweep suffers the cruelties of slaving for the owners of English country houses, Diamond and the little girl undergo the complementary cruelties of the city. As does Kingsley, MacDonald takes his child from a bitter life in this world to another, better existence through the door of ostensible "death."

Perhaps the most remarkable thing about *At the Back of the North Wind* is that MacDonald is trying, in fact, to justify death, that most inscrutable of the ways of God, to children. Diamond falls ill and nearly dies when exposed to the North Wind in winter through a crack near his bed over the stable. His coma is explained as the result of the fact that his spirit is journeying to the "hyperborean regions," an idea taken from Herodotus.[1] The North Wind, personified as a woman who takes Diamond on a sort of guided tour through her domains, is also the force which brings death. At one point, the little boy watches as a storm at sea sinks a ship, drowning all the passengers. North Wind explains why her nature includes such disasters:

> "I don't think I am just what you fancy me to be. I have to shape myself various ways to various people. But the heart of me is true. People call me dreadful names, and think they know all about me. Sometimes they call me Bad Fortune, sometimes Evil Chance, sometimes Ruin; and they have another name for me which they think the most dreadful of all."
>
> "What is that?"
>
> "I won't tell you that name... . Do you remember having to go through me to get into the country at my back? ... You were very near knowing what they call me then. Would you be afraid of me if you had to go through me again?"
>
> "No. Why should I? Indeed I should be glad enough, if it was only to get another peep of the country at your back." [363-64]

Here is another instance of MacDonald's preoccupation with natural disasters and his concern with analyzing and justifying them—a concern also manifested in the conventional novels. It is MacDonald's answer to Voltaire's answer (in *Candide*) to Leibnitz's idea that this is the best of all possible worlds. The natural disasters in the realistic works, however, are never so neatly "rationalized."

After coming so near death, Diamond recovers temporarily, but he then has a relapse and dies. MacDonald tries to explain to his child readers that death is not an end but a departure to another place which is a good deal more pleasant than the poverty in which Diamond had "lived." Here we have, perhaps, a seminal difference between the children's classics of the nineteenth century and the wishy-washy stories fed to the children in our own time: a hundred years ago a MacDonald *faced* the bitter fact of death and made his readers face it, while the authors of children's stories today seem, with a well-meaning but rather fatuous effort, to avoid subjecting their readers to "traumas"; and they expend their efforts in *denying* the reality of life's grimmer side.

And *At the Back of the North Wind* has a most peculiar attribute of plot, besides its bluntness of implicit content, to distinguish it from most saccharine books for children. Diamond, perhaps uniquely among the child-heroes of fairy tales, comes back again into this world after having had a glimpse of the Other World after death. This oddity is something present in *At the Back of the North Wind* that is absent from the otherwise similar *Water Babies* of Charles Kingsley (in which there is likewise a dual this-world, other-world setting and a blunt facing of death). The idea of trips to the other world sandwiched between returns to this is, as we shall see, typical of MacDonald and of some symbolic significance.

Endnote

1. Herodotus describes the Hyperboreans in book IV, 32-36. Wolff traces MacDonald's reference to the same idea to a verse by James Hogg (see *Golden Key*, 151 and 399n), but he does not tell us where Dante—another source mentioned by MacDonald—deals with it; I, too, have failed to locate the reference.

Works Cited

MacDonald, George. *At the Back of the North Wind*. London: Strahan, 1871.

The Imaginative Fiction

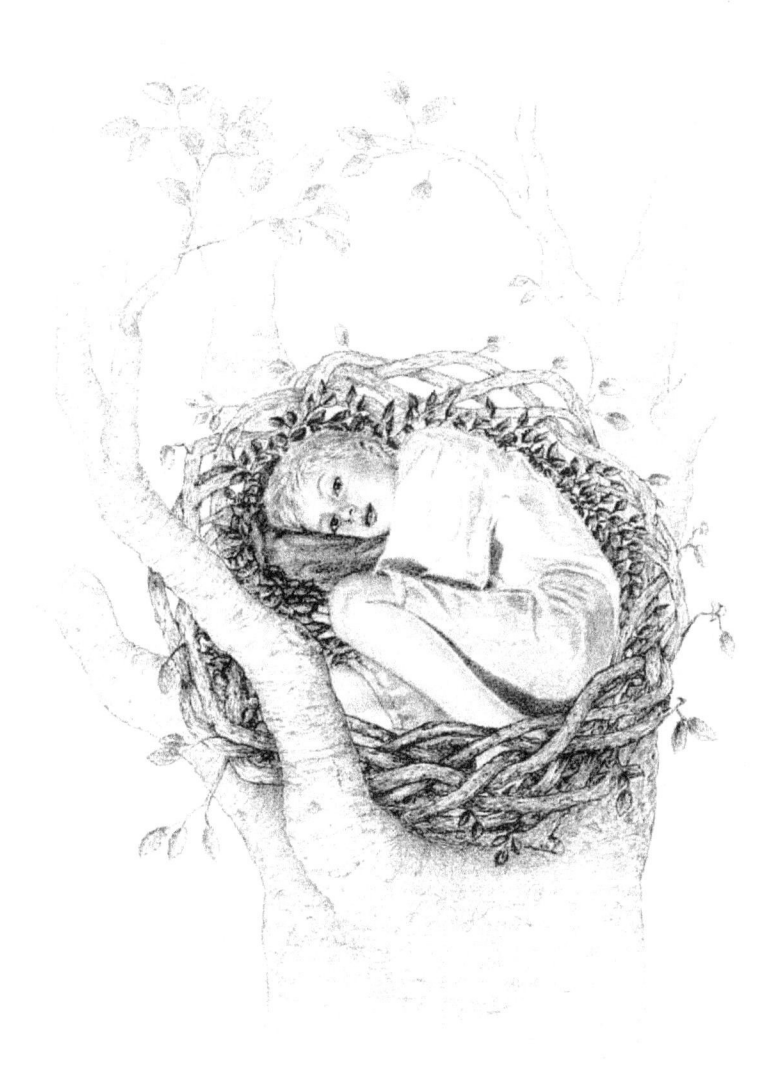

While I stood gazing, down from the sky came a sound of singing, but the voice was neither of lark nor of nightingale: it was sweeter than either: it was the voice of Diamond, up in his airy nest -

> The lightning and thunder,
> they go and they come;
> but the stars and the stillness
> Are always at home.

Illustration by Lauren A. Mills (© 1988)

Outward Signs of Inward Grace

From *The Harmony Within: The Spiritual Vision of George MacDonald*

Rolland Hein

We may use the term "sacramental," in a very broad sense, to describe MacDonald's view of God's relation to both the world of nature and the world of event and circumstance. MacDonald himself uses this term in a passage from his early novel *The Portent*, and in so doing gives us the kernel of his idea. He writes: "The very outside of a book had a charm to me. It was a kind of *sacrament*—an outward sign of an inward and spiritual grace; as, indeed, what on God's earth is not?" (italics mine).

A sacrament is an object or act that becomes a means whereby divine grace is, or may be, bestowed upon the recipient. Traditionally, Protestants reserve the term to refer to baptism and the Lord's Supper; Roman Catholics use it to describe seven essential rites of the Church. Whereas orthodox Christianity has tended to confine the application of the idea to very specific "sacred" acts, MacDonald suggests that it should have the widest possible application. Everything "on God's earth" is "an outward and visible sign of an inward and spiritual grace," in the sense that all circumstances and objects that surround a man on any given day of his life are invested by God with the potential to speak to him. Whether or not the potential that resides in a specific thing is realized by a specific man depends upon that man's present stage of spiritual development, his sensibility, and his attitudes. But God in grace is continually shaping outward circumstances to man's inner needs. "That which is within a man, not that which lies beyond his vision, is the main factor in what is about to befall him: the operation upon him is the event," MacDonald observes in *Lilith*.

In fact, all that is within a man sustains correspondences to all that is outside of him. MacDonald writes in *Orts*, a collection of his essays: "For the world is—allow us the homely figure—the human being turned inside out. All that moves in the mind is symbolized in Nature." These correspondences facilitate sacramental communication. A mystical life, a spirit from God Himself, courses through all nature and strives to communicate with man by using natural objects as symbols. In the novel *Thomas Wingfold* we read:

All about us, in earth and air, wherever the eye or ear can reach, there is a power ever breathing itself forth in signs, now in wind-waft, a cloud, a sunset; a power that holds constant and sweetest relation with the dark and silent world within us. The same God who is in us, and upon whose tree we are the buds, if not yet the flowers, also is all about us—inside the Spirit; outside, the Word. And the two are ever trying to meet in us... .

By virtue of the immanence of God in all things, as well as within man, there is a unity of substance between each man and the symbols he sees.[1]

That evil, in the form of adverse circumstances and events, may be sacramental is a strong theme in the children's fantasy *At the Back of the North Wind* ... . The imagery of the title suggests the equivocal nature of adversity, the north wind being a common image for what is adverse and unpleasant. However, to be at its back—that is, going with it rather than against it—is, as the story soon makes clear, a fascinating and salutary place to be.

This ambiguous nature of adversity, with the possibility of its having a charming "other side," is graphically portrayed in the opening scene of the story. Diamond is the small son of a poor London coachman, and his bedroom is a rickety structure built over the coach-house, affording meager protection from the cutting blasts of the North Wind. One particular night when the rushing wind is whistling shrilly around Diamond's bed, he seems to hear it speaking to him. Engaging it in conversation, he discovers the wind to be a fascinating woman of mighty beauty, with both anger and sweetness mingled in her looks. From her face comes light, as from the moon. On succeeding nights he accompanies her, flying with her over London ensconced in her long hair, while she fulfills her assignments. She carries out the bidding of a Higher Power, whose ways she herself does not firmly understand.

When he is confident she is not cruel, but good-intentioned, he asks her how it is she can bear bringing disaster, such as her present task of sinking a ship. She answers that she hears above the noise of the immediate disaster the "sound of a far-off song" that quite satisfies her concerning the present suffering, for it tells her that "all is right." When Diamond objects that what comforts her doesn't do her victims much good, she counters: "'It must. It must. It wouldn't be the song it seems to be if it did not swallow up all their fear and pain too, and set them singing it themselves with the rest.'" The principle that good can come of ill, thus illustrated in the opening scene, is then orchestrated throughout the course of Diamond's ensuing experiences.

Before the story reverts to realism, Diamond is taken to see the country at the back of the North Wind. The story makes clear that the trip occurs while he is seriously ill, and in a delirious state. She takes him far into the regions of the North, and then, in a memorable scene, he is commanded to pass directly through her person. Doing so, he enters a higher land in which nothing is wrong, but neither is anything quite right. This region, however, is pervaded with the certainty that everything is "going to be right some day." It is a land where there is peace and contentment intermingled with a patient waiting for a future fulfillment. The "good" dead are there, able to observe their loved ones back on earth, while anticipating fuller bliss in the Resurrection to come.

The experience of being in this higher land gives Diamond a moral and spiritual maturity beyond that normally acquired by anyone in this life, so that when he returns to health and the story progresses, he is shown to be a model of virtue. With impeccable obedience and industry Diamond works altruistically for the good of the poor, the sick, and the unfortunate—society's castoffs in the streets of nineteenth-century London. MacDonald's purpose is to show him realizing a fully harmonious cooperation with the principle already established—namely, that adversity and disaster are precipitated by a power that uses them as channels and instruments for an ultimate good to man. The concept itself is, of course, intriguing. But it is difficult, if not impossible, to work out in a believable manner in realistic fiction. For this reason, this section of the novel is considerably less appealing than the former section of fantasy.

It would seem, then, that symbolic art can succeed in suggesting the concept where realistic art cannot. For instance, the wanderings of Anodos in *Phantastes*, although they seem to be aimless and haphazard, and sometimes are terrifying, all work for his ultimate good, and the reader delights in the imaginative presentation of the principle in the fantasy world of Faerie. Similarly, as long as *At the Back of the North Wind* maintains a semi-fantastic setting, it also is charming and convincing; but at the point at which it seeks to demonstrate its theme in the real world of London coachmen, it fails to sustain one's acceptance.

This artistic dilemma is underscored by the success of the fairy tale "Little Daylight," which MacDonald nestles into the fabric of the realistic portion of the plot. A kindly poet who befriends Diamond visits a children's hospital and tells the patients there a fairy tale, the theme of which reinforces that of the book. "'I never knew of any interference on the part of the wicked fairy that did not turn out a good thing in the end,'" the narrator announces, and proceeds to tell the story of a princess named Little Daylight. At her christening, a wicked fairy cursed her, dooming her to sleep all day and to wake only at night, and then to be strong or weak according to the waxing or waning of the moon. Thus she grows up into a beautiful princess, dancing in the moonlight forests but never seeing the sun. A noble prince, who sees her in her nocturnal dances, falls in love with her. Later discovering her on a moonless night weak and ugly because of the curse, he befriends her, completely unaware that she is the same beautiful princess he has seen dancing, and out of pity he kisses her. The spell is thus broken, and her beauty returns, together with the privilege of at last enjoying the sun and, it is intimated, the prince's love. This tale is pleasant and satisfying, temporarily suspending any reluctance we may feel to accept the larger thesis of the book.

The book itself, however, recovers its charm in the closing chapters. Diamond's illness returns, and he dies. North Wind resumes her nocturnal visits to Diamond during his illness, and his death is depicted as his making a final trip to the "back of the North Wind." The aura of her presence in these closing scenes lingers in the mind, and many of her speeches give memorable expression to some of MacDonald's basic ideas. For instance, she answers Diamond's inquiry about whether dreams are to be trusted: "'The people who think lies, and do lies, are very likely to dream lies. But the people who love what is true will surely now and then dream true things. But then something depends on whether the dreams are home-grown, or whether the seed of them is blown over somebody else's garden wall... .'" Good people should trust their own deepest feelings and treasure their own highest hopes. How they shall come to fruition is a mystery, but one may safely hope they shall. Diamond articulates this hope in a song about the seasons:

> *Sure is the summer,*
> *Sure is the sun;*
> *The night and the winter*
> *Are shadows that run.*

MacDonald's view of the sacramental character of nature and event combines with his belief in the essential goodness of man's primary feelings and passions to produce a view of human experience quite different from that of much of historic Christianity. It opposes the ascetic tradition and solidly challenges the essentially Platonic assumptions upon which that tradition is based. The view that there exists an irreconcilable enmity between body and spirit, and that the body must be severely checked and chastised for the good of the soul, finds no sanction in MacDonald's thought. For him, what men must pit their spiritual energies against is the inferior selves of their beings, the undersides of their natures. The enemy is within us, is indeed *ourselves*... .

Endnote

1. *Thomas Wingfold*, Chapter 82. Reis sees antecedents for "MacDonald's views of God's self-expression in nature" in Emanuel Swedenborg, Jacob Boehme, and William Law (p. 38). Like so much nineteenth-century thought that speculates on the relation of the physical to the spiritual, MacDonald's conception derives in part from Swedenborg's thinking, such as is found in his *Heaven and Hell*. Greville writes that his father "knew enough of Swedenborg's teaching to feel the truth of *correspondences*, and would find innumerable instances of physical law tallying with metaphysical, of chemical affinities with spiritual affections . . ." (GMDW, p. 216; italics his). Thus Swedenborg seems to be the fountainhead of MacDonald's ideas, with some influence provided by Blake and Law. But his thought is most directly shaped by the German Romantics. Inasmuch as the French Symbolists also drew somewhat upon the thought of Swedenborg and the Germans, parallels may be drawn between the French Symbolists' idea of correspondences and MacDonald's. Yet in the material available to me, there is no evidence of MacDonald's drawing directly upon the French. The distinctive character of MacDonald's thought, and its chief interest for this study, is the Evangelical-pietistic emphasis MacDonald gives to this current of idea. Greville explains: "Once, forty years ago, I held conversation with my father on the laws of symbolism. He would allow that the algebraic symbol, which concerns only the three-dimensioned, has no *substantial* relation to the unknown quantity; nor the 'tree where it falleth' to the man unredeemed, the comparison being false. But the rose, when it gives some glimmer of the freedom for which a man hungers, does so because of its substantial unity with the man, each in degree being a signature of God's immanence" (GMDW, p. 482; italics his).

Works Cited

MacDonald, George. *At the Back of the North Wind*. London: Strahan, 1871.

MacDonald, Greville. *George MacDonald and His Wife*. New York: Dial, 1924.

Reis, Richard. *George MacDonald*. New York: Twayne, 1972.

Fiction for the Child

From *George MacDonald*

David S. Robb

It seems appropriate, perhaps even predictable, that a writer who gave the child such a central place in his ideology should have been the author of works now counted among the classics of Victorian fiction for children. Indeed, there is a seeming inevitability about the fact that it is MacDonald's children's books which have achieved the most sustained popularity—and availability in print—of all his writings. Clearly, his veneration for the child gave him more than a measure of sympathy with children, and the ability to address them effectively. Just as clearly, it was in this mode that his particular tastes and talents found the readiest acceptability: the fantasy-world of the fairy-tale was a ready-made medium for the imaginative freedom he so often needed. Writing for children, it would have been hard for him to do what he does so often elsewhere—namely to baffle and annoy sophisticated readers with the various denials of probability which most of his work evinces.

His children's fiction, therefore, seems to constitute a separate and especially successful category within his output. Yet its separateness from the rest of his work can be exaggerated and, indeed, the more one considers the matter the more integrated into the corpus of his writing it seems. The same characters-types, plot situations, images and symbols, apparently from a stock pool, occur throughout the body of his work. The dividing-line between the so-called "adult" fantasies and the writing for children is obviously narrow, if it really exists at all, but, more surprisingly, the gap between the 'realistic novels' and the writing for children is also much narrower than we might have expected. Among the Scottish novels, several (particularly *Alec Forbes* and *Robert Falconer*) have a major proportion of their lengths given over to the childhoods of their heroes and heroines, and are clearly close to the world of, say, *Ranald Bannerman's Boyhood*. Others, again, deal in whole or in large part with adolescent adventures (the above, plus, for example, *Malcolm*, *Donal Grant* and *Castle Warlock*). The genre of the adventure story for boys is palpably close in much of MacDonald's adult writing, and so is the world of fairytale.... Despite obvious but superficial differences of mode, all MacDonald's fiction patently comes from the same imagination and, its peculiar success notwithstanding, the writing for children is really no different.

Obviously, one cannot simply argue that there is nothing about the children's fiction which marks it out as "for children". The imaginative surfaces of these works are meant to appeal to the young, and can still do so: the fantasies about good and bad fairies and goblins, or many of the adventures of Ranald Bannerman, have a natural juvenile appeal. Just as important, MacDonald's consciousness of his young audience leads him (usually) to a more simple and direct style which can be more limpidly refreshing than much of his adult writing. Yet the over-riding feature which, at face value, seems to locate these works as for children—the fact that child characters are utterly central to them—is of little help in differentiating them from much else that MacDonald wrote. Furthermore, MacDonald can occasionally be seen forgetting that it is children he is supposed to be addressing as he lapses into discussions for adult readers, nowhere so obviously as at the end of Chapter 20 of *Ranald Bannerman's Boyhood*. ('But I find I have been forgetting that those for whom I write are young—too young to understand this. Let it remain, however ...') Here and often elsewhere, he cannot resist making points which seem to him to be true and important, however inappropriate they may be to his junior readers. Such moments occur sufficiently frequently for one to doubt whether his writing is being completely and securely controlled by a sense of the tender years of his audience. The task of writing specifically for children is less fundamental to him than the impulse to write as truly as he can—which is the goal he always sets himself elsewhere. His junior audiences often have to take him as they find him, just as his adult readers must.

This might appear to be a way of saying that his writing for children is also writing for adults, and we may be tempted to suspect that here we have the secret of his status as a classic children's author: such works as *Alice in Wonderland* and *Treasure Island* appear to have their stature depend, in part at least, on the esteem and interest of adults. Is there any great children's book which seems great because children, alone, have so designated it? C. S. Lewis said that 'I am almost inclined to set it up as a canon that a children's story which is enjoyed only by children is a bad children's story'.[1] In addition, the complex question of what makes for great children's literature is complicated by that occasional process whereby books written with a purely adult audience in view are relegated (the usual word) to the nursery to become children's classics. As Jacqueline Rose has recently pointed out, even *Peter Pan* was created for adult audiences.[2]

In MacDonald's case, we have an author who is constantly preoccupied with the largest issues, so it can seem inevitable that his children's writing is not just for children. Yet, as we have seen, his adult writing is not just for adults—it is for the child in each of them. Who, then, is MacDonald writing for? In an important sense, he is writing for himself. The discussion Ronald MacDonald reports ... can be taken to indicate not merely his father's profound sense of duty but also his inability to redirect his writing away from his own preoccupations and out towards the tastes and preferences of a readership. Not only do his works ceaselessly explore and articulate his own, very personal set of beliefs and priorities but, as we have frequently seen, they draw to an immense extent on his own memories and fantasies. To a considerable extent, MacDonald writes to explore and confirm, to himself, the meaning and significance of his own life, beliefs and recollections. *Phantastes*, his first major work of fiction, illustrates the process time and time again.

And it is in his writing for children, where his sense of a clear audience other than himself appears to be firmest, that we find him, I believe, at his most inward. For if the themes of his principal pieces of children's fiction are examined, we find that they are focused on insights or topics particularly liable to trouble the mind. Ever since his own lifetime, MacDonald has been regarded as offering a particularly optimistic message. Occasionally, in Greville's biography, we are allowed to glimpse his father's moments of doubt or difficulty and, strangely, it is in the writing for children that we find worries being confronted most directly. To illustrate this, let us look at his best work in this vein, and concentrate on the books he wrote for *Good Words for the Young* (Nov. 1868-Oct. 1872), the editorship of which he took over from Norman Macleod for the second, third and final volumes. Here appeared, among other MacDonald contributions, *At the Back of the North Wind*, *Ranald Bannerman's Boyhood* and *The Princess and the Goblin*... .

At the Back of the North Wind deals with an even more fundamental potential stumbling-block to the Christian believer than even fear or the difficulty of belief: it is about dying. It is the story of a dying child. Despite his apparent vitality, Young Diamond is a victim of poor living conditions which expose him to the cold which kills him. The lovely, motherly, but enigmatic North Wind, with whom he is so happy, is a complex figure standing for many things: she is an embodiment of nature and nature's power, she suggests the caring, motherly spirit within creation, and at times she seems akin to poetic inspiration. She is also what men often call fate, or bad fortune, or ruin, and she is a medium through which God's purpose is achieved, even when that purpose seems to involve death and disaster, as in the sinking of the ship with the loss of many lives and fortunes. All these things, however, are eventually seen as merged in one overriding identification, for men 'have another name for me which they think the most dreadful of all.' (ABNW, p. 386)

Death, of course, is frequently touched upon throughout MacDonald's works and is always more or less positively, even favourably, viewed, although the associated sadness is always acknowledged. Mossy's taste of death in the bath of the Old Man of the Sea, in 'The Golden Key,' is usually cited: Mossy pronounces death to be good, and is told that it is not better than life but, rather, is 'only more life'. In the novels, however, it is inevitable that death is presented from the point of view of bereavement, so that it is always a sad landmark. In *At the Back of the North Wind*, however, the reality of what is happening to Diamond is only very occasionally, and indirectly, glimpsed (as when his mother is described as being anxious about his state of health) and the positive side of his fate is given priority. Thus, his near-death while in Sandwich is presented as an opportunity for a marvellous journey, and the moment when he pitches out of the land of the living and into that of the dead is the moment of perhaps the most memorable encounter with North Wind. Even the open windows which kill him (the knot-hole in the thin partition at the beginning; the open bedroom window by which he waits for North Wind for the last time) are made to seem natural and positive things, with scarcely a hint of the danger which, from the mortal perspective, they represent. All North Wind's visits, in fact, are stages by which his health is steadily undermined. This is why Diamond 'must come for all that' (ABNW, p. 58): the opportunities to go with North Wind are understandably welcomed by Diamond, but just occasionally an underlying compulsion is to be glimpsed. Diamond must submit to the North Wind of death taking him away, just as those on the doomed ship have no choice in their cruel-seeming fate—and just as North Wind herself has no choice but bring about such devastation. This work is perhaps MacDonald's most drastic attempt to transform our vision of death, and to offer it as something to be wholeheartedly accepted, despite understandable mortal doubts.

Sleight-of-hand is needed to achieve this, however. Towards the end of the book, Diamond is gradually detached from his family, when they all move to Mr. Raymond's 'small place in Kent' along with Nanny and Jim, the two street Arabs whom Diamond has befriended. Within this larger family, Diamond is increasingly the eccentric, other-worldly odd man out. He is taken into service in the house itself, away from his parents, with never a backward look at them. MacDonald carefully organises a backward look, however, at his old home, the scene of the bulk of the book: it has changed somewhat, but not so much as Diamond's new, uncaring attitude towards it has: 'I thought I liked the place so much ... but I find I don't care about it' (ABNW, p. 396). The ordinary sense of rupture with beloved people and places which death usually entails has been muted to nothing, here, and the effect is heightened by bringing forward the narrator, hitherto transparent, as an observing character within the tale. When death finally comes to Diamond, it is a painless, desirable transition.

Behind the Back of the North Wind

At the Back of the North Wind is a more unequal work than the *Princess* books, not because it is partially dream-fantasy and partially a realistic novel with a social conscience, but because it is simply too long for its basic matter and consequently suffers from padding. Each *Princess* book has a natural narrative to tell, but the heart of *At the Back of the North Wind*, is simply a marvelous, static idea: North Wind herself as an image and as a compendium of all the many and contradictory meanings which we detect in her. As a result, MacDonald has to ceaselessly invent, and draw on source-material as diverse as nursery rhymes, Scots ballads, and his own disastrous northern cruise on the yacht *Blue Bell* earlier in 1869 when he had experienced, painfully and dangerously, the ferocity of illness to a degree which was new to him. The result is lacking in organic unity, as it veers from obvious moralistic allegory to realistic assaults on his reader's social awareness, from embarrassing dream-fables to weak attempts to revise and develop traditional nursery rhymes. Yet no reader would willingly forget the great passages of Diamond's experiences with North Wind: in them, MacDonald displays an inspired invention, combining visual and physical description with a profound, even severe, seriousness which is awe-inspiring. At the end, the work is in danger of making light of death, but in those moments when Diamond encounters North Wind at her most austere and enigmatic, there is no such danger.

There seems a curious discrepancy between writing books for children and writing with a focus on issues which are particularly troubling and difficult to come to terms with. Yet MacDonald's finest children's writing does seem to contain what is especially deep in him: his best non-fantasy work for young people, for example, *Ranald Bannerman's Boyhood*, has a wealth of autobiographical memories of Huntly that is equalled, in his output, only by *Alec Forbes of Howglen*. It avowedly sets out to describe a childhood, and to end when that childhood ends. 'Youth' eventually comes to Ranald when he realises that he is not yet 'a man'. And the touchstone which reveals these successive stages is death: Ranald (like MacDonald) loses his mother at an early age, but throughout the book he is essentially untouched by the loss until he returns from university to discover not only that his playmate Elsie Duff has died but that his friend Turkey had been engaged to her and is therefore sustaining a loss far beyond anything Ranald's life has yet challenged him with. Manhood comes, it seems, when one has faced up to death in the loss of loved ones. The essence of childhood, therefore, is that that challenge is unknown.

To MacDonald, therefore, an important part of the symbolic import of childhood is the absence of fear, or 'rats': childhood is a state of freedom from the anguish which plagues adults, which is why the subjection of children to terrors such as those which blight Annie Anderson's early years in Glamerton is such pollution. It can be difficult, however, to remain innocent of the heartache and the thousand natural shocks that flesh is heir to. As we have seen, childhood stands, in MacDonald's mind, for mankind at its most vulnerable, whether it is being threatened by the Liliths, or the rats, of creation. In the works examined here, it is as if MacDonald has been fending off his own rats, preserving the child in himself and his readers. Greville recalls how 'my father had a wonderful way of catching rats with his hand, thickly gloved' (GMDW, p. 327n). In these stories, in which mental rats are being caught, it is as if the conventions of writing for children, with their assurance of a happy outcome, and the control of the prominent narrator with his intimate, reliable adult voice, are being used as a thick glove. Writing of such matters for children gave MacDonald the secure stance he needed in order to contemplate difficulties and to reassure himself, once again, that it would be all right in the end.

Endnotes

1. Roger Lancelyn Green & Walter Hooper, *C. S. Lewis: A Biography*, London. 1974, p. 236.
2. Jacqueline Rose. *The Case of Peter Pan, or The Impossibility of Children's Fiction*. London. 1984. p. 5.

Works Cited

MacDonald, George. *At the Back of the North Wind*. London: Strahan, 1871; rpt. New York, 1950.

Old Wine in New Bottles: Aspects of Prophecy in George MacDonald's *At the Back of the North Wind*

From *For the Childlike*

Lesley Smith

George MacDonald's *At the Back of the North Wind* (1871) is the story of a little boy, Diamond, who makes friends with death, in the person of North Wind, and, while still a child, matures and then dies—fulfilling Job's melancholy prophecy:

> Thou liftest me up to the wind; thou causest me to ride upon it, and, and dissolvest my substance. For I know that thou wilt bring me to death, and to the house appointed for all living (30:22-23).[1]

Throughout the book, Old Testament prophecies of punishment are lived out—but in a way so irradiated by the New Testament ideal of love that by the time Diamond dies, it is a case of, "O death, where is thy sting?" (1 Cor. 15:55). MacDonald shows us the love behind the sternness mainly through the agency of the hero, a child whose role is angelic ("I do somehow believe that wur an angel just gone," says the drunken cabman [*North Wind* 183]), priestly (North Wind reminds him that his name is the sixth stone in the high priest's breastplate in the Book of Exodus [13]), and prophetic. Diamond is both a prophet himself, as is underlined by his many links with the prophet Daniel, and the sacrificial victim demanded by much Old Testament prophecy.

Diamond's relationship with North Wind begins when his family is living in The Wilderness and develops further when he (apparently) visits the country at her back. But, though North Wind's influence is considerable during the Bloomsbury section of the book, personal contact between the two is suspended; the boy never sees her when Horse Diamond is present or playing a key role, and in Bloomsbury, Joseph, who has taken to cab driving, is reunited with the horse, and Diamond must come fully to terms with the animal after which he was named. Paradoxically, it is during this period that Diamond's prophetic role develops, as his association with Daniel suggests. The process by which he fixes on a name for his baby sister is revealing:

> The baby had not been christened yet, but Diamond, in reading his bible, had come upon the word *dulcimer*, and thought it so pretty that ever after he called his sister Dulcimer (323).

The word *dulcimer* occurs three times in the Bible—all three in the third chapter of the Book of Daniel. This is not the first reference to Daniel, for near the beginning of *At the Back of the North Wind* Diamond's mother feels that "she would have gone into a lion's den ... to help her boy" (27).

There are several resemblances between the two books, though there is no precise allegory here or elsewhere; it is on the symbolic power of biblical myth that MacDonald draws. The most important links between Diamond and Daniel are not in the sphere of allusion but in those of character and role. What Diamond has gained from his sojourn at the back of the north wind is understanding—not the cleverness to which Mr. Raymond is at first inclined to attach too much importance ("Genius finds out truths, not tricks," says MacDonald [213])—and not the street wisdom of Nanny and Cripple Jim, but the understanding which can be derived only from reflection on intensely lived experience. In *The Hope of the Gospel*, MacDonald says: "Our whole life, to be at all, must be a growth in understanding." And he adds something which is clearly borne out in the life of Diamond: "Upon obedience our energy must be spent; understanding will follow" (19). Diamond is both obedient and consequently understanding, and this produces the Diamond "full of quiet wisdom" (345) vitally linked to Daniel, for the prophet is above all a man of understanding—"I am now come forth to give thee skill and understanding," says the Angel Gabriel (Dan. 9:22)—a man who is more sensitive to others than they are to themselves and who awakens them to the word which God is speaking to them as well as to him.

It is long before Diamond reaches this point, but from the very first chapter North Wind, through her nocturnal visits, begins to initiate him into the mysteries of life and eternity just as, in the Bible, "the secret [was] revealed unto Daniel in a night vision" (2:19). And Diamond, like Daniel, has "seen the vision, and sought for the meaning" (8:15). Daniel's role at first seems to be that of a good psychiatrist, helping Nebuchadnezzar bring his most deeply buried ideas into consciousness, and it is doubtful whether this can be said of Diamond. His association is basically with the interpreter of dreams who becomes a visionary, though in his case it is the other way round; he sees visions long before he becomes, not quite an interpreter of Nanny's dream of the moon, but a commentator who tries to convince her of its fundamental truth (297-98). Going one better than Nebuchadnezzar, Nanny does at least remember her dream—but Daniel has the advantage of dealing with someone who believes that his dreams have meaning. By the Mound section of *At the Back of the North Wind*, Nanny can say, "I never dreamed but that one [dream], and it seems nonsense enough, I'm sure Dreams ain't true." But her dream, rejected as it is, is not wasted, for Diamond meditates on it: "It wasn't nonsense," he answers Nanny. "It was a beautiful dream—and a funny one too, both in one" (355). From this time, his own interest in the moon increases significantly.

The apocalyptic passages of the Book of Daniel have no place in *At the Back of the North Wind*, but during the Bloomsbury section they are represented by allusions to the Book of Revelation (itself influenced by Daniel) which manifest themselves through the horses. Diamond's first assay at driving a cab is made with Mr. Stonecrop and his "nameless horse" (163), a mysterious animal whose color is not specified but who bears some affinity to the "pale horse" of Revelation: "His name that sat on him was Death, and Hell followed with him" (6:8).

> "What's the horses' name?" whispered Diamond, as he took the reins from the man.
>
> "It's not a nice name," said Mr. Stonecrop. "You needn't call him by it. I didn't give it him. He'll go well enough without it. Give the boy a whip, Jack. I never carries one when I drives old—"
>
> He didn't finish the sentence (162).

There is a suggestive parallel here with a subsequent conversation between Diamond and North Wind:

> "Sometimes [people] call me Bad Fortune, sometimes Evil Chance, sometimes Ruin; and they have another name for me which they think the most dreadful of all."
>
> "What is that?" asked Diamond, smiling up in her face.
>
> "I won't tell you that name" (363-64).

Soon after Diamond drives out of the yard, he narrowly avoids colliding with his father's cab:

> "Why, Diamond, it's a bad beginning to run into your own father," cried [Joseph].
>
> "But, father, wouldn't it have been a bad ending to run into your own son?" said Diamond in return; and the two men laughed heartily (163).

Father and son have narrowly escaped fulfilling one of the death prophecies of Jeremiah: "I will dash them one against another, even the fathers and the sons together, saith the Lord" (Jer. 13:14).

In Revelation, the rider of the red horse, and thus by association the horse itself, represents destruction; in *At the Back of the North Wind*, "Things ... did not go well with Joseph from the very arrival of [the horse] Ruby. It almost seemed as if the red beast had brought ill luck with him" (309-10). The worst misfortune, Ruby's month of lameness, is brought about by his deliberate spraining of his own ankle. His mission, as he sees it, is clearly spelled out: "It was necessary I should grow fat, and necessary that good Joseph, your master, should grow lean," he tells Horse Diamond (320), sounding remarkably like Isaiah: "And ... it shall come to pass, that the glory of Jacob [Joseph's father] shall be made thin, and the fatness of his flesh shall wax lean" (Is. 17:4). Subsequently it transpires that Ruby has misjudged his duty; his owner exclaims that he is "as fat as a pig" (327), which is undignified for an angel—but then, as Job says, "the price of wisdom is *above* rubies" (28:18; italics mine).

Horse Diamond has religious significance too. MacDonald does not specify his color, but he must be dark for a white lozenge to stand out on his forehead, and he certainly appears so in the Arthur Hughes illustrations. Revelation 6 goes on:

> And I beheld, and lo a black horse; and he that sat on him had a pair of balances in his hand. And I heard a voice in the midst of the four beasts say, A measure of wheat for a penny, and three measures of barley for a penny; and see thou hurt not the oil and the wine (6:5-6).

The black horse and its rider represent famine, and if Horse Diamond does not cause it, he certainly suffers from it in London. When Mr. Raymond inspects Ruby and Horse Diamond, they form an astonishing contrast:

> Beside the great red round barrel Ruby, all body and no legs, Diamond looked like a clothes-horse with a skin thrown over it. There was hardly a spot of him where you could not descry some sign of a bone underneath. Gaunt and grim and weary he stood, kissing his master, and heeding no one else (328).

But much more important than the apocalyptic overtones of the Bloomsbury episode is Diamond's growth in wisdom and maturity. The trials endured by his family in London help him "[take] his place as a man who judged what was wise, and [do] work worth doing" (251), and the value of suffering is underlined by MacDonald's reference to 2 Corinthians: "Diamond could not help thinking of words which he had heard in church ... 'Surely it is good to be afflicted,' or something like that" (254; *see* 2 Cor. 1:6).

The most important resemblance between Diamond and Daniel is that both are especially loved—a quality they share with Benjamin, "The beloved of the LORD." When North Wind carries Diamond in her hair, she is treating him as Moses prophesied Yahweh would treat Benjamin: "The Lord shall cover him all the day long, and he shall dwell between his shoulders" (Deut. 33:12). And Daniel is unique among Old Testament prophets not only in being visited by the Archangel Gabriel but also in being described as a man "greatly beloved" (Dan. 9:23,10:11,19). The Archangel's reasoning is crucial: "I am come to shew thee," he says, "*for* thou art greatly beloved: *therefore* understand the matter, and consider the vision" (Dan. 9:23; italics mine). Love is the key to all his prophetic gifts—and so it is to Diamond's.

Paradoxically, the fact that Diamond is loving and loved makes him an acceptable sacrifice in the Mound section of the book; and The Mound, though one of the little hills singled out in the Bible as places of rejoicing—"The little hills rejoice on every side," sings King David (Ps. 65:12)—is clearly to be Diamond's grave. It is here that the sternest prophecies are fulfilled, and many of them relate to those who, like Diamond, build their nests (at least figuratively) in tall trees—though their motives are very different from his: "Woe to him that coveteth an evil covetousness to his house, that he may set his nest on high, that he may be delivered from the power of evil!" says Habbakuk (2:9). And the nest-builders are usually told that they will be forced to descend: "Though thou shouldest make thy nest as high as the eagle, I will bring thee down from thence, saith the LORD," proclaims Jeremiah (49:16), and Obadiah is even more emphatic: "Though thou exalt thyself as the eagle, and though thou set my nest among the stars, thence will I bring thee down" (v. 4).

To Diamond his nests—one in the beech tree and one in the tower—are, as they have been ever since the night he flew in the "woven nest" of North Wind's hair (39), simply vantage points, and although he dies his fate is closer to the one hoped for by Job than to the downfall of those attacked by the prophets. If Diamond does not, like the man from the land of Uz, expect to "multiply [his] days as the sand" (Job 29:18), since he not only feels that he "should like to get up into the sky" (344) but that "the earth is all behind [his] back" (345), he fulfils Job's youthful anticipation that "I shall die in my nest" (Job 29:18).

The fall of the rotten elm tree in The Wilderness signifies the end of the status quo; the fall of a branch of the beech tree, struck by lightning at The Mound, foretells Diamond's death—as he recognizes when he immediately sings:

> The clock struck one,
> And the mouse came down.
> Dickery, dickery, dock! (351).

The identification of a tree or a branch with a man is so frequent in the Bible that the word *Branch* is used as a Messianic title (Is. 11:1). And in both testaments the severing of a branch from the tree suggests a curse: "The Lord, the LORD of hosts, shall lop the bough with terror" declares Isaiah sternly (10:33), and Jesus says that any branch that does not bear fruit will be cut away from the vine and burnt *(see* John 15:6). But in *At the Back of the North Wind* the curse is defused, although the seriousness of the situation is emphasized by the tutor's reflections: "I turned my steps a little aside to look at the stricken beech. I saw the bough torn from the stem . . ." 352). Death, which seems the ultimate curse, is Diamond's beloved, and he looks forward to nothing more than her visits through the window of his tower room. When he finally goes to the land at her back, some of Jeremiah's most frightening words are fulfilled without their sting: "Death is come up into our windows, and is entered into our palaces, to cut off the children from without" (Jer. 9:21).

St. Paul says of Jesus that "Christ hath redeemed us from the curse of the law, being made a curse for us" (Gal. 3:13), and through Diamond, too, a curse is transformed into a blessing.[2] He does not bear the guilt of others, like Jesus, but he absorbs the fearfulness of death; the ultimate message of the book is that, no matter what happens, there is nothing to be afraid of (cf. Reis, *George MacDonald* 84). Though there is great poignancy in the realization that North Wind can never share the eternity for which she has lovingly prepared Diamond, since she can never enter the country at her back—"There shall be no more death" in the New Jerusalem (Rev. 21:4)—Diamond has learned, as the tutor puts it, that "there is a still better love than that of the wonderful being you call North Wind" (376).

George MacDonald makes no attempt to elucidate the mystery of eternity, and it is intensified by the fact that Diamond's direct relationship is not with God, but with a creature who does not understand this mystery herself. The whole movement of the book is towards trust, which Diamond attains in such measure that he can peacefully let go of everything—even North Wind, even life. Though he goes to the "something that nobody knows" that the old princess sings of in *The Princess and Curdie* (67), we are not afraid for him; for the message of *At the Back of the North Wind* is to promise, as the final and culminating sentence of the Book of Daniel expresses it, that "thou shalt rest, and stand in thy lot at the end of the days"(12:13).[3]

Endnotes

1. Kathy Triggs, in *The Stars and the Stillness: A Portrait of George MacDonald*, cites a review of one of MacDonald's lectures which appeared in the Pittsburgh *Methodist Recorder* in February 1873 and which included the information that Mrs. MacDonald identified their son Maurice as "the lad who suggested ... by his quaint sayings, that weird writing, 'On the Back of the North Wind'" (122). This was sadly prophetic in view of Maurice's premature death in 1879 at the age of fifteen.
2. There are several references to Diamond as a Christ figure in Roderick McGillis's "Language and Secret Knowledge in *At the Back of the North Wind.*" Robert Lee Wolff, in *The Golden Key*, also considers Diamond Christ-like (291)—even to the extent of identifying his parents as Joseph and Mary instead of Joseph and Martha—but he diminishes the comparison by remarking that MacDonald "leaves somewhat ambiguous the question of young Diamond's sanity" (285).
3. The Book of Daniel is the first in the Old Testament to teach, specifically and in detail, the doctrine of the resurrection—which is no doubt one reason why MacDonald draws on it.

Works Cited

MacDonald, George. *At the Back of the North Wind*. London: Scripture Union, 1978. Facsimile of first edition. London: Strahan, 1871.
—. *The Hope of the Gospel*. London: Ward, Lock, Bowde, 1892.
—. *The Princess and Curdie*. London: Chatto & Windus, 1883.
Reis, Richard. *George MacDonald*. New York: Twayne, 1972.
Wolff, Robert Lee. *The Golden Key: A Study of the Fiction of George MacDonald*. New York: Yale UP, 1961.

Diamond and Kilmeny:
MacDonald, Hogg, and the Scottish Folk Tradition

From *For the Childlike*

William Raeper

It could be argued that George MacDonald's *At the Back of the North Wind* is more of a vision than a tale. For, what the reader takes away from the book is surely not a story or a sequence of events, but feelings—feelings about North Wind as an attractive and haunting form of death, or puzzlement as to the meaning of Diamond's and Nannie's [sic] suggestive and inexplicable dreams. The book strikes a continuing note of wonder in the imaginations of children, inviting them to respond to it, and it is this, perhaps more than anything else, which has kept MacDonald's book on household shelves for more than a century.

At the Back of the North Wind stands apart from MacDonald's other works for children in that it is set squarely in Victorian London and not, like the others, in a remote magical realm of bygone years. The world of cabdrivers and gentility, social problems and piety is pleasingly evoked. It is true, too, that Diamond, the book's focus, shares many features of the Victorian child hero—his saintliness in helping others, his cardboard priggery, and finally even his death. What saves Diamond, however, from a descent into complete and utter sickliness is that he becomes a fairy child—a Scottish brownie, in fact—going about the streets of London doing good. The reader does not have to accept Diamond as fact, but can enjoy him as fantasy. The book has a double story, superimposing two worlds, or perhaps two visions of the same world, on top of each other, and it is to MacDonald's credit that he uses the fairy to illuminate the mundane so successfully.

On a close inspection, the book does reveal a complex of learning and levels which are highly arresting as the reader perceives MacDonald translating his theological and imaginative ideas into language fit for children. Herodotus and his Hyperboreans are cited on the first page, for instance, and more than a passing reference is made to Durante (Dante), renamed by MacDonald to point up the universal value of his visionary poetry. Herodotus and Dante may seem weighty names to bandy about in front of children, but there is another, younger figure to complete the trio of pioneers who have recounted something of the back of the north wind, and this is a peasant girl called Kilmeny. Kilmeny, who shows many of the same changeling qualities as Diamond, could almost be seen as a Tangle to Diamond's Mossy, or as an Irene to his Curdie, the other half of a fairy pair.

Kilmeny was the subject of a poem in James Hogg's *The Queen's Wake* (1813). The setting of *The Queen's Wake*, an uneven collection of poems, is a competition of poets at a celebration in the honor of Mary, Queen of Scots. Though Hogg did not, in the end award the laurel to the poet who sang *Kilmeny*, history has certainly singled out his short poem as one of the greatest lyrics in Scottish literature. Generations of Scottish schoolchildren have had to learn it, and MacDonald, too, must have known it from boyhood. Briefly, it tells of Kilmeny, a young girl, who falls asleep in a wood and is taken by a spirit to "the land of thought." She remains there for seven years before returning home once more, but only for a short spell. "For Kilmeny was pure as pure could be." She is a magical virgin, a Beatrice, too good for mortal life and fit only for the highest reaches of heaven. MacDonald placed her and Dante side by side when he came to write *At the Back of the North Wind*:

> I will tell you something of what two very different people have reported, both of whom knew more about it, I believe, than Herodotus. One of them speaks from his own experience, for he visited the country: the other from the testimony of a young peasant girl who came back from it for a month's visit to her friends. The former was a great Italian of noble family, who died more than five hundred years ago... . Durante was an elderly man, and Diamond was a little boy, and so their experience must be a little different (113-114).

Then MacDonald goes on to quote some of Hogg's poem. In fact, Hogg's lyric appears to have provided a few of the salient features of the country at the back of the north wind. Though MacDonald claimed, "I have now come to the most difficult part of my story. And why? Because I do not know enough about it," he did, in fact, describe the back of the north wind in evocative detail, drawing on Hogg's description of the land that Kilmeny is taken off to:

> A land of love, and a land of light,
> Withouten sun, or moon, or night:
> Where the river swa'd a living stream,
> And the light a pure celestial beam:
> The land of vision it would seem,
> A still, and everlasting dream (*Selected Poems* 34).

Life as a dream is, of course, MacDonald's perpetual theme, taken from medieval literature and the writings of the German Romantics, but there are some closer parallels between the back of the north wind and the "land of thought" that Kilmeny wakes up in. There is no sun, for example, but "plenty of a certain still, rayless light" (*North Wind* 115). While Kilmeny is surrounded by spirits, similar to those who appear in MacDonald's "Parable of the Singer" in his long poem, *Within and Without*, the people at the back of the north wind are isolated though kind individuals who communicate without speaking. More important is the river. The river at the back of the north wind is a holy source of life, bubbling and singing. It is this river's song that Diamond continues to babble in his apparently nonsensical ballads throughout the rest of the book: "He insisted that if it did not sing tunes in people's ears, it sung tunes in their heads" (116). The river Kilmeny is laid in also has a song, and its waters bless her with eternal life, just as Diamond's trip to the back of the north wind "saints" him with another order of life which he must bring back to bless and improve the everyday world:

> Then deep in the stream her body they laid,
> That her youth and beauty might never fade;
> And they smiled on heaven when they say her lie
> In stream of life that wandered bye.
> She kend not where; but sae sweetly it rung,
> It fell on her ear like a dream on the morn:
> "O! blest be the day Kilmeny was born!"
> (*Selected Poems* 36)

There is a certain kind of Platonism mixed in with Diamond's and Kilmeny's experiences, as well as an inadequacy in describing the otherworldly scenes. For the country at the back of the north wind is only a picture of the true country where Diamond is destined at the end of the book, surely heaven, while Kilmeny's lofty "land of thought" (also heavenly) has a Greek ring to it. Both Kilmeny and Diamond eventually return to earth in different ways.

From this point on in MacDonald's book it becomes clear that it is not North Wind herself, but going to the back of her which is most important, for she is hardly in evidence for over two hundred pages after Diamond's return. Diamond journeys home, a saint and a fairy, to do the will of God in the London streets before finally departing this life because he is too good for it. Kilmeny, however, fulfills no such pious purpose. As in the traditional Scottish ballads, she vanishes (for seven years—Diamond is only gone for seven days, but in both cases a traditional note sounds) only to reappear briefly before returning once more to the spirit land. Paradoxically and similarly, Diamond is too good to live, while Kilmeny is too good to die. Yet Kilmeny and Diamond share more than just a surface similarity. Both spring from a shared consciousness—a Scottish consciousness—and this aspect of MacDonald's shaping as a writer has often been passed over. Even in MacDonald's long series of Scottish novels, critics have tended to look at the romantic or theological aspects of his fiction rather than at their distinctive Scottish flavor. At the same time, any examination of his fantasy writing has either scrutinized its German roots or else veered in the direction of Freud or Jung when looking for a theory. In effect, MacDonald's Scottishness has been overlooked and, for a Scottish writer who was so emphatically Scottish in his dress, speech and character, this is an uncomfortable blind spot when assessments are made of him as a writer.[1]

MacDonald was a farmer's boy from the northeast of Scotland, while Hogg was a shepherd from the border country of Ettrick. Though the two areas are separated by geography, they are not too widely separated by tradition. Both are lowland, both are steeped in ballads and folktales, and both are rural. In fact, the Huntly burn in the ballad of Thomas the Rhymer, which runs through the borders close to Hogg's home, is the same Huntly of MacDonald's birthplace, for the Gordons took the name with them when they moved from the Borders to Aberdeenshire after being granted lands there by Robert the Bruce.

In the countryside where Hogg and MacDonald grew up, the world of the ballad was the world of everyday life. Hogg claimed that his grandfather had seen fairies and that he had witches in his ancestry. MacDonald made no such claim, but there were witches alive when he was a boy and ghosts went out a-haunting in locales close by. Hogg first made a name for himself by collecting ballads for a volume of Sir Walter Scott's *Border Minstrelsy* and then, inspired by those, he sat down to compose his own in the same tradition. After a shaky start he enjoyed popular success with *The Queen's Wake* (which includes *Kilmeny*) and his career was launched.

MacDonald also set out to be a poet, beginning with *Within and Without*, which ran to two editions. He also composed ballads, notably within the structure of his rambling novels. These are also in a traditional style, but usually contain a theological and didactic emphasis in line with MacDonald's own priorities. MacDonald's ballads, it must be said, are notoriously bad. Often they are no more than thumping, jingling lines of undistinguished doggerel. Yet, on the one hand they play a fascinating intertextual role within the structure of his own novels and, on the other hand, it should be pointed out that the tradition of the "bothy ballad" was strong and peculiar to Aberdeenshire. In bothy ballads, ordinary people made up rhymes about their friends, employers, and events in everyday life. MacDonald was not just following a romantic impulse in writing ballads, he was doing something which would have come naturally to him from boyhood.

Ballads hold a unique and important status in the literature of any country. They are generally anonymous, being passed on by oral tradition in various forms, and this secures their place as poetry of the people. They usually tell a story and often deal with important events such as birth, death, and love, their own peculiar way, just as fairy tales do, ballads help people integrate their identity and order their inner experiences. It is true that ballads often include aspects of legend and fairy tale and vice versa. What Bruno Bettelheim writes of the fairy tale in his book *The Uses of Enchantment* may also hold good for the ballad:

It is here that fairy tales have unequalled value, because they offer new dimensions to the child's imagination which would be impossible for him to discover as truly his own. Even more important, the form and structure of fairy tales suggest images to the child by which he can structure his daydreams and with them give better direction to his life (7).

Even more suggestive is what Jung writes of fairy tales in *The Archetypes and the Collective Unconscious*:

As in alchemy, our fairy tale describes the unconscious processes that compensate the conscious, Christian situation. It depicts the workings of a spirit who carries our Christian thinking beyond the boundaries set by ecclesiastical concepts, seeking an answer to questions which neither the Middle Ages nor the present day have been able to solve (251).

In other words, fairy tales benefit us by helping us order our unconscious, inner processes. Surely, in the same way, the ballad, legend, and folktale tradition that both Hogg and MacDonald were drawing on, helps to do the same thing. Ballads are anonymous products of an imaginative consciousness. They exist outside of the church and the taboos of religion as expressions of ancestral voices, voices which reach out of the past and into the here and now. MacDonald, for one, was very conscious of his ancestral voices and knew them to be speaking in his writing. He allowed them to do this and did not always try to control what they were saying. Often, partly because of this, he did not give a meaning to his fantasy writing, but allowed the reader to draw his own from it, as from a well. This, especially in the area of his children's writing, is one of his chief characteristics. Of these voices of the past, however, MacDonald wrote:

In each present personal being we have the whole past of our generation enclosed, to be redeveloped with endless difference in each individuality. Hence perhaps it comes that, every now and then, into our consciousness float strange odours of feeling, strange tones as of by-gone affections, strange glimmers as of forgotten truths, strange mental sensations of indescribable sort and texture. Friends, I should be a terror to myself, did I not believe that wherever my dim consciousness may come to itself, God is there (*Paul Faber, Surgeon* 203-204).

MacDonald felt strongly that his ancestral voices be contained by his faith lest, perhaps, he succumb to their power.

If MacDonald's writing appears, however, to be romantic, that is because it is. Both Hogg and MacDonald had the example of Burns before them, that forerunner of the Romantics, the ploughman poet who became the voice of Scotland. Hogg actually knew Wordsworth and corresponded with Byron. In addition, both found that, owing to the currency that Wordsworth's and Coleridge's theories received, the form of poetry they were most familiar with the ballad, was thrust into the forefront of public taste. The ballad was heralded as the poem of the people, to be written in the language of the people and, along with the lyric, dislodged the forms of poetry, such as the epic, which had been popular in previous times. MacDonald found a theory therefore to give a spur to his writing of ballads, and it was a theory that served him well. Poetry in general became more "musical" with the poet as both player and instrument, recording his own *feelings* about the world around him. Poetry became, therefore, an invitation to *feel* with the poet and there was a return to the contemplation of nature accompanied the sighing melancholic music of the Aeolian harp. These views found their way into MacDonald's essay "The Fantastic Imagination," which dealt with the fairy tale as a literary form: "The best way with music, I imagine, is not to bring the forces of our intellect to bear on it, but to be still and let it work on that part of us for whose sake it exists" (*A Dish of Orts* 321-322).

Similarly, in his preface to *Dealings with the Fairies* (1867), a pocket-size book of the fairy colors of gold and green, MacDonald wrote: "Where more is meant than meets the ear." In effect, MacDonald married his folk tradition to Romantic theory and brought both of them to his children's writing. What is startling is that in his children's fiction he succeeded superbly, whereas in his poetry he failed. But, it must he asked, how did he succeed, and how did his Scottishness help him?

First of all, there is nothing very apparently Scottish about *At the Back of the North Wind*. Indeed, there are only a few details. Diamond's odd bedroom above the stable in The Mews is clearly a *chaumer* of the kind in which Aberdeenshire farm workers would sleep (those same men who sang the bothy ballads), and a connection is made with the traditional Scottish ballad *Tam Lin* when North Wind tells Diamond: "Nay, Diamond, if I change into a serpent or a tiger, you must not let your hold of me, for my hand will never change in yours if you keep a good hold" (14).[2]

In *Tam Lin*, Janet must hold on to Tam Lin while he changes into a variety of terrifying shapes and animals before turning back into a human knight. If she lets go, she will lose him; if she keeps hold then she can marry him. This motif is repeated in MacDonald's *The Carasoyn* where Colin must hold on to Fairy who turns successively into a snake, a white rabbit, a cat, a wood pigeon, and a dove.

But this is not enough to build a whole Scottish theory on. MacDonald's other fiction, his children's books, *The Princess and the Goblin* and *The Princess and Curdie* seem to be set in a distant, Scottish landscape, and the goblins in the first of these books possess unindividuated toes, a traditional Scottish feature. Ranald Bannerman's nurse is nicknamed "Kelpie" (a wicked fairy creature) in the book of the same name; while MacDonald's short fairy tale, *The Carasoyn*, with its portrayal of the queen of the fairies and the changeling girl, seems to owe a great deal to border legend. Sir Gibbie, in MacDonald's Scottish novel, is a brownie, and MacDonald's continual connection of the wizard, the horse, and the devil (in *Malcolm*, for example) owes much to local color quite apart from anything else. The Horseman's Word, a local secret society of farm workers, actually claimed to possess a word of power enabling its members, with the devil's backing, to hold sway over both horses and women. This society, active until the 1930s in Aberdeenshire and beyond, was particularly strong in Huntly. MacDonald must have known about it, and its supernatural elements, even though so far removed from the bounds of the kirk, must have intrigued him.

Yet, all these are ingredients, it could be pointed out, and not *substance*. And where is the bearing on MacDonald's *children's* fiction? A clue is to be found, perhaps, in the ballad of "Thomas the Rhymer." At the beginning of "Thomas the Rhymer," Thomas, a noted seer, is sitting by the Huntly bank when the Queen of the Fairies (surely at least a cousin of Princess Irene's great-great grandmother) appears to him and takes him off to Elfland. She tells him:

> O see not ye yon narrow road,
> So thick beset with thorns and briers?
> That is the path of righteousness,
> Tho after it but few enquires.
>
> And see not ye that braid, braid road,
> That lies across yon lillie leven?
> That is the path to wickedness,
> Tho some call it the road to heaven.
>
> And see not ye that bonny road,
> Which winds about the fernie brae?
> That is the road to fair Elfland,
> Where you and I this night maun gae
> (*English and Scottish Ballads* 65).

Thus there are *three* roads, not two, and the third, which is not an evil path, is the road to fairy land, or to the imagination. It exists between good and evil, heaven and hell, and appears to belong to either realm. Whatever fairies are (and whether they exist or not), they do show human imagination at work. There had been a time in Scottish history, before the Reformation, when the folk traditions and the old religion (where there was any religion) had been contentedly mixed up. T. C. Smout, the social historian, in his authoritative *A History of the Scottish People 1560-1830* writes:

> Medieval Scotland believed in saints, whose favour could be procured by sacrifice and pilgrimage: it believed in devils and fairies, whose quiescence at least could be procured by a libation of milk on the hillside, or by leaving a little grain in the ground for the "Old Gudeman." It believed in the power of priests, who served the saints, and likewise the power of witches, who were in communication with the devil and could control some of is supernatural

powers either to do good by healing or to do evil, by cursing and destruction (199).

The Reformation and the arrival of Calvinism in Scotland ended this truce between the church and the fairy folk. From then on there was no distinction between a good witch and a bad witch. The Mosaic text "Thou shalt not suffer a witch to live" was ruthlessly enforced and many women were put to death. The bright third way, the way of the imagination, was accordingly suppressed, to the continuing detriment of the arts in Scotland, and the fairies retreated to the woods and hills and vanished out of sight. But, perhaps it is a truth that while fairies can be hidden, they cannot be extinguished. They remained alive in ballads and stories, passed from mothers and nurses to each new generation of children and, though outlawed, they remained stubbornly in evidence. What this meant for writers like Hogg and MacDonald, growing up in rural areas where ballads and folktales were probably at their strongest, was that they imbibed, as children, a mixture of the Bible and fairy. Hogg, for example, recounted that his father was a strict religious man, while his mother was well versed in folklore and taught him ballads on her knee. He learned to read the Bible at an early age and memorized the ballads and the metrical psalms alongside each other. MacDonald, for his part, must have had similar childhood memories. Though he was better educated than Hogg, he would have heard folktales and learned ballads as a child, and it was this base which was galvanized into action when he finally encountered the library of German and romantic literature at Thurso Castle in 1842. *Within* met *Without* and the result was mingling of imagination, Romantic theory, and religion which was to serve him well in writing his children's fiction. In the fairy tale, as in poetry, MacDonald found that he did not have to be bound by the tenets of realistic fiction and was able to make his tales open-ended, Aeolian, as he pleased. At the same time, the subject of his children's books, the child, is also Jung's primal child. He is wise, eternal, and androgynous. This is a being who combines a knowledge of this world with an awareness of the other and is "given to metaphysics" (*North Wind* 83) just as Diamond is, and so is truly "father to the man," as Wordsworth claims.

In the Victorian era, children's fiction was largely prosy and instructive. Children were licked into shape in the nursery and anything to do with the imagination, especially fairy tales, was considered immoral and firmly out of bounds. Yet MacDonald was able to participate in removing these prejudices and there seem to be several reasons for this. On the one hand, his childhood acceptance of the fairy and the religious may have helped stifle any inhibition he may have felt against the fairy tale had he been brought up in the town. This is mere speculation, of course, but it might be true. It was also true that MacDonald was writing at a period when fairy tales were becoming more and more acceptable to the public at large. Yet, at the same time, it is MacDonald's legacy to have taken the fairy tale, in English, and given it a moral vision and to have written fairy tales and children's books which have never been out of print. This is a singular achievement and not a purely accidental one, as his essay on

"The Fantastic Imagination" bears witness. For MacDonald considered what he was about, and this particular essay marks the first time that someone has dared to posit a theory as to how a fairy tale should be written. Much of this essay draws on MacDonald's understanding of Romantic theory, but, at the same time, MacDonald's morality is equally important. As in all his writing, MacDonald was aiming at a religious form. Interestingly, one of MacDonald's favorite poets was Sir Philip Sidney (whom he anthologized in *A Cabinet of Gems* in 1891). Sidney's aim "to teach and delight" was one MacDonald took to heart and perhaps it helped his work become fit matter for the nursery. For, if MacDonald was imaginative, he was also religious and if he was a strong defender of the supernatural, he was also a teacher. This balance of apparent contradictions (contradictions to the Victorians, at least) is what may have helped his children's writing gain approval in the starchy world of the nineteenth century nursery. As a Scot, with his own flavor of the fairy and religious, he was able to respond imaginatively to the German and English Romantics and begin to reclaim that area of the imagination, that third way, which had been denied to children for so long.

MacDonald, the London dweller of the 1860s or the Sage of Bordighera of the 1880s, seems far removed from the country boy running around his father's farm. Yet it is the early years which are often the most formative in any life, something MacDonald was more than aware of as he wrote so powerfully and with such effect for children. In a period when interest in MacDonald is growing and when Hogg, too, is having more attention paid to him, perhaps that third way that they both learned about as children is one which needs pointing to again.

Endnotes

1. David Robb's book *George MacDonald* in the Scottish Writers Series at last makes a beginning in examining MacDonald's heritage, purpose, and achievement as a Scottish writer.
2. MacDonald's treatment of the animal in the human is given an evolutionary and spiritual aspect in *The Princess and Curdie*, where Curdie is given the gift of feeling the animal growing within, under the skin of a human hand (*see The Princess and Curdie*, Puffin Books, England, 1982, pp. 70-1). A more mystical, Swedenborgian twist is given to this idea in *Lilith*, where Mr Raven tells Vane:

   > Every one, as you ought to know, has a beast-self and a bird-self, and a stupid fish-self, ay, and a creeping serpent-self too, which it takes a deal of crushing to kill! In truth he has also a tree-self and a crystal-self, and I don't know how many selves more—all to get into harmony. You can tell what sort a man is by his creature that comes oftenest to the front (30).

Works Cited

Bettelheim, Bruno. *The Uses of Enchantment: The Meaning and Importance of Fairy Tales*. London: Thames and Hudson, 1976.

Child, F. J. *English and Scottish Ballads*. London: Harrop, 1922.

Hogg, James. *James Hogg: Selected Poems*. Ed. D. S. Mack. Oxford: Clarendon, 1970.

Jung, C. J. *The Archetypes and the Collective Unconscious*. New York: Pantheon, 1959.

MacDonald, George. *At the Back of the North Wind*. London: Strahan, 1871.

—. *A Dish of Orts*. London: Sampson, Low, Marston, 1895.

—. *Lilith*. Tring: Lion Publishing, 1982.

—. *Paul Faber, Surgeon*. London: Hurst and Blackett, 1879.

Robb, David. *George MacDonald*. Edinburgh: Scottish Academic Press, 1987.

Smout, T. C. *A History of the Scottish People 1560-1830*. London: Collins, 1969.

Diamond and Kilmeny

When she came close to where he stood, he no longer doubted she was human – for he had caught sight of her sunny hair, and her clear blue eyes, and the loveliest face and form he had ever seen. All at once she began singing like a nightingale, and dancing to her own music ...

Little Daylight

Illustration by Lauren A. Mills (© 1988)

Alice at the Back of the North Wind, Or the Metafictions of Lewis Carroll and George MacDonald

From *Extrapolation*

JOHN PENNINGTON

Lewis Carroll and George MacDonald. Or should it be George MacDonald and Lewis Carroll? Or just Lewis Carroll? Or George MacDonald? Do we need to distinguish George MacDonald the outcast preacher from George MacDonald the novelist, George MacDonald the poet, George MacDonald the fantasy and fairy-tale writer? And do we need to distinguish Lewis Carroll the quirky yet moralistic children's writer from the Reverend Charles Lutwidge Dodgson—Dodgson the mathematician and anti-vivisectionist, "Uncle Dodgson" the photographer? My playing with these authors' names is, I hope, more than a seemingly clever way to begin an article, for these men did indeed have various "signatures" in their lives and works: Lewis Carroll faintly disguised as the White Knight, George MacDonald's zealous religiosity encapsulated in his anagram "Corage! God Mend Al!" Both men are intriguing writers because they play multiple roles, especially when we realize that they influenced each others' work: *Phantastes* (1858) certainly influenced *Alice's Adventures in Wonderland* (1865); *Through the Looking-Glass* (1872) probably informed *Lilith* (1895). In *George MacDonald and His Wife*, Greville MacDonald fondly remembers his father reading the manuscript of *Alice*, Greville exclaiming that he "wished there were 60,0000 volumes of it" (342). That both men wrote fantasies and fairy tales suggests some sort of symbiotic imaginative relationship. In fact, William Raeper, in his critical biography of MacDonald, contends: "Doctrinally then, MacDonald and Dodgson were close and their theological interests led to other shared interests.... [They] informed one another at a profound level and they both held a common vision. Before Dodgson met MacDonald he showed no sign that he would one day set himself to writing fairy tales—for that is how he regarded *Alice*" (174-75).

Much of the interest in Carroll and MacDonald resides in the fact that they appear—even for all their Victorian "trappings"—so very modern. Many of Carroll's and MacDonald's works toy with narrative; such works become self-reflexive, and it is productive to analyze Carroll and MacDonald as metafictional writers. Their use of metafictional techniques creates a complex narrative web which links structural equivocation with thematic concerns. In her general survey of metafiction, Patricia Waugh defines the mode as a "fictional writing which self-consciously and systematically draws attention to its status as an artifact in order to pose questions about the relationship between fiction and reality" (2). Robert Alter in *Partial Magic* characterizes metafiction as that which "systematically flaunts its own condition of artifice and that by so doing probes into the problematic relationship between real-seeming artifice and reality" (x).

But self-reflexivity is more than just a playful pastime; it has literary and social implications. In *Fabulation and Metafiction* Robert Scholes argues that metafiction and the related mode of "experimental fabulation" (41) grow "out of an attitude which may be called 'fallibilism,' just as nineteenth-century realism grew out of an earlier attitude called positivism. Fabulation, then, means not turning away from reality which is fiction, but an attempt to find more subtle correspondences between the reality which is fiction and the fiction which is reality" (8). In fact, Scholes contends that such fabulators and metafictionists assume "the sense that the positivistic basis for traditional realism had been eroded, and that reality, if it could be caught at all, would require a whole new set of fictional skills" (4). In a similar vein, Waugh posits that "metafiction thus converts what it sees as the negative values of outworn literary conventions into the basis of a potentially constructive social criticism" (11) and achieves this by "re-examin[ing] the conventions of realism in order to discover—through its own self-reflection—a fictional form that is culturally relevant and comprehensible to contemporary readers" (18). Finally, in *Narcissistic Narrative*, Linda Hutcheon argues, "Metafiction parodies and imitates as a way to a new form which is just as serious and valid, as a synthesis, as the form it dialectically attempts to surpass" (25).

Metafiction, then, is on one level a reaction against literary trends and conventions, and metafictionists often undercut and parody these conventions to suggest that our sense of "reality" is tenuous. Carroll and MacDonald wrote in the nineteenth century when the realistic novel was vogue, the acceptable form that mirrored positivistic attitudes. Ironically, MacDonald struggled as a realistic writer, churning out one triple-decker novel after another (all mostly forgettable). In a letter to MacDonald, George Murry Smith, a publisher, admits: "If you would but write novels, you would find all the publishers saving up to buy them of you! Nothing but fiction pays" (Greville MacDonald 318). C. S. Lewis claims that such a dominant form as the realistic novel "seduced" MacDonald, when, in fact, his talents lay as "a mystic and natural symbolist" (232). By midcentury, however, and with the publication of Darwin's *Origin of the Species* (1859), a year after MacDonald's adult symbolic fantasy *Phantastes*, positivism began to crumble away, unearthing a radical skepticism. MacDonald and Carroll reflect this growing skepticism, and they mirror this by writing original, self-reflexive fairy tales and fantasies which are reactions against the positivistic attitude inculcated in the realistic novel. These authors, then, create a new literary form which questions the reader's conception of reality by depicting worlds that blur the distinction between reality and fiction, between dream and reality. Carroll and MacDonald predate Borges, who demolishes the reader's sense of stability by crafting *ficciones* which defy narrative cohesion.

Merely pointing out such hesitation over defining reality does not necessarily provide any strategy for living, however, and, as we know, Carroll and MacDonald were extremely concerned with morality and religion. Their experimental fabulations create uncertain, fallible worlds—in Carroll's case a nonsensical world—and they suggest in their radical narrative structures both hope and an ambiguous hesitation. MacDonald contends that reality is only found in other worlds, particularly a world after death, a Christian Platonic world analogous to Heaven. To MacDonald, hope is found in adventure, in the imagination, in the sheer power of creation which can construct mirror worlds reflecting the idealized world found through death. Carroll, on the other hand, seems less assured, and his fantasy world teeters on anarchy, where centers do not hold and where chaos is often loosed upon the world; his world narrows to nothingness. Both Carroll and MacDonald undercut realistic narrative conventions by confusing the reader's stable sense of reality, and their intent is to show that life is only a masking appearance for something beyond, for a world discontinuous from our own but one that is as vital and true. MacDonald's *At the Back of the North Wind* and Carroll's Alice books structurally and thematically provide a space for this alternative reality, and they achieve this primarily through metafictional means.

George MacDonald was a prolific author: he wrote sermons, poetry, realistic novels, and fairy tales and fantasies, for which he remains best known. Jack Zipes claims in *Fairy Tales and the Art of Subversion* that MacDonald "consciously sought to enter into the fairy-tale discourse on manners, norms, and values and to transform it" (104) by parodying and undercutting the classical fairy tales of Perrault, the Grimms, and Andersen. Such tales as "The Light Princess" and "The Wise Woman" parody "Rapunzel," "Sleeping Beauty," and "Little Red Riding Hood." But in these fairy tales MacDonald is conservative; he uses traditional fairy-tale structures and plays a variation on theme. Though these tales are self-reflexive, the focus is more on theme. The same case can be made for MacDonald's Curdie books. Yet in one of his most popular and endearing works, *At the Back of the North Wind*, MacDonald undertakes a more radical task: to redefine fantasy and fairy-tale discourse by dislocating structure through metafictional means.[1] Ultimately, MacDonald blurs the distinction between reality and fantasy and suggests that fantasy is also reality or another form of reality, and he eventually leads the reader to the land at the back of the north wind, which is, in essence, another term for death.

"*At the Back of the North Wind* is one of the most remarkable children's books in the English language," argues Michael Patrick Hearn. "[It] is as fascinating a fiction as any other produced in the Victorian Age" (303). Quite a claim about a work rarely read in the literature classroom. Mark Twain, an admirer of MacDonald, admits in a letter to W D. Howells:

> All these things might move and interest one. But how desperately more I have been moved to-night by the thought of a little old copy in the nursery of *At the Back of the North Wind*. Oh, what happy days they were when that book was read, and how Suzy [died in 1896] loved it! ... Death is so kind, benignant, to whom he loves, but he goes by us others and will not look our way. (Greville MacDonald 458)

Death as a kind friend is a central theme of *North Wind*, and MacDonald's approach in the text is not to merely discuss death thematically, but to provide an actual space for it within the structure of the text itself. In this sense, *North Wind* can be considered a subversive book which undermines narrative and thematic stability.

Realistic novels are based on frames. Readers are guided in such novels by clearly-marked frames—chapters, chronological narration, closure. MacDonald's juxtaposition of these frames from one reality to the next is integral to his metafictional approach. As Waugh suggests, "for metafictional writers the most fundamental assumption is that composing a novel is basically no different from composing or constructing one's 'reality.' Writing itself rather than consciousness becomes the main object of attention" (24). One method metafictional writers use to compose this reality, Waugh claims, is by "draw[ing] attention to the fact that life, as well as novels, is constructed through frames, and that it is finally impossible to know where one frame ends and another begins" (29). *North Wind* is constructed from multiple frames or boundaries. The book is a self-reflexive work about creation and the writing and interpreting of texts. MacDonald is able to fuse the real world of London with the land at the back of the north wind by providing a series of subtexts which undercut narrative stability, and he does this by confusing narrative boundaries, those very frames that readers use to separate fiction from life.

These series of subtexts combine to confound any narrative stability so that the reader views the fantasy world as "legitimately" as the realistic portion of the text. On the one hand, there is the realistic text which makes up about three-quarters of the book. In this text, the narrator describes with Dickensian accuracy Diamond's life in London, from his childhood, his father's sickness, his meeting of Nanny and Mr. Raymond, to his death. Here MacDonald uses a strict chronological framework so prevalent in the realistic novels of the day. And, it should be added, this section of the text often verges on the sentimental and didactic, which supports Lewis's claim about MacDonald's artistic talents. Another subtext, though, is the fantasy text: North Wind breaks into the narrative at random, sweeping Diamond across London, across the sea, finally to the land at the back of the north wind, which is death. In this section all chronology is destroyed; time and space are distorted and skewed, and physical laws are violated. North Wind can shift size at will, be inanimate one second, animate another; she can carry Diamond to any part of the world and have him back in his bed by morning. The narrative, then, becomes as disjointed. The fantasy subtext is presented side-by-side with the realistic narrative, and the narrator—who is actually retelling the story that Diamond has told him (a frame within a frame)—treats the fantasy subtext as a real text, and, thus, the reader must acknowledge this subtext as real, not the product of Diamond's imagination. Consequently, as the reader begins to feel comfortable and settled in with the realistic frame, the fantasy frame interrupts and forces the reader to shift narrative perspectives. As the text advances, the fantasy frame takes on more "reality" and supersedes the realistic text until Diamond's death in the real world becomes just another adventure to the land at the back of the north wind, a place that the reader has already visited. Whereas realistic novels strive for closure, *North Wind* subverts closure by ironically portraying death as a new and better beginning.

The realistic and fantasy frames dominate the structure of *North Wind*, but there exist other subtexts which are crucial in breaking down conventional narrative. After returning from the land at the back of the north wind, Diamond creates so-called nonsense poems to humor and instruct his little brother. These poems have no apparent structure; they are stream-of-consciousness rhymes of free association. However, these rhymes represent Diamond's otherworldly sensibilities and his exuberance over artistic creation, and these "poems" hint at the poetic genius generated from a journey to the fantastical realm (which is actually death). Diamond's images are random:

> baby's a-sleeping
> wake up baby
> for all the swallows
> are the merriest fellows
> and have the yellowest children
> who would go
> sleeping
> and snore like a gaby (123-24)

His poems approach the fluidity of North Wind's appearances; they use no punctuation and have no rational and orderly movement.

Besides creating poems, Diamond also reads nursery rhymes from other texts (again, a frame within a frame). From one book he finds on the beach, his mother reads a nonsense poem that goes on and on, seemingly to infinity:

> I know a river
> whose waters run asleep
> run run ever
> singing in the shallows
> dumb in the hollows
> sleeping so deep
> and all the swallows
> that dip their feathers
> in the hollows
> or in the shallows (108-09)

Diamond's mother, irritated by the poem's lack of meaning, stops reading and exclaims, "It's such nonsense! I believe it would go on for ever." Diamond answers: "That's just what it did" (114). It is worth noting Diamond's use of tense. He has been beyond the actual to the other, and now literature becomes a part of the actual experience, and even Diamond is influenced by the poem to write his own poems (note the repetition of *swallows*). The fluid movement of the river in the poem mirrors the movement of *North Wind*, and the emphasis in the poem on sleeping foreshadows Diamond's death, where the reader and the narrator find an alabaster Diamond "sleeping" on his bed. Roderick McGillis argues that Diamond's original poetry and the poetry he reads reflect his "secret knowledge" which "communicates the life cycle" (120): "Diamond is freed from the tyranny of poverty and nature through language .... The poem then is a manifestation in the actual of that dreamlike place Diamond visits with the help of North Wind" (121). Again, the narrative provides a structure that allows for such a fluid movement from one narrative frame to another.[2]

There is included in *North Wind* an original fairy tale, "Little Daylight," which is told by Mr. Raymond, the author of "the story of the Little Lady and the Goblin Prince" (273), who is George MacDonald. Thus, the reader gets a series of narrators within narrators—Diamond telling his story to the narrator proper (who eventually become a character in the story), who tells the story of Diamond and his adventures at the back of the north wind where there are interpolated poems and fairy tales told by other characters. The reader must remember that *North Wind* is told by a man named George MacDonald who inserts himself in the story as Mr. Raymond, a teller of fairy tales. To add more confusion to the narrative web, Diamond even retells his dreams, which take on fairy-tale qualities; of course, these dreams are real since they are a realistic depiction of Diamond's adventures at the back of the north wind, which is an actual place. Wheels within wheels—a quality of metafictional writing. Even MacDonald's use of traditional nursery rhymes—"Little Boy Blue" and "The Cat and the Fiddle," for example—suggests the complexity of this intertextuality. For as Waugh contends, "One way of reinforcing the notion of literary fiction as an alternative world is the use of literary and mythical allusion which remind the reader of the existence of this world outside everyday time and space, of its thoroughgoing textuality *and* intertextuality" (112). In fact, *North Wind*, the narrator tells the reader, is a retelling of the stories of Durante (Dante) and the peasant girl Kilmeny (from a James Hogg poem) (89).

Thus MacDonald creates a highly original and complex work that challenges the reader's narrative assumptions, breaks them, and provides the reader with a higher reality—death—which becomes, ironically, peaceful and beautiful. As the narrator says when he finally sees Diamond apparently dead: "I walked up the winding stair, and entered his room. A lovely figure, as white and almost as clear as alabaster, was lying on the bed. I saw at once how it was. They thought he was dead. I knew that he had gone to the back of the north wind" (302). Death now takes on an artistic permanence, and Diamond is now a work of art. MacDonald in effect provides an alternative Victorian death-bed scene, one not focusing on sentimentality and morbidity. Tolkien argues that fairy tales satiate our "deepest desire … the Escape from Death," and he writes that "death is the theme that most inspired George MacDonald" (67-68). MacDonald's conception of death as more life allows for escape from the mundane, and death becomes eucatastrophic by providing hope in the face of uncertainty and change. And MacDonald in *North Wind* uses metafictional techniques to provide this space for death. Hearn believes that *North Wind* "is a beautiful but also a baffling, disturbing work" (304), and much of this is due to MacDonald's complex narrative shifts.

To turn from *North Wind* to the Alice books is like moving from Charles Dickens in *Bleak House* to James Joyce in *Finnegan's Wake*: Dickens is a mild experimenter, Joyce a full-fledged radical. And in the Alice books Carroll undercuts the reader's narrative assumptions at virtually every level—thematic, structural, semantic. And like MacDonald, Carroll relies heavily on metafictional techniques. Carroll's intent in the Alice books is much more ambiguous than is MacDonald's, for in this ambiguity probably resides Carroll's purpose: like MacDonald, he creates a fantasy world that has a direct correspondence to the real world (he uses the typical portal device to enter Wonderland and Looking-Glass Land), but unlike MacDonald, Carroll constructs a world that deconstructs itself and real-world assumptions. In

Carroll's world danger lurks at every turn, and though much of this non-sense world is humorous, there is always the possibility of annihilation or non-existence (loss of being), a world certainly not as reassuring as MacDonald's. *Through the Looking-Glass* ends with

> In Wonderland they lie,
> Dreaming as the days go by,
> Dreaming as the summers die:
> Ever drifting down the stream—
> Lingering in the golden gleam—
> Life, what is it but a dream? (345)

MacDonald's *Phantastes* (1858) ends with a translation of Novalis: "'Our life is no dream; but it ought to become one, and perhaps will'" (182), and *Lilith* (1895) also ends with a similar sentiment (252). Dream, imagination, escape—death—these are the qualities that MacDonald and Carroll share, and in the Alice books Carroll, by using metafictional strategies, points to the dissolution between real and unreal.... .

These two Victorian writers were arguably experimenters in narrative form. Their use of metafictional techniques suggests an awareness that the traditional narrative forms found in the realistic novel were inadequate for presenting their specific thematic concerns, so they dislocate structure to create a space for theme. But here is where the similarities between the two men appear to end. MacDonald, a devout Christian who was disgruntled with hypocritical organized religion, found hope in death, in the land at the back of the north wind, and he experiments with narrative to provide that space for death. He makes death more life, beautiful, which is, in effect, an unusual and radical emphasis—though the world is bleak, death allows us to escape. Carroll, on the other hand, seems intent on destroying narrative stability, but his reasons for doing so are much more complex and elusive. Carpenter's claim, though highly speculative, is attractive, for Carroll does indeed show the un-creation of world and being. *North Wind*, though ending in death, seems so reassuring; the Alice books, though ending as dreams where Alice returns safe and snug in her world, seem, ironically, much more disturbing. Of course metafiction works on such paradoxes. In *Alice* the Duchess tells Alice, "Tut, tut, child! Everything's got a moral, if only you can find it" (120). The search for a moral, however, could be as fruitless as hunting for the snark or pursuing why a raven is like a writing desk. Or not. That is the purpose of criticism. And that is the purpose of literature. And it could very well be that my interpretation contrariwise misses the mark. But, then again, as the Red Queen stresses, "It's too late to correct it. When you've once said a thing, that fixes it, and you must take the consequences" (323).

Endnotes

1. MacDonald's adult fantasies, *Phantastes* and *Lilith*, also rely on metafictional techniques. In these works the main characters are constantly sliding from one reality to the next, never able to find secure footing in the narrative. Structure mirrors this chaos of being. It is interesting that MacDonald attempts a similar structure in *North Wind* that he "perfects" in his adult fantasies.
2. Christopher Ricks includes a version of MacDonald's nonsense poem in *The New Oxford Book of Victorian Verse*. But he fails to mention that the poem is an imitation of Robert Southey's "Cataract of Lodore." MacDonald's homage to Southey has metafictional implications: unlike Carroll, who often parodies poems through his own poems, MacDonald appears to respect Southey's children's poem and consciously or subconsciously draws upon it for inspiration. Thus MacDonald and Carroll seem to use parody and imitation for different ends: MacDonald to go to an idyllic past found in Southey's bucolic valley, Carroll to crush meaning and ridicule "tasteless" poetry. But even then, Carroll's parody of "Resolution and Independence" may only undercut form, not the theme of Wordsworth's poem. Such uses of parody and imitation depict the primary difference in the tone and method of *North Wind* and the Alice books.

Works Cited

Alter, Robert. *Partial Magic: The Novel as Self-Conscious Genre.* Berkeley: U of California P, 1975.

Carpenter, Humphrey. *Secret Gardens: The Golden Age of Children's Literature.* Boston: Houghton Mifflin, 1985.

Carroll, Lewis. *The Annotated Alice.* Ed. Martin Gardner. New York: New American Library, 1960.

Clark, Beverly Lyon. "Carroll's Well-Versed Narrative: *Through the Looking-Glass.*" *English Language Notes* 20.2 (1982): 65-75.

—. *Reflections of Fantasy: The Mirror-Worlds of Carroll, Nabokov, and Pynchon.* New York: Peter Lang, 1985.

Hearn, Michael Patrick. Afterword in *At the Back of the North Wind*, by George MacDonald. New York: New American Library, 1986, 303-14.

Hutcheon, Linda. *Narcissistic Narrative: The Metafictional Paradox.* New York: Routledge, 1984.

—. *A Theory of Parody: The Teachings of Twentieth-Century Art Forms.* New York: Routledge, 1985.

Jackson, Rosemary. *Fantasy: The Literature of Subversion.* London: Methuen, 1981.

Lewis, C. S. *The Allegory of Love.* London: Oxford UP, 1936.

MacDonald, George. *At the Back of the North Wind.* New York: New American Library, 1986.

—. *Lilith.* Grand Rapids, MI: Eerdmans, 1981.

—. *Phantastes.* Grand Rapids, MI: Eerdmans, 1981.

MacDonald, Greville. *George MacDonald and His Wife.* London: George Allen and Unwin, 1924.

McGillis, Roderick. "Language and Secret Knowledge in *At the Back of the North Wind.*" *Proceedings of the Seventh Annual Conference of the Children's Literature Association.* Ed. Patricia A. Ord. New Rochelle, NY: Children's Literature Association, 1980, 120-27.

Raeper, William. *George MacDonald.* Tring, England: Lion, 1987.

Ricks, Christopher, ed. *The New Oxford Book of Victorian Verse.* New York: Oxford UP, 1987.

Scholes, Robert. *Fabulation and Metafiction.* Urbana: U of Illinois P, 1979.

Southey, Robert. *Poems of Robert Southey.* Ed. Maurice H. Fitzgerald. London: Oxford UP, 1909.

Tolkien, J. R. R. "On Fairy-Stories." *The Tolkien Reader.* New York: Ballantine, 1966, 3-84.
Waugh, Patricia. *Metafiction.* London: Methuen, 1984.
Zipes, Jack. *Fairy Tales and the Art of Subversion.* New York: Wildman, 1983.

Endpapers for At the Back of the North Wind
Illustration by Jessie Wilcox Smith (David McKay, 1919)

Suffer the Children:
The Problem of the Loving Father in *At the Back of the North Wind*

From *Children's Literature Association Quarterly*

Naomi J. Wood

> Nietzsche stated the essentially religious problem of the meaning of pain and gave it the only fitting answer: if pain and suffering have any meaning, it must be that they are enjoyable to someone. (Deleuze 118)

> Surely it is good to be afflicted. *(At the Back of the North Wind* 223)

George MacDonald's mother-goddesses have figured so prominently in recent criticism that his commitment to patriarchy and to a Father-God has sometimes been neglected.[1] While maternal images figure prominently in MacDonald's imagination, to overlook the importance of the father in MacDonald's work is to risk misreading him. C. S. Lewis pointed out long ago that MacDonald's "almost perfect relationship with his father was the earthly root of all his wisdom. From his own father, MacDonald said, he first learned that Fatherhood must be at the core of the universe. He was thus prepared in an unusual way to teach that religion in which the relation of Father and Son is of all relations the most central" (1947, 10).

But in insisting on the "almost perfect relationship" between MacDonald and his father, Lewis overlooks MacDonald's more problematic father images. His novels for adults bristle with both positive and negative father figures: Robert Lee Wolff has noted that for every idealized image of a father, such as those found in *Ranald Bannerman's Boyhood* (1871) or *David Elginbrod* (1863), there is a corresponding image of a derelict, wastrel father or father-surrogate, such as those in *Robert Falconer* (1868) and *Alec Forbes* (1865).[2] In addition, while MacDonald's works for children frequently portray loving father-child relationships, these fathers are often absent, weak, or disabled when real crises occur. In the Curdie books (1870, 1882), Irene's father is absent for most of the first book and mentally and physically in the second, while Curdie's father simply supports his son from a distance. In *At the Back of the North Wind* (1871), Joseph often needs his son Diamond's help more than Diamond needs his. And even where strong father figures do occur, they are not always benevolent, for they take pleasure in arbitrary cruelty. If fatherhood is indeed "at the core of the universe," this insight is not entirely a consoling one.

Central to the idea of fatherhood in MacDonald's work and in his imagination is the problem of punishment: as most of his biographers have noted, the young MacDonald rebelled against the Father God of Calvinism by defying the doctrine of election. The challenge is repeated frequently in MacDonald's novels by young children who declare: "I dinna care for Him to love me if He doesna love ilkabody" (qtd. in Wolff 249). MacDonald stoutly affirmed that a loving God would not allow anyone to live forever out of his will; ultimately even the Devil would bow. In order to confront the ensuing difficulty of the problem of evil in the world, MacDonald imagines punishments that teach the one who is punished the lesson he or she most needs to learn. In MacDonald's theodicy, all mischance is designed specifically to bring each of God's children to repentance. In his works, all authority, whether supernatural or human, must inexorably stamp out evil. All good fathers—whether biological or surrogate—punish.

As MacDonald grew older and more pessimistic about goodness in the world, he seems to have decided that more punishment was necessary to elicit the proper repentance—Wolff comments on "the number and vividness of the whipping episodes in the later novels" (306). Further, in these novels punishment is a masculine prerogative: Wolff observes that with only one exception, the whipping in the realistic novels is done by men, who "lash the women, each other, and their children" (312). But in MacDonald's fantasies, the punishing is done by goddess grandmothers. Masochistic and sadistic images abound in MacDonald's work, centering on relationships between parents and sons. Psychoanalytic philosopher Gilles Deleuze argues that the masochistic universe is entirely separate from the sadistic one. Replacing the law-wielding father of sadistic fantasy actually enables the masochist to disavow the father and his power, supplanting him with the idealized, "supersensual" mother of the masochistic paradigm.

At the Back of the North Wind contains both masochistic and sadistic paradigms; this division attempts to resolve the problem of submission to a god who both loves and punishes. The work divides into two halves, two worlds, two modes. The first half is under the jurisdiction of motherly North Wind. The second half, the "realistic" part of the novel, features an ambivalent trinity of fathers: Mr. Raymond, the narrator, and MacDonald himself. In the first half, motherly North Wind punishes, kills, and thereby teaches Diamond that all things work together for good for those who love God and act according to his purpose (cf. Romans 8:28). Only after learning this lesson of submission is Diamond ready to submit to the more distant father figures in the second half of the novel and teach that submission to others. The first half of the story, in which Diamond travels on fantastic journeys with a sexual mother figure, is in tone, imagery, and mode remarkably analogous to the pre-oedipal, "Imaginary" phase described by Jacques Lacan, in which the infant, enjoying perfect unity with the mother, has not yet been catapulted into the Symbolic Order by the oedipal crisis. The second half of the story is given over almost entirely to the Symbolic Order, the order of the status quo and thus of realism.³ This latter half transfers agency to the three father figures, dramatizing issues of paternity, power, and punishment in relation not only to Diamond, but also to the readers; since this half is "realistic," it is more "applicable." The shift from the pleasure principle associated with the ideal mother to the reality principle of suffering associated with the ideal father, together with the demand that the audience enjoy this suffering, reflects the problem of address in children's literature in general, as articulated by Jacqueline Rose, namely who is speaking for whom, and to what purpose? Fatherhood, as expressed in MacDonald's work, poses fundamental questions about the meaning of authority, punishment, and submission. MacDonald goads his audience to ask: What do fathers want? What does it mean to have a father? What does it mean to love one?

I

Among the heirs of the puritan tradition during this period, fatherhood was both implicitly and explicitly associated with power and punishment. MacDonald, raised by Scottish Presbyterians, struggled with this concept his entire life. For these Protestants, using "the rod" liberally was considered a parental duty, one that was neglected at the peril of the child's immortal soul. Much literature for children was geared toward explaining the duty of parents to discipline without mercy and the duty of children to submit. Mr. Fairchild declared to his children in Mary Martha Sherwood's *The Fairchild Family* (1818), "I stand in the place of God to you, whilst you are a child" (149); the corollary was that God/Father's will was not to be questioned. Three-quarters of a century later, in 1894, one Rev. R. F. Horton was still explaining that the chief joy of childhood is "that children have no choice: 'Grown-up people have the burden of choosing whom they are to obey. That is chosen for *you* by Nature, by God. You have to obey your parents'" (qtd in Grylls 61). This attitude was an intimate part of MacDonald's upbringing and later life; he brought up his own sons in fear of the rod, regarding punishment as a true expression of love. His son and biographer Greville MacDonald wrote:

> My father, in the education of his children, put duty before everything. In spite of his repudiation of Calvinism, he upheld passive obedience as essential in training the young.... It made me look upon my father with some fear. He stood for the Inexorable. So that when appeal to an undeveloped moral sense failed, corporal punishment, sometimes severe, was inevitable. (27)

In this system, the child must learn to submit to authority without question, however constraining, demanding, illogical, or arbitrary it may seem. Ultimately, children are to strive for a submissive response to pain and sacrifice, assured by paternal voices that the rod can teach them the essential Christian lesson: relinquishing the self. These are the ideals of Christian child-rearing, as expressed in MacDonald's own books and life. Punishment teaches: it is the way a loving, fatherly God makes his erring children acceptable to him. What looks like evil is only the extreme expression of God's love—Hell is "only anither form o' love."[4] The true children of God, therefore, accept all that happens with the supreme confidence that it happens for their own good. But even if a person will not submit, he or she eventually will be compelled; in this version of divine paternalism, resistance is useless.[5]

This threatening and embracing authority was attributed to both paternal and maternal aspects of God. While MacDonald insists on the Law of the Father, he also imagines God as a punishing, commanding mother. Ironically, both the late nineteenth-century critic Thomas Gunn Selby and the middle twentieth-century critic Wolff castigate him for feminizing, sentimentalizing, and domesticating God without acknowledging God's status as disciplinarian (Wolff 258-60). A less gender biased look at MacDonald's texts, however, shows the motherly aspects of God to be remarkably stern; mothers can be just as harsh as the Father-God of Calvinism, though they couple this cruelty with loving seductiveness. In fact, there are marked affinities between MacDonald's goddess-grandmothers and Leopold von Sacher-Masoch's cruelly loving dominatrixes.[6] In his extensive analysis of Sacher-Masoch's works, Gilles Deleuze describes the paradigmatic torturer: "The trinity of the masochistic dream is summed up in the words: cold—maternal—severe, icy—sentimental—cruel" (51). North Wind too is cold, maternal, severe, sentimental, and what Deleuze calls "supersensual," a sensuality that belies its source. Like Sacher-Masoch's ideal women, North Wind kills without passion; like them, she stands for fantasy, enabling those who love her to disavow the Law of the Father, to act as though the father's law prohibiting love and sexual pleasure does not pertain. In MacDonald's work, however, these powerful goddesses are themselves under the direction of the God that he imagines as the source of all things. For all his subversive inversions noted by such critics as Jack Zipes, MacDonald is still supportive of cosmic authority.

In his most fully articulated expression of critical theory, "The Fantastic Imagination," MacDonald admits that he wishes to influence his own readers as a father would his children: "I do not write for children, but the childlike, whether of five, or fifty, or seventy-five" (25). To be childlike is to be submissive; MacDonald names women and children as his preferred audience—men "spoil countless precious things by intellectual greed" (28). His stated aim is to "assail the soul[s] of his reader[s]," overcoming their resistance and drawing them in (28). In essence, he wants readers who not only submit, but who revel in submission. Critical treatments of MacDonald emphasize his theology of love; I wish here to draw attention to the way MacDonald's love is defined by pain and humiliation.

II

In *At the Back of the North Wind*, parenthood is a power that loves, tests, and punishes. The motherly North Wind disciplines Diamond with icy blasts even as she conducts romantic trysts with him, initiating him into the pleasures of submission. In so doing, she prepares him for his meetings with fathers later in the book. After each encounter that Diamond has with North Wind, his parents note that he is not looking well, but Diamond desires her company more than he does his physical well-being. When Diamond visits the country at North Wind's back, he almost dies, and ever after his paleness and transparency are noted. Although in their first encounter North Wind promises Diamond that he will sustain no harm, his body immediately sustains the blow of "a long whistling spear of cold" that "str[ikes] his little naked chest [12]."[7] His first chilly encounter with North Wind foreshadows the end of his adventures with her: his death. The "spear of cold" that strikes his nakedness is only the first of a series of events leading to Diamond's intimate knowledge of cold; these experiences empty and deepen him to make him an ideal child, attracting to him the attention and ministrations of adults, particularly fathers.[8]

Although North Wind is the chief chastiser in the first part of the book, it is clear that she does not act on her own, She receives "orders" from a distant power and obeys. For instance, she tells Diamond: "I have got to sink a ship tonight.... It is rather dreadful. But it is my work, I must do it" (52). Later, when Diamond asks her what good will come of this, she replies, "I don't know. I obeyed orders. Good-by" (83). North Wind teaches Diamond to be the underling she is herself, not to question but to obey. He learns under her tutelage not to ask for reasons, justice, or logic. At first he is troubled by the inequality of the arbitrary disaster he sees her inflicting. When he questions her about sinking the ship, she replies that a far-off song she hears tells her, "that all is right; that it is coming to swallow up all cries."

> "But that won't do them any good—the people, I mean," persisted Diamond. "It must. It must," said North Wind hurriedly. "It wouldn't be the song it seems to be if it did not swallow up all their fear and pain, too, and set them singing it themselves with the rest." (65-66)

North Wind here seems strangely unsure of the truth of her own claims; her "hurriedness" carries over into many similar conversations with Diamond in which, unable or unwilling to answer his questions, she simply dismisses them. The vision she has of the song "swallowing" all the people, forcing them to sing along, suggests a power that none can withstand indefinitely. Punishment, chastisement, must inevitably attain its goal. Once Diamond has been to the back of the north wind himself, nearly suffering the ultimate chastisement of death, he no longer asks inconvenient questions and in fact begins to respond in North Wind's manner to the questioning people around him. Diamond has learned the Law that the Father has ordained and is now ready to be an instrument of that law. His adventures in the imaginary realm have prepared him to withstand the rigors of the realistic one. Midway through the novel, when Diamond returns from his journey to the country at North Wind's back, he is removed from the dream-world where North Wind ranges freely to the slums of London. Here he begins to spend more time with his father, here he meets the wealthy philanthropist Mr. Raymond, and here he encounters the narrator of the story.

III

This father-dominated "real" world is the world of nineteenth-century waif fiction: suffering here is concrete and material. Understandably, this half of the novel is much less discussed than the first half; it does not have the imaginative charm and sensuous pleasure of its predecessor, and it possesses in abundance the sentimentality and preachiness that often alienates modern readers of the Victorian novel. Although this section of the novel is loud in its praises of fathers, and although it proffers multiple father figures, their arbitrary power masked as pleasure estranges more than it seduces. Diamond must be bought by these fathers, whereas he has voluntarily gone with North Wind. It is impossible, however, to understand the full implications of the first part of the novel without confronting the sadistic antics of the fathers in the second.

Diamond's father has had to become a cabman after many years of secure employment by a rich gentleman, Mr. Coleman. The ship that North Wind sinks was Mr. Coleman's last attempt to save his fortune, and he becomes bankrupt. Joseph manages to buy Old Diamond, Mr. Coleman's horse and Young Diamond's "godfather," and a four-wheeled cab, and the family is introduced to the lives of the working—and nonworking-poor. But Diamond's biological father does not play a dominant role in this portion of the book. A working-class man struggling to make a living for his family, he is linked more with the old horse for whom he named his son than with the son himself. The love between man and horse almost supersedes other loves; Old Diamond is friend, servant, and son to Joseph, while Young Diamond operates on another plane entirely, close to influences and sources of which his father has no conception. Diamond loves his father and is as "grandly obedient" as Old Diamond (48).

There is the sense, however, that Joseph's name is no accident (Wolff 156). After his journey to the back of the north wind, Diamond seems no more human than the child Jesus, and he has a similarly ratified perspective. Although Diamond busies himself for his family's welfare, most notably driving the cab for two weeks while Joseph lies ill, we cannot imagine Diamond growing up to be a cabman like his father. Even their language is different—Diamond tends to speak standard English, unlike his father, even before he learns to read. Joseph, although he is known as a gentleman in North Wind's house (31), is not the locus of power in the story's second half.

Instead the middle-class father-figures who are attracted to Diamond's "still sweetness" (163) embody the symbolic power to which lesser forces in the novel must submit: powers of money, language, and writing. Masters of the media of exchange, these fathers demand submission from those beneath them in the social hierarchy and, in their kindly sadism, embody the spirit of the Law. The most conspicuous of them is Mr. Raymond, the philanthropist who rescues Diamond and his family from their poverty, but who toys with and humiliates Diamond's father in the process. Mr. Raymond displays his symbolic power by manipulating language, money, writing, and people. It is his attraction to Diamond that motivates the action in the second half of the novel. Although Mr. Raymond is described by Diamond and by the narrator as "the kindest man in London" (182), his philanthropy often verges on sadism.

Mr. Raymond is the epitome of the philanthropic gentleman found so often in waif stories. He takes an active interest in the lives of those who are less fortunate than he, rewarding small services with smaller tips: a penny for keeping a walkway clean, sixpence for learning to read. Mr. Raymond helps Diamond find a place in the Children's Hospital (to which he is a "large subscriber") for the street-sweeper Nanny when she is desperately ill from fever. When Nanny recovers, Mr. Raymond makes Diamond's father a proposition. For three months "Joseph should have the use of Mr. Raymond's horse while he was away, on condition that he never worked him more than six hours a day, and fed him well, and that, besides, he should take Nanny home as soon as she was able to leave the hospital, and provide for her as for one of his own children" (252-53).

Joseph is not very enthusiastic about taking the horse, Ruby; he considers the loan a close bargain, although he accepts the deal. Echoing North Wind's lessons to Diamond, the narrator tells us that Mr. Raymond has "reasons" for driving such a hard bargain with Joseph, although we are not told what those reasons are. Within a month the new horse has gone lame, because of a depression people take fewer cabs, and another baby is born. Joseph murmurs against the bargain he made with Mr. Raymond, while Diamond cheerily tells him, "I dare say he has some good reason for it" (284). After some months Mr. Raymond appears "with a smile on his face" (285). Joseph "receive[s] him respectfully, but not very cordially" (286-87) and is told he is responsible for his own misfortune. When Mr. Raymond sees Ruby, fat and glossy, he turns to Joseph and says, "Why ... you've not been using him well" (287). By this time, Joseph is humiliated and angry, but he knows better than to vent his rage at a rich man. The imbalance of power, of course, is crucial to the sadistic paradigm. Mr. Raymond banters ambiguously with Joseph until the latter is completely silenced: "too angry to make any answer" (288). Mr. Raymond then tells Joseph that he has been teasing him—he meant "using" in the sense of "making use" of not "taking care of." He offers to buy Old Diamond from Joseph and give him Ruby in return, but Joseph refuses. After continuing to harry Joseph for several more minutes with enigmatic statements, Mr. Raymond reveals that he wants to hire Joseph as his coachman in the country, support the entire family, and use Diamond and Ruby as the "pair to [his] carriage" (289). "A strong inclination to laugh intruded upon Joseph's inclination to cry, and made speech still harder than before" (290), but he manages to accept the offer.

Joseph attempts to reestablish some control by insisting that he be given first refusal if Diamond should ever be sold. However, Mr. Raymond ignores this plea by handing Joseph money; he is in full control, and does not need to answer. The scene concludes in the narrator's voice, explaining the "reason" for Mr. Raymond's initial stinginess and his unaccountable delay:

> He had meant to test Joseph when he made the bargain about Ruby, but had no intention of so greatly prolonging the trial. He had been taken ill in Switzerland, and had been quite unable to return sooner. He went away now highly gratified at finding that he had stood the test, and was a true man, (291).

All is well: "reasons" have been revealed, and Diamond's family is safe again under the protective wing of an upper-class father. Joseph and his family weep and laugh together, relieved from want after many months of anxious deprivation and after having their feelings wrought up to the highest possible key for the "gratification" of their benefactor. Mr. Raymond's actions in this exchange, indeed throughout the process, seem unaccountable, except for the fact that he obviously is enjoying himself. When Old Diamond and Ruby are brought out together, for instance, "Mr. Raymond could hardly keep his countenance..." (288-89). Baiting Joseph with riddles until Joseph cannot speak, he gradually reveals his god-like design. Like North Wind's overseer, Mr. Raymond has "reasons" only gradually revealed to the persons they most affect, Diamond's serene faith is vindicated even while his father is reduced to infantile dependence and silence.

This core scene demonstrates the problem of the father in *At the Back of the North Wind*. Readers are urged to believe that misfortune is punishment "for our own good." In an effort to prove this doctrine, MacDonald disavows the reality of injustice in the material world by insisting on the justice of the ideal world. Mr. Raymond may bait Joseph, but Joseph is better for it in the long run, having exercised patience and resignation. North Wind may buffet the crossing-sweeper mercilessly, but she has her orders, and all will be right in the end. Misfortune is sometimes a consequence of having done things to deserve it (as in the case of Mr. Coleman), but sometimes simply a matter of "testing," a process that "refines" the person who experiences it. The general theory of "reasons" is problematized, however, by the way the father-figures of the novel appear to enjoy toying with, and teasing, the people over whom they exert control. Mr. Raymond's first challenge to Diamond is that he learn to read; the second is to solve a riddle—which because of his lack of education he is unable to do. Mr. Raymond helps Diamond to enter the Symbolic Order by interpreting the meanings of his songs in the most repressive ways: "they must kill the snake, you know"; "People may have their way for a while, if they like, but it will get them into such troubles they'll wish they hadn't had it" (185). "Reasons," in short, seem always to require the obedience of the uninitiated.

A second powerful father figure is the narrator himself; he too enjoys the power of aggression and of language. The narrator's first action within the story exhibits his pleasure in the rather domineering teasing that MacDonald associates with paternal power; he sees Diamond reading under a tree, oblivious to all around him. The narrator sneaks up on him and speaks "suddenly, with the hope of seeing a startled little face look round" (301). Disappointed of startling the boy, the narrator is fascinated by Diamond's empty depth, a quality he has been discussing throughout the novel. But the narrator also claims obedience for himself. The first sentence of the novel is "I have been asked to tell you about the back of the North Wind" (7). The narrator positions himself as the standard paternal voice so common in children's literature of the period, commenting on Diamond's actions and generally dispensing moral advice with a liberal hand. In one example of many, after describing how Diamond learns to drive a cab, the narrator pontificates:

> Some people don't know how to do what they are told; they have not been used to it, and they neither understand quickly nor are able to turn what they do understand into action quickly. With an obedient mind one learns the rights of things fast enough; for it is the law of the universe, and to obey is to understand. (141)

It comes as a surprise when, in chapter 35—only two chapters before the book's conclusion—the narrator actually appears as a character, another lover of Diamond. He never tells the reader *who* has asked him to tell the story, or what his qualifications are for doing so, but he does insist throughout the text upon his own symbolic authority, as evinced by his learning versus the unletteredness of the children, Diamond and Nanny, whose fantasies he describes. Although the narrator repeatedly remarks that he cannot relate the true story of Diamond's experience at the north wind's back because "I do not know enough about it" (98); still, "I have been to school, and although that could never make me able to dream so well as Nanny, it has made me able to tell her dream better than she could herself" (255). The narrator claims to be able to translate and even to improve the words that a child may have thought: "I do not mean that [Diamond] thought these very words. They are perhaps too grown-up for him to have thought, but they represent the kind of thing that was in his heart and his head. . ." (130). Even while the narrator gives credit to children for experiencing things he is spiritually not able to experience, he also claims linguistic priority and establishes his dominance in the text. At the same time, however, he acknowledges language's inadequacy to tell such stories as he has been told. For all his symbolic wealth, this father-figure, like Mr. Raymond, desires something that Diamond's fantasy world possesses.

Several narrative clues suggest that both Mr. Raymond and the narrator are stand-ins for MacDonald himself. Mr. Raymond writes fairy stories for children, including one about "the Little Lady and the Goblin Prince" (301)—MacDonald's own *The Princess and the Goblin* was published the year after *At the Back of the North Wind*. Again like MacDonald, Mr. Raymond is willing to believe that animals will go to heaven (*North Wind* 250; Raeper 94). Mr. Raymond acts as MacDonald's surrogate in the book. MacDonald is, after all, the one who wishes to "assail the souls" of his childlike readers, while Mr. Raymond clearly is equally interested in assailing and overpowering the people with whom he comes in contact. Moreover, the narrator is a tutor, an occupation MacDonald held at one time (*North Wind* 301), and a poet. Finally, both the narrator and Mr. Raymond have the arbitrary power of philanthropists, of North Winds, of gods—and of authors.

With all this power, it is something of a puzzle what these fathers want of Diamond. Mr. Raymond openly desires the child. After being initially attracted to Diamond's "still sweetness" (163), he invests increasingly in this singular child: he buys Diamond's attention initially by telling him that when he has learned to read, he will give him sixpence. As their relationship continues, Mr. Raymond buys Diamond's friend Nanny, Old Diamond the horse, and Diamond's father, until he eventually succeeds in getting Diamond into his house. What is it about Diamond that Mr. Raymond wants to buy? What could a father, in charge of such a wide range of symbols, want of a small boy? The narrator, too, has an absorbing interest in and involvement with Diamond as an object of desire. He lovingly describes Diamond's attributes and conversations and openly desires his experiences. He neglects crucial information and then draws the reader's attention to it as evidence of Diamond's overriding importance: "I was so full of Diamond that I forgot to tell you a baby had arrived in the meantime" (129). Being "full of Diamond," he can dispense with narrative chronology. The narrator describes the effect Diamond-in-the-flesh has upon him:

SUFFER THE CHILDREN

> The whole ways and look of the child, so full of quiet wisdom ... took hold of my heart, and I felt myself wonderfully drawn towards him. It seemed to me, somehow, as if little Diamond possessed the secret of life, and was himself what he was so ready to think the lowest living thing—an angel of God... . A gush of reverence came over me, and with a single *good night*, I turned and left him in his nest. (304-305)

The passage clearly illustrates the narrator's intense investment in Diamond as a source, a place of origin—"the secret of life." Because of this quality in the boy, the narrator is "wonderfully drawn" to the latter's "quiet wisdom," expressed in his ability to see angels in anything. The narrator's "gush of reverence" substitutes for more corporeal ejaculations. Diamond's access to the "secret of life" is a result of his removal from the bonds of educated language and thought. Although the narrator emphatically claims linguistic priority and omniscient knowledge of his characters' thoughts and motivations, the origin of language, and indeed of life, is elsewhere: it is projected upon Diamond, the idealized child who has been disciplined by his journey to and from the country at the back of the north wind. Possessing Diamond, Mr. Raymond and the narrator hope to possess the source.

Diamond's attractiveness seems universal (to the "good," at least), and particularly so to the middle-class men around him. The quality they desire is described in different ways: Mr. Raymond calls it "genius," but the working-class folk call it "silliness," though in either case Diamond is "God's baby" (186, 162). The last epithet may be closest to the truth, for, as we have seen, Diamond seems not to be connected with his parents as a product of that working-class environment. More refined than they, thanks to North Wind's predations, Diamond moves into higher social circles, and is treated with respect as well as desire by the gentry. However, even as he moves upward, taking his family with him, Diamond never actually becomes part of middle-class society; he remains fundamentally removed from the Symbolic Order even while he is subject to its rigors.

In fact, *At the Back of the North Wind* attributes babies with power drawn from the very origins of the world. North Wind tells Diamond that East Wind told her that "it is all managed by a baby" (53), when he questions her about the source of her orders.[9] At several points in the novel, when new babies appear to stretch the meager family funds even closer to the breaking point, both Diamond and the narrator insist that "babies always take care of their fathers and mothers" (158). Diamond, not surprisingly, has a special affinity with babies that none of the other children in the book have. As he plays with them, he makes up long, rhyming songs that he claims are a joint project between them: "We make them [the songs] together, you know. They're just as much baby's as mine. It's he that pulls them out of me" (186). Roderick McGillis argues that poetry is the originary and motivating force of the novel and that the land at the North Wind's back is the "source of poetry" (McGlllis 196), but it is even more than that: it is the source of all origins, Diamond enters this country by walking between mother-North Wind's knees, into and through her body. Once Diamond has been to the source, he takes on the qualities he finds there and himself begins to represent that point of origin which in MacDonald's mind is always and equally associated with death, the end point. Diamond's originary babyhood, like similar inversions of parent-child relationships in the novels of Charles Dickens, allows him to be the locus of origin, the answer not only to theodicical questions, but also to the question of where we all come from. Fathers in *At the Back of the North Wind* finally look to babies for insight about the meaning of the world.

IV

To look to babies as embodiments of the meaning of life, however, is a disingenuous move on MacDonald's part, and one which throws into question the liberation and autonomy true masochism offers the "victim." Deleuze points out that in the masochistic universe, the most important writing is the contract, which represents the "victim's" own desires. The masochist follows the letter of the law, triumphantly finding pleasure in the very punishment that seeks to eradicate desire. By contrast, in MacDonald's work, the father addresses the child not in order to rear him properly, but in order to force him to surrender the authenticity with which the father himself has invested him. The logic of punishment in this context is to purify the child to make it ready (by emptying it of human desire and subjectivity) to bear the weight of the metaphysical desires of the adult. *At the Back of the North Wind* disavows adult power and knowledge by asserting the priority of the "celestial wisdom" and the power that "God's babies," the completely passive, possess.[10] The contract, however, here written by the father-punisher rather than by the child-victim, works not to express the child's desires, but rather those of the father.

In a late novel, *There and Back* (1891), Thomas Wingfold, MacDonald's "ideal preacher" (Wolff 311), punishes his son ferociously:

> "I told him I must whip him; that I could not bear doing it, but rather than he should be a damned, mean, contemptible little rascal, I would kill him and be hanged for it ... Well, what do you think the little fellow said? 'Don't kill me, papa,' he cried. 'I will be good. Don't, please, be hanged for my naughtiness! Whip me, and that will make me good.... ' I cried .... The child took out his little pocket-handkerchief and dried my eyes, and then prepared himself for the whipping. And I whipped him as I never did before, and I hope in God I shall never have to do it again. The moment it was over, while my heart was like to burst, he flung his arms around my neck and began kissing me, 'I will never make you cry again, papa!' he said." (367-68)

The interaction could be a script from a child pornography movie: here, the child is the assertive one, guiding his own punishment. He assures the father of his love, consoles him, removes his own trousers, and tenderly allows his father to spend his passion in lashing his buttocks. Afterwards, the child expresses only love: the two are described as partners in the same enterprise. Throughout his work MacDonald positively asserts the didactic benefits of punishment as a way both of expressing love and of coming to know the Good. At the same time, there is more than a little sensual investment in the scene. Does the father punish *because* he loves, or *in order to* love, his child? James Kincaid has shown how adults invent the child who will welcome these attentions (255-63); is this fantasy directed at the child or at the adult who reads this novel?

At the Back of the North Wind, then, is a masochistic contract written for the victim by the torturer. A true masochistic contract would allow the victim also to be the director and scriptwriter. In MacDonald's grammar, the father who beats reveals his own desires even as he invents the child who desires beating. It is not a matter of love, but of power. Even the experience of MacDonald's own sons belies the power of the father to compel pleasure in submission. As Greville MacDonald, who was nothing if not a dutiful son, recalls his own experience of punishment: "It compelled submission, but never made me repentant. Certainly it did not encourage my brains. But worse, it made an over-sensitive child craving for love, so truly afraid of his father that more than once I lied to him" (27). George MacDonald's fantasies of pleasurable punishment must not be interpreted as wholly effective, but rather as the expressions of a fundamentally conflicted ideology of fatherhood.

But there is even more at stake. When such fantasies are incorporated into children's texts, they become more menacing, and demand interrogation. Throughout his work, MacDonald describes punishments lovingly and characterizes the victims, especially when they are children, as voluntary participants in the act. Five-year-old "Phosy," in "The Gifts of the Child Christ," repeatedly asks for the pleasure of God's chastisement: she takes seriously her minister's assertion that affliction "is the chastening of the Lord, a sure sign of his love and his fatherhood" (31). Diamond observes in *At the Back of the North Wind* that chastening "refines" children and makes them "higher" than they were before. He remembers the minister preaching "Surely it is good to be afflicted"; such chastisement turns rough Nanny into a child "so sweet, and gentle, and refined, that she might have had a lady and gentleman for a father and mother" (223).[11] Children who learn this lesson well will welcome all disaster as the means to "refinement" and upward mobility. What is more, powerful fathers take much more pleasure in this wasted, ethereal kind of beauty.

The strongly voyeuristic aspect of the fathers' fascination with Diamond belies the assertion that all punishment is for the child's own good; it seems rather for the father's enjoyment. MacDonald's narrators frankly acknowledge the pleasure that observing and manipulating children and their punishments gives. For example, the narrator of "The Gifts of the Child Christ" covets Phosy's dreams of the Valley of Humiliation, and imagines penetrating and being enveloped by them: "Right blessedly would I enter the dreams of such a child—revel in them, as a bee in the heavenly gulf of a cactus-flower" (48). The curious image of a cactus-flower raises the possibility that impalement on its spines would be an equal pleasure to drinking its nectar—or perhaps part of the same thing. The cactus-flower suggests the simultaneous pleasure and pain of being devoured by the "heavenly gulf," which on the one hand signifies the "empty" child herself, but on the other evokes the powerlessness to which such children are being condemned. The many evidences of an adult narrator's pleasure in the pain and submission of these objectified children suggest that these narratives are more for adults' enjoyment than for children's benefit.

Thus, in *At the Back of the North Wind* and other fantasies by MacDonald, power is only *attributed* to babies: the material power of the book is solidly in the hands of the white middle-class men who make things happen. They focus upon the child as an object of desire, but this is not designed to give power to the child reader. Instead, *At the Back of the North Wind* offers us the attempted seduction of a little boy, promising true pleasure if he will empty himself and submit. The narrator, Mr. Raymond, and MacDonald himself, the male trinity directing the plot, pursue rather more sadistic goals. Theirs is not the language of the victim, but that of the torturer, who, as Georges Bataille tells us, "necessarily uses the hypocritical language of established order and power" (qtd. in Deleuze 17). They use the language of authority to pursue their own desires, to possess the "sweet stillness" of Diamond's depths, and thereby to satisfy their own thirst for origins.

At the Back of the North Wind has been enthusiastically recommended by educators and parents for over a century. At once a lyric fantasy and a call for social justice, it expresses potent fantasies of childhood power and sexuality. The tale becomes sinister only when we begin to question the ways that authority justifies itself in the text. Diamond is vampirized by his putative benefactors, who spend his vital force to satisfy their own desires. Readers are expected to register that fathers love empty children most, children who are pure, ideal, dying, or dead: children who have been constricted by adult demands that they enjoy and participate in their pain. Nanny and Jim, both of whom are "full" children, repudiate Diamond's empty metaphysics and so survive, shut out of the narrative's perilous scope. However, MacDonald's most potent nexus is that between power, pleasure, and pain, a web he unselfconsciously offers his readers "for their own good." The pleasure and pain of dominant and submissive relationships are so integral to MacDonald's vision that we cannot understand his work without them. As a text for children, then, *At the Back of the North Wind* exhibits most clearly the "impossibility" of the demand it makes of its readers to evacuate the self in order to take on the qualities of "true" "good" children.[12]

I wish to question MacDonald's disinterestedness, his innocence. The problem of the father in his work indicates a deep ambivalence about the apparent simultaneity of love and punishment. *At the Back of the North Wind* attempts to persuade the victim that peace and pleasure are only found in submission to arbitrary power and pain. At the same time, the novel founders on the split between the child and the adult, between the masochist and the sadist, the fantastic and the realistic. The problem with the father and his relationship to his sons is the metaphysical problem of theodicy. When we see "fathers" so evidently enjoying their "children's" pain, we must ask who benefits most from the relationship. As a man who deeply believed in love and equality, MacDonald still could not resolve the contradictions that resulted from trying to "justify the ways of God to man." As an apology for the presence of pain and evil in a good father's world, *At the Back of the North Wind* attempts to persuade its readers to relinquish their reasoning power and submit to the pleasures of authority's chastisement. During the course of its didactic purpose, however, the book also reveals the delight of the torturer and calls into question his disinterestedness. The torturers themselves lack what their idealized victims offer. God's masculine stand-ins—the narrator and Mr. Raymond—try to possess Diamond, and his ascribed originality, not for his good, but in order to fulfil their own desire. The fathers in *At the Back of the North Wind* are not willing to empty themselves as Diamond has been emptied, or to be chastised as he has been; they cannot finally establish their own innocence, and Diamond escapes them to go to the back of the North Wind, whose innocence is marked by her failure to delight in teasing. For all MacDonald's assertions about the efficacy and pleasure of the father's punishment as an expression of love, even he retreats to the Imaginary world of the mother in the end; the true consolation of death is the return to the womb, a final avoidance of the Law of the Father. MacDonald's repressive fathers, for all their professions of love, cannot finally persuade their victims of punishment's efficacy.

Endnotes

1. Humphrey Carpenter, Nancy Willard, and Judith Gero John have all treated MacDonald's motherly goddess figures at length, and they are frequently discussed elsewhere.
2. Wolff is too often dismissed by more recent critical discussions of MacDonald simply on the basis of his Freudianism and not on the basis of his interpretations. I have found Wolff's work extremely useful in formulating my own thoughts about MacDonald in connection with this project, particularly his detailed treatment of fathers. Although I do not agree with all aspects of his thesis, as the present discussion makes clear, his work provides a groundwork and impetus for my own.
3. I am using a Lacanian model; therefore "Law of the Father," "Imaginary," and "Symbolic (Order)," as I use them in this essay, are intended to have Lacanian valences.
4. A quotation from *David Elginbrod*, spoken by David, who is the ideal father of that novel. He is based, according to Greville MacDonald, on George MacDonald's father (qtd. in Wolff 194).
5. The high costs of this philosophy of child-rearing are discussed by Alice Miller in her psychoanalytic treatments of the causes of fascism and other social ills, e.g. *For Your Own Good: Hidden-Cruelty in Child-Rearing and the Roots of Violence*.
6. The Austrian Leopold von Sacher-Masoch, from whose novels the word "masochism" was coined by Richard von Krafft-Ebing, is best known for *Venus in Furs* (1870).
7. Though Roderick McGillis has pointed out the inadequacies of the Puffin edition, I have chosen it as the most generally available one.
8. James Kincaid's provocative book, *Child-Loving*, exposes the essential eroticism of our culture's construction of the empty child. My work shares many assumptions with Kincaid's, particularly the need to question our basic notions of what children are. But while Kincaid's book focuses on a variety of cultural artifacts from the Victorian era, I question the power of MacDonald's asymmetrical relationships. My inspiration comes from "the theorization of relationships of domination" and submission as they are explicated in the work of Deleuze, Jessica Benjamin, and specifically in children's literature, by Rose.
9. In MacDonald's famous fairytale "The Golden Key" (1867), the "oldest man of all," the "old man of Fire," who lives deep within the earth and is by implication the source of all things, is "a little naked child" with

"an awfulness of absolute repose on [his] face" (172).

10. Kincaid delineates the ways in which Victorian culture, and we as its inheritors, make pedophilia both inevitable and damned. Kincaid's examination of power has particular relevance, although I am not following the same trajectory. Kincaid seeks to disrupt the operations of power by refusing to allow its seriousness to inhibit pleasure, particularly mutual sexual pleasure. I want to expose MacDonald's exploitative view of the working classes (frequently infantilized, as I argue), one that surfaces with regularity in an otherwise radically socialist oeuvre. *At the Back of the North Wind* in particular seems almost to be a plea from power (religious, class, adult) to desire to be cooperative and submit.

11. Nanny's case offers a contrast with Diamond's. Although she is "refined" and "chastised" by her illness, she does not take the necessary steps to live "at the back of the north wind," in spirit. She is too full of herself, her confidence in her own abilities, her interest in her work, and her love for the crippled Jim to be the emptied, "good" child for long after she recovers. In her dream of the beautiful lady in the moon, a dream she later dismisses as silly, she disobeys orders and is thrown out, never to give credence to fantasy again. Nanny never "rises" out of the working class and is seemingly incapable of having all the "mire" removed from her beginnings. Instead, she and Jim happily play with each other and laugh at Diamond's airy-fairy fantasies.

12. The term "impossibility" of course refers to Rose's book.

Works Cited

Benjamin, Jessica. *The Bonds of Love: Psychoanalysis, Feminism, and the Problem of Domination*. New York: Pantheon, 1988.

Carpenter, Humphrey. *Secret Gardens: The Golden Age of Children's Literature from Alice in Wonderland to Winnie-the-Pooh*. Boston: Houghton Mifflin, 1985.

Deleuze, Gilles, and Leopold von Sacher-Masoch. *Sacher-Masoch*. Trans. Jean McNeil. New York: Braziller, 1971. Rpt. as *Masochism: "Coldness and Cruelty" and "Venus in Furs."* New York: Zone, 1989.

Grylls, David. *Guardians and Angels: Parents and Children in Nineteenth-Century Literature*. London: Faber and Faber, 1978.

John, Judith Gero. "Searching for the Great-Great Grandmother: Powerful Women in George MacDonald's Fantasies." *The Lion and the Unicorn* 15 (1991): 27-54.

Kincaid, James. *Child-Loving: The Erotic Child and Victorian Literature*. New York: Routledge, 1992.

Lewis, C. S. Preface. *George MacDonald: An Anthology*. By George MacDonald. New York: Macmlllan, 1947. 10-22.

MacDonald, George. *At the Back of the North Wind*. 1871. London: Puffin, 1984.

—. "The Fantastic Imagination." 1893. Glenn Edward Sadler, ed. *The Gifts of the Child Christ*. 31-60.

—. "The Gifts of the Child Christ." 1882. Glenn Edward Sadler, ed. *Gifts of the Child Christ*: 31-60.

—. *The Gifts of the Child Christ: Fairytales and Stories for the Childlike*. Ed. and Intro. Glenn Edward Sadler, Vol. 1. Grand Rapids, MI: William B. Eerdmans, 1973.

—. "The Golden Key." 1867. Glenn Edward Sadler, ed. *The Gifts of the Child Christ*: 151-77.

—. *There and Back*. Boston: D. Lothrop & Co., 1891.

MacDonald, Greville. *Reminiscences of a Specialist*. London: Allen and Unwin, 1932.

Marcus, Steven. *The Other Victorians: A Study of Sexuality and Pornography in Mid-Nineteenth-Century England*. New York: Basic Books, 1964.

McGillis, Roderick, "Language and Secret Knowledge in *At the Back of the North Wind*." *Durham University Journal* 73 (1981): 191-98.

Miller, Alice. *For Your Own Good: Hidden Cruelty in Child-rearing and the Roots of Violence*. Trans. Hildegarde and Hunter Hannum. 3rd Edition. New York: Farrar, Straus and Giroux and The Noonday Press, 1990.

Raeper, William. *George MacDonald*. Tring, Herts: Lion, 1987.

Rose, Jacqueline. *The Case of Peter Pan: Or, The Impossibility of Children's Fiction*. London: Macmillan, 1984.
Sherwood, Mary Martha. *The History of the Fairchild Family*. 1818. London: James Nisbet & Co., 1889.
Willard, Nancy, "The Goddess in the Belfry: Grandmothers and Wise Women in George MacDonald's Books for Children." *For the Childlike: George MacDonald's Fantasies for Children*. Ed. Roderick McGillis. Mecuchen, NJ: The Children's Literature Association and The Scarecrow Press, 1992.
Wolff, Robert Lee. *The Golden Key: A Study of the Fiction of George MacDonald*. New Haven: Yale UP, 1961.
Zipes Jack. *Fairy Tales and the Art of Subversion: The Classical Genre for Children and the Process of Civilization*. New York: Heinemann Educational Books, 1983. Rpt. New York: Routledge, 1991.

Outworn Liberal Humanism:
George MacDonald and "The Right Relation to the Whole"

From *North Wind: A Journal of George MacDonald Studies*

Roderick McGillis

"what an end lies before us"—George MacDonald

The case of George MacDonald is curious. On the one hand, he continues to sit on the margins of mainstream canonical literature, finding his place by virtue of his undoubted skills as a writer of fantasy. On the other hand, he continues to hold the imaginations of a specialized group of readers—both academic and non-academic—who look to him for spiritual guidance. For this group of readers, MacDonald is important for what he has to say about matters of spirit and devotion. For some readers who glance at his work as interesting but minor examples of an "other" Victorianism, MacDonald represents either a tradition of liberal humanism or a tradition of Christian spirituality that looks distinctly old-fashioned in these days of cultural construction and decentered selves. Terry Eagleton refers to this humanist tradition with its autonomous human subject as "embarrassingly out of gear with certain alternative versions of subjectivity which arise more directly from the late capitalist economy itself" (377). Capitalism, late or early, as far as I can tell, wants willing producers and compliant consumers. As far as fantasy is concerned, the capitalist enterprise welcomes projections that envisage utopia in such a way that they do not, as Rosemary Jackson points out, "directly engage with divisions or contradictions of subjects *in-side* human culture" (154; Jackson's emphasis). In other words, the fantasy of a unified psychic order as well as a unified social order is well and good as long as it remains at a remove from action in the world we must adapt ourselves to. We need never worry about changing this world we actually live in when we have visions of better (and worse) worlds available to us in fantasy. And fantasy such as George MacDonald's diverts us from engaging in social critique and hence social action by looking always toward a metaphysical reality independent from the economy of our workaday world.

My drift implies that MacDonald presents us with a vision that is, again as Jackson suggests, deeply conservative and non-threatening to the social and economic status quo precisely because of his faith in individual perfectibility, his belief in the unified individual, his intense gaze at a transcendent rather than an actual world-in short, because of his belief in a liberal and humanist sensibility. It is this sensibility Colin Manlove refers to when he states that the "whole orientation of MacDonald's fantasy is towards the spiritual and metaphysical" (155). If indeed I seem to be implying this, then let me quickly disclaim my implication. What I wish to argue here is that MacDonald's fantasy (or at least the example of it I intend to examine) presents the reader with a radical critique of totalizing systems—whether these systems be political, economic, or religious—and an understanding of the self as a function of desire. My focus is one scene in MacDonald's fantasy for children, *At the Back of the North Wind* (1871).

The scene I have in mind is in Chapter 8, "The East Window"; in the previous chapter North Wind leaves Diamond in a cathedral by himself while she continues on her mission to sink a ship. Before she leaves him, North Wind informs Diamond that "a beginning is the greatest thing of all" (65). In MacDonald's world, a beginning is the condition in which main characters almost always find themselves. Beginnings are a function of desire, the desire to get somewhere or something. We might view beginnings as teleological, as oriented by their very nature toward ends, but the condition of beginning defers ending, just as the elusive nature of self eludes fixity or the odour of music (cf 61) hints at but does not deliver clarity of meaning. When I speak of desire, then, I invoke a Lacanian lack. In MacDonald's romantic worlds, the self is a desiring self and is in consequence incomplete, always experiencing simulations. Even Diamond's trip to the back of the North Wind early in the book shows him (we later learn) "[o]nly a picture" of that place (278). Finality can only come after endings, and endings are not for time-bound existence this side of the grave. Here there are no endings, only beginnings. Or if endings do occur, they are "endless endings" such as we have in the last chapter of *Lilith*. The end of the fiction that is *At the Back of the North Wind* is the beginning of Diamond's new life and the beginning of the reader's search for understanding. We begin something because we desire something. Desire is the motivation for beginning. In *At the Back of the North Wind*, young Diamond desires, and one manifestation of this desire is his eagerness to understand the things North Wind shows and tells him. She initiates in Diamond the beginning of knowledge. The book does the same for the reader.

And so what does Diamond begin to learn inside the great cathedral as a storm rages without? He falls asleep near the east end of the building, beneath the great Apostles' window, and thinks he wakes to hear the Apostles in this window whispering about him. Before we consider what they say, we might examine this window and the others MacDonald mentions. Diamond hears the Apostles from the east window talking, and St. Peter says that he thinks he saw him earlier in the evening in the gallery near the Nicodemus window. Shortly after, St. Luke joins the conversation "from the next window" (68). The mention of the Nicodemus window draws attention to late night conversations concerning truth, the flesh, and the spirit. Nicodemus, like Diamond, has a difficult time understanding the words of a miracle worker; he wonders how one can "enter the second time into his mother's womb, and be born" (John 3.4). From a psychoanalytical perspective, Diamond's trips with North Wind are manifestations of his desire to return to (or perhaps to remain in) the womb; from a spiritual perspective, they are reminders of the manner in which spirit intersects with this material world in which we live. Diamond, like Nicodemus, is a doubter; he needs to learn how to understand that living in doubts and uncertainties need not mean living without hope and faith. The participation of St. Thomas in the conversation also makes this point about doubt. Diamond is a doubter who must learn trust and acceptance.

His conversations with North Wind in the previous chapter remind me of Asia's conversations with Demogorgon in Shelley's *Prometheus Unbound*, in that Demogorgon speaks in riddles. Riddles, we will learn later in *At the Back of the North Wind*, are of two kinds—the kind that are tricks (162) and the kind that lead to mysterious truths. Demogorgon, like North Wind, is riddle itself, an amorphous shape, a shape without shape. He must take the form of him or her who perceives him; the same is true of North Wind. My pronoun here in reference to Demogorgon is a mark of uncertainty since the deep truth is not only imageless but also genderless. The genderless quality of deep truth may have something to do with MacDonald's well-established construction of the deity as both female and male. Diamond perceives a maternal and yet erotic female in North Wind because this figure best meets with his own desiring self. Asia perceives a male Demogorgon because this figure best meets with *her* desiring self. I invoke Shelley remembering that Shelley's *Prometheus*, for MacDonald, contains "fundamental ideas" that are "grand" (*Dish of Orts* 278). Perhaps the grandest vision of all in *Prometheus Unbound* is the connection of metaphysical with physical truths. Shelley's poem plays out in a mythic and fantastic landscape, but it deals with concrete social, economic, and political realities. The same is true of *At the Back of the North Wind*.

The Nicodemus window, then, might remind us of a stage in Diamond's life that he will pass through. In Christian language, he learns what it means to be born again; he experiences a new birth. Diamond passes from beneath this window in the gallery down into the nave and along to the east end of the cathedral where he comes near two other windows: the Apostles' window and the one from which St. Luke speaks. The narrator mentions several persons by name: St. Peter, St. Matthew, St. Thomas, and St. Luke. The text implies that at least one other unnamed Apostle speaks. What strikes me about the men named is the various occupations they represent: Peter, a fisherman; Matthew, a tax collector; Thomas, a carpenter; Luke, a physician. Nicodemus, we might recall, is a Pharisee and member of the group who opposed Jesus. The men the narrator names form a disparate company, and yet they all have something in common: their devotion to truth and understanding. What I argue here is that this disparate company presents something akin to the disparateness of North Wind herself. The notion of a self for MacDonald is, undoubtedly, related to the notion of the perfectible individual, the unified self of the liberal humanist tradition. But the unified person is not a person we meet here in this sublunar world. MacDonald tells us in his sermon on "The New Name" that each person's "true name" is "the *meaning of* the person who bears it" (*Unspoken Sermons* 106; MacDonald's emphasis), and that this name can only come directly from God because "no one but God sees what the man is or even, seeing what he is, could express in a name-word the sum and harmony of what he sees" (106-07). The unified person is an aspect of human becoming, and becoming proceeds into an indefinite future, as perhaps the fantasy *Lilith* expresses as well as anything in MacDonald's work. MacDonald reminds us many times of the several selves inherent in each person, even while he gestures toward a time when these several selves find harmony and unification in "right relation to the whole" (*Anthology* 190).

The group of Apostles and the Gospel-writer Luke speak in a manner that indicates to Diamond that they are not who they appear to be. He imagines that they can "only be the sextons and vergers, and such like, who got up at night, and put on the robes of deans and bishops, and called each other grand names, as the foolish servants he had heard his father tell of call themselves lords and ladies, after their masters and mistresses" (69). The invoking of the carnivalesque in this passage might remind us of necessary reversals and shifting roles. What interests, me, however, is the melding of characters. The scene is replete with such dissolves. Apostles become sextons and vergers who in turn become foolish servants, waking becomes sleeping and vice versa, the cathedral becomes a stable with horses and hay, night becomes day, storm becomes calm, identity shifts. Instability is the order of things here. The "right relation to the whole" remains elusive.

In *At the Back of the North Wind*, the layers of narrative voice also communicate the lack of a unified subject beyond the imaginary of Diamond's still unmirrored life. From title page to final paragraph of the novel, we have a complex author-relationship to the text. Obviously, the author of this book is George MacDonald; the cover and title page inform us of this fact. But our sophisticated understanding of narrative prompts us to separate the named author from the narrator of the fiction. When we begin reading the work, we encounter the voice of an extradiegetic narrator, someone who has "been asked" (11) to tell this story. Near the end of the story, however, this extradiegetic narrator turns into a homodiegetic narrator, someone who actually interacts with the characters in the narrative. The narrator is both inside and outside the narrative. But a further complication occurs with the presence in the narrative of the character named Mr. Raymond. Mr. Raymond is a writer, one of whose books is the *Little Lady and the Goblin Prince* (261), a reference to a book by the author George MacDonald which is as yet unpublished. When it does appear it will have the title, *The Princess and the Goblin*. In other words, George MacDonald the author distances himself from the narrator of this fiction and at the same time duplicates himself in the person of Mr. Raymond. This raises the question: who is George MacDonald? How does one identify an author? What is an author? At the very least, this splitting of authorship raises the notion of constructed selves. The author of a book is no more unified, no more in a "right relation to the whole," than anyone else in this incomplete world.

Raising questions is what this book is all about. And one of the questions it raises has to do with authorship itself. We might recall that authorship has something to do with authority, and in MacDonald's world authority comes under question. The narrator remarks at one point: "I don't know what I know, I only know what I think" (119). And he confesses at the beginning of chapter 36 that he could not regard Diamond's experiences with North Wind "in exactly the same light as he [Diamond] did" (270); in other words, he could not see these experiences illuminated with the same clarity as Diamond. Diamond is the only character in the book who approaches a "right relation to the whole," and he is about to depart this world for a place we cannot know about first hand. As long as we remain on this side of death, we are only moving toward that right relation. As long as we remain on this side of death, we are in a world of mundane concerns. And so speaking of mundane concerns, I return to the Apostles.

Earlier I referred to at least one unnamed Apostle. This one complains of North Wind's "disrespectful" conduct. He also confesses that he does not "understand that woman's conduct" (69). This confession fits with my theme of incompletion. But what is more striking here is the Apostle's complaint. He notes that he and his fellows have "enough to do with our money, without taking care of other people's children." And he goes on to say that taking care of other people's children is not "what our forefathers built cathedrals for" (69). In a similar vein, a voice (it is not clear whether this is the same voice or another one) remarks that North Wind's goings on have dirtied his blue robe and that it "will cost me shillings to clean it" (69). Of course, we learn right away that these are the voices of sextons and vergers and such-like, and not apostles, but the fact that we learn this only after the words concerning the money and North Wind's disrespect have been uttered (apparently by at least one of the Apostles) requires that we consider how the words might appropriately fit these authority figures. The reader of *At the Back of the North Wind* might either remain perplexed or else move on to take for granted that the words are not the Apostles' but are decidedly those of falsely pious church authorities. Readers who know MacDonald's distaste for "sharp-edged systems" (*Expression of Character* 51) or his difficulty with the congregation at Arundel during his only official pastorate will not find it difficult to realize he might have reason to criticize the church. The church as an institution has financial concerns just as businessmen do. When we take finance into account, we might remember that the scene in *At the Back of the North Wind* takes place while North Wind is out sinking a ship, and the sinking of the ship has something to do with business and economic practice of the time. Lurking in this critique of Mammon-worship is an implicit invocation of imperialism. The Church, no less than other institutions of the state apparatus, is in the business of colonizing.

The indictment of Church and State is evident in the transformation of the cathedral into the stable. Implicit in this transformation is a privileging of the small and meek over the powerful and authoritarian. MacDonald communicates this privileging in a number of ways, not the least of which is parody. The stable is, in effect, a parody of the cathedral. The child holds a parodic position in terms of the adult. The horses, Diamond and Ruby, parody humans. North Wind parodies Demogorgon and Romantic immanence generally. Mr. Raymond's story of "Little Daylight" parodies "Sleeping Beauty" and other fairy tales. Intertextual references to Herodotus, Dante, and James Hogg imply more in the way of parodic elements in the book. In some curious way sleep parodies waking, death parodies life, and fantasy parodies reality. This is not simply a way of saying one thing is reflective of another in this book; rather, the force of the parodic here undermines the stability of "sharp-edged systems." Parody, as Linda Hutcheon argues, "contests our humanist assumptions about artistic originality and uniqueness and our capitalist notions of ownership and property" (92).

Parody gives a curious twist to desire. I suspect that the parody reflects the parodist's desire to be that which he or she parodies. Rarely does parody choose an inconsequential or ephemeral object for its reproduction. It reproduces that which has value, however we may articulate that value. And so when MacDonald parodies the fairy tale, we can, I think, take it for granted that he finds something of value in the old stories. When he parodies the Apostles, we can rest assured he knows they offer us something of value. When he parodies the human desire for completion, we may rightly assume he believes in the possibility of completion. Entelechy is, for MacDonald, reality. It is only that we have yet to fulfill that form towards which we are growing. The unfinished aspect of MacDonald's vision of human life is apparent at the end of the book in North Wind's seeming inability to answer Diamond's questions. He insistently asks her to tell him that what he has experienced has not been a dream and that she herself is a reality, but she just as insistently avoids stating anything outright. She offers tentative statements of what she thinks, and she avows that she is "looking for something to say all the time" (276). She resolutely refuses, however, to answer Diamond's questions categorically. A similar ambiguity adheres to the question of the body. Responding to North Wind's distinction between "brain" and "mind," Diamond remarks that she cannot know of what she speaks because she has not "got a body" (285). She quickly assures him that he could not know her if she did not have a body. The words "know" and "body" remind us of the pleasures of the flesh necessary for reproduction. Production and reproduction are aspects of this world's economy, and they often reflect a masculine ethos. What North Wind does is to remind Diamond and the reader of an economy based not so much on production as on expansion. And I refer to an expansiveness of the self outward to others. Truly to produce is to give of the self, not to gain for the self. MacDonald says as much throughout his work, and in his depiction here of Diamond who helps his family both inside and outside the home, who comes to Nanny's aid, and who changes the life of the Drunken Cabman. Diamond produces the only thing worth producing in MacDonald's scheme of things: good deeds. These good deeds set Diamond on a direct path to the right relation to the whole.

Works Cited

Eagleton, Terry. *The Ideology of the Aesthetic.* Oxford: Basil Blackwell, 1990.
Hutcheon, Linda. *The Politics of Postmodernism.* London: Routledge, 1989.
Jackson, Rosemary. *Fantasy: The Literature of Subversion.* London: Methuen, 1981.
Lewis, C. S. *George MacDonald: An Anthology.* London: Geoffrey Bles, 1946.
MacDonald, George. *At the Back of the North Wind.* (1871). New York: Airmont, 1966.
—. *A Dish of Orts.* London: Sampson, Low, Marston, 1895.
—. *Lilith: A Romance.* London: Chatto & Windus, 1895.
—. *Unspoken Sermons.* London: Alexander Strahan, 1867.
Manlove, Colin. "MacDonald and Kingsley: A Victorian Contrast." *The Gold Thread: Essays on George MacDonald.* Ed. William Raeper. Edinburgh: Edinburgh UP, 1990, 140-162.
Sadler, Glenn Edward, ed. *An Expression of Character: The Letters of George MacDonald.* Grand Rapids, MI: William B. Eerdmans, 1994.
Shelley, P. B. *The Poems of Shelley.* Ed. Thomas Hutchinson. London: Oxford UP, 1965.

Imagining the Afterlife:
The Fantasies of Charles Kingsley and George MacDonald

From *Dante and the Victorians*

Alison Milbank

MacDonald's equivalent of *The Water Babies* both in subject matter and Dantesque frame is another tale, *At the Back of the North Wind*, published serially in 1868-69. In the form of a beautiful maiden, the North Wind takes a poor coachman's son, Diamond, on a number of journeys, but especially to an arctic region which is literally at the back of the north wind. Diamond is not the first visitor; a 'great Italian' had preceded him:

> He had to enter that country thro' a fire so hot that he would have thrown himself into boiling glass to cool himself. This was not Diamond's experience, but then Durante—that was the name of the Italian, and it means lasting, for his books will last as long as there are men in the world worthy of having them—Durante was an elderly man, and Diamond was a little boy, and so their experiences must be a little different.

So the child named after the imperishable diamond is a junior Dante, and he finds, surprisingly, no arctic landscape but Dante's earthly paradise in all its vernal particulars, including the river 'that flowed not only through but over grass', imitating Lethe's clarity. There he meets 'a little girl belonging to the gardener, who thought he had lost her, but was quite mistaken'. Eventually, Diamond himself dies and the North Wind carries him in her arms, as Matelda does with Dante, along the river, singing to him the story of his life. Like Kingsley's operators of divine law, the North Wind is a complex personification because she is the harbinger of death who sinks ships at sea, as well as the bringer of health to the smog-filled diseased air of London. A divine housekeeper, like Dickens's Esther in the similarly plague-suffering London of *Bleak House*, she 'sweeps the cobwebs from the sky'.

In contrast to Kingsley's Dantesque amalgams and ambiguous setting, MacDonald's 'Back of the North Wind' is the actual earthly paradise of Dante. However, whereas in Dante it was the prelude to the soul's ascension into its place in the heavenly rose, in MacDonald it is the growing-place for those who die young, and prepare for the beatific vision. With society as it is constituted, the natural development of the poor child is possible only after death, although the novel charts the rescue of Diamond's father from penury to secure employment in Kent. Like Kingsley, MacDonald turns to Dante for an educative model of development in the afterlife, and similarly includes an element of the erotic in leading the soul to a fuller understanding of the divine. Yet whereas Kingsley seeks a recapitulation of human origins in lower forms of life, MacDonald uses Dante's re-creation of the Garden of Eden for his more Platonic conception of the soul's original existence in God. However, both writers took a high view of the married state as the restoration of the unity of the soul which would continue into eternity: 'And thou shalt be mine, my spirit's bride / In the ceaseless flow of eternity's tide', MacDonald wrote in a poem to his wife, while Kingsley's drawings and letters on the subject are similar in content and with a continuation of physical sexual relations... .

The achievement of Kingsley and MacDonald lies in their success in defamiliarising both this world and the life to come. Just as in their other worlds the operation of the natural moral law by a series of quasi-divine feminine personifications enables a direct relation of act and consequence, so their narrative technique eschews and even sometimes collapses plot development, yet remains precise and believable because it mirrors stylistically the *contrapasso* element in their moral system. While their narratives tend, in unDantesque fashion, to elide the division between temporal and extra-temporal modes of existence, their reliance upon Dantesque principles of figuration protects them from the presiding fault of much contemporary imaginative anticipation of the afterlife: the reproduction of human society in an unaltered form in the next world.

Erasing Borders:
MacDonald's *At the Back of the North Wind*

From *Ventures into Childland*

U. C. Knoepflmacher

Written after *The King of the Golden River*, *The Rose and the Ring*, "The Light Princess," and *Alice in Wonderland*, George Mac-Donald's sprawling fantasy-novel ran serially in *Good Words for the Young* from 1868 to 1869 and was reissued in book form in 1871, the same year in which *Through the Looking Glass* was published. The diffuseness and length of a fairy tale that takes up thirty-eight full-blown chapters certainly offers a sharp contrast to the tightly controlled texts of Ruskin, Thackeray, and Carroll, as well as to MacDonald's own well-honed "The Light Princess." Any reader expecting to find a straightforward narrative will be thwarted by the story's abrupt shifts and turns and interpolations.

The book's original publication in separable units, each enhanced by Arthur Hughes's superb woodcuts, partly accounts for its meandering quality. Yet MacDonald's apparent unwillingness to tighten or compress *At the Back of the North Wind* upon reissuing it as a book also suggests that the looser format brought about by the serial mode of publication suited a narrative that challenges our habitual notions of structure even more than "The Light Princes."...

At the Back of the North Wind ... counters [an] earlier emphasis on the maturation of a child-protagonist. Since the boy who calls himself "Little Diamond" at the outset does not have to grow into manhood, he seems an ostensible throwback to Ruskin's *The King of the Golden River*, closer to the arrested "little Gluck" than to the maturing princes and princesses of *The Rose and the Ring* and "The Light Princess" or even to an Alice whose growth Carroll reluctantly comes to accept. Both Gluck and Diamond perform domestic tasks for elders to whom they defer as much as to the personified natural forces with whom they form a special relationship. Nonetheless, Diamond differs substantially from Gluck. Unlike the boy whom Ruskin chooses to reimplant in a this-worldly Eden, MacDonald's dream-child is primarily defined by his obsessive desire for the overpowering female figure who eventually translates him into a numinous order beyond life and death.

... The opening of *At the Back of the North Wind* ... furnishes MacDonald with an immediate opportunity to distance himself from the gender stereotypes embedded in *The King of the Golden River*. For MacDonald rejects Ruskin's equation of femininity with an idealized passivity. Apparently recalling the episode in which an avenging gale ravages the bedroom of Schwartz and Hans, MacDonald rewrites the scene from a perspective that establishes the absolute rule of the goddess-figure who will dominate his own narrative.

MacDonald carefully rearranges Ruskin's scene. Gluck's "shivering" brothers found their rooms violated by the intruder who left his calling card, South-West Wind, Esquire. Little Diamond, too, discovers that the blowing wind he has thrice tried to shut out has entered his own sleeping quarters. To avoid the "long whistling spear of cold" that strikes his "little naked chest," Diamond hides his head under the bedclothes. Although the "voice" he hears now seems gentler, even "a little like his mother's," Diamond assumes that he is being addressed by a male invader. Showing Gluck's own deference towards South-West Wind, Esquire, he respectfully addresses "Mr. North Wind," as if his visitor were that earlier figure's brother (*BNW*, chap. 1, 6-7). Yet the intruder quickly corrects the boy's mistake ... .

Since the child still mistakes the sexual identity of his visitor, the voice asks him, "just a little angrily," to peek out from under the bedclothes. When he refuses, a "tremendous blast" sweeps off Diamond's clothes. The denuded boy must now confront the full-size figure whom MacDonald goes on to describe as combining a maternal authority with something that resembles Diamond's own childlike vulnerability:

> He started up in terror. Leaning over him was the large beautiful pale face of a woman. Her dark eyes looked a little angry, for they had just begun to flash; but a quivering in her sweet upper lip made her look as if she were going to cry. What was most strange was that away from her head streamed out her black hair in every direction, so that the darkness in the hay-loft looked as if it were made of her hair; but as Diamond gazed at her in speechless amazement, mingled with confidence—for the boy was entranced with her mighty beauty—her hair began to gather itself out of the darkness, and fell down all about her again, till her face looked out of the midst like a moon out of a cloud. (*BNW*, chap. 1, 8)

Given MacDonald's close personal and literary relations with both Ruskin and Lewis Carroll, it hardly seems unwarranted to read this scene as a friendly corrective of their fearful ambivalence about adult female power. MacDonald had submitted "The Light Princess" to the scrutiny of both men, and had come in conflict with Ruskin over its representation of sexual "passion." He soon twitted Ruskin for his prudery in *Adela Cathcart* and apparently could not resist poking fun at Carroll's self-representation in the opening verses to *Wonderland* as a rower debilitated by female freight. Indeed, as I shall later suggest, it is possible to regard Mr. Raymond, the wealthy bachelor and children's author who becomes Diamond's benefactor, as an amalgam of both Ruskin and Carroll.

By reinstating in a children's book the mighty female presences of his adult fantasies, MacDonald signals the obsession he shares with Ruskin and Carroll. But his two predecessors had resisted the seductive, yet angry, maternal authority to which MacDonald has Diamond submit. Indeed, the boy's initial resistance of North Wind captures Ruskin's and Carroll's own ambivalent response to overpowering women. Ruskin kept female figures out of the all-male cast of *The King of the Golden River*; Carroll confronted Alice with those hideous emblems of maternity, the Duchess and the Queen of Hearts. MacDonald, too, acknowledges that an overwhelming maternal figure can be intimidating. The "mighty beauty" who towers over Diamond at first scares the boy as much as a towering Alice intimidated a trembling White Rabbit. But North Wind's "quivering" lip suggests something that Diamond can learn only after his visitor willingly reduces her size; for, like Alice, she too can be naive and vulnerable. North Wind's childlike aspects help to level the differences between herself and the frightened boy. Just as Diamond's regressive imagination furthers the "education" of "a brother-baby" and, later, of a "sister-baby" (*BNW*, chap. 31, 252), so does North Wind often seem more like an older sister. She and Diamond are coworkers, willing agents for an inscrutable power that lies beyond the comprehension of each.

Although Diamond bypasses the process of sexual maturation, MacDonald implies that North Wind's stimulus and tutelage will allow the short-lived boy a privileged existence. In the last third of his narrative, MacDonald repeatedly hints that the unusual child who bears the nickname of "God's baby" may actually have been sent on a special mission during his brief stay among ordinary mortals. Passive during his initial period of apprenticeship, Diamond soon turns into a tiny social activist who succeeds in mending broken lives and inspiring grown-ups by his cheerful rejection of their skepticism and despair. Unlike the dozing Alice or a Gluck immobilized by his older brothers, Diamond is never idle. In the middle portion of the book, he helps redress the destitution caused by his father's joblessness and sickness, the degradation suffered by his friend Nanny (MacDonald's female version of Jo in Dickens's *Bleak House*), the physical abuse inflicted on horses and battered wives, the ennui of the Victorian upper class. Although his abiding cheerfulness often strikes others as odd or even crazy, he inevitably gains their respect—so much so that, in the book's last chapters, a narrator-turned-hagiographer avidly records the boy's last pronouncements.

This unabashed endorsement of Diamond may seem much closer to Charles Lutwidge Dodgson's verse tributes to an adored dream-child than to Lewis Carroll's ironic handling of Alice's misconceptions and blunders. Yet MacDonald's narrator is quite unsentimental about his "goody-goody" hero; he delights in Diamond's many misperceptions and stresses the child's difficulties in articulating, let alone interpreting, the meanings of his dream-encounters. The narrator, however, does not at all feel superior to this slightly addled little boy. Quite to the contrary, he welcomes Diamond's openness to possibilities the adult mind has discarded. The narrator thus repeatedly insists that he respects the elusiveness of meanings that Diamond finds so difficult to express. Such meanings, the narrator acknowledges, cannot really be captured by his own linear narrative. And, by professing to be wholly dependent on Diamond's own accounts, MacDonald as narrator-editor avoids the controlling authorial presence always implied in Carroll's reader-wary narratives... .

Unlike Carroll, MacDonald is quite in earnest when he has his narrator defer to the greater authority of a dreamy child-protagonist. The narrator who readily admits his inadequacies as interpreter of North Wind's and Diamond's gnomic utterances almost exults in his lack of control over a story that moves in seeming randomness through stops and starts and diversions. The narrator's deferential relation to Diamond therefore mirrors Diamond's own awed relation to North Wind. Yet North Wind herself, whose visits become fitful and unpredictable after she returns Diamond from the land at her back, professes to serve inscrutable powers far more knowing than herself. Her own authority, she insists with childlike trust, is superseded by these unknown superiors. Like Diamond and the narrator, North Wind thus welcomes a reality impervious to penetration by an adult intellect... .

Though written long after *At the Back of the North Wind*, the essay on "individual development" helps to explain some of the roles MacDonald assigns to Diamond after the boy's return from "the good place" he has internalized (*BNW*, chap. 10, 88). With North Wind gone during the middle third of the book, her former pupil takes over her identity as teacher of the uninformed. MacDonald delights in Diamond's perverse unreason. He suggests that the child's return from a borderland between life and death has given him the authority—and a newly found "Will"—to challenge experiences his mother regards as axiomatic. When Martha tries to impress upon Diamond the gravity of hunger, he shocks her by parading his incomprehension:

"There *are* people in the world who have nothing to eat, Diamond."

"Then I suppose they don't stop in it any longer. They—they—what you call—die—don't they?"

"Yes, they do. How would you like that?"

"I don't know. I never tried. But I suppose they go where they get something to eat."

"Like enough they don't want it," said his mother petulantly.

"That's all right then," said Diamond, thinking I dare say more than he chose to put in words. (*BNW,* chap. 13, 101)

The narrator's last remark seems puzzling. Is the resurrected boy thinking of his contentment, "better than mere happiness," in the land at the back of North Wind? When questioned about "the people there" by the narrator who will become his biographer, Diamond allows that they looked "quite pleased," albeit a "little sad" at finding themselves in a mere way station, between their past and a "gladder" future (*BNW,* chap. 10, 88). Even Diamond's unwillingness to verbalize the knowledge he has gained stems from his kinship with figures who can silently communicate when they "only look at each other, and understand everything" (*BNW,* chap. 10, 87).

His anti-verbal stance, however, also allows Diamond to undercut his mother's condescending use of the stale similes she deems appropriate for a child of his limited understanding. Provoked by his quietism, Martha insists that hunger and death are not abstractions, but directly applicable to the family's predicament. She tries to rattle the boy by telling him that "we shall have nothing to eat by and by" (*BNW,* chap. 13, 101), and becomes exasperated when he points to a piece of gingerbread in the basket before them:

"O you little bird! You have no more sense than a sparrow that picks what it wants, and never thinks of the winter and the frost and the snow."

"Ah—yes—I see. But the birds get through the winter, don't they?"

"Some of them fall dead on the ground."

"They must die some time. They wouldn't like to be birds always. Would you, Mother?"

"What a child it is!" thought his mother, but she said nothing. (*BNW,* chap.13,102)

Martha's underestimation of a child who has just come back from a journey through "frost" and "snow" becomes apparent in the chapters that follow. For Diamond not only acts as the family's chief provider but also takes care of other victims, such as the much-abused Nanny and her crippled friend Jim. When Diamond decides to find Nanny's dwelling place in a foul London slum, a policeman urges him to stay away from the place, lest accompanied by an adult. The unabashed boy ignores the advice. On finding Nanny gravely ill in her filthy lodgings, he is promptly attacked by vicious denizens of the

Victorian underworld. The policeman, who has warily followed Diamond, afraid that the child might get "torn" apart, routs the assailants. Gently reproaching Diamond for his excessive trust, he points out that the boy might have suffered great harm "if I hadn't been at hand." Diamond's prompt reply is disarming: "Yes; but you were at hand, you know, so they couldn't." The narrator glosses this truism by saying, "Perhaps the answer was deeper in purport than either Diamond or the policeman knew" *(BNW,* chap. 21, 163).

MacDonald seems to recognize, however, that he must rely on something more than such dialogues between coy Innocence and wary Experience if he is to succeed in vindicating Diamond's unconscious awareness of a "deeper purport." He therefore suggests Diamond's consonance with higher harmonies through more symbolic means. The river sounds that still flow in Diamond's mind have made him attuned to unheard melodies. Whereas earlier, the boy still needed North Wind to explain that a poet was someone "glad of something," he now responds to the incantatory rhythms of a certain kind of free-flowing and free-associational verse. The automatic, self-propelling rhymes he tries to master, even before learning how to read and write, strike Diamond as a better medium for his intuitions than the linguistic precisions demanded by adults. In its preference of sound over sense, this formless type of poetry conveys the feelings of well-being and trust that Diamond finds so difficult to articulate through causal and linear discourse.

Diamond's first experience of such a different mode of utterance occurs, significantly enough, when he is still at the seashore debating with his mother. Pointing to "something fluttering" in the sand, he gets his mother to retrieve what turns out to be "a little book, partly buried in the sand" *(BNW,* chap. 13,104). When Diamond asks her to read aloud to him what she identifies as nursery rhymes, Martha is frustrated by a poem that strikes her as incomprehensible. She offers to "find a better poem," but a puff of wind thrice blows "the leaves rustling back to the same verses," and Diamond, "of the same mind as the wind," urges her to continue reading. After more than two-hundred lines (and five pages of printed text!) of euphonious, unpunctuated, repetitious yet ever varying combinations of a limited number of words, Martha has had enough; unlike the pleasantly lulled Diamond, she cannot relax her expectations of direction or meaning:

"It's such nonsense!" said his mother. "I believe it would go on for ever."

"That's just what it did," said Diamond. (*BNW,* chap. 13, 112)

The nameless song that so stimulates Diamond is MacDonald's own version of Carroll's "Jabberwocky." Already displaying the adult's interest in definitive meanings, Alice wanted Humpty Dumpty to decode the words of the elusive poem that so intrigued her. Diamond, however, prefers to submit himself to the sounds and rhythms of a catalogue of nouns and verbs that yield no action, no crowning event in which *"somebody* killed *something"* (as Alice so shrewdly noted). We are offered no vorpal sword cutting through gordian knots, no climactic welcoming of a "beamish boy." The never-ending song that the mother of a radiant boy dismisses as errant "nonsense" features no human agent.

Despite occasional conjunctions ("and," "or," "but") and connectives that seem to suggest some causal logic ("for," "so," "and so"), the poem MacDonald has Martha ascribe to a "silly woman" is the kind of antinarrative that Julia Kristeva would call a "genotext": the attempted reconstruction of a process that is "ephemeral" and "unstable" as it "organizes a space" and moves through zones that have only "relative and transitory borders."[1] The only threads that can be said to run through this drawn-out canticle are provided by its opening reference to "a river" and by the recurrent introduction of "the wind" that becomes identified with that river. The flowing river whose waters "run run ever" (line 3) blends with the blowing wind found everywhere: "it's all in the wind / that blows from behind / and all in the river / that flows forever" (lines 199-203). But this fluidity has neither a source nor a destination: "but never you find/ whence comes the wind / that blows on the hollows / and over the shallows / where dip the swallows / alive it blows / the life as it goes / awake or asleep / into the river / that sings as it flows / and the life it blows" (lines 129-140). There is no middle or end or beginning to the circularities that Diamond finds so familiar (*BNW,* chap. 13, 106-111). No longer in need of Martha's rendition of the verses, Diamond chants snippets from it before falling "fast asleep and dreaming of the land at the back of the north wind" (*BNW,* chap. 13, 112). He is in that state described as an entry into a "higher life" in MacDonald's 1880 essay on the growth of a boy's mind: upon recognizing "certain relations, initiated by fancies, desires, preferences that arise within himself" in the "world that is not his mother," the boy opens himself to an "existence and force of Being other and higher than his own."[2]

Yet the narrator of *At the Back of the North Wind* is as slippery as ever when he warns us that the verses he has reproduced are not to be construed as the actual words that fluttered in a seaside breeze: "Now I do not know exactly what the mother read, but this is what Diamond heard, *or thought afterwards that he had heard*" (*BNW,* chap. 13,104; italics added). Lines that MacDonald has obviously composed himself thus are divested of any authorial imprint. The letter of the text is unimportant. It is Diamond's receptivity that is being stressed when the narrator reminds the reader that Diamond was, after all, "very sleepy" at the time and that, although "he thought he understood the verses" recited to him, "he may have been only dreaming better ones" (*BNW,* chap. 13, 104-105).

Later, when Diamond's father uses "those very rhymes" as a "lesson-book" to teach the boy how to read, Diamond immediately hunts for "the poem he thought he had heard his mother read." He fancies he might identify it merely from "the look of it," yet even after he can make out individual words, the poem continues to elude him. He therefore settles for verses that also appeal to him, although they "were certainly not very like those he was in search of" (*BNW*, chap. 20, 150). Unlike the earlier poem, this enigmatic retelling of "Little Boy Blue" has a slight narrative thread: like Carroll's slayer of the Jabberwock, a little boy triumphs by vanquishing a snake. Diamond readily identifies the snake with the biblical serpent; still, he halts his exegesis by confessing that he cannot extract much more. When Martha calls him "a silly" for taking the poem so seriously and for holding it "true," he responds: "That killing of the snake looks true. It's what I've got to do so often" (*BNW*, chap. 21, 159). The snake, he implies, stands for a negativity he daily combats in others.

Chapter 13 marks a division between the obedient child who had deferred to North Wind as well as to Martha and the newly resolute boy who navigates throughout a bleak Dickensian London, armed only by his faith in an unseen North Wind. MacDonald now validates Diamond's credentials by giving us more instances of his unusual poetic consciousness, and by making us privy to a dream that suggests the boy's subconscious awareness of otherworldy origins. At the same time, however, we follow Diamond's activities as a social worker whose engagements with the everyday world also validate his visionary status. Dream and actuality now intersect. They can no longer be kept apart if a child's innocence is to act as a guide for the higher Innocence that MacDonald, like Blake before him, regards as the vanquisher of empirical Experience.... .

Diamond's unbroken dream, Nanny's dream fragment, and Mr. Raymond's story of "Little Daylight" are competing versions of the core fantasy that shapes the plot of *At the Back of the North Wind*. For each of these interpolated narratives dramatizes the same yearning for incorporation with a female Other that so powerfully fuels MacDonald's imagination. Each story centers on a wanderer's venture into a magical space. Diamond first dreams about "waiting for North Wind" in the "old garden" in which he met her when he was smaller. Vainly looking for her in a lush and ever-expanding landscape—"a beautiful country, not like any country he had ever been before"—he settles contentedly under a "rose-bush" to be transported into a more exotic realm in a new dream-within-a-dream (*BNW*, chap. 25, 186, 187). Nanny, who claims to have been affected by the role the moon had played in Mr. Raymond's story, dreams of exchanging London's moonless, muddy streets for a beckoning "garden place with green grass, and the moon shining upon it!" (*BNW*, chap. 30, 236). The young prince in Mr. Raymond's tale is even more volitionless. "[C]ompelled to flee for his life, disguised like a peasant" after a massacre of his country's patriarchy, he comes to "the outside of the forest" he merely wants to traverse, when he, too, stumbles upon a "lovely spot" that is moon-bathed and grassy (*BNW*, chap. 28, 213, 215).

Each of these three travelers has been specially chosen to enter a space that offers unexpected sights to their aroused imaginations. Diamond hears "a child's voice" inviting him to "come up" to an unseen location he finds by intuitively choosing to go down (*BNW*, chap. 25, 187, 188). Nanny and the young prince, however, lack Diamond's ability to "look through the look of things," and therefore require the assistance of adults to get to their destinations. When a huge, shiny moon descends next to Nanny, "a curious little old man" steps out to "fetch" the paralyzed girl (*BNW*, chap. 30, 239). This dwarf, Nanny soon discovers, is her superior, though himself a servant to the beautiful lady of the moon. Just as Nanny's servitude is mirrored by the dwarf, so the prince's reliance on a lowly disguise is adopted by the "very nice tidy motherly woman" who feeds him yet refuses to show him how "to get out of this wood" (*BNW*, chap. 28, 214). The matronly figure is actually a fairy who wants to steer this young man towards her ward, Princess Daylight.

The new setting entered by the dreaming Diamond reverses the image of draining that MacDonald had dramatized in "The Light Princess." Lifted by the waters of an upward bubbling stream, Diamond pushes his way out of a subterranean hole into an open place where he is embraced by a host of shouting "naked little boys" with wings (*BNW*, chap. 25, 189). Feeling light and carefree in the company of other children, Diamond seems at the opposite extreme of the sad and uncomfortable prince who had risked death when he "corked" the hole in Lake Lagobel. The prince had demanded a kiss from the child-woman whose gravity—and adult sexuality—he helped restore. Diamond, however, cavorts with levitating angel boys whose kisses make his heart melt "from clear delight." He has regained a prenatal Eden.[3] The place where a wind blows "like the very embodiment of living gladness" seems superior to the windless realm at the back of North Wind (*BNW*, chap. 25, 190). Possibly the "gladder" haven that travelers such as Kilmeny and Durante had yearned for (*BNW*, chap. 11, 88), it seems a place of origination that Diamond has half-forgotten in his waking life. His angelic dream-companions, however, recognize him as one of their own; by "constantly coming back to Diamond," they acknowledge him "as the centre of their enjoyment, rejoicing over him as if he had been a lost playmate" (*BNW*, chap. 25,190).

MacDonald uses the remainder of this joyful dream to tease us into constructing a mythic genealogy for Diamond that neither the boy nor the narrator ever propound. Diamond may indeed be a wingless angel boy who—like one of the playmates he observes—has zoomed to earth through a hole created by digging "up a small star" of a color to his liking (*BNW*, chap. 25,

191). The shining lumps of precious stones unearthed by these boy miners—rubies or emeralds or amethysts—may, in effect, influence their naming after their incarnation in the world below. That everyday world, however, has given Diamond an awareness that the angel boys lack: "I don't see any little girls," he astutely remarks. His companions are baffled, having never met such complementary beings. They allow that "those others—what do you call them?—" may do repair work to undo the damage the boys cause by their own digging and trampling. But if so, they reason, these creatures must make their rounds whenever "we fall asleep." Diamond eagerly awaits the arrival of "girl-angels," since "I, not being an angel, shall not fall asleep." But sleep overcomes him as much as the others. The best he can do is try to remember some of the "nonsense" verses sung by the boy-angels; still, the few lines he recalls are "so near sense" that he doubts their genuineness (*BNW,* chap 25, 192, 193, 194).

The female sexuality that Diamond's dream manages to erase plays a more prominent role in Nanny's dream and altogether dominates the plot of Mr. Raymond's "Little Daylight." Both narratives offer variations of the concern with the passage from girlhood to womanhood that had preoccupied MacDonald's three male predecessors, Ruskin, Thackeray, and Carroll. Nanny's dream dramatizes a pubescent girl's difficulty in negotiating this passage without the support and example of a maternal model. The tale of "Little Daylight," on the other hand, dramatizes a male perspective that MacDonald well understood from his contacts with Ruskin and Carroll: Mr. Raymond's true protagonist is not the story's titular heroine, but rather the prince who must overcome his aversion to menstrual women. Through Nanny's dream and by revising his own story of "The Light Princess," MacDonald subtly repudiates the hankering for ever-pure little girls harbored by his two fellow fantasists.

There were several reasons why MacDonald may have wanted Nanny's dream to follow, rather than precede, Mr. Raymond's story. He implies that the emotional needs of this maltreated street-child cannot really be met by a story that merely reshuffles the habitual trappings of fairy tales familiar to well-read Victorian middle-class children. But more than a gap in class affiliations is involved. For MacDonald also seems to hint that the male point of view that shapes the erotics of "Little Daylight" is of dubious help to any girl on the threshold of puberty. Although Nanny derives her imagery from Mr. Raymond's tale of still another cursed princess released by a lover's kiss, the dream itself has been induced by her hypnotic attachment to a ruby ring that a kind lady visitor has temporarily lent the sick child. This philanthropic gentlewoman, who eventually rescues Mr. Raymond himself from perpetual virginity, is transformed into a yearned-for, yet ultimately inaccessible, figure of female authority in Nanny's dream. The dwarf's "beautiful mistress," the "moon-lady," seems too removed from the lowly servant pressed into service at her lunar abode (*BNW*, chap. 30, 240).

After Nanny tells her dream, Diamond asks her to fall asleep again and try to complete what she has aborted. His response seems justified. Nanny's account painfully thwarts the reader's desire to witness a fulfillment of the wishes of a child whose psychological health requires something other than the nostrums prescribed by a Victorian middle-class culture that stressed the importance of virtuous parental control and example. After her trials in Wonderland, a waking Alice could return to the comforts offered by her elders. Nanny, however, finds that her dream-trials are no different from those she experiences in her everyday life. Tested in her dream as window cleaner by the dwarf who has become too old for the job, Nanny desperately wants to please the motionless white lady of the moon who averts her "whole face" from her new servant. Although Nanny wants the lady to turn her head "full upon me, or even to look at me" (*BNW*, chap. 30, 245), she accepts the disdain as a mark of her own unworthiness. Her fears of inadequacy come true when she opens, Pandora-like, a box of fiery bees that should have remained shut.

Although the moon-lady professes to pity Nanny, she banishes her from her feminine domain. A girl who cannot "be trusted" to repress her impulse to experience the forbidden, she declares, is "only fit for the mud" (*BNW*, chap 30, 247). Further aggravating Nanny's guilt feelings, the employer in the dream accuses her of having stolen the ring she is wearing and orders the dwarf to twist it off. Unable to protest her innocence, a profoundly "ashamed" Nanny wakes up. Diamond's assurances that she might still have "nice talks with the moon-lady" strike her as impossible. "Sal's Nanny" cannot become the moon-lady's ward. Although she finds herself cared for, hereafter, by Mr. Raymond and his bride, she will prefer the acceptance of "Cripple Jim" to the company of the "little girl-angels" that the cheerful Diamond is sure she might have met (*BNW*, chap. 30, 240).

Mr. Raymond centers his story of "Little Daylight" on the predicament of a princess whose health is tied to the cycle of the moon. But his narrative seems almost as removed from its feminine sources as Nanny was when banished by the moon-lady. Claiming to be unable to come up with the "true story" demanded by a girl auditor, Mr. Raymond complies, instead, with a little boy's request by offering "a sort of a fairy tale" (*BNW*, chap. 27, 205). His fantasy about a young woman whose appearance degenerates every month exaggerates the revulsion over female aging so prevalent in Victorian male fantasies from *Alice in Wonderland* to Rider Haggard's *She*. Princess Daylight is more of a freak than her counterpart in "The Light Princess." Asleep during the day, this night creature, too, finds ways of "enjoying her moonlight alone" (*BNW*, chap. 28, 212). But the child-woman who steals away on nightly swims proves irresistible to the prince who so quickly "falls in" with her. In "Little Daylight," however, it seems "inconceivable" that "any prince" might "find and deliver" a princess whose monthly cycles transform a fresh beauty into a wizened monster:

> ... The more beautiful she was in the full moon, the more withered and worn did she become as the moon waned. At the time at which my story has now arrived, she looked, when the moon was small or gone, like an old woman exhausted with suffering. This was the more painful that her appearance was unnatural; for her hair and eyes did not change. Her wan face was both drawn and wrinkled, and had an eager hungry look. Her skinny hands moved as if wishing, but unable, to lay hold of something. (*BNW*, chap. 28, 212)

The "something" this hungry, almost vampiric creature desires whenever her "change" comes upon her is a fresh prince who might replenish her waning life-blood. Yet as soon as her vitality is restored by a crescent moon, a male lover becomes inconsequential. Self-sufficient, ecstatic, the princess celebrates the full power of her femininity in a private ritual, "singing like a nightingale, and dancing to her own music, with her eyes ever turned to the moon" (*BNW*, chap. 28, 215-16). The good fairy who draws the disguised prince into the forest glade to watch this performance makes sure that he will see a figure of radiant Innocence, "a girl dressed in white, gleaming in the moon-shine," before he ever faces the loathly hag he eventually must kiss (*BNW*, chap. 28, 215). As voyeuristic and sentimental as his counterpart in "The Light Princess," the young idealist at first resists the notion that this apparition may be as human as himself. He dares not approach her, lest "she should vanish from his sight." After more furtive gazings, he becomes "incapable of thinking of anything" but this beautiful dream-child (*BNW*, chap. 28, 216, 218).

Only an accident emboldens the prince to approach the object of his desire. A lightning bolt—no doubt unleashed by the fairy to whom Mr. Raymond assigns a role akin to that which MacDonald assigns to North Wind—leads the young man to assume that the princess has been stunned or even killed. Their brief exchange ends when she makes "a repellent gesture" which only exacerbates his desire (*BNW*, chap. 28, 221). Like Diamond patiently waiting for North Wind to reappear, he abides his time. But the creature he finally meets on a "night in which there was no moon at all" (*BNW*, chap. 28, 223) is not the seductive figure he has expected:

> The countenance was that of an old woman, but it had a fearfully strange look. A black cloak concealed her hair, and her eyes were closed. He laid her down as comfortably as he could, chafed her hands, put a little cordial

from a bottle, also the gift of the fairy, into her mouth; took off his coat and wrapped it about her, and in short did the best he could. In a little while she opened her eyes and looked at him—so pitifully! The tears rose and flowed down her grey wrinkled cheeks, but she said never a word. (*BNW,* chap. 28, 224-25)

Here ... the flow of tears proves to be redemptive. Yet instead of the weeping Light Princess who nurtures an inert prince with the aid of her old nurse, it is the prince himself who uses the "motherly" fairy's bottle to revive the bundled figure, light as a child, whom he cradles in his arms. Convinced that the moaning creature is about die, the young man, "very near crying," implores her to stay alive. His pity is overpowering: "'Mother, mother!' he said. 'Poor mother!' and kissed her on the withered lips." His spontaneous act of love breaks the spell. Abasing himself once again, he falls at a young woman's feet, not daring to "look up until she laid her hand upon his head" (*BNW,* chap. 28, 225).

Even before Mr. Raymond begins this fantasy of recuperation, the narrator steps in to question its appeal: "I do not know how much of Mr. Raymond's story the smaller children understood; indeed, I don't quite know how much there was in it to be understood, for in such a story everyone just has to take what he can get" (*BNW,* chap. 27, 206). Given the tale's adverse effect on Nanny as demonstrated by her subsequent dream, and given, too, Diamond's failure to respond to it, the narrator's remark adds still another note of distrust to MacDonald's habitual reservations about fairy tales for children. The insertion of "The Light Princess" into *Adela Cathcart* supposedly allowed an adult heroine to recover a childlike faith; the insertion of "Little Daylight" into *At the Back of the North Wind,* however, only underscores the freshness of Diamond's nonliterary imagination. The narrator snidely stresses Mr. Raymond's derivativeness: "I cannot help myself thinking that he was somewhat indebted for this to the old story of The Sleeping Beauty" (*BNW,* chap. 27, 206).

Why does MacDonald express hostility towards a tale he readily acknowledged as his own in other collections? And why is his grave narrator so unappreciative of its fine Thackerayan wit? Diamond's earnest biographer seems deaf to the wonderfully comic deflation of standard fairy-tale paraphernalia in the story's early portions; nor does he appear willing to concede that "Mr. Raymond" freshens, not just "Sleeping Beauty" or "The Frog Prince," but also the subtext of the tale which Chaucer assigned to his Wife of Bath. As I have been suggesting, the ironic handling of Mr. Raymond's imagination allows MacDonald to distance himself from falsifying constructions of female purity that he recognized in other male fantasists. The "gentleman-prince" who worships a distant figure in white must be taught what Mr. Raymond himself has to learn—namely, that "femininity" involves more than aestheticized female shapes gazed from afar. The prince's voyeurism resembles that of two gentlemen of MacDonald's acquaintance. Princess Daylight's story has much to do with Lewis Carroll's wishful constructions of perennially young dream-children and with Ruskin's confessions to MacDonald about the shattering discovery that Effie Gray had become a menstrual woman.

Yet MacDonald's attempt to distance himself from Mr. Raymond's fantasy can also be read as an act of self-protection. For the prince who kisses the dying woman he thrice calls "mother" enacts the same incestuous yearning dramatized when Diamond penetrated the cold body of a seemingly dead North Wind. MacDonald's implied critique of Carroll and Ruskin for allowing their stories to be shaped by adult preoccupations can, after all, be applied to his own work. For MacDonald cannot refrain from using Mr. Raymond's fairy tale as a vehicle for the same obsessive longing that eventually leads him to grant Diamond the fulfilling death-embrace the novel has so long delayed.

Read in this fashion, "Little Daylight" satisfies a male's desire to resuscitate a mother associated with death. The transformation of an old woman into a desirable bride demands the parallel transformation of a young prince into a maternal nourisher. Just as Diamond nurses his infant brother and sister as an expression of his unfulfilled desire for North Wind's comforting breast, so does the orphaned prince who stills a sobbing, child-sized woman seek compensation for his own lack. Both figures therefore enact MacDonald's lifelong yearning for the lost young mother who pitied the crying infant she had been forced to wean.

It seems significant that MacDonald has little left for Diamond to do after the telling of "Little Daylight." Like the prince who patiently waits for the princess to reappear, Diamond lapses into his earlier passive stance. He has become useless to others. Replaced by a second baby in his parents' home and by lame Jim in Nanny's heart, he is "installed as a page" in the country house of Mr. Raymond and his new bride (*BNW*, chap. 35, 277). His main function in the home called "The Mound" is to delight his employers with his pretty appearance in "a suit of blue" that nicely brings out the pallor of his skin. He also acts as Mr. Raymond's consultant by giving his "opinion" on the children's books that gentleman continues to write. Diamond cannot tell stories that others call "clever" apart from those they call "silly," but he always knows whether he likes a story or not. It remains unclear, however, whether he likes the "story of the Little Lady and the Goblin Prince" that the narrator finds him reading (*BNW*, chap. 35, 277). For he dies before he can pass judgment on what is obviously MacDonald's next work, *The Princess and the Goblin*, serialized in 1871.

The last chapters of *At the Back of the North Wind* restore the dialogic form of Diamond's earlier exchanges with North Wind. The boy now worries that the moon-bathed figure who revisits him after her long absence may be unreal: "How am I to know that it's not a dream?" Her answers no longer seem to satisfy him ... . When, in the novel's final paragraphs, a weeping Mrs. Raymond leads the narrator to Diamond's room at the "top of the tower," he finds the boy frozen into a "lovely figure, as white and almost as clear as alabaster," an image of North Wind herself (*BNW,* chap. 38, 308)... .

    MacDonald ... wants to convert a mortal "Jack"—an ordinary, humble boy—into a Christlike immortal. The child whom the narrator beatifies cannot be soiled by the residues that weigh down Nanny or his own mother. Having discharged his earthly duties, he can be carried off by North Wind into a mystic abode. Despite its originality and power, there is something complacent about a fantasy that ultimately extricates Diamond from further engagement with error, poverty, and evil. And, despite his apparent efforts to distance himself from a Carrollian worship of an arrested female innocence, MacDonald's own privileging of the virginal boy he refuses to ironize makes him open to rather similar charges of distortion... .

ILLUSTRATION BY F.D. BEDFORD (MACMILLAN COMPANY, 1924)

Endnotes

1. Julia Kristeva, "Revolutions in Poetic Language," in *The Kristeva Reader*, ed. Toril Moi (New York: Columbia University Press, 1988), 121.
2. MacDonald, "Sketch of Individual Development," 45-46.
3. Unlike the Greek word *paradises* (a walled garden), the Hebrew *edhen* simply means "delight."

Works Cited

MacDonald, George. *At the Back of the North Wind*. New York: Macmillan, 1964.

Behind the Back of the North Wind

From Chapter IX "How Diamond Got to the Back of the North Wind"
Illustration by Gertrude A. Kay (David McKay Company, 1909)

Child's Work Is Child's Play:
The Value of George MacDonald's Diamond

From *Children's Literature Association Quarterly*

Lisa Hermine Makman

I. New Toys

At the end of the eighteenth century, a "toy" was a trifling thing. The word often referred to a diminutive but accurate copy of an object, sometimes constructed from luxury materials. Such a toy was a decorative item to be displayed, defined in terms of its uselessness and lavish attractiveness. In the nineteenth century, as "toy" came more frequently to denote a child's plaything, children themselves became toy-like, at least in the eyes of adults, who saw them increasingly as precious objects. This transformation took place at precisely the time that children's legal right to work was curtailed.

Between the 1860s and the 1920s, as legislation increasingly limited child labor and enforced school attendance, children gradually ceased to have concrete economic value. As their earning power diminished, they came to be seen as expenses—part of the world of consumption rather than production, toy-like objects for whom to buy.[1] During this period, as Viviana Zelizer has detailed, the idea of an economically worthless but emotionally priceless child emerged. A carefree, labor-free childhood came to be understood as a fundamental right of all children regardless of their social class; simultaneously, childhood became an increasingly popular locus for fantasies about leisure and freedom for adults. Children's literature written at the time participates in this emergent vision of childhood—registering, reinforcing, and in some cases reconfiguring new ideas about children. George MacDonald's *At the Back of the North Wind* (1871) not only presents the new toy-child but, strikingly, replays in its narrative the progressive development of the fantasy that children are toys. Over the course of the novel, the value of MacDonald's child-hero, Diamond, shifts; his ability to produce literal wealth for his family transforms into a capacity to produce abstract "wealth"—emotional and spiritual value—both for his family and for a broader community.

The unusual nature of MacDonald's hero and the curious nature of his name are stressed throughout the tale. The name "Diamond" immediately raises the question of the child's value. Initially, it seems to indicate that he is highly valued, a treasured jewel. One soon discovers, however, that Diamond has been named after a favorite horse, which the boy's coachman father drives for his employer. Diamond the horse is a devoted servant and a committed laborer. Diamond the boy is, initially at least, a "toy" version of this horse. In the early part of the narrative, MacDonald stresses that Diamond is a child of leisure (in part by contrasting him with a working child, Nanny); even though the boy's family is quite poor, he does not need to work. Yet over the course of the novel, after a journey to the back of the north wind,[2] Diamond comes into a vocation, first as a laborer and finally as a sort of savior. His transformation brings to light complex divisions and links between notions of child's work and child's play in MacDonald's day.

For MacDonald's original readers, the name Diamond would not only signify a precious stone. In England at the time MacDonald wrote his story, the slang expression "diamond cracking" referred to work in coal mines, and coal was dubbed "black diamond." "Coleman," the name of the man who employs Diamond's father, also suggests a connection with coal mining. Thirty years earlier, exposés about child miners had shocked all of England into producing legislation strictly limiting child labor in mines (see *Children's Employment Commission*, First and Second Reports). But although Diamond's name may have conjured up images of child miners for the nineteenth-century reader, MacDonald's hero is not initially depicted as a laborer. He looks the part of the gem rather than the pitch. His skin is eerily pale, almost translucent (378). Diamond's name thus contains the divergent images of children in circulation at the time: the idealized toy-child, inherently valuable, necessarily good, and the piteous child-slave, toiling to produce value, potentially corrupt, and in dire need of rescue.[3]

At the time that MacDonald's novel was first circulating among English readers,[4] almost a third of the nation's population was under the age of fifteen. Public debates raged about what to do with England's highly visible population of poor children, many of whom were workers. During the writer's lifetime (1824-1905), the idea that work is morally good for children slipped into its opposite: labor came to be seen as corrupting. By the 1860s, although idleness in children was still generally perceived as a threat to orderly society, school, not work, came to be seen as the ideal place to socialize poor children; indeed, the schooling offered to these children often included instruction in hygiene and manners (Horn 83-85).[5] *At the Back of the North Wind* was written during the period just before the Education Acts of 1870 and 1876 converted these new conceptions of children into law by forbidding work for children under the age of ten and making labor for children between ten and thirteen conditional on the presentation of a certificate indicating that the child had received sufficient education. MacDonald's novel is part of the cultural climate that gave rise to this legislation. It suggests how Diamond and his ilk move from the quarry to the display case.

II. Child's Work Is Child's Play

In the new genre of child psychology journals that appeared after the Education Acts and before the turn of the century (journals such as *Child Life* and *The Paidologist*) child's "play" was increasingly the focus of discussion. In these periodicals, child's play is often described as an essential prelude to and aspect of work. It differs fundamentally from work in that it is non-instrumental; its value, like that of the toy, is not connected to a function in the everyday world. According to one writer for *Child Life*, play has "no further intentional end than the action itself (Murray 170). Nevertheless, the child's spontaneous, non-instrumental activity was commonly construed as a model for adult work. As E. R. Murray insists in a 1901 *Child Life* article on games, "Men are slaves unless they carry into life-work the spirit, the life, the freedom with which a child flings himself into his so-called play" (170). Whereas in contemporaneous socialist thought a takeover of the means of production was seen as necessary to liberate alienated workers, writers for child psychology journals suggested that with the proper education (an education *by* children) workers would be saved from this wretched fate of enslavement and alienation.

Similarly, in *At the Back of the North Wind* child's play, portrayed as inherently good, is shown to be a paradigm for adult activity. As such, play in the novel comes to contribute to the reform of moral corruption in adults, thus bettering society for all. The London that MacDonald depicts in his story is in economic and moral crisis. Adults in this world fail to provide authority and order for themselves and their children. In a telling analogy, Londoners are described as "Those careless, greedy, untidy children [who] make [the world] such a mess" (38). With his playful labor and industrious play, Diamond functions as a model for dissolute adults and strives to redeem the fallen grownup world. His interventions in adult society are enabled by his relationship with a fantastical female spirit, North Wind, and by his access to the magical land that she represents.

To learn that work is play and to reach North Wind's realm, Diamond must cross borders between material world and dream-world, between reality and fiction, between the realm of the living and the realm of the dead. After he travels to the back of the north wind, a land of dreams and death, he returns to the human world to do the "work" of a human angel. During his imaginative sojourn away from home, Diamond neither works nor plays. Instead, his spirit rests, at leisure: he feels "so still and quiet and patient and contented that, as far as the mere feeling went, it was something better than mere happiness"

(116). In this state, all desire is sated. But while in his mind Diamond visits the back of the north wind, his body remains at home, where he almost dies from a severe illness. His proximity to death, like that of other fictive Victorian children, grants him a special power, the power to transform his world and to create in it a secure home.

MacDonald leaves his reader unsure as to the ontological status of the land at the back of the north wind. Does Diamond merely dream about this place? Is it an allegorical representation of the child's imagination? Is it some sort of afterworld, a purgatory perhaps?[6] All of these suggestions remain possibilities. What is clear from the start of the book, however, is the land's role as the source of Diamond's moral and spiritual authority. Moreover, this place can be viewed as an emblem for child's "play" as it came to be understood by educators and child psychologists around the turn of the twentieth century. Writing in the journal *Child Life*, John Dewey describes child's "play" as a state of mind instead of an activity: "[play] denotes the psychological attitude of the child, not his outward performances" (5). According to Dewey, play consists of the child's "mental attitude in its entirety and unity" ("Principles" 6). This conception of play—a child's "unified" inner realm—bears a strong resemblance to MacDonald's representation of play as it is manifest in the magical land Diamond finds at North Wind's back.

It is North Wind herself who makes possible Diamond's voyage. She constitutes a boundary between realms, a threshold that Diamond must cross to reach the country at her back—a country to which she herself has no access. Just as Diamond's biological mother brought him into the world, this surrogate brings him out of it. Diamond's passage through North Wind is a reversal of birth, a sort of death. MacDonald writes,

> When he reached her knees, he put out his hand to lay it on her, but nothing was there save an intense cold. He walked on. Then all grew white about him; and the cold stung him like fire. He walked on still, groping through the whiteness. It thickened about him. At last, it got into his heart, and he lost all sense. I would say that he fainted—only whereas in common faints all grows black about you, he felt swallowed up in whiteness. (112)

Diamond's association with whiteness throughout the tale is epitomized here in this merger with the wind's inner whiteness. The boy's whiteness here and elsewhere in MacDonald's text is associated with death, with becoming an object. But Diamond's death-walk through North Wind also proves to effect a rebirth. Inasmuch as North Wind is identified with Diamond's imagination, his death/rebirth through her is an act of autogenesis, of self-creation, and thus the boy is closely linked to feminine reproductive power—though what he reproduces is himself.

Nevertheless, MacDonald identifies the spirit as a mother throughout the story. She reminds Diamond of his own mother and refers to him as her "baby" (358). But while MacDonald emphasizes North Wind's maternal attitude toward Diamond, he contrasts her with Diamond's earthly mother. Whereas Diamond's mother is impotent and morose, the wind is all-powerful, playful, and often erotic. Whereas for Diamond's mother work is labor, necessary to acquire money, for North Wind work is play—a natural and spontaneous activity, pleasurable in and of itself, and, importantly, morally productive.

After Diamond travels to the back of the north wind, he adopts North Wind's playful approach to work. But the child's interactions with the spirit not only change his attitude toward labor, they also alter his experience of pleasure and desire. Both his desire and pleasure come to be fixed on the figure of the wind and all that she brings to him.

MacDonald sets up his account of the land at the back of the north wind in opposition to what he claims is an alternative version of this story, Herodotus's report of the Hyperboreans in the *Histories*.[7] He begins his novel, "I have been asked to tell you about the back of the north wind. An old Greek writer mentions a people who lived there, and were so comfortable that they could not bear it any longer, and drowned themselves. My story is not the same as his" (1). If the world of the Hyperboreans self-destructs because it privileges luxury over all else, the magical world that MacDonald depicts persists because it exists to serve the dreary world of urban England; the pleasures generated by the land at the back of the north wind will advance a higher good. In MacDonald's story, the threat posed by too much pleasure is localized in and controlled by the figure of Diamond, whose body mediates between the world of pleasure and the "real" world. This "real" world, the London of MacDonald's novel, can only tolerate small doses of pleasure, which can be used to oil the machinery of work and productivity. Although MacDonald maintains that Herodotus "had not got the right account of the [back of the north wind]," he seems to perceive in his own society the same threat of drowning in bliss that appears in his version of the ancient Greek tale. Thus Herodotus's mythical land stands in for MacDonald's London, which, toward the end of the nineteenth century, increasingly privileged the values of consumerism— the joys of the marketplace. MacDonald's story then becomes an attempt to marshal Herodotus's hedonistic vision, and that of Victorian England, toward a socially redemptive vision. MacDonald imaginatively combats this vision in *At the Back of the North Wind* by imposing a division of labor. He invents a field of work and a field of play, between which the child Diamond negotiates, bringing the spirit of play into the adult's world of work yet containing the potentially anarchic energies of play.

III. Classes of Children

Before considering how MacDonald elaborates the fantasy of the child savior in *At the Back of the North Wind*, it is fruitful to consider his work alongside that of his immediate predecessors. How had previous authors of fantasies for children represented work and play? MacDonald's novel is one of the first full-length fantasies for children. Arguably, its only significant precursors are Charles Kingsley's *The Water Babies: A Fairy Tale for a Land Baby* (1863)[8] and Lewis Carroll's *Alice's Adventures in Wonderland* (1865), both of which introduce motifs of children's work and play that *At the Back of the North Wind* explores. In addition, both *Water Babies* and *Wonderland*, like MacDonald's novel, develop whimsical fictions about realms set apart from the mundane adult world, realms in which child's play takes center stage ... .

Kingsley's novel anticipates *At the Back of the North Wind* in its melding of realistic and fantastical styles, the central role given to a magical domain of play, and the function of the female goddess/teacher in that play-realm. But while Kingsley emphasizes the mysterious nature of the play-world and its inhabitants, MacDonald focuses more on the mysterious nature of the child who can enter that world. Carroll, who in *Wonderland* eschews the moral vision favored by the other writers, shares with MacDonald this focus on the child: Wonderland is inconceivable without Alice. Carroll's narrative foregrounds Alice's idiosyncratic reactions to her bizarre environment.... .

In *Alice's Adventures in Wonderland* Carroll introduces the concept of play as noninstrumental activity, an idea that would be developed by later children's writers such as J. M. Barrie and Beatrix Potter.

In *At the Back of the North Wind* MacDonald combines elements from the works of his predecessors, drawing from Kingsley's didacticism and from Carroll's linguistic play. But MacDonald's play-world differs from those depicted by Kingsley and Carroll in that it has a dynamic relationship with the actual world. Unlike Alice, who returns from her dream of *Wonderland* unchanged but with an amusing tale to tell, and unlike Tom, who ascends from the water-world heavenward to his own redemption, Diamond returns from the back of the north wind to play an active role as a redeemer in the human world.

In the arms of the Wind or nested in her hair, Diamond has a bird's-eye view of London at night and of "the misery that trie[s] to get in the windows and doors" of homes, including his own. All the while, the Wind performs her "work"—she "sweeps" her "room" (38, 41), which includes the entire city of London, performing a sort of moral cleansing. During her flight over the city, she and Diamond spy another sweeper of a more prosaic sort, a tiny street sweeper named Nanny, blown about in the wind while trying to cling to her broom. In order to rescue this waif, Diamond leaves the safety of the Wind's embrace. This response of extreme pity at the sight of this lone and apparently homeless child laborer marks Diamond as a social type familiar to MacDonald's audience—the child-rescuer.[9] Diamond soon discovers that Nanny is parentless and lives with a drunken old woman named Sal. Thus the child laborer here also takes a form easily recognizable to MacDonald's first readers, a miserable shape that inspires pity. Henry Mayhew, in his famous classification of London workers, *London Labour and the London Poor* (1861-62), categorizes street sweepers as a particularly pitiable and honorable type of worker, although he also denigrates sweeping as "an excuse for begging" (465). In contrast, MacDonald represents street sweeping as honest hard work—his sweepers earn the change they are given. But his story suggests that even such honest work is not suitable for a child, especially a girl. It brings out in Nanny a malignant precocity that Diamond later labors to correct.

When Diamond and the young sweeper first converse, she assumes that he too is a sweeper. After determining that he does not have a "crossing" to sweep,

> "What do you do, then?" asked she. "You ain't big enough for most things."
>
> "I don't know what I do do," answered he, feeling rather ashamed.
>
> "Nothing, I suppose. My father's Mr. Coleman's coachman." (45)

Nanny is shocked to discover that Diamond has a father and thus has no need to work at all. Struck by his life situation and simplicity, she refers to him as a "kid." MacDonald writes, "She called him a *kid*, but she was not really a month older than he was; only she had had to work for her bread, and that so soon makes people older" (49).

The figure of the sweeper girl suggests how children's labor fosters a horrible precocity, a perversion of the laws of nature. In the mid-Victorian period, a longer childhood was being encouraged by scientists and moralists alike. According to Herbert Spencer, a brief childhood ineluctably leads to a barbarous adulthood.[10] In "The Comparative Psychology of Man," Spencer links precocity to the "uncivilized" or "savage." He writes,

> In conformity with the biological law, that the higher the organisms the

> longer they take to evolve, members of the inferior human races may be expected to complete their mental evolution sooner than members of the superior races; and we have evidence that they do this. Travelers from all regions comment, now on the great precocity of children among savages and semi-civilized peoples, and now on the early arrest of their mental progress. (191-92)

Ultimately, a voyage to the back of the north wind enables Diamond to perform work without becoming precocious, and later to educate and thus to civilize Nanny. He trains her to be a part of his family; she is domesticated, renewed, transmuted from "rough girl" to "gentle maiden" (254). By teaching her how to sweep house instead of sweeping the street, Diamond shows her that a girl's proper place is in the home.

Diamond's voyage enables him to help his own family as well. Their London is an unstable world in which parents cannot provide economic security for their children. In the course of the story, Diamond's parents suffer financial crises several times. When Diamond's father, who has gone into business for himself as a cabbie, falls ill and can no longer work, the boy tries to soothe his despairing mother by singing her a song from a pamphlet of rhymes carried to him by North Wind. The song tells the story of a young "early bird" who "gets the worm" when his mother cannot. Diamond's mother responds wistfully, "I wish you were like that little bird, Diamond, and could catch worms for yourself" (216). Her child takes the hint. The next morning, before his parents awaken, he sets off to work in his father's cab, effectively becoming the early bird bringing home the worm. Diamond's "work" here is shown to be playful, natural, and spontaneous. By working, the boy not only labors to bring home money for his parents; he also joyfully replays the story from the song. Importantly, the song that serves as Diamond's script does not belong to the debased adult world; according to Diamond, this song and the others in the pamphlet were generated by the river that flows through the back of the north wind. Furthermore, Diamond's association with the bird stresses his own separateness from the human world and its monetary economy. He works within a symbolically "natural" economy that is inherently moral.

Diamond's parents, nevertheless, are trapped in the monetary economy. They first suffer financial woes as a pathetic sacrifice of the careless capitalist Mr. Coleman, who brings trouble on himself and his family and "most people he has to do with" by "making haste to be rich" (130)—by speculating excessively. When Mr. Coleman loses his wealth, Diamond's father loses both his home and his livelihood. And yet if the old man drains away capital, a child can retrieve it. In this process, literal capital is transformed into figurative capital, that is, moral value.

Thus the point of children's "work" is to undo damage, financial and moral, perpetrated by adults. MacDonald divides moral labor between the Wind and her protégé Diamond; while the spirit punishes fallen humanity, the child heals by undoing harm perpetrated by the fallen. For instance, whereas North Wind makes the Coleman family pay for its shady economic practice by sinking the ship that contains the last of Coleman's assets, Diamond continues the Wind's work but in a less destructive and punitive manner. While helping out his own family by driving his father's cab, he facilitates a reunion between Miss Coleman and her betrothed, a man believed to have been drowned when Coleman's ship sank. This reunion enables the triumph of "right" values—human love is more important than material wealth. Diamond's "work" thus has moral consequences. It cures social ills and fills in for inadequate authorities. For instance, when Mrs. Coleman fails to give a penny to Nanny when the latter sweeps the street for her, Diamond, who observes this interaction, leaps to the rescue and awards the girl a penny that Mrs. Coleman had previously given to him.

Diamond also contributes to the moral and financial reform of his family's neighbor, an inveterately drunken cab driver who beats his wife and neglects his baby. Here, Diamond seems to have angel-like access to all the places North Wind took him during their flight across London. Believing that the cabman is asleep, Diamond simply walks into his neighbor's apartment unnoticed, calms a screaming child, and delivers a sermon on the effects of alcohol to the baby. The cab driver, who is in fact conscious, takes to heart Diamond's words, imagining that the boy is an angel. As he preaches indirectly to the cabman, Diamond explains the role of children in the lives of adults: he says to the baby, "There's nobody in the house to take care of [mother and father] but baby; and you *do* take care of them, baby—don't you, baby? I know you do. Babies always take care of their fathers and mothers—don't they, baby? That's what they come for—isn't it, baby?" (182).

Although children in this story are presented as victims of irrational and corrupt adults, they are also saviors; indeed, this is their primary calling. They possess, through their imaginative capabilities, the power to save. It is Diamond's connection to a world apart—a world beyond degraded London—that allows him to serve this function.

IV. Agents of Transformation

MacDonald identifies the back of the north wind, the land of dreams and endless leisure, as the origin of stories. It is the source of creative powers, of what Mr. Raymond, a wealthy child-rescuer and author of children's stories, deems Diamond's "genius." When Diamond returns from the back of the north wind, his work often takes the form of singing songs and storytelling. For Diamond storytelling is a collaborative act, and so it demands the presence of an active audience. When Mr. Raymond asks the child to give him an example of the songs he invents, Diamond explains that he "couldn't make a line without baby on my knee. We make them together, you know. They're just as much baby's as mine. It's he pulls them out of me" (212). Once these songs are "pull[ed] out" of Diamond, they cannot be reproduced; Diamond cannot remember them. The products of Diamond's imagination thus resist commodification. They offer a stark contrast to the tales of Mr. Raymond and those of MacDonald himself, which are replicated and packaged in books.

Throughout the novel, Diamond cites the eternal song of the river at the back of the north wind as the place in which he finds the songs he sings. This is the meta-linguistic source of Diamond's songs. The moral codes of the novel, which are conveyed in these songs, are thus naturalized, as if they do not constitute a specific set of precepts but merely denote the absence of corruption in a pristine nature. Supporting this connection between a beneficent nature and the values associated with play is North Wind herself, whom MacDonald presents as an embodiment of both natural forces and the spirit of play.

Like the songs, Diamond's dreams point to the natural aspect of his work and have a direct impact on the "real" world—the world of his family and friends. In a dream brought to him by North Wind, Diamond participates in the "work" performed by souls before they are born, joining a troop of boy-angels in their play and in their labor. These boys are merry miners. First they sing and play, and afterwards they "dig for stars" with pickaxes; it is "hard" work but pleasurable (241). The child-work depicted here conveys a nostalgia for work as it was imagined to have been practiced in a mythical pre-industrial era, when laborers were free and not alienated, when communities were integrated. Values commonly associated with play are emphasized in this scene—spontaneity, passion, group participation. Such values, no longer acceptable in *workers* in the late nineteenth century and after, were increasingly encouraged in adult *consumers*; here, MacDonald has these values fuel a non-monetary economy of supernatural work, a sort of play that brings new souls to earth. Diamond here plays the roles of miner and mined; he is both mining angel and unearthed soul. As a result, once again Diamond enacts in a play-realm his own coming-into-being, his own birth. Importantly, the dream does not distract him from his mundane labors but rather motivates him to continue them. MacDonald writes, "His head was full of the dream he had dreamed; but it did not make him neglect his work, for his work was not to dig stars but to drive old Diamond and pick up fares" (243).

Throughout the novel, MacDonald stresses that Diamond's play-values motivate work and not consumption. In a scene that takes place in a toy store, the author takes pains to exhibit that his hero is not a consumer, that he values North Wind's version of play over the play that toys can purchase, and that he values North Wind herself over toys.[11] Diamond has befriended the store's proprietor and often stops by the shop to chat with her, even though he has no money to spend on her goods. One day, the boy enters the store and finds himself alone, surrounded by toys. The wind, invisible, arrives on the scene as a sort of spirit of play:

> Around him were a great many toys of all prices, from a penny up to shillings. All at once he heard a gentle whirring somewhere amongst them. It made him start and look behind him. There were the sails of a windmill going round and round almost close to his ear. He thought at first it must be one of those toys which are wound up and go with clockwork; but no, it was a common penny toy, with the windmill at the end of a whistle, and when the whistle blows the windmill goes. But the wonder was that there was no one at the whistle end blowing, and yet the sails were turning round and round—now faster, now slower, now faster again. (98)

Although Diamond initially fails to recognize his friend, he is transfixed by the moving toy. MacDonald privileges the value of the wind's gifts over the value of inanimate toys; the wind, introduces an element of play into life and an element of life into toys. Significantly, she manifests herself in one of the cheap toys, thereby reinforcing the notion that the principle of play defies the conventional assumption that value is always commensurate with price.

The narrative makes clear that it is the wind rather than the toys (or other treats) that excites Diamond's desire. Indeed North Wind breaks some of the toys in the store, because, she says, the shop's owner is overvaluing her toys: she is "thinking too much of her new stock" (100). After the spirit's dramatic departure, Diamond joylessly goes home. This scene picks up an antimaterialist strain that rims throughout the novel. At the beginning of the story, after Diamond plays in a toy carriage made from two broken chairs and a cradle, he thinks, "It is not fine things that make home a nice place, but your mother and your father" (29).

V. To the Display Case

MacDonald's story concludes with a pastoral fantasy of redemption. At the end of the novel, Mr. Raymond and his new bride bring Diamond and his family (including Nanny and her fellow sweeper Jim) to live and work at his newly purchased country estate, "The Mound," a title that evokes the serenity and solemnity of death. For Diamond, life in this rustic atmosphere takes a familiar shape; it "was more like being at the back of the north wind than anything he had known since he left it" (337). Here MacDonald's narrative points to ways in which Victorian discourses of childhood incorporate and develop ideas and imagery celebrated by the Romantic poets, as epitomized in William Wordsworth's "Ode: Intimations of Immortality" (1807). Like Wordsworth's nature, both the child's imagination and the supernatural land that nourishes it serve a magical healing function. MacDonald's story seems to answer the Romantics' call for a return to a pre-industrial order where children's work occurred at home under kindly parental eyes. At the estate, there is no talk of wages. All of the working folk flourish naturally under the paternalistic regime of Mr. Raymond.[12]

At the Mound, Diamond is employed to do what he does best—play: to read, sing songs, tell stories, and dream. Nominally, he is hired as a page, and we learn that "he was dressed in a suit of blue, from which his pale face and fair hair came out like the loveliest blossom" (340). In fact his "job" is to be a flowerlike object of wonder and beauty, gazed upon lovingly by his adult admirers—his employers. MacDonald writes, "Mrs. Raymond confessed that she often rang her bell just to have once more the pleasure of seeing the lovely stillness of the boy's face, with those blue eyes which seemed rather made for other people to took into than for himself to look out of" (345). As the story comes to a close, Diamond is increasingly depicted as an unmoving object that brings pleasure with its passive existence: a sort of toy.

As a toy, Diamond is not entirely useless. Like the toy, a commodity, he stimulates desire, but unlike the toy he awakens compassion rather than passion to spend and possess. The narrator, who enters the story as a character at this point, meets Diamond and appraises his worth as a treasured "toy," highlighting the value inherent in the boy's physical presence and in his inner life. The encounter is the last in a series of scenes in which Diamond's peculiar gentleness and awesome truthfulness astonish adults in the narrative, attract them to him, and alter their behavior. These scenes resemble conversion stories, in which Diamond catalyzes the inner change of his adult interlocutor. For instance, when Diamond first works to earn money for his family, he has a distinct transforming effect on the cabbies with whom he works. MacDonald writes, "At first [Diamond] heard a good many rough and bad words.... they did not even stick to him, nor to say get inside him. He never took any notice of them, and his face shone pure and good in the middle of them, like a primrose in a hailstorm" (166). Diamond's natural refinement, his diamondlike purity and imperviousness to bad influence, leads the cabbies to idolize him, and as a consequence they stop using "rough" language around him. Once again, MacDonald uses the image of a flower to describe the boy, a figure that here conveys Diamond's planted-ness along with his "natural" attractiveness and innocence.

At the end of the novel, when the narrator first espies Diamond, the child is sitting against a beech-tree with his nose in a book. The man creeps up behind the boy and suddenly asks, "What are you reading?", cruelly hoping "to see a startled little face look round at me." Diamond slowly turns to face the narrator, and the child's calm countenance "rebuke[s] [the man's] unkind desire and ma[kes] [him] ashamed of it" (341). Subsequently, the narrator plummets into mortification as he comes to recognize Diamond's uniqueness and worth. Diamond's otherworldly qualities mark him as belonging to a different class—both a different social class and a different order of beings. The narrator reports, "The whole ways and look of the child, so full of quiet wisdom ... took hold of my heart, and I felt myself wonderfully drawn towards him. It seemed to me, somehow, as if little Diamond possessed the secret of life and was himself what he was so ready to think the lowest living thing—an angel of God with something special to say or do. A gush of reverence came over me" (345). Like many literary children of his day, Diamond produces in adults a transformative recognition. In sentimental Victorian literature, children often effect moral "conversions" in adults because of their legible innocence and pathos, and one may discern a link between the adult's sighting of a child and that adult's consequent inner change. In *Oliver Twist*, for example, Nancy is converted by the "sight" of Oliver. Charles Dickens writes that "the sight of the persecuted child has turned vice itself and given it the courage and attributes of virtue" (336). Diamond is a new version of Dickens's pitiful innocent. With Diamond, what you see is not all of what you get.

In MacDonald's novel, it is not only Diamond's legibility—his evident stillness and ingenuousness—that inspires the narrator's "conversion." It is also his inscrutability. Because he possesses knowledge held by no other living being, he is an enigma, a curiosity and a kind of curio, a desirable object. This aspect of Diamond points to a shift in nineteenth-century idealized portraits of the child: more and more the child's treasure comes to be seen as *buried* treasure.

VI. White and Black Diamond

A diamond is a thing, a highly valued thing, but a thing nevertheless, cold and hard. At the end of MacDonald's tale, Diamond the boy also becomes a cold, hard thing—he is dead. The narrator reports, "I walked up the winding stair, and entered his room. A lovely figure, as white and almost as clear as alabaster, was lying on the bed. I saw at once how it was. They thought he was dead. I knew that he had gone to the back of the north wind" (378). Like Peter Pan and like Tom the sweep, Diamond will never grow up. And like these other eternal children, he is not accessible to the adults who so ardently desire him. In *Peter Pan* the grownups are left covetously fingering Peter's black shadow; in *The Water Babies*, they are left weeping over Tom's blackened "shell"; in MacDonald's story, the adults can view only Diamond's smooth, hard form, his diamondlike carcass. The child dies into an image, becoming an icon: the eternal child. Diamond will never enter the world of adult corruption. His body is the sign and seal of a moral economy founded on compassion and goodwill, valued bourgeois attributes. In order for the child to fit into a moral economy, to produce itself as symbolic capital, its energies must be silenced, stilled. Diamond must die *because* his death transfers his secret knowledge to the adult storyteller.

In the December 1868 issue of *Good Words for the Young* between installments of *At the Back of the North Wind*, Hugh Macmillan published a short educational article entitled "A Lump of Coal." In this piece, Macmillan explains the origins of coal to his young readers. The story introduces the trope of childhood as precious treasure in a way that strikingly parallels MacDonald's presentation of childhood, suggesting that quasi-scientific texts drew from and produced the same mythology of childhood found in MacDonald's text. Several qualities characterize both natural resources and the child as they appear respectively in the texts of Macmillan and MacDonald: they are raw material; they are sui generis; they are profound and somewhat perplexing; and, finally, they are freely giving of their bounty, so that no labor need be expended to extract their value. Macmillan writes, "The page of the earth's history book that tells us the history of coal is a very extraordinary one. If is to the familiar appearance of the world at the present day what the fairy story-books of childhood are to the sober duties and enjoyments of grown up men" (101). This "page," which carries the story of coal, is a hidden page, buried deep in the ground and associated with the distant past. Significantly, Macmillan compares this "page" to a fairy tale.

Coal, the hero of Macmillan's scientific story (the story inscribed on the aforementioned "page"), bears some resemblance to MacDonald's hero Diamond. Like Diamond, Macmillan's coal is a "precious treasure"; it is deeply mysterious, the emissary of a distant world associated with the magic of childhood. Like Diamond, it has a positive effect on those exposed to it; coal, Macmillan writes, "does one's heart good" (102). And like Diamond, it produces magical stories: the burning coals themselves become fairy-tales, "those castles and rocks, the abodes of giants and dragons" (102). According to Macmillan, not only is the *story* of coal associated with children, but coal itself is the child of a "child"—the young earth: "The earth has its ages just like a human being. It has its childhood and youth, and it is of the fresh green youth of the earth that the coal burning in the grate speaks" (101). But if coal "speaks" of and originates in an edenic past, how does it make its way into the present?

In Macmillan's narrative, coal apparently makes the journey from earth to hearth without human labor. The only worker in this story is the sun, personified as a generous contributor to human comfort: "The source of all labour is the sun; and we get the benefit of his labour when we burn the coal or the wood in which he has condensed and preserved it" (102). Although human labor is entirely erased from this narrative, the images that accompany Macmillan's text hint that people must expend energy to reap the benefits of coal. A dark image that depicts laborers at work in a mine is juxtaposed with a bright image of children at a hearth, placing a bit of coal in the fire. Macmillan explains that when we burn coal we "set free" light that has been "caged and imprisoned" in it (102). The image links children with this process of liberation. The literal children as they are imagined here inhabit a realm of pleasure entirely removed from the black nether world of miners—the adult world of labor. This fantasy of distance covers over the actual proximity of these domains. In spite of legislation limiting child labor in the mines, in 1871 there were thousands more children working in mines than there had been twenty years before (see 1851 and 1871 Population Census Reports).

Fantasies such as *At the Back of the North Wind* support the idea that the adult's sphere of work and children's sphere of pleasure are discrete and distant—children still in the workforce are being "saved," removed from the adult world, to healthy environments. But the situation of children in MacDonald's novel after Diamond's death points to the illusory nature of this division. At the time of Diamond's demise, Nanny remains a worker, although the nature of her work has changed, become invisible. As a domestic worker, she performs "natural" duties attached to her gender, household duties that are meant [to] prepare her for her future as a wife and mother. In MacDonald's England, domestic labor performed by young girls was on the rise. While in 1851 about fifty thousand girls between the ages of ten and fourteen reported themselves as working in domestic service, in 1871 almost twice as many claimed to be performing this labor.[13] Certainly, countless girls served as "little mothers" without reporting their labor to the census enumerator. Likewise, the work of boys and girls who moved from regulated industries to sweated trades disappeared from official records. This sort of "buried" treasure seems to hold little interest for MacDonald.

Epilogue

By the end of the Victorian era, poor children were no longer widely available in England as a legal source of labor. Yet they, along with their wealthier counterparts, came to be seen as another sort of valuable resource—a natural resource, a possession "more precious than gold" (Montessori 5). Organizations devoted to analyzing this resource and exploring ways to put it to use burgeoned and nourished in Europe and in America. At the International Labor Conference in Berlin in 1890, a "universal" minimum age for work (twelve years old) was declared for the countries of northern Europe. At the Chicago World's Fair in 1893, English and American "child-study" associations proclaimed children the principal "wealth" of all nations. In the decades that followed, the source of this "wealth" was ever more frequently positioned within the child's imagination. The influential educator Maria Montessori (1870-1952) writes, "The child's true constructive energy, a dynamic power, has remained unnoticed for thousands of years. Just as men have trodden the earth, and later tilled its surface, without thought for the immense wealth hidden in its depths, so the men of our day make progress after progress in civilized life, without noticing the treasures that lie hidden in the psychic world of infancy" (5). This "psychic world of infancy," a child's inferiority, was ardently celebrated and gleefully charted not only by Montessori but also, by scores of her contemporaries—educators, psychologists, imaginative writers, historians, and even advertisers and commercial artists. In Anglo-American public discourse, "child-lovers" of every stripe chimed in with their ideas about the perimeters and mystical contents of the child's imagination. Their representations of children express a fervid, almost religious, belief in the mystery, power, and redemptive potential of the inner life of the child. The child's mind—a "treasure" and virgin source of wealth—can, Montessori suggests, be plumbed and plundered: "The child is endowed with unknown powers, which can guide us to a radiant future. If what we really want is a new world, then education must take as its aim the development of these hidden possibilities" (4). Thus Montessori and others found new "work" for the child, enlisting it in a utopian scheme.

The "inner child" that Montessori describes, often construed as magical and enigmatic, was thought to become manifest in the child's new form of work: play. Increasingly, child's play was conceived as a state of mind as well as an activity, and this state of mind had immeasurable value. But who summons this "value" from children—children themselves, or adults such as MacDonald and Montessori? Although children at the end of the century were no longer consigned to abject labor conditions, they were still defined by their role in an adult economy, albeit a moral or symbolic rather than a financial economy. This is a new form of subjugation, one that is, of course, disavowed by the adults, who, like Montessori and MacDonald, claim that children themselves voluntarily offer their inner bounty to an ailing adult world.

Child's Work is Child's Play

Endnotes

1. See McKendrick for a discussion of how children become consumers and come to be seen as "leisure items" with the advent of consumer culture in the late eighteenth century (ch. 7).
2. In this article I will refer to the "north wind" as both a place and a character. Following MacDonald, I will capitalize the words "north wind" only when referring to the character.
3. In the first half of the nineteenth century, child-labor reformers frequently employed the language of abolitionists. During this period, analogies between working children and enslaved Africans were commonplace; see Cunningham, ch. 4.
4. *At the Back of the North Wind* was serialized between November 1868 and October 1870 in Strahan and Company's children's periodical *Good Words for the Young* which MacDonald edited from 1869 to 1872 (when MacDonald's editorship ended, the publication changed its name to *Good Things*).
5. Reformers believed that too much work led to the physical and intellectual stunting of children.
6. Before presenting Diamond's account of the land at the back of the north wind, MacDonald's narrator summarizes reports of that place by "two very different people," a "great Italian" named "Durante" (a stand-in for Dante Alighieri), and a "very young peasant girl" named Kilmeny (the title character in James Hogg's poem "Kilmeny: A Fairy Legend").
7. MacDonald's reference here is wrong. Although MacDonald names Herodotus as the author of this report, the latter's account of the Hyperboreans in the *Histories* bears no resemblance to the description MacDonald attributes to the "old Greek writer." The Hyperboreans are also mentioned in Pindar's odes (*Olympia* 3, *Pytlna* 10, and *Istlmtia* 6) and in Hesiod's *Catalogue*. The classical description of the land at the back of the north wind closest to MacDonald's account is that in *Olympia* 3: "Never the Muse / is absent from their ways ... Neither disease nor bitter old age is mixed / in their sacred blood; far from labor and battle / they live."
8. Kingsley also published in *Good Words for the Young*.
9. At the time that MacDonald was writing, middle- and upper-class men were plunging into London slums to "save" indigent children. For instance, Thomas Barnardo, nicknamed "the father of nobody's children," rose to fame in the 1870s for his

efforts to pluck London's "street Arabs"—homeless children—off the streets at night and provide them with homes and work.
10. Critiques of precocity analogous to Spencer's (but without his racism) continue to inform contemporary discourses of childhood, as in Neil Postman's *The Disappearance of Childhood*.
11. To be sure, North Wind is herself described as a "toy" lady early on in the story, when she appears in a diminutive form.
12. It is important to note that although the novel celebrates Mr. Raymond as a hero, it also compares him unfavorably with Diamond both as child-rescuer and as moral authority.
13. This information is based on census reports; the numbers are therefore underestimates. Casual and part-time child laborers as well as those performing work in their own families probably did not report their occupation to the census.

Works Cited

Carroll, Lewis. *Complete Works of Lewis Carroll*. New York: Vintage, 1976.

Children's Employment Commission, First Report: Mining. Parliamentary Papers XV, 1842.

Children's Employment Commission, Second Report. Parliamentary Papers XIII and XIV, 1843.

Cunningham, Hugh. *Children of the Poor: Representations of Childhood Since the Seventeenth Century*. Oxford: Blackwell, 1991.

Dewey, John. "Froebel's Educational Principles." *Child Life* 3.9 (15 January 1901): 5-10.

—. *Child Life*. 3.9 (15 January 1901): 5-10.

Dickens, Charles. *Oliver Twist*. 1837. Oxford: Clarendon, 1966.

Horn, Pamela. *Children's Work and Welfare, 1780-1880*. Basingstoke: Macmillan, 1994.

Kingsley, Charles. *The Water Babies: A Fairy Tale for a Land-Baby*. 1863. Boston: Burnham, 1870.

MacDonald, George, *At the Back of the North Wind*. 1871. Whitehorn, CA: Johannesen, 1993.

Macmillan, Hugh. "A Lump of Coal." *Good Words for the Young* (December 1868): 102-5.

Mayhew, Henry. *London Labour and the London Poor*. Vol. 2. 1861-62. New York: Dover, 1968.

McKendrick, Neil, John Brewer, and J.H. Plumb. *The Birth of a Consumer Society: The Commercialization of Eighteenth Century England*. London: Europa, 1982.

Montessori, Maria. *The Absorbent Mind*. 1949. New York: Delta, 1989.

Murray, E. R. "On Kindergarten Games." *Child Life* 3.1. Conference Supplement (15 July 1901): 169-71.

Spencer, Herbert. "The Comparative Psychology of Man." *Popular Science Monthly* 8 (1876). Rpt. *Images of Race*. Ed. Michael D. Biddiss. Leicester: Leicester UP, 1979. 257-69.

Zelizer, Viviana A. *Pricing the Priceless Child: The Changing Social Value of Children*. New York: Basic, 1985.

THE TWO-WORLD CONSCIOUSNESS OF *NORTH WIND*:
UNITY AND DICHOTOMY IN MACDONALD'S FAIRY TALE

From *Studies in Scottish Literature*

FERNANDO J. SOTO

In the past decade, there has been increasing work devoted to George MacDonald's books, including his enigmatic "children's tale" *At the Back of the North Wind*. From the more general studies we have received insights into the methods and materials MacDonald chose to utilize in many of his books, while from the more focused researches, there have emerged some interesting readings, explaining individual aspects of *North Wind*. For all that, *At the Back of the North Wind* remains enigmatic and suggestive of deeply hidden ethereal meanings. So, how is the curious reader to interpret the linguistic eddies and mythological whirlwinds still left behind by this long intriguing fairy tale?

A general exposition of one of MacDonald's main recurring themes is provided by Stephen Prickett's "The Two Worlds of George MacDonald." Just as the title of this article suggests, MacDonald, according to Prickett, was very interested in separate yet inter-related realities or worlds that could be visited by some of the characters in his stories. This insight is helpful in understanding many of MacDonald's works; however, Prickett appears to visualize the two worlds mainly in spatio-temporal terms.[1] In a similar vein, Nancy Willard's "The Goddess in the Belfry: Grandmothers and Wise Women in George MacDonald's Books for Children" (*Childlike*, pp. 67-74) and Nancy-Lou Patterson's "*Kore* Motifs in *The Princess and the Goblin*" (*Childlike*, pp. 169-82) have identified or intuited MacDonald's recurring use of Greek mythological material, although this has not been thoroughly studied nor expanded to include *At the Back of the North Wind*.

On the other hand, more particular and focused insights into MacDonald's tale are provided by Roderick McGillis in his "Language and Secret Knowledge in *At the Back of the North Wind*" (*Childlike*, pp. 145-59) and by Lesley Smith's "Old Wine in New Bottles: Aspects of Prophesy in George MacDonald's *At the Back of the North Wind*" (*Childlike*, pp. 161-68). McGillis's and Smith's articles are helpful; however, they appear to explain only parts of one side of the story. McGillis puts most of his emphasis on a Christianized reading of a poetic language as it relates to secret knowledge

The Two-World Consciousness of North Wind

at the expense of other types of language and knowledge. Smith, in similar fashion, concentrates solely on the Judeo-Christian mythological material to the detriment of the wealth of Greek mythological dimensions in the book.

Scholars appear well aware of the wealth of Judeo-Christian references and allusions in *At the Back of the North Wind*.[2] Little attention, however, has been devoted to the equal if not more important direct and indirect Greek references and allusions present in the story. In the first short paragraph of *North Wind*, MacDonald introduces some of the important Greek mythological material he will use in his story. By using a direct reference to Herodotus, the indirect reference to the Hyperboreans, and by mentioning the strange fate of these mythic people, MacDonald underscores the crucial importance of Greek mythology for his book. In addition, by drawing attention to the supposed mass watery deaths of the Hyperboreans, something which does not appear to be mentioned anywhere by Herodotus, MacDonald makes sure to convey to the reader that his story will give an extremely creative reading of some interesting yet obscure and sometimes confused Greek mythological stories and traditions.[3]

Some of the main references in MacDonald's book are those to the Greek god Boreas, the north wind itself/himself. The ancient Greeks did not leave us much material on Boreas, their personification of the north wind. Much of the mythological material the Greeks did provide, however, appears to have inspired MacDonald when he wrote his *North Wind*. Some of this inspiration may be gleaned by reviewing parts of the mythology surrounding Boreas:

> Boreas ... The god of the North Wind. He lived in Thrace which to the Greeks represented the ultimate in a cold climate. He is depicted as a winged demon ... In one image he is shown, like the Roman Janus, with two faces looking in opposite directions ... Boreas, in the shape of a horse, is said to have sired by the mares of Erichthonius twelve colts ... Boreas also sired swift horses by one of the Furies as well as by a Harpy.[4]

Thus, the Greeks generally associated their North Wind with horses, and more particularly with a black steed as we read in *The Iliad*:

> For him were pastur'd in the marshy mead,
> Rejoicing with their foals, three thousand mares;
> Them Boreas, in the pasture where they fed,
> Beheld, enamour'd; and amid the herd
> In likeness of a coal-black steed appear'd;
> Twelve foals, by him conceiving, they produc'd.
> These, o'er the teeming corn-fields as they flew,
> Skimm'd o'er the standing ears, nor broke the haulm;

And, o'er wide Ocean's bosom as they flew,
Skimm'd o'er the topmost spray of th' hoary sea[5]

Black is not only the color of the mythological Boreas in the form of a horse. It is also the color that Arthur Hughes, the original illustrator of MacDonald's book, perhaps with the help of the writer, chose to use in his depiction of Diamond the horse.[6] That old Diamond is black is also found to be significant with regards to the mythic symbolism a black horse has for modern scholars (Smith, *Childlike*, pp. 164-5). More importantly, just as Boreas is closely associated with a black stallion in Greek mythology, so is North Wind identified with old Diamond in many parts of the book.

Similarities and intricate connections between North Wind and old Diamond abound. Smith sensed some connection between these two characters, but did not pursue the matter in this passage:

> Diamond's relationship with North Wind begins when his family is living in The Wilderness and develops further when he (apparently) visits the country at her back. But, though North Wind's influence is considerable during the Bloomsbury section of the book, personal contact between the two is suspended; the boy never sees her when Horse Diamond is present or playing a key role (*Childlike*, pp. 161-62).

MacDonald prevents old Diamond and North Wind from meeting because they are very closely related and may at times merge into one and the same being. This merging becomes more and more apparent as we continue to consider the web of connections between old Diamond and North Wind.

One of the easiest connections to consider between the two is in the way they are both portrayed in relation to young Diamond. It may be recalled that there are only two creatures on whose backs the boy mounts: old Diamond and North Wind. It must also be remembered that the Greek name "Hyperborean" means "over the north wind" or "one at the back of Boreas/North Wind" and that MacDonald, in the first page of the book, makes the reader aware that young Diamond sleeps directly above the back of old Diamond: "For Diamond's father had built him a bed in the loft with boards all around it … and Diamond's father put old Diamond in the stall under the bed… ."[7] Therefore, every night young Diamond is directly over or "at the back of old Diamond," and insofar as the boy is a "Hyperboraean,"[8] his natural place is also at the back of the North Wind or Boreas.

MacDonald, however, goes further: he has the boy compare the two entities: "To have a lady like that for a friend—with such long hair, too! Why it was longer than twenty Diamonds' tails!" (*North Wind*, p. 21). The boy also appears intuitively aware of some connection between North Wind and old Diamond from the beginning of his encounters with North Wind. Young

The Two-World Consciousness of North Wind

Diamond not only consciously stops following North Wind and uses the ladder leading to old Diamond instead of the one "he would naturally have gone down" (*North Wind*, p. 21), but he also talks to both creatures in a similar fashion. Furthermore, young Diamond notices the peculiar coincidence of being driven to exactly the same spot—by the wall—on two separate occasions by both old Diamond and North Wind (*North Wind*, p. 31).

The similarities continue as young Diamond soon actively begins to climb on the back of both creatures. Diamond first climbs on the horse's back in Chapter 3 before attempting a similar feat at the back of North Wind in Chapter 4. MacDonald describes these related events in similar terms:

> 'I'll give old Diamond a surprise,' thought the boy; and creeping up very softly, before the horse knew, he was astride of his back. Then it was young Diamond's turn to have more of a surprise than he had expected; for as with an earthquake, with a rumbling and a rocking hither and thither, a sprawling of legs and heaving as of many backs, young Diamond found himself hoisted up in the air, with both hands twisted in the horse's mane. The next instant old Diamond lashed out with both his hind legs, and giving one cry of terror young Diamond found himself lying on his neck, with his arms as far round it as they would go. But then the horse stood as still as a stone, except that he lifted his head gently up, to let the boy slip down to his back (*North Wind*, p. 28).

The first time Diamond is placed on North Wind's back, this important event is described thus:

> She took him in her hands, threw him over her shoulder, and said, 'Get in, Diamond.'
>
> And Diamond parted her hair with his hands, crept between, and feeling about soon found the woven nest. It was just like a pocket, or like the shawl in which gipsy women carry their children. North Wind put her hands to her back, felt all about the nest, and finding it safe, said,—
>
> 'Are you comfortable, Diamond?'
>
> 'Yes, indeed,' answered Diamond.
>
> The next moment he was rising in the air. North Wind grew towering up to the place of the clouds. Her hair went streaming out from her, till it spread like a mist over the stars. She flung herself abroad in space.
>
> Diamond held on by two of the twisted ropes which, parted and interwoven, formed his shelter, for he could not help being afraid (*North Wind*, pp. 38-9).

There are many similarities between the two events and some interesting horse riding references in the account of Diamond at the back of North Wind. For instance, some of these similarities are: the throwing over the shoulder, the violent rising up in the air, Diamond twisting his hands in the hair of both creatures. Comparing North Wind's hair to two twisted ropes is also a curious method of describing what young Diamond held in his hands, unless MacDonald had the reins or a bridle in mind. MacDonald's verbal descriptions are further accentuated in Arthur Hughes' jockey-like depiction of Diamond on the back of North Wind.

In Chapter 5, Diamond is placed on old Diamond's back by his father, very much as he had previously been placed on the back of North Wind. Here, once again, there is an emphasis on young Diamond reaching for old Diamond's bridle (*North Wind*, pp. 48-9). More important, however, is what follows: the direct comparison or confusion by Nanny of old Diamond and North Wind. This is what takes place once young Diamond drops in on her once off North Wind and once off old Diamond:

> He had a penny in his pocket, the gift of the same lady the day before, and he tumbled off his horse to give it to the girl ... She thought first: "Then he *was* on the back of the North Wind after all!' but, looking up at the sound of the horse's feet on the paved crossing, she changed her idea, saying to herself, 'North Wind is his father's horse! That's the secret of it! Why couldn't he say so?' (*North Wind*, p. 50).

This should make us reconsider the identity of North Wind and old Diamond, and also the role of Nanny, who is not so shallow and dense as she has been portrayed by some scholars. Momentarily she correctly identifies North Wind with old Diamond—something which young Diamond never consciously appears able to do.

The similarities between North Wind and old Diamond go much deeper than merely having both entities ridden by young Diamond and identified by Nanny. Both North Wind and old Diamond, in classic Greek tradition, appear to be flesh/meat eaters.[9] The reader of *At the Back of the North Wind* is reminded at least twice of old Diamond's proclivities or appetite for flesh/meat. The first instance is found in Chapter 1, when young Diamond fears being eaten by the horse:

> Diamond's father put old Diamond in the stall under the bed, because he was a quiet horse, and did not go to sleep standing, but lay down like a reasonable creature. But, although he was a surprisingly reasonable creature, yet, when young Diamond woke in the middle of the night, and felt the bed shaking in the blasts of the north wind, he could not help wondering whether, if the wind should blow the house down, and

The Two-World Consciousness of North Wind

he were to fall through into the manger, old Diamond mightn't eat him up before he knew him in his night-gown (*North Wind*, pp. 11-12).

Here is what Euripides wrote:

> [Heracles] mounted on a car and tamed with the bit the steeds of Diomede, that greedily champed their bloody food at gory mangers with jaws unbridled, devouring with hideous joy the flesh of men ... [10]

The second instance is a much more direct reference presented by the narrator, not by a scared and imaginative, yet intuitively perceptive, child:

> During all that month, they lived on very short commons indeed, seldom tasting meat except on Sundays, and poor old Diamond, who worked hardest of all, not even then—so that at the end of it he was as thin as a clothes-horse (*North Wind*, p. 241).

On the other hand, the reference to North Wind as a flesh/meat eater is not as pronounced. In Chapter 3, while young Diamond believes that North Wind has eaten a child, she first leaves him in suspense and only later denies the charge of cannibalism:

> 'Surely,' he thought, 'North Wind can't be eating one of the children!' Coming to himself all at once, he rushed after her with his little first clenched ... Before he reached the head of the stair, however, North Wind met him, took him by the hand, and hurried down and out of the house.
>
> 'I hope you haven't eaten a baby, North Wind!' said Diamond, very solemnly.
>
> North Wind laughed merrily, and went tripping on faster . . .
>
> 'No,' she said at last, 'I did not eat a baby' (*North Wind*, p. 35).

These references to old Diamond and North Wind eating flesh/meat both reflect the other possible meaning of the name Boreas—"Devouring" (Graves, p. 384)—and the general way the ancients visualized the double-edged power of the winds. For instance, here is how a more modern scholar explains the way the power of the winds was understood:

> It is easy enough to see how winds were conceived of as Snatchers, death-demons, but why should they impregnate, give life? It is not, I think, by a mere figure of speech that breezes ... are spoken of as 'life-begetting' ... and 'soul rearing'. It is not because they are in our sense life-giving and refreshing as well as destructive: the truth lies deeper down. Only life can give life, only a soul gives birth to a soul; the winds *are* souls as well as breaths ... (Harrison, p. 179).

Behind the Back of the North Wind

Both old Diamond (the "reasonable creature") and North Wind possess the power of speech. Young Diamond is able to speak to them and can understand then in turn. However, old Diamond does not, as might be expected, speak English. A possibility is that old Diamond may follow Boreas, the Greek god of the north wind and father of horses, by speaking Greek. When young Diamond first hears old Diamond speak, this is the way the narrator describes the peculiar event:

> He heard the two horses talking to each other—in a strange language, which yet, somehow or other, he could understand, and turn over in his mind in English. The first words he heard were from Diamond (*North Wind*, pp. 246-7).

This type of flesh/meat eating, speaking horse is reminiscent of some of the ancient Greek-speaking horses such as Boreas in the form of a stallion or, among others, Xanthus, Achilles' horse, or the horses of Diomedes.

Many ancient sources agree that Boreas, as a horse and giver of life, was the father of flesh/meat eating and talking horses, but several of these sources are confused or incomplete regarding Boreas' parentage or progeny. David Kravitz lists the following under the heading of Boreas:

> The north wind. Son of Eos and Astraeus. Had many offspring. 1. Father of the horses of Ares, by one of the Erinnyes. 2. Father of the horses of Erechtheus, by one of the Harpies. 3. Father of the immortal horses of Achilles, Balius and Xanthus, by the Harpy, Podarge. 4. Father of twelve fast horses by the twelve mares of Dardanus ... Boreas was renowned as a father of horses because of their speed.[11]

There are numerous sources that agree that many of the above horses ate flesh/meat, while at least Xanthus is well known for his speaking abilities, but not so well know for his flesh/meat eating tendencies (Graves, 130.a and 130.1).[12] Even though a few of the above equine sexual exploits are credited in some sources to Boreas' brother Zephyr, the west wind, this would still make the former a grandfather, father or uncle to many of the flesh-eating and talking horses.[13] Merely by scratching the surface of some obscure Greek traditions, it becomes apparent that MacDonald borrowed much from Greek mythology for his *At the Back of the North Wind*. This revelation should not come as a surprise to readers, as similar Greek mythology is used by MacDonald in several of his books for children, and because the mythology dealing with Boreas/North Wind, as stated earlier, is directly alluded to in reference to Herodotus, the Hyperboreans, and North Wind.

In order to understand the more obscure connections between North Wind/Boreas and his equine prodigy, we need to probe further into some of the mythological traditions emerging out of and dealing with Thrace. It is in Thrace, a northern region for the Greeks, where most of the traditions of gods and mortals associated with Boreas/North Wind and flesh/meat eating, talking horses, are placed.[14] For instance, the flesh-eating horses of Ares—originally a Thracian war god—which were passed on to the Thracian king Diomedes, were Boreas' offspring.

MacDonald may also have had in mind traditions which trace many of North Wind's characteristics to his mother, Eos. Some obscure traditions have Eos, not Zeus, kidnap Ganymedes (in a whirlwind?), the young and beautiful son of Tros, and it is to repay this boy's father for the abductions that two flesh-eating and talking horses, Balius and Zanthus, are provided (Graves, 29.c; 75.5; 130; 137.5, and 153.e)[15] In addition, Boreas, like his mother also was a kidnapper; however, he did not direct his attention only to beautiful females: he is also known to have fallen in love with Hyacinthus. In this myth, Boreas falls in love with him and later kills him through the action of the wind when the boy chooses Apollo instead of the god of the north wind (Lemprière, p. 119).

Another aspect which should be apparent is that MacDonald follows some of these Greek traditions of naming different beings by the same name and then proceeding to confuse their characteristics and identities. For instance, the name Xanthus was, among others, the name of one of King Diomedes' flesh-eating horses, Hector's horse, Achilles' horse, and as well another name for the river Scamander which/whom Achilles fought in *Iliad* XXI.[16] Interestingly, Scamander/Xanthus was the father of the wife of Tros/Laomedon—the king who in some traditions was given the horse Xanthus in return for his son Ganymedes. On the other hand, Podarces, who later became Priam, was the son of Laomedon and in turn Hector's father, which would tend to make Ganymedes Hector's uncle! In addition, Podarge (for whom Podarces/Priam was named) was supposed to be the daughter and/or mate of Boreas—who through her or by her became a grandfather, father, or uncle to Achilles' Xanthus. This all seems very incestuous and confused, and while MacDonald only confuses a few names/characters, he nevertheless manages to keep the mood and flavor of the Greek tradition of overlapping histories, names, and identities.

According to William Raeper:

> MacDonald's stature as a Scottish writer (and his use of tradition and dialect) has still to be fully assessed. As a Victorian, MacDonald's fantasy writing and novels comprise a collection of texts that must be increasingly valuable to anyone interested in that age.[17]

There are many more types of worlds to discover in MacDonald's book. In "Language and Secret Knowledge in *At the Back of the North Wind*"

McGillis outlines the use of poetry and secret knowledge in MacDonald's book (*Childlike*, pp. 145-59). However, while poetry plays a role in transmitting some secrets to the boy, another world of hidden language appears to have been completely overlooked. Just as there is an earthier, darker Greek aspect to strongly counter-balance the light Judeo-Christian one, there is a folksy prose and an earthy dialectal secret language to counter-balance the elevated poetic language.

One of the best examples of this, as it relates to language and young Diamond's and North Wind's relationship to secret knowledge, occurs in the first chapter of the book. Here it is young Diamond who attempts to impart to North Wind a linguistic secret and it is she who misunderstands him. When North Wind is confused by young Diamond's use of, and the value he attaches to, the word "Diamond," the following exchange occurs:

> 'Diamond is a very pretty name,' persisted the boy, vexed that it should not give satisfaction.
>
> 'Diamond is a useless thing rather,' said the voice.
>
> "That's not true. Diamond is very nice—as big as two—and so quiet all night! And doesn't he make a jolly row in the morning, getting up on his four great legs! It's like thunder.' (*North Wind*, p. 17)

This knowledge regarding the horse, passed on from young Diamond to North Wind, is just the beginning of Diamond's attempts to share certain knowledge with his airy godmother. Even though North Wind appears to think she is the only one sharing a secret knowledge with the boy regarding his name, a deeper type of secret linguistic knowledge is missed by her. Parts of this hidden lesson may be seen in the following conversation:

> 'Our window opens like a door, right over the coach-house door. And the wind— you, ma'am—came in, and blew the Bible out of the man's hands, and the leaves went all flutter flutter on the floor, and my mother picked it up and gave it back to him open, and there—'
>
> 'Was your name in the Bible,—the sixth stone in the high-priest's breast-plate.'
>
> 'Oh!—a stone, was it?' said Diamond. 'I thought it had been a horse—I did.'
>
> 'Never mind. A horse is better than a stone any day. Well, you see, I know all about you and your mother.' (*North Wind*, pp. 19-20)

What Diamond appears to know due to his rural upbringing is that a horse was not better but equal to a stone! *The English Dialect Dictionary* makes this equality clear. Thus a stone, in some dialects of Scotland and England, was linguistically equal to a stallion or a horse.[18] And it is this dialectal knowledge of a stone being a stallion that young Diamond appears to want to refer to, instead of the Biblical, and perhaps useless, precious stone North Wind has in mind. However, North Wind does not appear to understand this other type of earthier, secret linguistic knowledge and thus retains her idea of a gem throughout the conversation.

The next major debate between the rustic young Diamond and the airy North Wind involves the nature of poetry. Here, once again, there appears to be much more to Diamond's position than meets the eye. There is some rational linguistic method to Diamond's thinking when he argues with North Wind in the following exchange:

> 'You darling!' said Diamond, seeing what a lovely little toy-woman she was . . .
>
> 'I am quite as respectable now as I shall be six hours after this, when I take an East Indiaman by the royals, twist her round, and push her under.' . . .
>
> 'But look there!' she resumed. 'Do you see a boat with one man in it—a green and white boat?'
>
> 'Yes; quite well.'
>
> "That's a poet.'
>
> 'I thought you said it was a bo-at.'
>
> 'Stupid pet! Don't you know what a poet is?'
>
> 'Why, a thing to sail on the water in.' (*North Wind*, p. 54)

Diamond, in response to the ambiguity created by North Wind, appears to be concentrating on two linguistically interesting things: the word "man" used to describe a boat (as the "East Indiaman" mentioned by North Wind, or the more common merchantman, man-o-war, man-at-arms, or just plain "man" used to describe a boat during Victorian times), and the poetship or the poet craft involved. These types of clever linguistic connections become more apparent when North Wind "gets wind" of Diamond's meanings as she continues the above discussion:

> 'Well, perhaps you're not so far wrong. Some poets do carry people over the sea. But I have no business to talk so much. The man is a poet.'
>
> 'The boat is a boat,' said Diamond (*North Wind*, pp. 54-5.)

As Diamond had not mentioned a sea-going craft (i.e., a "man"), it may be safe to guess that North Wind, who had just used the word "Indiaman," may be intuiting some meaningful parts of the man-boat relationships or the special craft used by poets to carry people over a metaphorical sea. It would not be illogical for Diamond to suppose that if a poet is a man and a man is a boat, then a poet must also be a boat. Furthermore, if poets are to carry anyone over the sea, this transportation would most likely be performed with the poet's ship or by the poet's craft (i.e., poetry). For the creative and logical young Diamond, a poet is a boat, and as the boy cannot spell very well, it is easy to see how for him the poetship may very well be the poet's ship and the poetcraft may be the poet's craft. Therefore, the reader may assume that Diamond is not as simple as he has been portrayed by scholars, nor is North Wind the omniscient entity who attempts to teach a somewhat dull and opinionated boy.

Given the above arguments, I believe that McGillis' theory that North Wind attempts to teach Diamond the language of poetry and the secret knowledge this entails should be expanded to include Diamond's attempts to teach her the creative wisdom and logic inherent in his rural speech. In other words, North Wind's conclusion, presented early in the book that "you see I know all about you and your mother" need not be accepted uncritically. North Wind, as it will be shown later, knows young Diamond's mother intimately, but she does not appear to know all about Diamond. She could stand to learn something from her pupil.

The dichotomies in *At the Back of the North Wind*, while very important for MacDonald, are only one part of his project in the book. Separation is balanced by unity in the book. Both Diamonds and North Wind have already been presented as the uniters of disparate things or mediators of the different worlds, but MacDonald also attempts at many levels to join other characters and parts of the book.

One of the connections made in numerous episodes in the book is that involving North Wind and Martha, Diamond's mother. In the first chapter the narrator tells the reader that young Diamond thought that North Wind's gentle voice "sounded a little like his mother's" (*North Wind*, p. 16). In the same chapter, North Wind tells Diamond that she knows and loves his mother, that she was present at his birth, and that she had a part in naming him (p. 19). Later on we are reminded by Diamond of the possible friendship between North Wind and his mother (p. 48) and that North Wind's voice is as close as it can be to his mother's (p. 58). It is the narrator who next reminds the reader of this connection—when the boy is forsaken in the cathedral (p. 71). The relations between both females appear to become strong as the book progresses: North Wind, when Diamond does not recognize her at the toy shop, compares young Diamond to "a baby that doesn't know his mother in a new bonnet" (p. 81). Later, along the way to her back, North Wind tells Diamond: "Coil yourself up and go to sleep. The yacht shall be my cradle, and you shall be my baby" (p. 86).[19] The last instance to be noted here involves the transportation of a very ill Diamond from the arms of North Wind to his sickbed, where he holds and is

The Two-World Consciousness of North Wind

held by his mother (p. 101). It is difficult to know why MacDonald associated Martha, the good housewife, with North Wind.[20] This connection also helps to explain other enigmatic parts of the book.[21]

There are other references to Diamond being like North Wind's baby and these may help explain another little understood, but important and recurring reference. Diamond is referred to as God's baby, North Wind's baby, and once as old Diamond's godchild (*North Wind*, p. 136). All of these can now be accounted for given that North Wind is closely associated with Martha, that North Wind may see herself breathing life into young Diamond at his birth, that North Wind is very closely related if not identical to old Diamond, and finally, that North Wind is the Greek god Boreas. An inkling of his parentage may account for young Diamond's accepting the supposed insult, with which he is continually confronted, as a compliment instead. Here is one of the instances:

> "The cabbies call him 'God's baby,'" she whispered. "He's not right in the head, you know. A tile loose."
>
> Still Diamond, though he heard every word, and understood it too, kept on smiling. What could it matter what people called him, so long as he did nothing that he ought not to do? And, besides, *God's baby* was surely the best of names! (p. 149).

Diamond, therefore, may not only be "'God's baby,' a Christ figure who spread his message of love, obedience, and duty through his actions and his words," according to McGillis. Diamond also shares aspects of his father's, the Greek god Boreas', character.[22] Another set of clues regarding young Diamond's associations with Boreas emerge as one considers the interesting games young Diamond plays near the beginning of the story. Two of these are described by MacDonald:

> Although the next day was very stormy, Diamond ... was busy making a cave by the side of his mother's fire with a broken chair, a three legged stool, and a blanket, and then sitting in it (p. 13).

The second game is this:

> He played all his games over and over indoors, specially that of driving two chairs harnessed to the baby's cradle (pp. 30-31).

Both of the games fit well with Diamond's status as Boreas' son because not only was the God of the north wind closely associated with horses but he, like all of the other winds, was generally known to live in a cave. Given the above evidence, Diamond may very well be God's baby, Boreas' son. What also follows from these conclusions is that both Diamonds are intricately related if not unified in parts of the book and that MacDonald appears to be conflating

Martha and North Wind into one character.[23]

The Martha-North Wind connection also explains something that McGillis picks up on but has some trouble explaining: the misunderstanding between mother and son ("Language," p. 145). This parallels not only the identification of Martha with North Wind but also the lack of understanding on the parts of North Wind *and* Martha in regards to Diamond's prosaic and poetic outbursts. Thus, Diamond's mother(s)—Martha/North Wind—individually appear to miss both types of secret knowledge emerging from her/their son. However, this is not so much because "Diamond ... is with Christ in not caring for the morrow. He has befriended the spirit of change, North Wind" ("Language," p. 145), but probably because he was with his father, Boreas, and may be partaking of the God of the north wind's essence, flux itself.

It is this type of obscure set of references to ancient mythology which gives further support to the arguments regarding a connection between North Wind and Martha. First, another linguistic puzzle found in the book should be explained in order to give further weight to the connection between both mothers. It must be remembered that in *At the Back of the North Wind*, there are several references to old Diamond's associations with a stone. These references have already been explained by the dialectal connection between a horse/stallion and a stone. This information, then, can be further used to explain the curious name of the mysterious horse owner, Mr. Stonecrop. And, while MacDonald is very secretive regarding the name of the horse owned by Stonecrop—something which would have proved helpful for identification purposes—he does supply relevant information in other parts of the book. If a stone is a horse, then the name Stonecrop may mean horse crop. This interpretation is supported by the fact that MacDonald appears to be playing with exactly this meaning (i.e., horse crop/whip) when he has Stonecrop state: "Give the boy a whip, Jack. I never carries one when I drives old—" (*North Wind*, p. 130). This name can be further analyzed by reviewing the close linguistic connections between the word crop and the word head. Thus, the name Stonecrop may also mean horse head. Interestingly, there are many signs of the existence of Thracian cannibalistic horse worshiping cults where the devotees wore horse masks during the ceremonies (Graves, 130.1). It was probably some of these masked rituals which gave rise to much of the mythology of flesh-eating, verbose Thracian horses fathered by Boreas. If even part of the above is accepted, then Martha as the mother of Diamond may be seen as related to the horse cults and thus can, be wearing a horse mask, represent North Wind Him/Herself while retaining her own identity.

It is not only in his fiction (with the help of Stonecrop) that MacDonald is secretive regarding the name of a horse. In one of his letters it becomes

The Two-World Consciousness of North Wind

apparent that MacDonald named one of his own female ponies Zephyr, while remaining tight-lipped regarding the name of the other (brother/sister or son/daughter?) horse. Some of this somewhat ironic information, from the perspective of *North Wind,* is gathered from a letter MacDonald wrote to William Cowper-Temple in 1879, some eight years after publishing his airy tale.

> Now about your guests the highly privileged ponies. I am sorry to hear they have so little to do for that shows they have not been so useful as I had flattered myself they might be ... I wish they had been useful and then we could have *begged* you to keep them. Now we can only ask you whether you know of any one who would buy them or accept them. There is this difficulty about selling them, that Zephyr is really worth nothing, and the other though not eight quite, I fancy is not worth much without her. I should not like to part them, and much rather than do so I would give them to anybody who would be kind to them ... .[24]

Thus the mystery horse, perhaps related to Zephyr (i.e., the Greek West Wind), is never named, and s/he appears to have been born at approximately the same time as was the fictive Diamond, sometime in 1871.[25]

MacDonald appears to know not only about the ancient cannibalistic horse-masked women, but also about the purpose and later changes to the rituals involved. One of these was the replacement of an old king by a new one. This ritual is paralleled to some degree by both Diamonds replacing their parents in the middle of the book. The horse Diamond, as noted by Lesley Smith,[26] becomes prominent in the Bloomsbury section of the book when North Wind is not present. On the other hand, young Diamond takes on the role of his father as cab driver and provider for the family. Both of these events are portrayed as anything but unnatural in the book. Graves (in sections 71.1, 101.g and 109.J, and 130.1) goes on to describe how the ritual was changed by Heracles from a cannibalistic one to one having to do with an organized chariot crash. It is young Diamond, in the company of Stonecrop, and his father who almost crash into one another as the former is learning to drive a cab (*North Wind,* p. 131). It should also be noticed Joseph hands over the reigns of his own cab/chariot to Diamond after this close call which may represent a rite of passage from boy to man in MacDonald's tale. A few chapters after this incident Diamond replaces his father Joseph as cabman and bread-winner.

Another dichotomy which appears to be called into question is the role of gender in *At the Back of the North Wind.* Not only are old Diamond (a stallion), and North Wind (a female deity) continually confused, but young Diamond, after first meeting her and stating that North Wind's voice sounded like his mother's, appears to recall the male god Boreas when he calls her Mr. North

Wind (pp. 16-17). This gender confusion is expanded by MacDonald as even young Diamond's gender appears to be ambiguous. It is Diamond's mother who first makes a remark regarding her son:

> 'Why, Diamond, child!' said his mother at last, 'you're as good to your mother as if you were a girl—nursing the baby, and toasting the bread, and sweeping up the hearth!' (p. 125).

After this compliment, Diamond is told by one of the cabmen that he looks like a girl:

> 'Well, you're a plucky one, for all your girl's looks!' said the man; 'and I wish ye luck.' (p. 177)

Even Diamond appears to view himself in an ambiguous manner in terms of gender. Near the end of the book, Diamond is once again in the habit of nursing his brother and sister when the narrator makes the following comment:

> Sometimes he would have his little brother, sometimes his little sister, and sometimes both of them in the grass with him, and then he felt like a cat with her first kittens, he said, only he couldn't purr—all he could do was to sing (p. 262)

These examples of gender ambiguity would be strange were it not for all of the gender confusion present in much of the ancient Greek mythology MacDonald uses in his book. And while there are many other instances in the ancient traditions of transgendered and/or hermaphroditic gods, humans, and animals, MacDonald only hints at this in his story, just enough to keep the flavor of the old traditions which saw unity where we see dichotomies.

The last topic to consider in this paper involves the death of young Diamond. Throughout the story there are constant reminders of Diamond's illness and the proximity of death. His constant excursions with North Wind/Boreas, as the boy becomes ill, partially prepare the reader for Diamond's ultimate odyssey with North Wind at the end of the book. Interestingly, Diamond is not the only hero to travel to the Greek land of death with the aid of North Wind. In *The Odyssey*, Homer, through the mouth of Circe, includes the following directions to the "groves of Persephone" and the "home of Hades":

> 'Son of Laertes and seed of Zeus, resourceful Odysseus,
> let no need for a guide on your ship trouble you; only
> set up your mast pole and spread the white sails upon it,
> And sit still, and let the blast of the North wind carry you.
> But when you have crossed with your ship the stream of the Ocean,
> you will find there a thickly wooded shore, and the groves of Persephone,

and tall black poplars growing, and fruit-perishing willows;
then beach your ship on the shore of the deep-eddying Ocean
and yourself go forward into the moldering home of Hades.[27]

This reference makes clear that MacDonald was well versed in Greek mythology and the ancient conception of the topography of the world. This knowledge allowed him to provide a guide for Diamond when the boy twice made his journey to the land of death. The first journey resembles that of Odysseus' in a ship, while the means used to get to the back of the North Wind the second time is the much more common type, death.

George MacDonald's *At the Back of the North Wind*, while being "understood" and enjoyed by children, offers adult readers some staggering meanings, allusions, and messages. This is a very complex book which will require much in-depth study for future readers to understand. And while scholars have commented on the fact that MacDonald attempts to place himself in a complex theological tradition, in a Christian tradition, and in a tradition of the "poetic," there are other traditions which MacDonald chose to enter into. There are darker and earthier aspects to *At the Back of the North Wind* which counterbalance the sweet, safe, and perhaps childlike Christian readings of the book. It is these deeper, darker/aspects which are beginning to be illuminated, unearthed and understood by scholars and readers. While we sometimes note the close similarities between MacDonald and Dante, we ought not to forget that Dante continually merged Greek and Roman mythology/history with his Christian stories. While MacDonald was guided by Dante, he also allowed Virgil, Herodotus and other Greek historians and mythographers to lead him. This type of myth exploration allowed MacDonald into the deep, dark genius of the ancient Greek mind when he wrote his *At the Back of the North Wind*.

While some of this complex book's dark secrets have been noted in this article, it is far from a complete reading of *North Wind*. It is, however, hoped that now scholars will have more, and perhaps better, tools at their disposal when evaluating the ultimate meaning—if any overall meaning exists—of *At the Back of the North Wind*. Finally, I hope that two related conclusions appear certain: that Greek mythology and rural Victorian language will play very prominent parts in any new understanding of MacDonald's book, and that *At the Back of the North Wind* must be studied carefully, and from several other dimensions or worlds than merely the Christian or the poetic, if we are to deepen our understanding of this enigmatic book and its writer.

Endnotes

1. Stephen Prickett, "The Two Worlds of George MacDonald," in Roderick McGillis, ed., *For the Childlike* (Metuchen & London, 1992), p. 17. Henceforth *Childlike*.
2. See Robert Lee Wolf, *The Golden Key* (New Haven, 1961), p. 291; Michael Mendelson, "The Fairy Tales of George MacDonald and the Evolution of a Genre," in *Childlike*, p. 33; John Townsend, *Written for Children* (Harmondsworth, 1983), p. 101.
3. MacDonald claims that the Hyperboreans committed mass suicide because they were too comfortable. This is a very creative but misleading interpretation of the tradition. According to the myth, once the older Hyperboreans had lived a long and prosperous life, they individually committed suicide by jumping from a cliff into the sea. In similar fashion MacDonald will give his own creative readings of other Greek myths throughout the book.
4. Pierre Grimal, *The Dictionary of Classical Mythology*, trans. A. R. Maxwell-Hyslop (Oxford, 1996), p. 77.
5. Homer, *The Iliad and Odyssey*, trans. Edward, Earl of Derby, and William Cowper (London, 1933), p. 351, lines 254-63. For some of the chthonic aspects of blackness associated with the winds, see Jane Harrison, *Prologomena to the Study of Greek Religion* (Cambridge, 1903), p. 67. Henceforth Harrison.
6. Even though the color of old Diamond is never directly mentioned by MacDonald, Arthur Hughes, perhaps at the author's instigation, depicted a black horse. This can be further deduced insofar as MacDonald does tell the reader that North Wind's hair is black (p. 18) while old Diamond's coat always appears darker than North Wind's hair in Hughes' illustrations.
7. George MacDonald, *At the Back of the North Wind, The Princess and the Goblin, The Princess and Curdie* (London, 1979), p. 11. Henceforth *North Wind*.
8. According to the definition given in *Lempriére's Classical Dictionary*, as revised by F. A. Wright (London, 1990), p. 319, Diamond, by living in a cold climate, may very well qualify as a Hyperborean: "The word Hyperborean is applied in general to all those who inhabit any cold climate." Since Hecateus, through Diodurus Siculus, places the Hyperborean region in Britain, MacDonald may have had even more reason for assigning

The Two-World Consciousness of North Wind

Diamond the title of "one at the back of the north wind" (i.e. a Hyperborean). For this latter information, see Robert Graves, *The Greek Myths* (New York, 1957), section 21.1. Henceforth Lempriére and Graves.

9. MacDonald appears to follow the ancient Greek lack of differentiation between some of the higher animals, such as horses, and humans, and also in the lack of distinguishing between meat and flesh.
10. Euripides, *Heracles Mad*, trans. E. P. Coleridge, in *The Plays of Euripides*, ed. R. M. Hutchins (Chicago, 1952), p. 368, lines 382-5.
11. David Kravitz, *Who's Who in Greek and Roman Mythology* (New York, 1976), p. 46.
12. Homer does not assign Xanthus' paternity to Boreas nor discuss the flesh eating tendencies of Achilles' horse, many other sources do so.
13. Timothy Gantz, *Early Greek Myth* (Baltimore & London, 1993), p. 18.
14. For an account of the spreading of the Boreas Cult see Graves, 48.3. It should also be noted that Thrace was the "kingdom" just south of the Hyperborean region. This is probably the reason why North Wind, as Boreas, cannot get to "her own back."
15. In regards to Eos' snatching of young men and disease, Graves makes the following connection which may be relevant for our understanding of North Wind: "Eos's constant love affairs with young mortals are also allegories: dawn brings midnight lovers a renewal of erotic passion, and is the most usual time for men to be carried off by fever" (Graves, 40.2).
16. For an explanation of how Xanthus, Achilles' horse, could have been identified with Xanthus, Hector's horse, see Graves 29.1. For the information on Xanthus, one of King Diomedes' flesh-eating horses, see Carlos Parada, *Genealogical Guide to Greek Mythology* (Joncered, Sweden, 1993), p. 184
17. William Raeper, ed. *The Gold Thread* (Edinburgh, 1990), Introduction, p. 9.
18. MacDonald appears well aware of the connection between a stone and a horse. In at least two other instances he compares old Diamond to a stone, while Ruby is also associated with stone in the latter part of the book—see *North Wind*, pp. 28, 129 and 229.
19. It is interesting to note that MacDonald appears to know and

use the very ancient Chthonic associations between North Wind/Boreas and snakes. In the above, North Wind implies that Diamond must coil himself if he is to play the part of her baby while in Chapter 1 (p. 20) she tells Diamond that she has the power to change into a serpent. For some of the snake nature of north wind/Boreas see Harrison, p. 181, and Graves, 1, a and b.

20. There is at least one more connection between Martha and North Wind. North Wind is continually described as a lady and the meaning of the name Martha, in Aramean, is "a lady."

21. One explanation may have something to do with the unifying tendency present by having both the boy and the horse named Diamond. As North Wind appears to recognize her role as the possible parent of young Diamond, then she also becomes the mother of the other Diamond. The mythological parentage of the flesh/meat eating, talking horses suits Boreas/North Wind quite well and so may provide an affinity between the two mothers of the respective Diamonds. Diamond calls his sister Dulcimer (or sweet air) and this implies that she is also a daughter of North Wind.

22. Roderick McGillis, "Language and Secret Knowledge in *At the Back of the North Wind*," in *Childlike*, p. 145 (henceforth "Language"). It may be due to an intuition of the incongruity between the ancient Greek and the Christian aspects of Diamond that gave rise to the very different and surprising scholarly opinions regarding him. For instance Stephen Prickett in his *Victorian Fantasy* (Hassocks, Sussex, 1979) does not appear to like Diamond and ends up calling him a prig. This is almost in direct opposition to McGillis who seems to like and revere Diamond as he casts the mantle of Christ over him in his article. However, the so called angelic or Christian aspects of the boy may also be accounted for by referring to his Greek winged father as well as to the mild manners Diamond learned by traveling to the Hyperborean regions—a land known for its highly civilized people and institutions. For MacDonald's descriptions of the "free and so just and so healthy" Hyperboreans, see *North Wind*, p. 92.

23. MacDonald appears to be reverting to some mythological ideas regarding the ancient unifying conception of things. In Greek mythology many categories accepted today were not as rigid at an earlier time. Natural forces, animals, people, and gods were

not as separate in the ancient Greek mind as they are today.
24. George MacDonald, *An Expression of Character: The Letters of George MacDonald*, ed. Glen Sadler (Grand Rapids, 1994), pp. 288-9.
25. MacDonald gives one of his horses in *A Rough Shaking* very special human attributes and an extremely significant name, Memnon. Memnon it the almost human horse that is intelligent enough to be sent on his own to deliver messages. It is interesting to note that the mythological Memnon was black, a son of Eos and thus a half brother to Boreas and Zephyr. Furthermore, by being named after Memnon—the son of the ever-babbling Thitonus (and Eos)—who is himself a brother of Priam/Podarces—this particular horse, like old Diamond/Boreas/North Wind, may, in MacDonald's mind, deserve to be considered almost human and linguistically able to deliver messages.
26. See Lesley Smith, "Old Wine in New Bottles: Aspects of Prophesy in George MacDonald's *At the Back of the North Wind*," in *Childlike*, pp. 161-62.
27. Homer, *The Odyssey*, trans. Richard Lattimore (New York, 1967), p. 165, lines 504-12.

A Reading of *At the Back of the North Wind*

From *North Wind: A Journal of George MacDonald Studies*

Colin Manlove

MacDonald's *At the Back of the North Wind* (1871) was first serialised in *Good Words for the Young* under his own editorship, from October 1868 to November 1870. It was his first attempt at writing a full-length "fairy-story" for children, following on his shorter fairy tales—including "The Selfish Giant," "The Light Princess," and "The Golden Key"—written between 1862 and 1867, and published in *Dealings with the Fairies* (1867). *At the Back of the North Wind* is in fact longer than either of the "Princess" books that were to follow it, *The Princess and the Goblin* (1872) and *The Princess and Curdie* (1882). It tells of the boy Diamond's life as a cabman's son in a poor area of mid-Victorian London, and of his meetings and adventures with a lady called North Wind; and it includes a separate fairy-tale called "Little Daylight," two dream-stories, and several poems. Generally well received by the public, it has hardly been out of print since.

At the Back of the North Wind is MacDonald's only fantasy set mainly in this world. In *Phantastes* (1858), Anodos goes into Fairy Land and in *Lilith* Mr Vane finds himself in the Region of the Seven Dimensions. In the Princess books we are in a fairy-tale realm of kings, princesses, and goblins; and the worlds of the shorter fairy tales are all full of fairies, witches, and giants. But Diamond's story nearly all happens either in Victorian London or in other parts of the world where North Wind takes him. By weaving together these two contexts, the one urban and organised, the other natural and violent, MacDonald is trying to show how both ordinary human life and the wild elemental forces of this world are joined in God. This mingling of order and disorder, structured city life and rough nature also suggests that our organised lives and our random-seeming sufferings are alike parts of a larger reality than we know. North Wind says that she does what she often does as part of a larger plan that she does not understand. In the city, the order made by man produces as much real chaos as North Wind only seems to, with "gentlemen" such as Diamond's father at the bottom of society, and children forced to work as crossing-sweepers: yet chance, if not man, may sometimes level things a little, as a shipwreck makes the rich Colemans poor, or a poor cab driver's son one day takes Mr Raymond as a fare.

In *At the Back of the North Wind* MacDonald can be seen as trying to reconcile the idiom of the novels of "real life" he had been writing since *David Elginbrod* (1864) with the remoter-seeming worlds of his fantasy stories. Two of the novels written at the time of *At the Back of the North Wind*—*Robert Falconer* (1867) and *Guild Court* (1868)—concerned the miseries and temptations of London life and the need for Christian faith to look beyond them. Now MacDonald tries to show that for those who have eyes to see—and for him that usually means children and some mothers—the world is full of ultimately benign supernatural forces that control its workings.

In this he is close to Charles Kingsley, in his strange "fairy-tale for a land-baby," *The Water-Babies* (1863), which is the main source for *At the Back of the North Wind*, and which introduces us to the "great fairies" who run the world. Kingsley's little hero Tom is a poor child, a chimney sweep's boy, living in a hard world in Victorian Yorkshire. One day Tom runs away to the moors, falls into a stream, and is turned into a water-baby. Thereafter he travels down to the sea, where he meets the grand ladies Mrs Bedonebyasyoudid and Mrs Doasyouwouldbedoneby. They are the laws of action and reaction, which work both physically and morally: if you hit a tree, it hurts you; if you hit somebody else, the world will find a way of punishing and improving you. The parallel in MacDonald is North Wind, but the sufferings she causes people often seem much less deserved; MacDonald's universe is less evidently just than Kingsley's.

Tom later meets Mother Carey, who sits frozen on an ice throne in the Arctic, "mak[ing] things make themselves" (149): she is the generative urge. MacDonald's North Wind sits just like this as a block of ice when Diamond goes through her to the country at her back, but in his story she symbolises death. As a naturalist Kingsley is more interested in this world than in the world beyond, though he insists on that too. MacDonald, however, gives us an account of the land behind the North Wind. Kingsley comes closest to the more mystical MacDonald at the end of his story, when Tom meets the greatest of the fairies, and finds that she contains all the others, and shines with so blinding a light that he cannot yet read her name.

Kingsley sees the deity as a rational scientist as much as a mystic and loving God, who has designed his creation so that, read aright by the human intelligence, it will reveal both its order and God's existence. *The Water-Babies* progresses from physical to moral to divine principles, ending with an intuition of the being that is all of them and much more. Kingsley's procedure is fundamentally analytic, going deeper and deeper (as in the deepening waters of the story, from stream to river to ocean), where MacDonald works much more from immediate intuition. For MacDonald God is not found beneath or behind nature, but right on top of it. North Wind appears to Diamond in the very first chapter of his story, on its surface. "The show of things is that for which God cares *most*, for their show is the face of far deeper things than they ... It is through their show, not through their analysis, that we enter into their deepest truths" (MacDonald, *Unspoken Sermons* 350). MacDonald is not an evolutionist like Kingsley. He looks for God at the source rather than the end of rivers, as at the end of *Lilith*. His North Wind goes backwards to her home in the north, and Diamond then goes through her to a land that lies behind her.

If we recall that this was the time when Darwin's *Origin of Species* (1859) was causing so much consternation, we will see how MacDonald's story may be an attempt, like Kingsley's, to refute the materialistic implications of Darwin's theory—namely, that the universe is merely the physical setting for the working out of the natural laws of selection. Both want to "show," in Kingsley's words, "that there is a quite miraculous and divine element underlying all physical nature" (*Letters*, II 137). Kingsley shows this in the element of water, MacDonald in that of air. But the procedures by which each sets about this are radically different (Manlove, "MacDonald and Kingsley").

MacDonald hardly ever refers to Darwin in his work, and yet as a trained scientist Darwin's ideas would have been deeply interesting to him. The plain reason for this omission was that arguments for or against the existence of God were for MacDonald nothing to do with Christian faith. "No wisdom of the wise can find out God; no words of the God-loving can reveal him. The simplicity of the whole natural relation is too deep for the philosopher" (MacDonald, *Hope of the Gospel* 153-4). "To know Christ is an infinitely higher thing than to know all theology, all that is said about his person or babbled about his work" (*Unspoken Sermons* 350). No one can come to a belief in God through a mere proof of his existence: belief only comes from knowing Him, from a relationship. And for MacDonald the same thing would go for "proofs" against God: they miss the point. Follow in God's ways, MacDonald says, and you will find Him; be faithful and you will find truth.

The present writer once saw MacDonald's repudiation of arguments about God as a self-protective silencing of his intellect in order to save his faith (*Modern Fantasy* 58-60; 63-4). But it is now clear to him that MacDonald believed that Christianity had much more to do with lived than with proved truths, and with faith through obedience rather than certainty. MacDonald always disliked theology, which for him attempted to reduce God to a system; and he disliked even more those Christians of his day who let their faith be shaken by mere argument. "Oh, the folly of any mind that would explain God

A Reading of At the Back of the North Wind

before obeying Him! That would map out the character of God, instead of crying, Lord, what wouldst thou have me to do?" (*Unspoken Sermons* 504). MacDonald even ignored the whole structure and doctrines of Christianity—the six-day creation, the original innocence and fall of man, the devil and hell as final realities, the idea of a last judgement; he had little time for churches and the ecclesiastical establishments of any faith; and he did not see the Bible apart from the Gospels as being the word of God (Manlove, "MacDonald's Theology"). *At the Back of the North Wind*, though it deals intensely with the God-man relationship, says nothing about any of these, apart from criticising a cathedral and showing the biblical references of the names "Diamond" and "Dulcimer" (MacDonald, *North Wind* 11; 227).

Religions and churches are ways by which men try to impose form and certainty on the ineffable. But MacDonald does not want such settled schematics, nor such human interpositions between people and God. He wants a living, changing faith based simply on a direct relationship. Such a faith makes uncertainty as much a part of our relation with God as assurance. This is the subject of MacDonald's sermon "The Voice of Job": "Doubts are the messengers of the Living One to rouse the honest.... Doubt must precede every deeper assurance; for uncertainties are what we first see when we look into a region hitherto unknown, unexplored, unannexed" (*Unspoken Sermons* 355). Man is meant to be unsure in order that he should look for certainty. Man is meant to argue with God, as part of an ongoing friendship with him.

And this is what we have imaged in lesser degree in Diamond's friendship with the lady of the North Wind who, like assurance itself, comes and goes. Diamond is never quite sure that North Wind is real. She visits him at night when he is asleep, and he has to wonder whether she is only a dream, an illusion. Other people too think he may be a little touched in the head: his friend Nanny thinks he may have "a tile loose," and even his mother worries that his fever may have affected his mind. Some call Diamond "God's baby," which, unknown to them, may be literally true. He has to live as an oddity, marked out from his fellows. Doubt as to the reality of North Wind afflicts Diamond to the last, even while his relationship with her grows ever closer. He says to her, "I can't help being frightened to think that perhaps I am only dreaming, and you are nowhere at all. Do tell me that you are my own real beautiful North Wind" (310).

If God would not give Job any answers, North Wind cannot satisfy Diamond. She is uneasy at his questions, and admits there are many things she does not understand herself. She argues that Diamond could not have loved her truly, if she were only a dream, "You might have loved me in a dream, dreamily, and forgotten me when you awoke, I dare say, but not loved me as a real being as you love me" (311). She says she has many forms beside the one she shows to Diamond. And she claims that somewhere every dream has its reality. But at the end Diamond is still not "quite sure yet" (314). Later, the narrator becomes involved in the story, telling Diamond that "Even if she [North Wind] be a dream, the dream of such a beautiful creature could not come to you by chance" (324). Still Diamond is left "more thoughtful than satisfied."

All these arguments, good though they are, are in the end really there to demonstrate their own limitations. Proofs and reasons will never bring us to conviction; and the cynicism of others will not alone shake our belief. In the end love, trust and faith will take us far closer to the reality of God. The best answer North Wind gives Diamond is that he could not have been in love with a lie: the relationship between her and Diamond is the ground of her—and his—reality and truth. One way the book could be said to work on us is by using the frustrations of intellectual uncertainty to drive us towards simply testing the water through a relationship with God. And actually Diamond's friendship with North Wind proves the point: for in order to ask her whether she is real or not, he must already believe that she is; one could not ask for a truth from an illusion. All through the story he has been taught to trust her when she has borne him into the air, he has put himself literally in her hands, as man must with God. Reality exists in their relationship itself, in the giving to each other of two individuals. MacDonald believed that "The bond of the universe ... is the devotion of the Son to the Father.... For the very beginnings of unity there must be two. Without Christ, therefore, there could be no universe" (*Unspoken Sermons* 428). Equally, relationship between two supposes distance, which is the ground of doubt, as Christ experienced it on the Cross. Without such doubt, faith could not exist. But always such relationship implies intimacy: "Here and here only, in the relation of the two wills, God's and his own, can a man come into vital contact with the All-in-all" (*Unspoken Sermons* 310).

At the Back of the North Wind is unique among MacDonald's fantasies in putting doubt at its core beside faith. To the end Diamond cannot be sure of North Wind's reality nor we of Diamond's sanity; and in his early death we can only trust that he has gone to the back of the North Wind. In other of MacDonald's fairy tales for children everything ends happily and with assurance. Mossy and Tangle in "The Golden Key" reach "the land whence the shadows fall," the princess is rescued from her curse and the prince from near-death in "The Light Princess," in the Princess books Princess Irene is saved from the goblins, and she and her father the king from the evil counsellors. Only *The Wise Woman* (1875), where just one of two children being spiritually educated is reformed, is different. In the adult fantasies *Phantastes* (1858) and *Lilith* (1895), the protagonists do not doubt the reality of their wonderful experiences while they are having them, but only at the end, when they are abruptly returned to this world and now have to believe in the other.

Part of the reason for the continual doubt in *At the Back of the North Wind* is that Diamond does not live in a fairyland where marvellous or supernatural events are relatively common, but in a material world that does not believe in such things, and sees all his experiences with North Wind as delusions. MacDonald is trying to bring his fairy vision together with real life. Equally, however, he is working the other way round, to show that what we take to be real life is just as wonderful, just as much a thought in God's mind, as an imagined world.

North Wind is to be seen as a creature not just of dream but of vision, which for MacDonald means that she can be more true than true, in that she is the world seen most deeply. She can come to Diamond because as a young child he sees with his innocent imagination rather than with his intellect or reason; when he is a boy, he does not see her again until he is dying and his rational mind goes away. While he is a child, Diamond lives easily in the world of the imagination; when he is a boy the adventures with North Wind stop and he enters more into the material human world of sense perception. His commitment to the truth of North Wind remains, but now in her absence. Rather than finding her within his own life, he meets her at one remove, through poems, visions and the fairy tale "Little Daylight."

MacDonald writes *At the Back of the North Wind* in such a way as to throw us out of our conscious, organising, formalising selves. He wants to break down our way of reducing life and art to schemes and patterns, and to respond at a much more intimate level. For him the discovered meaning of a story can get in the way of its *being*. That is why he writes the book for children, who put no structures between themselves and direct experience.

> To reveal is immeasurably more than to represent; it is to present to the eyes that know the truth when they see it ... to see God and to love him are one. He can be revealed only to the child; perfectly, to the pure child only. All the discipline of the world is to make men children, that God may be revealed to them. (*Hope of the Gospel* 153)

And that is the object of *At the Back of the North Wind*: it seeks to take us back to the way of seeing of an innocent child. That vision perceives the world directly, without connecting things together with the mind and so distancing them. Moreover everything is seen as strange, so that a lady called North Wind breaking into Diamond's sleep at night is not much more odd to him than having the family horse stabled downstairs, or a poet in a rowing boat. It is just our habit of making connections among things rather than regarding them for themselves, that MacDonald wants to remove, so that we can perceive the world not only as wonderful, but as a miracle continually being worked by God.

How does MacDonald do this? He writes a fantasy. And in his case this means that he makes a book that in part embodies the imagination that is the source of his fantasy, being an apparent chaos, full of interrupted narratives, songs, strange dreams, visions, and fairy-stories; a book that often frustrates its readers' desires for sense and clarity, and drives them to a more intuitive and intimate experience of its material. As in *Phantastes*, but here in a different mode, he partly follows Novalis's view of the ideal art form, the fairy tale, which has no form at all: "A fairy tale is like an unconnected dream picture, a wonderful collection of things and events, like a musical fantasy, the harmonious patterns of a wind-harp, or nature itself."[1]

The particular way in which *At the Back of the North Wind* works to wear away our intellects is through subversion, the undermining of our assumptions. Our sense of what is the "norm" is being constantly upset. For in *At the Back of the North Wind*, we do not entirely lose a norm, a "reality" against which to see things, as we do in *Phantastes*. We feel that Diamond is a child in a mid-Victorian world, son of a poor London family, and eventual assistant to his father in the cab-driving trade. Indeed we do not leave the earth itself for any magic place, except once, when Diamond travels to the back of the North Wind.

At first we experience Diamond's dreams as departures from his main life. But such departures are not single and once for all as in *Phantastes*, when Anodos leaves one world and enters another only at the beginning and the end of his story. Here they happen again and again with every visit of North Wind, every interpolated dream or fairy story. When Diamond is in the middle of trying to answer the prim stained glass Apostles in the cathedral by the sea, he suddenly finds himself back in his own bed in London with the old horse Diamond rising and shaking himself below him. When he returns from the back of the North Wind, he is back again in Sandwich by the sea; when he visits the children's hospital where Nanny is, she tells him the story of her dream about the Man in the Moon. The result of all these changes is to make the story continually subversive: we have the ground taken from us and then replaced before being taken away again. And we are not sure which world is real, the Victorian one, or the fantastic ones.

As for the story as a sequence of events, no sooner do we feel there is such a sequence than it is gone, and the other way round. In the first part of the book North Wind comes to Diamond only at odd intervals. As the wind, we suppose, she is variable; and as a child, so is he. She visits him first when he is asleep, and tells him to get up and follow her, but he stops to stroke the horse Diamond in the stall under his room, and when he goes out she is gone—although a cold wind blows him along a path and through a door into the next-door garden of his father's employers the Colemans. He is seen in the garden by the Colemans' old nurse, and taken in and returned home. Immediately he wakes up, he hears the horse moving below, and goes down and gets into difficulties climbing on to his back. He is not surprised by these transitions, but we are.

Thereafter Diamond is kept indoors for some days and we watch him play. Then he is allowed out; and shortly after that, North Wind comes back to him again at night, and takes him flying with her over London, in her work of sweeping the streets with her "great besom" (34). But when Diamond sees a little girl being blown about by her, he asks to be set down to help her. So that abruptly ends that contact too, and we are back with the "real" world again. Again we follow Diamond's everyday life for some time; until, a few months later he finds North Wind in the garden next door, chasing a sleepy bee out of a tulip. They talk together, until Diamond finds that she has gone. And so it goes on. We do not know why North Wind has attached herself to Diamond, often what she does seems inconsequential, we can never settle with her before she is away, and we are kept flickering between outings with her and Diamond's daily family life.

However the mere fact of there being such a figure as North Wind adds excitement to the story, and we suppose that there is some purpose to her visits yet to be seen. And we begin to realise that by alternating the episodes with North Wind and Diamond's family life, MacDonald is suggesting that the one is not necessarily more exciting or momentous than the other, and that the wonderful is interwoven with the fabric of this world. Also linking the different episodes is the developing relationship between Diamond and North Wind: at first she is a little imperious or else mocking, but as Diamond gets to know her he realises some of her weaknesses and they become more equal and loving. Last, there is a sequence at a deeper level: for each of Diamond's journeys with North Wind takes him further and further from home. At first he finds himself in the Colemans' garden next to his house, next he travels round the streets of London, the third trip takes him to the Kent coast, and the last to the North Pole and the country behind North Wind's back. Each journey takes him further out of himself; each shows him more of the wonders of the world and the mystery that surrounds it; and each deepens his love and trust in North Wind, while making him more painfully aware of the sufferings she causes.

But when Diamond returns from the country at the back of North Wind, she disappears altogether from the story; and we enter on an entirely new prospect concerning Diamond's later boyhood in London, and the changing fortunes of his family. This part of the book is less a continuous story than a sequence of vignettes, for it is still continually interrupted by fantastic episodes, poems, and stories—a visionary experience Diamond has with some star-children, a long fairy story, "Little Daylight," a dream of Nanny's about visiting the Man in the Moon, a conversation between two horses, one of which is an angel in disguise, a long poem, and numerous nursery rhymes. Every one of these interpolations is mysterious, and has no explanation or interpretation. Just as in the first part of the book, we are still being switched continually between Victorian reality and fantasy. And at the end of all this, without much introduction, North Wind returns and Diamond is shown to be dying.

There is no evident connection between the first section of the book with North Wind and the rest, apart from Diamond's continuing to be the central figure. And we have moved away from dreams to waking, from night to day, and from the world of the mind to one that is much more of the body and its needs—cab driving that moves people about, houses for shelter and security, hospitals for sick children, babies to be fed and cleaned, men who beat their wives. Diamond's father loses his job after the Coleman family is ruined, and the family move to Bloomsbury; Diamond then helps at home with the new baby, learns how to drive a cab, is taught to read, takes over the cab driving from his father when the latter falls ill, and supports the family; then his father's fortunes change and he is made coachman to Mr Raymond at his country house. The randomness of the story is now coming from its realism as much as its fantasy, for it will not turn life into a fiction, will not make a plot that dominates everything and stops us attending to the immediate moment. MacDonald says that God cares only for the present action, not for the future, "the next is nowhere till God has made it" (*Unspoken Sermons* 211). There are no plans, for where life is subject to continual revision there cannot be. This is a story of a boyhood in Victorian London, of everyday life on the edge of poverty, of chances that help and accidents that hinder, and of good acts occasionally rewarded.

Thus while the book as a whole gives us an underlying story concerning Diamond's young life, that life is so multifarious and peculiar as to challenge sense. In this way *At the Back of the North Wind* refuses certainties, and demands to be read at an intuitive level. MacDonald said of the fairy tale that we are to read it as a child would, for whom the connections among things are not logical but magical:

> The best way ... is not to bring the forces of our intellect to bear on it, but to be still and let it work on that part of us for whose sake it exists. We spoil countless things by intellectual greed ... If any strain of my "broken music" make a child's eyes flash, or his mother's grow for a moment dim, my labour will not have been in vain. (*Orts* 322)

A Reading of At the Back of the North Wind

The unsettled manner of *At the Back of the North Wind* helps to wear our minds away so that we may feel the story at a deeper and more intimate level. Intimacy is the thing, for it is our standing back that is wrong. MacDonald always felt that closeness with people and things was the only way to understand them aright, and for him that closeness came from the body rather than the mind. "It is by the body that we come into contact with Nature, with our fellow-men, with all their revelations of God to us" (*Unspoken Sermons* 161). For him "the deepest truths of nature are far too simple for us to understand. One day, I trust, we shall be able to enter their secrets from within them—by natural contact between our hearts and theirs" (*Unspoken Sermons* 351). This emphasis on understanding through intimacy is founded on MacDonald's belief in loving relationship as the heart of life. In *At the Back of the North Wind* it is seen in Diamond's often physical closeness to North Wind, feeling the cold of her breath, being pulled up to her by her huge arm, being warm when he is close to her, being kissed and hugged by her, flying with half buried in her hair.

The scrambling of sequence in the book, and the continual uncertainty, is seen in small as in large. The book begins with an "I" narrator telling us enigmatically that he has been asked to write about the country at the back of the North Wind. He mentions Herodotus's account of a people who lived there and found it so pleasant that they drowned themselves. But then he says he is not going to tell that story because Herodotus did not have the right account of the place. In fact, "I am going to tell you how it fared with a boy who went there." We wonder who has asked this narrator to write about the other country Diamond visits, and why. Then all his statements seem rather ill fitting. He introduces Herodotus only to set him aside. He tells us of a people who killed themselves because they were "so comfortable." And in the end it seems he is not going to tell us about the country as about "how it fared with a boy who went there."

In the next paragraph the narrator sets a scene that is the reverse of comfortable. He says his boy hero lived in a room above a coach house, but he describes no more of this room than one thin and rotten wall against which the north wind blows. Then he says,

> Still, this room was not very cold except when the north wind blew stronger than usual: the room I have to do with now was always cold, except in summer, when the sun took the matter into his own hands. Indeed I am not sure whether I ought to call it a room at all; for it was just a loft where they kept hay and straw and oats for the horses. And when little Diamond—But stop: I must tell you that his father, who was a coachman, had named him after a favourite horse, and his mother had no objection: when little Diamond lay there in bed he could hear

the horses under him.... .

We are told how biting the wind was against the thin wall; then that the room within was not usually so cold at all; then that there is another room that is to be our main concern; then that this unlocated room is not properly a room at all. He tells us it is always cold, and then retracts, "except in summer." When the narrator starts to describe this last place he happens on little Diamond, who could as well be a horse as a boy (which in fact is true), and then veers off to tell us how he got his name and what his mother thought of it. He uses orotund phrases, "took matters into his own hands," "had no objection." In and out of this ill-fitting assemblage of rambling statements details gleam, "always cold, except in summer," "where they kept hay and straw and oats for the horses," "he could hear the horses under him." Everything no sooner is, than in a sense it is not, and slips from our grasp. Nothing is articulated without a qualification. And in fact this sense of things slipping out of reach is going to be uniquely appropriate to describing Diamond's strange and mystical experiences in this book. He will always be just on the edge of what he saw and heard at the back of the North Wind, but unable quite to recall or articulate it.

At the same time we are made unsure of the identities of things. The constant mingling of fantastic elements with the "reality" of Diamond's family life in London begins to make uncertain the final difference between them. This is added to by London itself being made strange, when we find that besides Diamond's family this is a place that has a Mr Dives or a Mr Raymond in it, not to say one that is peopled with alchemical symbolism in the names Mr Coleman, Old Sal, Diamond, and Ruby. Even a lazy cab horse maintains that it is an angel in disguise. This is a world that for all its apparent Victorian solidity, is also based in ancient signatures of the mind and the imagination.

And who is Diamond? However honest and good his parents are, this well-spoken, angelic child seems hardly the product of his impoverished background. Is he more a child of God than of man? Is he, born to poor parents and living above a manger, a kind of Christ? Here even the fact that his family are living in the grounds of a house called "The Wilderness," from which they later move, may recall the journey back from the refuge from Herod. MacDonald has Wordsworth's view of the child as nearest to God, and has to reconcile this with the real life child who lives in urban Victorian poverty. Diamond as an innocent child is attuned to the spiritual world, and able to see and speak with the beings of that world. Yet at the same time we also have to accommodate the possibility that he is deluded, and maybe not quite right in his head.

Who also is North Wind? She tells Diamond that she is not always so pleasant as she is to him, particularly when she has to ruin or kill people in storms. She has two selves, or, as she says, she is two "me's" in one. To

A Reading of At the Back of the North Wind

Diamond's "Here you are taking care of a poor little boy with one arm, and there you are sinking a ship with the other," North Wind says that she cannot be two people, but is simply the same person with different faces. Therefore since Diamond is sure of the goodness of one of her selves, the other must be good too, however ugly it may look. It is a fair argument, but arguments do not really get rid of feelings. And there is a reverse argument from her other harsher side, namely that she is really bad all through and that her "kindness might be only a pretence for the sake of being more cruel afterwards" (60). At which notion Diamond clings to her terrified, crying, "No, no, dear North Wind; I can't believe that, I don't believe it. That would kill me. I love you, and you must love me, else how could I come to love you?"

Even this argument is but a straw in the wind herself. It is the logic of a child who has never met and fallen in love with a Lilith. All arguments are for MacDonald helpless to prove either the existence or the nature of God. So we cannot finally be certain which kind of being North Wind is, and her two selves remain as irreconcilable to mortals as their sufferings at the hands of a supposedly loving God. An interpretation of this book that said that North Wind was a form of the devil tempting Diamond as Christ, and bringing him to eventual ruin could not be disproved. Certainly, "nice kind lady" aside, North Wind must remain a problematic, Janus-like figure to our intellects, for it is only through faith that one can feel and trust in her essential goodness.

Part of the reason for this uncertainty is that, alone of all the great female figures in MacDonald's fantasies, North Wind is not omniscient. She says she is only the agent of a greater power whose purposes she does not fully understand. Often when she is consoling Diamond, she is also trying to reassure herself. Nor is she in the position of authority that the all other great ladies have. Irene's grandmother is the wellspring of spiritual truth in the "Princess" books, the Wise Woman is the arbiter of the moral fates of Rosamond and Agnes in *The Lost Princess*, but North Wind has been left to fend for herself as a force of nature, with only "a far-off song" to reassure her. Even Kingsley's fairy Mrs Bedonebyasyoudid, North Wind's natural equivalent in *The Water-Babies*, is more confident of her role "I never was made, my child; and I shall go on for ever and ever; for I am as old as Eternity, and yet as young as Time" (*Water Babies* 108). But North Wind can only say, "I don't know. I obeyed orders" (79). In *At the Back of the North Wind* MacDonald has dared to do without an authority figure who gives us certainties.

Another "two-faced" aspect of the book lies in the way in what we think to be real at one time is later said to be a fiction. When we first read the story Diamond seems actually to go on his adventures with North Wind. We do not doubt in the reality of his flight with her over London and his being set down with the little crossing sweeper Nanny: how else could he know what London looked like from above, and what otherwise would he be doing so far from home in the streets? It is as real as a helicopter flight over the city would be to us. But then he asks himself whether it was a dream, which reminds us that North Wind comes to him when he is in bed; and this introduction of doubt is not helped by Nanny's plain disbelief.

Then again Diamond seems to have been with North Wind on his later journey to the cathedral by the sea, for how else could he know of it? The shipwreck North Wind later tells him she caused seems real enough, especially since it has a real enough outcome in impoverishing Mr Coleman. Later Diamond's journeys on two successive ships going towards the Arctic seem very solid and real,[2] but then when he passes through North Wind's ice-cold body to the country at her back he enters a dream-like world that he cannot fully describe. After this journey North Wind is gone from Diamond for some time, and people around Diamond begin to doubt whether he is "all there," which increases the uncertainty about her. Altogether we are left with the conflicting sensation that Diamond both travels and does not, both has what is literally a bosom friend and remains alone; for both readings are given equal validity.

And then we have the dual status given to dreams themselves. Does dreaming your experiences necessarily make them unreal? Diamond wants to believe not, but is made unsure by others, particularly Nanny, until she herself has a dream that exposes her moral nature to her. At the end of the story we are left with two realities, a mentally unbalanced child who has died, and a child who has gone to the back of the North Wind. For MacDonald there is no difference in solidity between the "real" world and the dream world because each is a thought in the mind of God (*Orts* 2-5) but his own resolution of the duality is not offered here. In the world of *At the Back of the North Wind* he stands back, far more than in any other of his children's books. Like Diamond, we are to find our own way through and beyond this world, in which opposites can both be true.

All this makes for a measure of relativism in the book. It is seen in poor houseless Nanny who is helped by Diamond and taken to hospital when she is ill: we are inclined to see her as (streetwise) innocence wronged, but she is not only that, for later on she turns against Diamond when she is with her boyfriend Jim, and in her dream she shows herself untrustworthy when she opens a box of bees that cause trouble. In the opposite direction the cabman who is a brutal drunkard and a wife-beater comes to see some of the error of his ways, and helps Diamond when he is once in difficulties with cabmen at another station. The Colemans seem good benefactors to Diamond's family, yet they do not provide them with good lodgings, they do not care for children, and Miss Coleman does not give Nanny a penny at the crossing she sweeps for her. Even Mr Raymond—"Light of the World"—may from one point of view be the rescuer of Diamond's family from misery, but from the human point of view he is cruel, testing Diamond's father by giving him a bad horse to see how well he survives.

The book's relativism is partly expressive of its having several realities—London, travels with North Wind, the country at her back, a fairy story, dreams, poems about another world. With so many different contexts there are bound to be opposed ideas of what is real. These stories, poems, and dreams are partly symbolic versions of what is happening to Diamond in his London and North Wind lives, but they are not just narrative adjectives. They are just as "real" experiences for Diamond as London itself. MacDonald never divided fiction or dreaming from experience, but saw them both as another and deeper form of being. We have to consider *At the Back of the North Wind* as a collection of different realities, or, equally, different fantasies. In that sense the world of the nursery rhyme Diamond reads about Little Boy Blue is as real as the world in which Nanny is shut out in the cold London streets by her grandmother.

Just as we have narratives that are continually interrupted, and adventures that are both dreams in bed and journeys abroad, so we find a juxtaposition of stillness and movement throughout the book. North Wind frequently tells Diamond that she has no time to stop and must be about her business, before stopping indeed to have a conversation with him (27, 31, 52, 63, 68). When Diamond is left by North Wind in the cathedral while she goes off to sink a ship, the still figures of the Apostles in the stained glass windows move down from their frames to talk disapprovingly about him; and meanwhile Diamond lies still on the altar steps, at once asleep and conscious, and unable to move. At her home in the Arctic, North Wind, whose essence lies in movement, is turned into a motionless block of ice. In the inset fairy tale "Little Daylight," the princess dances in the full moon and is torpid and still when the moon wanes. Little Boy Blue in the poem about him calls together all the creatures and leads them out into the country, only to reveal that he does not know what he wants to do with them, and that they can all go home again: all the movement ends in stasis. Diamond the horse works all he can when pulling a cab, but the other horse Ruby is fat and idle. A policeman forever tells people to "move on" who have nowhere to go. Diamond's family moves house in the middle of the story, but then his father becomes bedridden and "still" with illness. Diamond's song about the stream flows ever onward, and ends where it began, moves forward only to stay. And whenever Diamond is at the heart of movement with North Wind, he is still: with her in a storm, "nestling in … [the tempest's] very core and formative centre,"

It seemed to Diamond … that they were motionless in this centre, and

> that all confusion and fighting went on around them. Flash after flash illuminated the fierce chaos, revealing in varied yellow and blue and grey and dusky red the vaporous contention; peal after peal of thunder tore the infinite waste; but it seemed to Diamond that North Wind and he were motionless, all but … [her] hair. It was not so. They were sweeping with the speed of the wind itself towards the sea. (61)

The experience is at once physical, an anticipation of human flight, and mystical, partaking in the nature of the unmoved mover.

The oscillation between stillness and movement is also seen in the way there both is and is not a story of spiritual growth in the book. Diamond is the perfect innocent from the outset, and yet his innocence is also seen as inadequate, needing refinement. From one point of view Diamond does not develop, or become better, throughout the narrative, even if he gains more knowledge, because he is perfect already: he is "God's baby" both when he starts and ends, which is why North Wind comes to him; and his very name, Diamond, suggests the unchanging and pure. When he becomes a cab driver, his simple goodness, humility and charity still shine through, bringing even the most brutish driver among his fellows to amend his life. And at the end he is still the child nestling to North Wind's bosom and asking to be comforted. And North Wind herself, who has been continually subversive in appearance, now tiny, now vast, now omnipotent, now helpless, now a wolf or a tiger and now a loving woman, is still to Diamond the same mixture of teasing girl, beautiful lady and caring mother as she was when he first met her.

Yet at the same time, there may be a contradictory pattern beneath the story suggesting that Diamond *is* purified, and that there is movement through growth. This pattern comes from alchemy, with which MacDonald was familiar from his reading of Paracelsus and particularly Jacob Boehme. There are three stages in the narrative that parallel the three of alchemical transformation, *nigredo* (black), the breakdown of the original substance, *albedo* (white), or the making of a new substance out of this reduced material, and *rubedo* (red), the purification of the new substance to the *prima materia*. In *At the Back of the North Wind* these stages are first, Diamond's adventures with North Wind, nearly all by night (black); then his life in London, almost all in daylight (white[3]); and last the ruby ring Nanny is given in hospital by a lady visitor, the ruby glass in her dream and the arrival of horse Ruby (red).[4]

Diamond also moves away from the ignorance of early innocence. Where at first we see him taught by North Wind and in a position of inferiority, later he is able to hold his own in looking after his family, and finally as able to impart wisdom to others. And we could say that in the first part, his old self and assumptions about the world are broken down as he comes to believe in North Wind; that in the second, he moves away from personal experiences

A Reading of At the Back of the North Wind

towards a new and social self that helps others; and that in the last part he is refined to the point of being ready to leave this world and enter another. It is a steady move outwards. The book begins with Diamond's snug bed in the hay, reached through a maze of hay bales in the attic, yet with only a thin wall of rotten wood between it and the outside world. It is a perfect symbol of the complacent self in what it thinks is security, but with only a thin film between it and wild reality. North Wind breaks in on Diamond, chills him, and leads him out into the garden beneath, where he loses her. Back she comes later, and again, to take him from his bed to travel the streets. Then as we have seen, on further visits he goes on progressively longer journeys with North Wind, until on his return from the country at her back he is ready to move out of himself without help: for now he begins to help in the family, and later travels the streets beyond home, as a cab-driver. Here Diamond's initial naïve innocence has been modified and strengthened by experience, without changing its heart.

Diamond is an odd mixture quite apart from his being both pure innocence and educated ignorance. Though he seems so unworldly, so much the "baby" as Nanny sees him, he is far more practical than most. Even as a child he adapts the family's broken furniture to make for himself a two-horse cart. While still a young boy, he learns how to drive a cab to help the family when his father is ill. He becomes a skilful driver, and he knows how to drive an honest bargain (187-9). In this way Diamond comes more alive, more a part of the world, during the narrative. He has often shown himself ready to jump into life with both feet, as when he has North Wind set him down so that he can help Nanny in the streets, or when later he intervenes to stop some boys tormenting a girl (who turns out to be Nanny again).

Yet at the same time Diamond's whole journey is a process of dying. Not just physically dying, for his illnesses come as randomly as North Wind, but rather spiritually, inasmuch as he increasingly moves away from the world and speaks from his knowledge of another. He plays with his baby brother because he loves his strange songs and seems to Diamond to have arrived freighted with joy from another place. He begins his adventures with North Wind by following her out of his loft into the garden; and ends by moving to a nest in the treetops, where he can be nearer to her. His early journey to the country at North Wind's back pulls at him for the rest of his short life, during which he is rather like Marvell's soul in "The Garden" that leaves his body and flies into a tree:

> There like a Bird it sits, and sings,
> Then whets, and combs its silver Wings,
> And, till prepar'd for longer flight,
> Waves in its Plumes the various Light.

So when in the end Diamond dies, his death comes partly because he wishes it. The whole duality of Diamond's life-ward and death-ward histories is caught up in North Wind herself, who is at once life-giving energy and death-dealing inertia.

At the Back of the North Wind is full of double views and contradictions. It is also the most argumentative of MacDonald's fantasies: there is none in which people are so continually stirred up and "got at" by others. The book is full of conversations and arguments; everybody has a different point of view, and they all "bounce off" one another in continual contradiction. The story begins with North Wind waking Diamond up and telling him he must follow her downstairs, when there seems no reason why he should. Diamond pesters Nanny with his visions until she herself has a discomposing dream. Meanwhile she continually mocks him. The Apostles in the cathedral window stand over the sleeping Diamond and criticise both him and North Wind. Even the horses Diamond and Ruby in their stable have a long squabble about Ruby's sloth and greed. People are continually doing violence to one another: Old Sal beats Nanny and shuts her out in the streets, a drunken cab driver strikes his wife, some boys attack Nanny and Diamond is beaten by them when he intervenes, cab drivers and thieving women assault Diamond, some East End idlers try to throw him off his box and steal his money. And the whole book is packed with questions. Why are things as they are? Is North Wind real? Is she good? Is Diamond mentally disturbed? Everybody is forever challenging each other—as in the following snippet, when Diamond is listing his father's friends, and includes the brutal cabby and his family next door:

> "They're no friends of mine," said his father.
>
> "Well, they're friends of mine," said Diamond.
>
> His father laughed.
>
> "Much good they'll do you!" he said.
>
> "How do you know they won't?" returned Diamond.
>
> "Well, go on," said his father. (157)

Or again, when a policeman saves Diamond from being robbed by the poor women—

> "You came just in the right time, thank you . . ."[said] Diamond. "They've done me no harm."
>
> "They would have if I hadn't been at hand, though."
>
> "Yes, but you were at hand you know, so they couldn't."
>
> Perhaps the answer was deeper in purport than either Diamond or the policeman knew. (173)

A Reading of At the Back of the North Wind

Even the narrator cannot resist putting in his pennyworth.

As for North Wind's relationship with Diamond, that is often an argument, or mockery, or doubt. When she is a very small zephyr trying to get a bee out of a tulip Diamond thinks North Wind is a fairy, and she retorts that size is no determinant of anything, ending, "You stupid Diamond! Have you never seen me before?" (47-8). She teases him like a girl when he will not come out of his bed, or cannot jump over a wall, or does not know the difference between a boat and a poet. At other times North Wind is the grand lady who must sink a ship at sea, and Diamond cannot accept this, even when she argues that in the end she is doing as much good and kindness here as she is doing more obviously and immediately to Diamond himself. Diamond's sympathy for the drowning people makes him unable to take North Wind's Olympian view of things. The often ruffled friendship of the two is some reflection of what MacDonald said of God's relation to his creation: "there can be no unity, no delight of love, no harmony, no good in being, where there is but one. Two at least are needed for oneness" (*Unspoken Sermons* 298). In his sermon "The Voice of Job" MacDonald declares that it was far better that Job argued with God. In the quarrel with God lives a relationship; only by challenging him may we come to accept him (*Unspoken Sermons* 355). Such a relationship is no settled thing however, for in this life it is based on continual oscillations between assurance and doubt.

At the Back of the North Wind also unsettles us by its frequent use of inversion. North Wind tells Diamond that the hole she makes into his hayloft bedroom is for her a window out from her world into his, whereas Diamond thinks of windows as looking outside to the wide world of North Wind (5). When Diamond and North wind enter the cathedral on the coast by a door in the tower, this door is so described that it seems they are going out, not in by it (64). The painted Apostles of the cathedral's eastern window are angry at North Wind because she blows their windows in, but they face only inwards, not outwards like true apostles. In dreams Diamond and Nanny have they see people look in at them from the stars or the moon, but for these people this is looking out, both star-realm and moon being described as spheres. Later we have Diamond reaching the stars by going underground (200-03): he pulls up the "plumb-line [of] gravitation" (208). The aim behind this is that distinctions between inside and out, "here" and "there," or "up" and "down," all divisions between this world and others, should finally dissolve. This is partly why we have such strangely named people as Mr Dyves, Mr Raymond, or Diamond himself in the London world, for it too is part of another world, and vice versa. The fixity implied in making divisions is opposed by the story. So too is fixity of size and, by implication, importance. North Wind constantly changes size according to whether she is a breeze or a gale. When once Diamond sees her in tiny form, he makes the mistake of seeing her as a fairy, at which she scolds him (47-8).

Other forms of inversion come from the nature of North Wind herself. The further away from her one moves, the more one feels the cold of her breath; but when one is right up close to her, as Diamond often is, the wind is still, and one can be quite warm. This is itself an inverted analogy to MacDonald's idea that it is only when we are at a distance from God that his love burns us (*Unspoken Sermons* 18-33). Then there is the odd situation whereby North Wind is least "herself" when she is at home: she becomes weak and helpless, and freezes to a block of ice. For all she is North Wind is always going from and not to the north: she can only get there by shrinking backwards practically to nothing. She flies southwards to find a ship that will take Diamond northwards. And in her very act of blowing southwards she provides sailing ships with the power to travel north. Paradox upon paradox, some found in embedded in the nature we know, some in a nature we have not yet seen. And all of them turn the world into a perpetual surprise.

When the world is seen this way, when down is up and out is in, the separate things in it begin to come together, and to share their natures with one another. North Wind's hair is indistinguishable from the wind itself, houses seen from North Wind's back become "a great torrent of bricks and stones" (33), a poet is a boat (51). Nothing then stands on its own, for the world is founded on relationship and the exchange of love. In the poem about a river that Diamond's mother finds in the sand by the sea, everything in it, flowers, swallows, lambs, wind, clouds and grass, joins with the flowing water in one long unpunctuated sentence with neither beginning nor end:

> it's all in the wind
> that blows from behind
> and all in the river
> that flows for ever
> and all in the grasses
> and the white daisies
> and the merry sheep
> awake or asleep
> and the happy swallows
> skimming the shallows
> and it's all in the wind
> and blows from behind (119)

"It's all in the wind / that blows from behind": "The whole system of the universe," declared MacDonald, "works upon this law—the driving of things upward towards the centre" (*Unspoken Sermons* 132). Where creatures join in love they partake in love's creator, who reconciles all things, draws all things to him.

And yet to common sight how little do daily things seem to share with one another like this. London is a hard place of often cold hearts, where one man jostles another. Life is governed by a struggle to find work and feed one's family. Lower down the scale her grandmother Old Sal shuts Nanny out of her house. But even the rich, seen by Nanny passing in their carriages, are bitter: "Oh my! How they do look sometimes—fit to bite your head off!" (43). Everyone, but for stray occasions of love, cuts themselves off from a wider community: even Diamond's father will only have the friends he chooses. People are divided by their class and their money; everybody is concerned with their own interests; the only reality is a physical one. The city, an image of people living together, also separates them from one another. It takes the pure love of Diamond to show some of the people around him what they lack; yet still Nanny and her friend crippled Jim, for both of whom Diamond has done so much, later spurn him as an idiot. In such a world Diamond's evident goodness makes him something of an angel or a freak. In the more normal way of things, such charity as there is goes disguised, and even compromised with evil, as when Mr Raymond leaves the idle horse Ruby to the care of Diamond's father in a cruel-seeming test. Here things seem not joined in their separation but rather at odds with one another.

Hard too are the houses and roads. Only when North Wind flies over the London streets and the roofs of the buildings below are they turned to seeming water by her speed. Houses can cut off the self from the world, and as manufactured objects they are images of the conscious mind. North Wind's house by contrast is the open air under the sky, and she is always trying to look out of her "windows" into what is to her the outside world of house interiors. She is forever breaking in to them, whether to bring Diamond outside, or to punish a wicked nurse, or to coax a bee out of a tulip, or to try to shatter the windows of the cathedral. The home of the gin-soaked Old Sal is a dark basement with filthy windows and no less filthy interior, where the sick Nanny is abandoned to die. "The Mews" in Bloomsbury, where Diamond's family go after his father has become a cab driver, looks out on "a dirty paved yard" into which North Wind rarely penetrates because "there was such a high wall, and so many houses about the mews" (126). The best houses are those high up, like that of the Man in the Moon, with many well-cleaned windows to see out of: Nanny is delighted at the recall of it, "Oh, it was beautiful! There we were, all up in the air, in such a nice clean little house!" (257). And the country house of the Raymonds is very high on a mound, so that one can see a long way out into the world and the sky. Diamond is given a room at the top of it with which he is very pleased, but he soon forsakes even this for a nest he makes for himself at the top of a high tree in the grounds. He has "got out" in a final sense, for he has now entered North Wind's house. In this sense the impulse of the book is a Platonic one towards elevation above the world.

But it is not so much houses themselves that are problem, but the souls they express. As houses in fact, can also be good things. They keep us out of the wind and the cold—though as MacDonald shows with Diamond and Nanny that an old barrel will serve as well at need. They are the sanctuaries of our private lives, good or bad, and essential to the rearing of families. Diamond's parents are good people, and out of the wretched homes in which they live come happy children. Though many have closed their eyes to the truth, the city is not outside God's love, it is as much a part of it as the wild world of North Wind or the country at her back. And within the city good is still done, if often it does not seem that way. North Wind sinks Mr Coleman's ship to amend his life. Though Diamond's father loses his position, his new job as cab driver and his later illness produce acts of love from Diamond that would otherwise not have been seen. And sometimes seeming chance will throw good fortune as well as bad in our way—hence Mr Raymond. And hence too Diamond, whose innocence lights people's lives, whose love helps bring them together. All are parts of the city.[5]

And nothing, not even houses, stays still in this book. Everything that seems so solid and enduring is in movement, symbolised in North Wind and in Diamond's constant journeying with her; everything, bricks, walls, streets, cities, is "moving on." The four different houses Diamond lives in—the stables at the Colemans, the Bloomsbury house, "The Mound," and finally the tree-top nest shift from one to another like time itself. The changes from "waking" to "dream," from poetry to prose, from "reality" to "fantasy" and from life to death, not only show all these categories moving towards one another, but also that all worlds are contingent in the mind of God. For in the end the shifts of reality and subject in the book reflect the nature of God himself, who can freely change his plans as he will, because he "lives by the vital law of liberty":

> What stupidity of perfection would that be which left no margin about God's work, no room for change of plan upon change of fact.... See the freedom of God in his sunsets—never a second like one of the foregone!—in his moons and skies—in the ever-changing solid earth!—all moving by no dead law, but in the harmony of the vital law of liberty, God's creative perfection. (*Unspoken Sermons* 241-2)

And later, "If we can change, God can change, else is he less free than we" (244).

And this brings us to the act of reading the book *At the Back of the North Wind*. Just as Diamond has to live through his doubts about North Wind, so

A Reading of At the Back of the North Wind

do the readers of MacDonald's story. We will feel partly that it is a fantasy, meaning that is not true. But for MacDonald, fantasy, which of its very nature invites disbelief, is actually the sole means of awakening it. Fantasy is like dreaming and imagining, but dreams can come from the deepest truth. "When a man dreams his own dream, he is the sport of his dream; when Another gives it him, that Other is able to fulfil it" (*Phantastes and Lilith* 420). Without the imagination, man becomes spiritually dead. For MacDonald this was happening in his own time: science with all its achievements was held to be the product of reason, to the detriment of the imaginative faculty and therefore of the soul. In 1867, a year before he began writing *At the Back of the North Wind*, he wrote an essay, "The Imagination: Its Functions and its Culture" to warn against this. He argued that scientific discovery came not from reason but from the very imagination that nourished poets and children; and he showed that the imagination had moral as well as perceptual value.

> In very truth, a wise imagination, which is the presence of the spirit of God, is the best guide that man or woman can have; for it is not the things that we see the most clearly that influence us the most powerfully; undefined, yet vivid visions of something beyond, something which eye has not seen nor ear heard, have far more influence than any logical sequences whereby the same things may be demonstrated to the intellect. (*Orts* 28)

It is to show this that *At the Back of the North Wind* is written. The perceptual issue concerning the imagination—is it true or false?—is present throughout Diamond's discussions of dreams with North Wind. The importance of the imagination to human spiritual health is the underlying subject of the fairy story "Little Daylight" told by Mr Raymond to the young patients in the children's hospital. As a fairy tale this story deals with essences, and shows what is fundamentally needed in the society of the book. It describes a princess cursed at her christening by a wicked fairy to sleep by day, wake at night, and wax and wane with the moon, until a prince comes and kisses her without knowing who she is. It is because her family have cut themselves off from the dark wood of the imagination, that the princess is cursed with her inverted half-life, both night and moon being symbols of the imagination. Eventually she begins to live in the forest that surrounds the royal palace. Thither chances one day a dispossessed and disguised prince—both adjectives symbolising that his life is in the imagination rather than in controlling reason. This prince finally breaks the spell that holds the princess by kissing her when she is in the form of a withered and sick old woman, at which she regains her native beauty. Thus restored to itself in the unity of prince and princess, the world of the imagination can come out of the dark wood back into its own in the sunlight.

It is no accident that this vision is conveyed through a fairy tale, for a fairy tale is in MacDonald's view one of the highest forms of the imagination, and using one here is a way of further celebrating that faculty.

"Little Daylight" symbolises almost exactly what MacDonald felt had gone wrong with Victorian scientific and materialistic culture, and what was needed to put it right. What was real, MacDonald felt, had sunk to the level of what could be grasped or used; and the imagination, which was the source of all love, had been degraded as illusion. Shortly following the fairy tale, we are given another image of the illness of the day in the dream Nanny has about the moon while in hospital. This dream describes how the conscious self so often damages the imagination. Nanny dreams that the moon comes down to her, and the Man in the Moon helps her inside to meet his lady, while they fly upwards. The dream is full of alchemical symbolism, but the main point for us is that the moon Nanny enters is her own imagination, which she eventually betrays. She is asked by the old Man in the Moon to clean the windows of its sphere, which may be construed as opening her imagination more fully to the wonder about it, but while doing so she disobeys the advice he gave her against opening a strange humming box of bees, who may be the light of the moon, and so is thrown out of the moon and her dream. She the meddling intellect that will not let a thing be, but must possess it and seek to unlock its secret, to reduce it to her way of seeing. She is like Anodos in *Phantastes*, who seizes a little girl's strange musical globe and so destroys it. "Caught in a hand which does not love its kind," MacDonald said of fairy tale, "it … can neither flash nor fly" (*Orts* 319).

By such symbolic means as this MacDonald puts over the essential value of the imagination, and shows how the conscious greedy self that wants to possess and know everything is death to it. But more than this, he heightens our sense that our own entry into the "sphere" of his own book has itself been as much a climb into the imagination as Nanny's. Thus, the disconnected form of the book, and its constant undermining of our assurance, serves not only to draw us in by subverting our conscious minds, but to supply an image of the chaotic, metamorphic imagination itself. Such intimacy with his texts is what MacDonald desires: "A fairytale, a sonata, a gathering storm, a limitless night, seizes you and carries you away: do you begin at once to wrestle with it and ask whence its power over you, whither it is carrying you?" (*Orts* 319).

And whither is *At the Back of the North Wind* carrying us? Into whose imagination is it drawing us? North Wind talks of a far-off music she hears behind everything she does, coming nearer all the time: but perhaps in a sense it has arrived, indeed has always been here. Here we come to the very root of *At the Back of the North Wind*. For MacDonald believed that both our so solid-seeming world and our imaginary creations are all present thoughts in the mind of God. So far this is, if Platonic, not wholly unconventional theology. But MacDonald goes further than this metaphysical statement. For him God is immediately present in the human imagination, and the origin of all our best dreams and creations. These images and ideas are always felt by human dreamers and artists to come not from themselves, but from some unknown source; and that source is not merely the the imagination on its own:

> From that unknown region we grant they come, but not by its own blind working ... God sits in that chamber of our being in which the candle of our consciousness goes out in darkness, and sends forth from thence wonderful gifts into the light of that understanding which is his candle. (*Orts* 24-5)

But the divine origin of such gifts is too often hidden from us, no more felt than the existence of an emerald under a mountain. It is only in such things as music, or wild storms, or fairy tales that the presence of God can most be felt, because these are all images of "that chamber of our being where the candle of our consciousness goes out in darkness." And even then, it is only the child and not the rationalising adult to whom these things speak.

It is to make us such children that *At the Back of the North Wind* has the form that it does. And if this does not quite succeed for us, we have a child at its centre to point the way. There is no other fantasy of MacDonald's that places quite so much importance on the vision of a child, nor that tests it so hard against reality. Diamond indeed is by being a perfect child more than a child. As the story proceeds his spiritual insights become deeper than those of the wisest of old men. When he tells the convalescent Nanny that she is coming to live with his family, and she says, "That's too good to be true," he answers,

> "There's very few things good enough to be true ... but I hope this is. Too good to be true it can't be. Isn't *true* good? And isn't *good* good? And how, then, can anything be too good to be true?" (252)

These are the words of a child who has never really left the country at North Wind's back. These are the words of the sort of child MacDonald saw as God in man:

> God is represented in Jesus, for that God is like Jesus: Jesus is represented in the child, for that Jesus is like the child. Therefore God is represented in the child, for that he is like the child. God is child-like. In the true vision of this fact lies the receiving of God in the child. ("The Child in the Midst, *Unspoken Sermons* 12)

At the Back of the North Wind is in part a celebration of the childlikeness in Diamond that is also the essence of God's nature. Our experience of Diamond is here not to be just with an innocent child, but with a child who embodies the divine nature. We are ideally to have a continuing mystical relationship with Diamond.

In truth, therefore, while we may think that North Wind is the great "supernatural" figure of the book, really it is Diamond. His preternatural innocence may mark him out for mockery, but he has nothing to do with the preciousness of a Fauntleroy. True, he is an "ordinary" child living in relative poverty in a city, but the so was Christ, and Christ would have behaved with the same innocent purity as Diamond. MacDonald has managed to create in Diamond a child who at once makes himself part of the workaday world he lives in, and yet has a nature quite above that of any other person about him. Those who judge by human standards will see him as a little mad, as Nanny does, or as an odious goody-goody as do some readers. But to see Diamond in human terms only is to misunderstand him (126). This is a child who perfectly embodies that childlikeness which MacDonald saw as the essence of God's nature and of Christ in and through him. This is a Victorian Christ, if one whose life creates no converts.

At the Back of the North Wind is unique in its mixture of historical and fantastic realities. What MacDonald is doing here is showing that our own everyday world is surrounded and interpenetrated by others, and that the distinctions we make to keep reality separate from fantasy are empty. Fiction itself in the form of this story, dreams, poems, inset fairy tales, all are as solid as our "real" world, all bring us news of another world to which we more truly belong. In a larger view our world is a dream in God's mind as much as Diamond's experiences with North Wind. In the smaller world of struggle to which most of the characters are confined, life seems enmeshed in uncertainties and contradictions. And yet out of its impoverished heart Victorian London produces a child who is God's baby, a new Christ whom those about him fail to understand, a dia-mond or two-world soul who increasingly moves towards a world beyond ours. Meanwhile London itself is inhabited by living alchemical symbols, that transform it from a meaningless assemblage of colliding selves to a crucible of slow refinement. Deep within the world the incarnation continues, reminding those who have eyes to see that the ultimate truth of the universe is that heaven and earth are married.

A Reading of At the Back of the North Wind

Endnotes

1. MacDonald's translation of Novalis in the epigraph to *Phantastes*.
2. The description of Diamond stowed away beneath the decks of the first northward-bound ship, listening for days to the trampling of the crew's feet above and all the noises of the ship itself (85) must owe its vividness of detail to MacDonald's own below-decks journey north to Trondheim on the yacht Bluebell in June 1869, when he was so ill that he had to spend the entire trip in bed in a windowless cabin (Raeper 267-8).
3. The long poem Diamond's mother reads to him on the beach at Sandwich just after his return from North Wind's back (114-19) is dominated by the colours white and yellow (light and sunlight). It is in a strange book whose pages they see fluttering in the wind, and which is probably brought to them by North Wind's agency, for Diamond is sure it is the song he heard in the world at her back.
4. Alchemical symbolism (*AI*, passim) has a child as one symbol of the stone that is changed; has coal as the fuel of the furnace and as a symbol for the blackness of the *nigredo* (the Colemans, first employers of the family); it sees a house, particularly a glass house, as the alchemical vessel; views wind as an essential part of the reaction; considers bees to be the fiery action by which metals are transformed to the "prima material" that makes the philosopher's stone; regards trees as symbols for the growth of the stone, and nests as the alchemical vessel in which it is engendered. All these items are prominent in *At the Back of the North Wind*, together with other alchemical symbols such as the moon or Luna, the sun (Mr Raymond, "light of the world," angels (Ruby the horse, the dragonfly in the well), circles (the princess's dances in "Little Daylight"), sand and sea (Diamond at Sandwich), star (Diamond's dream), stream (the long poem), garden (the Colemans'), serpent (the poem about Little Boy Blue), tower (The Mound), thick and thin (the fat and lean horses (274)).
5. In this MacDonald is close to the vision of Charles Williams, who knew his work.

Works Cited

Abraham, Lyndy. *A Dictionary of Alchemical Imagery*. Cambridge: Cambridge UP, 1998.

Kingsley, Charles. *His Letters and Memories of His Life*. Ed. Frances E. Kingsley. 2 vols, 1st ed. London: Kegan Paul, 1876.

—. *The Water-Babies*. Ed. Brian Alderson. London: Oxford UP, 1995.

MacDonald, George. *A Dish of Orts, Chiefly Papers on the Imagination, and on Shakspere*. London: Sampson Low Marston, 1893.

—. *At the Back of the North Wind*. London: Dent, 1956.

—. *The Hope of the Gospel*. Whitethorn, CA: Johannesen, 1995.

—. *Phantastes and Lilith*. London: Gollancz, 1962.

—. *Unspoken Sermons, Series I, II, III*. Whitethorn, CA: Johannesen, 1997.

Manlove, Colin. "MacDonald and Kingsley: A Victorian Contrast." *The Gold Thread: Essays on George MacDonald*. Ed. William Raeper. Edinburgh: Edinburgh UP, 1975: 140-62

—. "MacDonald's Theology and his Fantasy Fiction." *Inklings Forever, V: A Collection of Essays Presented at the Fifth Frances White Ewbank Colloquium on C. S. Lewis and Friends*. Upland, IN: Taylor University, 2006: 175-8

—. *Modern Fantasy: Five Studies*. Cambridge: Cambridge UP, 1975.

Raeper, William. *George MacDonald*. Tring, Herts: Lion, 1987.

Realism, Fantasy and a Critique of Nineteenth Century Society in George MacDonald's *At the Back of the North Wind*

From *A Noble Unrest*

Jean Webb

George MacDonald's *At the Back of the North Wind* (1871) can be situated between two seemingly opposite lines of literary evolution in English literature in the nineteenth century: the realist social problem novel, as exemplified by Elizabeth Gaskell's novel for adults, *Mary Barton*, (1848) and the burgeoning of fantasy writing for children in the 1870s, for example Charles Kingsley's *The Water Babies* (1863), and Lewis Carroll's *Alice in Wonderland* (1864). Kingsley and Carroll have been designated under the title of writers of "Nonsense"; however, embedded in their work is a critique of 19th century society. Similarly MacDonald is perceived as a writer of fantasy, and similarly MacDonald engages in a philosophical and moral discussion and critique of the contemporary Victorian English society.

In her novel *Mary Barton* Elizabeth Gaskell was intent upon raising awareness of the deplorable conditions under which the poor lived in Manchester in the 1840s. Such conditions were also recorded by Friedrich Engels in his journeys around England at the time.[1] In terms of design of the city, (as in London), Manchester was particular in that due to the ergonomic patterns it need not be necessary for the rich to come into contact with the poor, since they lived and worked in separate areas. Gaskell was married to a Unitarian Minister, thus her work would have taken her into the places shunned by others of the middle classes. She also demonstrated a high level of moral and social conscience and a sensibility towards the ignored poor. Benjamin Disraeli had previously brought such division to the notice of the reading public in his novel *Sybil or The Two Nations* (1845) stating that England was comprised of two nations, the rich and the poor.

In her Preface to *Mary Barton* Elizabeth Gaskell ponders on the lives of the poor as follows:

> I had always felt a deep sympathy with the care-worn men, who looked as if doomed to struggle through their lives in strange alternations between work and want, tossed to and fro by circumstance, apparently in a greater degree than other men. (*Mary Barton* xxxv)

> [. . .] I bethought me how deep might be the innocence of some of those who elbowed me daily in the streets of the town in which I resided. (*Mary Barton* xxxvi)

Gaskell demonstrates an humanitarian approach to the poor, setting the lives of her characters in the turbulent social and political contexts of the 1840s which was a decade of boom and bust in manufacturing. The Chartist Movement was also pushing for the franchise for working class men. Gaskell's characters are fully engaged in the political action, the tension and understandable dissatisfaction which led to riot and social unrest. Again she records this awareness in her Preface:

> I saw they were sore and more irritable against the rich, the even tenor of whose seemingly happy lives appeared to increase the anguish caused by the lottery-like nature of their own. (*Mary Barton* xxxv)

Thus her protagonists struggle with the poverty of their everyday working lives and strive for the movement towards greater political equality. Disraeli also focused on political economy and the impact such had on the working classes. Both writers had strong moral and humanitarian drives underpinning their work, which they integrated into the realist depiction of their characters and the decisions they made.

By the 1870s some movement had been made in the improvement of working conditions and the franchise; however, there was still much to be done, especially in social conditions for the poor. Charles Kingsley's *The Water Babies*, (1863), brought the plight of the child chimney sweeps to the notice of the reading public. Kingsley's novel is a combination of realism, fairytale and the surreal, as the narrator observes Tom on his journey of moral redemption from boy chimney sweep, to water baby, to a Great Man of Science. *The Water Babies* is also a critique of nineteenth century society, in terms of the cruelties and working conditions for these child sweeps (for some of them were girls), and of the morality of the contemporary world. A great work in the genre of fantasy and surrealism, Kingsley's intention is not to explore the nature of the imagination as was that of George MacDonald, who, amongst other matters, was concerned with morality, both social and individual, and the nature of humanity. Kingsley's fantasy world was a parallel one, for characters and related events from the "real" world are transposed and continued into the fantasy creation which translates the debates of the period, and those Kingsley was having with himself concerning Darwinism, for example, and notions of creation. Kingsley does not offer any practical solutions. His answers lie in the morality of the individual; the moral education of Tom. In *At the Back of the North Wind*, the agent for change is Diamond, who is morally pure and innocent. MacDonald's world of fantasy is better described as an adjunct world, for Diamond moves to the back of the North Wind, yet the happenings there are not observed by the reader, nor can Diamond clearly transpose such into reality. This country lies within the imagination of the reader, and is recalled by Diamond through the poetry and music he brings back with him as a memory of his experiences.

George MacDonald's essay 'The Fantastic Imagination' (1893) can be read in conjunction with *At the Back of the North Wind* as a discussion of the imagination which enlightens the reading of MacDonald's novel for children. In 'The Fantastic Imagination' he writes:

> The natural world has its laws, and no man must interfere with them in the way of presentment any more than in the way of use; but they themselves may suggest laws of other kinds, and man may, if he pleases, invent a little world of his own, with its own laws ('Fantastic Imagination' 5)

And invent a little world is what MacDonald does in the novel, both in his realist creation and in the world beyond the North Wind. MacDonald's discursive thoughts relate to the narrative structure of *At the Back of the North Wind*. There are no magical happenings which change the real world for the better; all change is derived from a logical cause and effect mode conducive to realist writing. The inclusion of the North Wind enables MacDonald to invent "a little world of his own" for the interaction of Diamond and the North Wind in order to explore the otherness of the imagination; yet even that world does not transgress the laws which govern over both reality and imagination, as will be discussed further. What is enhanced by Diamond's interaction with the North Wind is his ability to effect change by the ambiance of his personality. Despite the desperations of poverty into which Diamond and his family descend, Diamond creates harmony. Here there is a direct relationship with MacDonald's theorising on the writing of fantasy:

> His world once invented, the highest law that comes next into play is, that there shall be harmony between the laws by which the new world has begun to exist. ('Fantastic Imagination' 6)

The root of such harmony is with Diamond's close relationship with the natural world, epitomised in the personification of the North Wind.

In his introductory paragraph MacDonald emphasises the difference between his conceptualisation of the back of the North Wind and that recorded by Herodotus, which suggests that it was "so comfortable" that "a people who lived there" "drowned themselves" (*North Wind* 11). A playful implication here is that Herodotus, who is regarded as a founding father of historians, actually got it wrong. This is especially ironic in that the Victorian period was one particularly interested in the formulation of the writing of history, with the work of Thomas Carlyle et al. A further implication is that an excess of "comfort" cannot be transposed into the real world, which is certainly not the case in MacDonald's text, for Diamond brings great comfort to all who know him.

Diamond's sleeping accommodation in a room over the coach-house where Old Diamond, the horse, is stabled is not comfortable by modern standards but it is so for the boy because he is in close proximity to nature. He luxuriates in the warmth and smell of the hay and the security of the horse below. MacDonald's description of the flimsiness of the boards which separate his sleeping quarters from the outside world and the domain of the North Wind is emphasised by the image of the wind slipping through the slit in the boards made by a penknife like a "cat after a mouse" (*North Wind* 11). The closeness to nature is thereby introduced and gently stressed from the very beginnings of the narrative. Furthermore, and more importantly, Diamond is closer to the horse than to his family in those private hours, when he settles and sleeps, and it is with the horse that he shares a close understanding and relationship. Even their name is shared. Horse and boy; boy and horse become synonymous, as it were. Yet interestingly, MacDonald elected to limit this relationship to one which refused to enter into say, magical conversations between the two. The equine Diamond is an instrumental factor in the realist narrative, not the fantasy. The greater force of Nature embodied in the North Wind which surrounds both boy and horse is the conduit into the world of the imagination.

Diamond's first experience of meeting North Wind is one which develops through natural association. She emerges as a presence firstly in her "normally" natural state:

> The wind was rising again, and getting very loud, and full of rushes and whistles. (*North Wind* 13)

The logical development is the emergence of a voice, that of North Wind herself. Structurally the narrative is rational, easing the reader from realism into fantasy and the imagination. MacDonald abides by the classical unities of time, place and character, in strong contrast to the fantasy creations of his contemporary, Lewis Carroll whose *Alice in Wonderland* certainly has its own logical construction which is based on syllogism and moving beyond the constraints of time and place.[2] MacDonald's technique dissolves those boundaries, fusing together the real and fantasy worlds, thus conveying that sense of the imaginary/fantasy space which can be in the actual as well as another place.

From his first sight of North Wind, Diamond is "entranced with her mighty beauty" (*North Wind* 18). The physical description MacDonald assigns to

Realism, Fantasy and a Critique of 19th Century Society

North Wind brilliantly produces a solidity out of the wind which as Christina Rossetti observed in her poem "Who has seen the wind?" (1893) could only normally be materialised in the effect on objects, such as the trees. MacDonald's personification of the wind is a combination of physical attributes, such as her flowing hair and the description of her face which looked "out of the midst of it like a moon out of a cloud" (*North Wind* 18).

Their conversation had circulated upon Diamond's unusual name, which North Wind thought "funny" (*North Wind* 16), a response to which Diamond objects. The expectation of the reader in association with the word 'diamond' is to think of the precious stone; however, for Diamond his connection is with the 'great and good horse' (*North Wind* 17). Both of them have to come to know each other, further than the representation of their names; as MacDonald comments: "For to know a person's name is not always to know the person's self" (*North Wind* 17),—which in many ways is the crux of the text, for MacDonald is creating a child protagonist who will mean more than the materialistic associations with his name. In fact the character of Diamond is a rejection of the materialism and capitalism which drove and blighted human experience in the Victorian period, and which in many ways still does today.

North Wind logically has to be a beautiful woman, for as MacDonald wrote in 'The Fantastic Imagination':

> Law is the soil in which alone beauty will grow; beauty is the only stuff in which Truth can be clothed; and you may, if you will, call Imagination the tailor that cuts her garments to fit her ('Fantastic Imagination' 6).

Beauty, Law and the Imagination are fused together in the figure of North Wind. Through their interaction Diamond is initiated and educated into such understanding, which he will disseminate to those with whom he communicates. Following his first meeting with North Wind, Diamond is found in the courtyard and taken into the warmth of the drawing-room, for they think he has been sleep-walking. He mistakenly thinks that Miss Coleman is his North Wind, and is then disappointed. Here the fusion between reality and imagination is emphasized; the transposition of the world of fantasy back into reality, which is then in itself unsatisfactory. The process of moving into the fantasy world is gradual and logical: a child's dream, perhaps, on a stormy night, or the initiation into an other worldliness which exists outside normality.

Diamond's next meeting with North Wind is pre-figured by his return to the yard where North Wind had left him. Having been confined to home because of bad weather for a week, his experience of going outside to play before sunset is one of a bountiful re-union with nature. He is described as "flying from the door like a bird from its cage" (*North Wind* 31). MacDonald provides a luscious description of the sunset over the stable-yard:

And Diamond thought that, next to his own home, he had never seen any place he would like so much to live in as that sky. (*North Wind* 31).

MacDonald is bringing together the elements of the narrative in a logical construction, so that it is acceptable when Diamond is so happy at the back of the North Wind, and that he is deeply embedded in the love of his family. What is also emphasized is the Romantic relationship with nature. Diamond is a Romantic child; he is emotionally affected by his natural surroundings; an innocent who moves from innocence to experience through both his relationships with North Wind, in terms of the imagination, the spiritual, and with those he meets and affects in his "real" life.

The world of the imagination is brought into Diamond's consciousness and confirmed as being part of his reality when he returns to the yard and remembers "how the wind had driven him to the same spot on the night of his dream" (*North Wind* 31). He stoops down to look at a primrose, "a dwarfish thing", focusing on the diminutive size of the plant, which is itself stirred by a "little wind" (North Wind 31). The centre of the primrose is described as being "one eye that the dull black wintry earth had opened to look at the sky with" (*North Wind* 31). In his own way, Diamond will be an eye through which his family and close companions will be "able to look at the sky" or rather "into" the sky when he recounts later his journey to the back of the North Wind. Diamond will become the "eye" through which others may see.

The emphasis on size in this passage is an instrumental introduction to the changing size and power of the North Wind. She is diminutive at sunset, in this case, and will grow to a mighty raging storm, as we all change in emotional power at different points of experience. The primrose acts as a referent in the later conversation which Diamond has with North Wind:

"But you're no bigger than me."

"Do you think I care how big or how little I am? Didn't you see me this evening? I was less then."

"No. Where was you?"

"Behind the leaves of the primrose. Didn't you see them blowing?"

"Yes." (*North Wind* 33).

North Wind's ability to change size is a responsive approach to the demands of natural conditions, rather than the happenstance of changes in body size to which Carroll's Alice is subjected. Diamond is also, through such conversations and experiences with North Wind, learning of the multiplicity of the self. As an aside, I also think that the analogy with the North Wind and the variations in levels of energy in response to situations, parallels the levels of energy, both emotional and intellectual which one may feel "inside one's head" at different times, and the energies created by engagement with the creative imagination. Physically, emotionally and spiritually we are not static beings.

North Wind is certainly not static, as said. Diamond accompanies her on a journey through the environs, as her energy increases she becomes a "full-grown girl" (*North Wind* 35) and then a wolf which frightens a drunken woman who should have been caring for a child. Here MacDonald incorporates a direct moral warning against the excesses of drink, whilst also including a discussion of the perception of "good" and "bad" and the differences between person and necessary action. Following her appearance as a wolf North Wind comments to Diamond:

> "Good people see good things; bad people, bad things."
>
> "Then are you a bad thing?"
>
> "No. For *you* see me, Diamond, dear," said the girl, and she looked down at him, and Diamond saw the loving eyes of the great lady beaming from the depths of her falling hair. (*North Wind* 36)

Diamond's relationship with the North Wind is an educative one. In the episodes in the "real" world Diamond is given broadening experiences which he may not fully understand, because they lie outside of the rationality in which Diamond can operate, and also how as human beings we cannot 'know' the reasons for everything. Time spent with North Wind is not always comfortable and easy; he has to learn to trust her, to develop a Keatsian negative capability in not being able to "know" the rational answers to natural disasters, such as the sinking of the passenger ship. The emotional veracity of MacDonald's writing communicates how Diamond has to struggle with his doubts and fears, until he can fully trust North Wind. Initially lessons to develop this confidence in her are placed in the real world; later this trust will transpose directly to the imagined world at the back of the North Wind, where there will be no direct contact with recognised reality. MacDonald thereby takes his reader on a process of learning as he does with Diamond, and in so doing to learn more about urban society and morality, or in many cases the lack of it. Trust is established through the physical relationship between Diamond and the North Wind. On, for example, the stormy night in London, she weaves her hair together to make a warm nest for him.

> It was just like a pocket, or like the shawl in which gypsy women carry their children. (*North Wind* 38)

North Wind is a "natural" nomad, a gypsy of the sky. Diamond is technically flying with her, in the quasi-situation of being her baby cradled on her back, safe from the elemental furore below, which she is creating.

> There was a great roaring, for the wind was dashing against London like

a sea; but at North Wind's back, Diamond, of course felt nothing of it at all. (*North Wind* 39)

On being questioned as to the cause of the noise, North Wind replies gently:

> "The noise of my besom. I am the old woman that sweeps the cobwebs from the sky; only I'm busy with the floor now." (*North Wind* 39)

The logical link is established between this moment with North Wind and seeing the little sweeper girl, struggling against the wind, dragging her broom, for it is Nanny who will figure so greatly later in the realist part of the narrative. Diamond asks if North Wind will help the child; however, at that time there are other duties for his guardian companion, who answers saying that she must not leave her work. His question is one born of his compassionate nature: "But why shouldn't you be kind to her?" North Wind points out that she is actually helping the child in one way by "sweeping the wicked smells away" (*North Wind* 41).

It will later be the influence of Diamond's kindness which saves Nanny's life and brings her a better way of living. The implied lesson communicated by North Wind is that there are actions which are appropriate at certain times, and others which are not. Here North Wind is employing a broad brush, to cleanse the city; Diamond will later employ his compassionate nature to, as it were, cleanse little Nanny's life of the tawdry lifestyle with her grandmother. MacDonald is also, through such narrative sequencing, demonstrating the cause and effect between events which may seem minor, or meetings which may be fleeting, or coincidental and then develop into important and life changing relationships.

In order to fully be prepared for the ways in which Diamond's life will change, for example, when he takes over his father's cab driving business, Diamond has to learn physical courage. The early episode in the cathedral is where North Wind tests Diamond; on trusting her; trusting his own senses and trusting his own measure of courage. North Wind leads him into one of the towers and onto a gallery to wait for her while she has to go about her duty of sinking the ship, He is, understandably, greatly afraid of falling. North Wind questions his seemingly irrational fear, for he had not quavered when nestled in her hair traversing the skies but a few moments previously. Although he is now being held by her he is upset because he is walking on his own legs, which might slip. Even though he directly states that he does not like this albeit knowing that she would be down after him and save him should he slip, North Wind lets go of his hand, wherewith Diamond screams and is "bent double with terror". "She left the words, 'Come after me', sounding in his ears." (*North Wind* 68)

The Biblical echoes here are very strong of Christ calling his disciples to demonstrate their faith in Him, to leave their normal lives and follow. The phrasing of this short sentence is also interesting, for the situation of the command is within Diamond as a physical presence. MacDonald could have more conventionally written: "North Wind called Diamond to follow her"; however, this phrase would not have carried the emotive weight of the fear Diamond is entrapped by and which is within him. At such heightened traumatic moments, one does experience differently; time slows, sound becomes transposed into one's physicality, that fusion of event and emotion and the body. Diamond does survive and "pass" this test, for he walks alone, whilst realising that he had been helped by the wind blowing into his face to make him brave. She did not hold him, but she had not left him. As North Wind says afterwards:

> "You had to be taught what courage was. And you couldn't know what it was without feeling it: therefore it was given you. But don't you feel as if you would try to be brave yourself next time?"
>
> "Yes, I do. But trying is not much."
>
> "Yes, it is—a very great deal, for it is a beginning. And a beginning is the greatest thing of all." (*North Wind* 70)

North Wind passes on great wisdom to the young Diamond. The narrative structure of MacDonald's novel also imparts the philosophical perceptions which he discusses in "The Fantastic Imagination". Diamond has overcome a great fear of falling; he has discovered courage within himself, a courage which was dormant, for as MacDonald states in his essay:

> The best thing you can do for your fellow, next to raising his consciousness, is—not to give him things to think about, but to wake things up that are in him; or say, to make him think things for himself. ('Fantastic Imagination' 9)

The conversation between North Wind and Diamond which follows the incident on the ledge demonstrates that there cannot be absolute understanding of all states, events and consequences. They discuss how the breath of North Wind had the power to awaken courage in Diamond:

> I knew it would make you strong.... But how my breath has that power I cannot tell. It was put into me when I was made. That is all I know.' (*North Wind* 70)

Interestingly North Wind "knows" the power, but cannot "tell"; she is unable to articulate an explanation. Here MacDonald returns both to the rationality of his writings on the creation of the imaginary, that certain laws cannot be traversed, there has to be a logic within the created world and also to a demonstration by North Wind of negative capability. To 'know' is all she and thus Diamond, need "to know". As MacDonald states:

> In physical things a man may invent; in moral things he must obey—and take the laws with him into his invented world as well. ('Fantastic Imagination' 7)

Morally North Wind would have misinformed or misled Diamond had she made up a reason for why her breath has so much power. By honestly sharing her "ignorance" North Wind refrains from falsely setting herself up as all-powerful and all-knowing.

By this stage in the novel MacDonald has established a completely trusting relationship between the boy and the wind. The realist context of the harshness and inequality of nineteenth century working class life in London has also been introduced, at this point with some distance from Diamond himself, for it is later in the narrative when Diamond takes over his father's position as cab driver. The reader thus far, has an insight into Diamond's strengths and frailties, and is, in other words, getting to 'know' Diamond. High incidence of child illness and mortality was a sad reality during the nineteenth century. MacDonald's own experience and that of his family is testament to the ravages of tuberculosis, for example. Diamond's first visit to the back of the North Wind is associated with his being very ill, of the fragility of child health during the period.

MacDonald's rendering of these sections of the novel take reality—serious illness and near-death experiences, and death itself—and explore that which we cannot know through the imaginative process. Diamond is taken by his mother to Sandwich on the coast to recuperate, and to try to prevent his illness becoming more acute. He meets North Wind again in a toyshop, where she stirs the sails of a windmill. That afternoon Diamond falls very ill. He sleeps and in his doing so "found himself in a cloud of North Wind's hair" (*North Wind* 82). Body, elements and sky-scape are merged. Diamond wants to go to the back of the north wind. North Wind explains that it is not possible for her to go there, since she always blows in a southerly direction, from the north, and so she "never gets farther than the outer door" (*North Wind* 83). This is very logical, whilst being conceptually puzzling and disturbing, her namesake "home" is one she can never enter; a place of "otherness" for the North Wind herself. The way she can reach the boundary is explained by her as follows:

> "... I have only to consent to be nobody, and there I am. I draw into myself, and there I am on the doorstep." (*North Wind* 83)

She has to agree—with whom the reader does not know, nor needs to know—to give up her body, to become "no-body", and to relinquish her identity.

Realism, Fantasy and a Critique of 19th Century Society

The image of withdrawal is very powerful. When serious illness overtakes the individual, there is such a withdrawal from the energy of life, as portrayed by the activities of North Wind, and following the increasing withdrawal into the self, which then ceases to exist as a projection into the social world, as the patient lies in a state of suspended animation. They are a sick body with a silenced "self". Diamond travels north by sea with the aid and company of North Wind. On reaching their destination North Wind is disappearing:

> Diamond stared at her in terror, for he saw that her form and face were growing, not small, but transparent, like something dissolving not in water, but in light. He could see the side of the blue cave through her very heart. (*North Wind* 88)

North Wind is landscape, ice, light and nothingness, her being is all around and within her, yet she is not. Looking into the heart of light, one has all light, yet 'sees' nothing. Interestingly, for me, this pre-figures T.S. Eliot's lines in *The Wasteland*:

> … I could not
> Speak, and my eyes failed, I was neither
> Living nor dead, and I knew nothing,
> Looking into the heart of light, the silence.
> *Oed' und leer das Meer.*
> (trans. Desolate and empty the sea[3])
> (*The Wasteland* 40-43)

Eliot's post-World War I image is negative and without hope, in contrast to the experiences Diamond brings back with him. At this stage, however, before he has entered that country at the back of the north wind, he has to surmount his terror, and feels that North Wind does not care for him any more.

> "Yes, I do. Only I can't show it. All my love is down at the bottom of my heart. But I feel it bubbling there." (*North Wind* 90)

This sums up the dilemma of the human condition, when feelings are suppressed for various reasons and the expression of love becomes concealed, lying dormant and inanimate.

MacDonald has an honesty which is communicated through the narrative voice. He addresses the reader directly, as seemingly the omniscient, all-knowing narrator, yet what he has to say is that he does not know.

> I have now come to the most difficult part of my story. And why? Because I do not know enough about it. (*North Wind* 91)

The narrative role is given over to Diamond who has been to the back of the north wind, whereas the "official" narrator has not. Diamond, at this point, becomes an unreliable narrator,

> Because, when he came back, he had forgotten a great deal, and what he did remember was very hard to tell. Things there are so very different from things here! (*North Wind 91*)

Diamond's problem is that things are so different that he has no reliable referents.

> The people there do not speak the same language for one thing. Indeed, Diamond insisted that there they do not speak at all. I do not think he was right, but it may have appeared so to Diamond. (*North Wind* 91)

The conversational, confiding tone of "the"narrator is somewhat amusing, whilst also introducing a clash of power and status, between the adult narrator and the child narrator. The knowledge of Diamond is actually being overruled by someone who cannot know the truth. "The" narrator returns to the techniques derived of History and of Law: accounts given by different people which verify "the" Truth, yet in truth, verify difference according to experience. Yet again, a return to the 'Fantastic Imagination' raises the philosophical and, indeed, political position of the differences in reading according to the individual reader: the liberation from a singular mode of reading and understanding.

> Everyone, however, who feels the story, will read its meaning after his own nature and development: one man will read one meaning in it, another will read another. ('Fantastic Imagination' 7)

Diamond's account of his experience has to be recounted by using referents with which *he* is familiar. His guide, North Wind, cannot be there with him. This has to be his interpretation and translation. The referents pertaining to the elements and landscape which MacDonald has used throughout which have enabled the description of North Wind do not exist in the same form for Diamond to use:

> The sun too had vanished; but that was no matter, for there was plenty of a certain still rayless light. Where it came from he never found out; but he thought it belonged to the country itself.... . He insisted that if it (the river) did not sing tunes in people's ears, it sung tunes in their heads, and proof of which I may mention that, in the troubles which followed, Diamond was often heard singing... , "One of the tunes the river at the back of the north wind sung." (*North Wind* 93)

The omniscient narrator is reclaiming his author-ity from Diamond by asserting that he has proof of the un-provable. MacDonald refuses to take an "easy option" with this section of recounting Diamond's memories; he could have defined the landscape at the back of the north wind, by using oppositions in a parallel world, much as Carroll did in his reversed world in *Through the Looking-Glass*. Instead he aligns this world beyond with this one, yet shifts the 'concreteness', giving softness to the landscape, where the river flows through grass, not rocks. There is also an emphasis on interiority as the river sings tunes "in" the head, fusing body and landscape as he has done so before.

When Diamond is back with his mother following his visit to the back of the north wind which was in the real world of physicality a severe illness, she reads poetry to him. Despite her efforts to find a better one than the "nonsense" she has before her, "the wind blew the leaves rustling back to the same verses" (*North Wind* 110). MacDonald is again fusing landscape, language, reality and imagination. The leaves of the book become as leaves from a tree, wind-blown and rustling.

> Now I do not know what the mother read, but this is what Diamond heard, or thought afterwards that he had heard. (*North Wind* 110)

The long poem is a harmonious fusion, where one element of nature flows into another linked by the repetition of words and rhythmic sounds. In his essay MacDonald discusses the relationship between music and words. His imagined opponent retorts:

> "But words are not music; words at least are meant and fitted to carry a precise meaning!"

To which MacDonald answers:

> It is very seldom indeed that they carry the exact meaning of any user of them! ... Words are live things that may be variously employed to various ends... . They are things to be put together like the pieces of a dissected map, or to arrange like the notes on a stave. ('Fantastic Imagination' 8)

The elements of the landscape which occur in the poem—the river, shallows, hollows, dust, and daisies for example—are like the pieces of a map which becomes populated by the nesting activities of the swallows and the gambolling lambs. The river runs throughout "singing" this natural celebration of life and provides the musicality like a recurrent theme in a composition. Linguistically the poem returns to an almost repeated patterns of words like the subtle change in harmony in music. For example:

> for he loves her best
> with the nicest cakes
> which the sunshine bakes (*North Wind* 111)

becomes a little later:

> for the nests they make

> with the clay they cake
> in the sunshine bake (*North Wind* 113)

The emphasis in the poem is on the musicality and harmony, rather than rationality. The patterning is repetitive and circular, the poem finishing with the lines

> and its all in the wind
> that blows from behind (*North Wind* 115)

MacDonald is using language in the place of music, for as he states in 'The Fantastic Imagination', using a common Romantic association between the Aeolian harp, the wind and the imagination:

> where his (the writer's) object is to move by suggestion, to cause to imagine, then let him assail the soul of the reader as the wind assails the Aeolian harp. ('Fantastic Imagination' 10)

Approximately one third of the novel has been given to Diamond to reach this point, where he can realise the country at the back of the north wind in an extended poem which narrates the harmonies of nature. When he sleeps he sleeps in that country, yet at this point MacDonald returns the reader to the actualities of nineteenth century working class life, and a realist narrative. Reality and the imagination become fused through Diamond, for he is active in the domain of the working cabbies whilst increasingly strongly "living" in the country at the back of the north wind. The result is that the enhanced experience of Diamond increases the effect he has upon the working and social communities.

Diamond's father's working situation has changed and he decides to go into business for himself as a cab driver. Here the impact upon changes in working conditions become evident, and the emphasis moves to the self-employed, in accord with the ethos of Samuel Smiles' *Book of Self Help* (1859). The responsibility falls more greatly upon the individual to effect change in their lives and on those of others. The responsibilities of Diamond's parents per se also increase with the birth of a new baby. Diamond extends great love, celebrating joy with his little brother, demonstrating a feminine caring approach. Diamond also eventually assumes the position of bread-winner for the family when he takes up the cab driving business due to his father's illness. Whilst scrupulously honest and hard working he is also a good business man, ensuring, politely, that he is paid a fair remuneration for his work (*North Wind* 178). His loving, caring and socially responsible attitude is thus effective in both feminine and masculine roles. Through Diamond's meeting Mr. Raymond, a gentleman, Diamond's father becomes aware of the importance for Diamond to be taught to read. MacDonald's decision in introducing Diamond to literacy emphasises the holistic approach embedded in this novel: that dissemination of imaginative experiences is related to literature and thereby the necessity for the child to be able to read. It also illustrates the need for the adult to take responsibility for all aspects of child welfare and development. However good, loving and responsible Diamond is, his innocence needs to be accompanied by experience and knowledge which will serve him in this real world.

The shift into the living conditions of the working classes with the visit to the slum cellar dwelling of Nanny and Sal, and events of Diamond's working life take the reader into an oppositional world of violence and ugliness in comparison with the serenity, beauty and love embodied in the country at the back of the north wind. However, Diamond's influence variously enables good to out and positive change to come about, not only enacted by himself, but also by the adults who are influenced by him, especially pertinently Mr. Raymond, the rich man. Whereas in Gaskell's *Mary Barton* there is a physical as well as a social divide between the classes, in MacDonald's novel the wealthy are seen to act in a philanthropic vein, bringing relief to the poor. There is no "jealousy" extended towards the rich as with Gaskell's observation, for they willingly work together. Diamond could also be said to be the embodiment of the "deep innocence" Gaskell observed in working class people she "elbowed" in the street. Diamond's spiritual benevolence derived of his innocence, is transposed into material action, which is reminiscent of the innocent character Gluck in John Ruskin's fairy tale "King of the Golden River" (written 1841, published 1851). On taking up the agricultural management of the valley, post the changing of his brothers into black stones, Gluck puts into action a socially supportive programme. This model embodied Ruskin's ideas of a social welfare system which eventually came into actuality a century later in the Welfare State–which proves that fairy tales can "come true".

The ending of the novel with Diamond's death, however, seems to deviate from the traditional notion that fairy tales always end happily, with the young innocent protagonist triumphing and receiving great reward in this life. Through Diamond's dying MacDonald maintains the integrity of his text. He refuses to perform a magical saving and return to robust health for the child. Instead, Diamond's death reflects the probability of child mortality conducive with the period, an experience which sadly MacDonald could attest to in his own life. By Diamond's pre-pubescent death, his innocence is preserved. There is also an implied critique of Victorian society in this sad ending, suggesting that such wealth and concentration of innocence in itself, symbolised by Diamond, has no place in the real world. Charles Kingsley transformed his chimney sweep's boy Tom into a Great Man of Science; the reader knows not how because Tom was blindfolded going 'up the back stairs'. Tom's future is predictable in this practical mode since the nineteenth century was a great time for scientific discovery, engineering and industrialisation. He is not, however, allowed to marry Ellie, merely be friends, since she is of a higher class, despite his rise in status. Kingsley's recognition of the horizon of expectation stops with class; MacDonald's with morality and humanity which can totally override class barriers, eradicating poverty, ignorance and the depravities of life. MacDonald has given some hope in demonstrating that this is to some extent possible, but complete social change was in the future, and still is, for the divide between rich and poor continues to exist in the twenty first century in the United Kingdom, despite the Welfare State. Where MacDonald gives the reader the possibility of vision is in the final line of the text: "They thought he was dead. I knew that he had gone to the back of the north wind" (*North Wind* 292). The country of the imagination is where Diamond now lives, in a state which can be no other than bliss. What the adult narrator and the reader have is this experience translated into reality by Diamond and potentially to be continued in the ways in which individuals can transpose such through their own imaginative processes. As the omniscient narrator affirms, the back of the North Wind does exist, and certainly is not nonsense.

Endnotes

1. Frederick Engels *The condition of the working class in England: from personal observation and authentic sources*. First published in Great Britian in 1892, Granada, 1969.
2. See for example Jean Webb "Alice as Subject in the Logic of Wonderland." Cogan Thacker, Deborah and Webb, Jean (2002) *Introducing Children's Literature: Romanticism to Postmodernism*, London, Routledge.
3. Thanks to Dr. Catherine Neal, University of Worcester, for this translation.

Works Cited

Carroll, Lewis. *Alice's Adventures in Wonderland and Through the Looking-Glass*. Roger Lancelyn Green, (ed.). Oxford: Oxford University Press, 1982.

Disraeli, Benjamin. *Sybil or the Two Nations*. Oxford: Oxford University Press, 1926.

Gaskell, Elizabeth. *Mary Barton*. Oxford: Oxford University Press, 1987.

Kingsley, Charles. *The Water-Babies*. Oxford: Oxford University Press, 1995.

MacDonald, George. *At the Back of the North Wind*. In *George Macdonald*. London: Octopus Books Ltd, 1979. 5-292.

"The Fantastic Imagination." *The Complete Fairy Tales*. Ed. U.C. Knoepflmacher. London: Penguin Books, 1999. 1-14.

T.S. Eliot. *T.S. Eliot Selected Poems*. London: Faber and Faber, 1954.

Behind the Back of the North Wind

But the next time he came up with the cat, the cat was not a cat, but a hunting-leopard. And the hunting-leopard grew to a jaguar, all covered with spots like eyes. And the jaguar grew to a Bengal tiger. And at none of them was Diamond afraid, for he had been at North Wind's back, and he could be afraid of her no longer whatever she did or grew.

Illustration by Lauren A. Mills (© 1988)

Selected Bibliography

* indicates books excerpted from or essays included in this collection

Letters

Sadler, Glenn Edward. *An Expression of Character: The Letters of George MacDonald.* Grand Rapids, MI: Eerdmans, 1994. Print.

Biography and Critical Biography

*Hein, Rolland. *The Harmony Within: The Spiritual Vision of George MacDonald.* Grand Rapids, MI: Eerdman's, 1982. Print.
Johnson, Joseph. *George MacDonald: A Biographical and Critical Appreciation.* London: Sir Isaac Pittman, 1906. Print.
Lewis, C. S. Preface. *George MacDonald: 365 Readings.* New York: Macmillan, 1947. xxi-xxxiv. Print.
MacDonald, Greville. *George MacDonald and His Wife.* London: George Allen and Unwin, 1924. Print.
—. *Reminiscences of a Specialist.* London: George Allen and Unwin, 1932. Print.
MacDonald, Ronald. *From a Northern Window.* London: James Nisbet & Co., Limited, 1911. Print.
Phillips, Michael R. *George MacDonald: Scotland's Beloved Storyteller.* Minneapolis: Bethany House, 1987. Print.
Prickett, Stephen. "Adults in Allegory Land: Kingsley and MacDonald." *Victorian Fantasy.* 2nd ed. Waco, TX: Baylor UP, 2005. 139-171. Print.
Raeper, William. *George MacDonald.* Tring, England: Lion, 1987. Print.
*Reis, Richard. *George MacDonald.* New York: Twayne, 1972. Print.
*Robb, David S. *George MacDonald.* Edinburgh: Scottish Academic Press, 1987. Print.
Saintsbury, Elizabeth. *George MacDonald: A Short Life.* Edinburgh: Cannongate, 1987. Print.
Triggs, Kathy. *George MacDonald: The Seeking Heart.* London: Pickering and Inglis, 1984. Print.
—. *The Stars and the Stillness: A Portrait of George MacDonald.* Cambridge: Lutterworth, 1986. Print.
*Wolff, Robert Lee. *The Golden Key: A Study of the Fiction of George MacDonald.* New Haven: Yale UP, 1961. Print.

Bibliography

Bulloch, J. M. "A Centennial Bibliography of George MacDonald." *Aberdeen University Library Bulletin* 5 (1925): 679-747. Print.
Hutton, Muriel. "The George MacDonald Collection: Brander Library, Huntly." *The Book Collector* 17 (1968): 13-25. Print.
—. "Sour Grapeshot." *Aberdeen University Review* 41 (1965): 85-88. Print.
Shaberman, R. B. *George MacDonald's Books for Children: A Bibliography of First Editions*. London: Cityprint Business Centres, 1979. Print.
—. *George MacDonald: A Bibliographical Study*. Winchester: St. Paul's Bibliographies, 1990. Print.

Collections of Essays

Harriman, Lucas, ed. Lilith *in a New Light: Essays on the George MacDonald Fantasy Novel*. Jefferson, NC: McFarland, 2008. Print.
Himes, Jonathan B., ed. *Truths Breathed Through Silver: The Inklings' Moral and Mythopoeic Legacy*. Newcastle, England: Cambridge Scholars, 2008. Print.
McGillis, Roderick, ed. *For the Childlike: George MacDonald's Fantasies for Children*. Metuchen, NJ: Scarecrow, 1992. Print.
—, ed. *George MacDonald: Literary Heritage and Heirs*. Wayne, PA: Zossima, 2008. Print.
Raeper, William, ed. *The Gold Thread: Essays of George MacDonald*. Edinburgh: Edinburgh UP, 1990. Print.
Webb, Jean, ed. *A Noble Unrest: Contemporary Essays on George MacDonald*. Newcastle: Cambridge Scholars Publishing, 2007. Print.

Literary Studies of At the Back of the North Wind

Adams, Gillian. "Student Responses to *Alice in Wonderland* and *At the Back of the North Wind*." *Children's Literature Association Quarterly* 10.1 (Spring 1985): 6- 9. Print
Johnson, Rachel. "'A Sort of Fairy Tale': Narrative and Genre in George MacDonald's Little Daylight." *A Noble Unrest: Contemporary Essays on the Word of George MacDonald*. Newcastle, England: Cambridge Scholars, 2007. 33-43. Print.

Selected Bibliography

*Knoepflmacher, U. C. "Erasing Borders: MacDonald's *At the Back of the North Wind*." *Ventures into Childland: Vicotorians, Fairy Tales, and Femininity*. Chicago: U of Chicago P, 1998. 228-68. Print.

*Makman, Lisa Hermine. "Child's Work Is Child's Play: The Value of George MacDonald's Diamond." *Children's Literature Association Quarterly* 24.3 (1999): 119-29. Print.

Maiwald, Patrick. "*At the Back of the North Wind*." *The Journey in George MacDonald's Fiction*. Trier: WVT, 2008. 87-105. Print.

May, Jill P. "Symbolic Journeys toward Death: George MacDonald and Howard Pyle as Fantasists." *Proceedings of the Thirteenth Annual conference of the Children's Literature Association*. Ed. Susan R. Gannon and Ruth Anne Thompson. West Lafayette, IN: Purdue, 1988. 129-34. Print.

Manlove, Colin. "George MacDonald's Fairy Tales." *Christian Fantasy: From 1200 to the Present*. Notre Dame, IN: U of Notre Dame P, 1992. 164-82. Print.

*—. "A Reading of *At the Back of the North Wind*." *North Wind: A Journal of George MacDonald Studies* 27 (2008): 51-78.

*McGillis, Roderick. "Outworn Liberal Humanism: George MacDonald and 'The Right Relation to the Whole.'" *North Wind* 16 (1997): 5-13. Print.

—. "Language and Secret Knowledge in *At the Back of the North Wind*." *For the Childlike: George MacDonald's Fantasies for Children*. Ed. Roderick McGillis. Metuchen, NJ: Scarecrow, 1992. 145-60. Print.

*Milbank, Alison. "Imagining the Afterlife: The Fantasies of Charles Kingsley and George MacDonald." *Dante and the Victorians*. Manchester: Manchester UP, 1998. 176-82.

*Parsons, Coleman O. "The Progenitors of *Black Beauty* in Humanitarian Literature." *Notes and Queries* 19 (April 1947): 156-58. Print.

*Pennington, John. "Alice at the Back of the North Wind, Or the Metafictions of Lewis Carroll and George MacDonald." *Extrapolation* 33.1 (1992): 59-72. Print.

Persyn, Catherine. "'And all about the courtly Stable/Bright-Harnessed Angels Sit': Eschatological Elements in *At the Back of the North Wind*." *North Wind: A Journal of George MacDonald Studies* 20 (2001): 1-29. Print.

—. "A Person's name and a Person's Self; or, Just Who is North Wind." *North Wind: A Journal of George MacDonald Studies* 22 (2003): 60-83. Print.

—. "Sous le signe d'Astarté: Voyage Initiatique au Pays du Vent du Nord." *Cahiers Victoriens et Edouardiens* 57.16 (Apr 2003): 115-34. Print.

—. "'In My end Is My Beginning': The fin-Negans Motif in George MacDonald's *At the Back of the North Wind.*" *Mythlore* 24 (Winter-Spring 2006): 53-69. Print.

—. "'Never Was There a Happier Partnership': les Illustrations d'Arthur Hughes pour *At the Back of the North Wind* de George MacDonald." *Cahiers Victoriens et Edouardiens* 64 (Oct. 2006): 183-264. Print.

Prickett, Stephen. "The Two Worlds of George MacDonald." *For the Childlike: George MacDonald's Fantasies for Children*. Ed. Roderick McGillis. Metuchen, NJ: Scarecrow, 1992. 17-29. Print.

Hearn, Michael Patrick. Afterword. *At the Back of the North Wind*. By George MacDonald. New York: Signet, 1986. 303-16. Print.

Hilder, Monika."George MacDonald's Education into Mythic Wonder: A Recovery of the Transcendent." *Sublimer Aspects: Interfaces between Literature, Aesthetics, and Theology*. Ed. Natasha Duquette. Newcastle, England: Cambridge Scholars, 2007. 176-93. Print.

John, Judith Gero. "Searching for Great-Great-Grandmother: Powerful Women in George MacDonald's Fantasies." *The Lion and the Unicorn* 15.2 (Dec. 1991): 27-34. Print.

*Raeper, William "Diamond and Kilmeny: MacDonald, Hogg, and the Scottish Folk Tradition." *For the Childlike*. Ed. Roderick McGillis. Methuen, NJ:Scarecrow, 1992: 133-44. Print.

Riga, Frank P. "From Time to Eternity: MacDonald's Doorway Between." *Essays on C. S. Lewis and George MacDonald: Truth, Fiction, and the Power of the Imagination*. Ed. Cynthia Marshall. Lewiston, NY: Mellen, 1991. 83-100. Print.

Sadler, Glenn E. "*At the Back of the North Wind*: George MacDonald, a Centennial Appreciation." *Orcist: Bulletin of the University of Wisconsin J. R. R. Tolkien Society* 3 (1969): 20-22. Print.

Salmon, Edward "Literature for the Little Ones." *The Nineteenth Century* 22 (October 1887): 563-80. Print.

Scott, Tania. "Good Words: *At the Back of the North Wind* and the Periodical Press." *North Wind: A Journal of George MacDonald Studies* 29 (2010): 40-51.

*Smith, Lesley "Old Wine in New Bottles: Aspects of Prophecy in George MacDonald's *At the Back of the North Wind.*" *For the Childlike*. Ed.

Selected Bibliography

Roderick McGillis. Metuchen, NJ: Scarecrow Press, 1992: 161-68. Print.
*Soto, Fernando J. "The Two-World Consciousness of *North Wind*: Unity and Dichotomy in MacDonald's Fairy Tale." *Studies in Scottish Literature* 33-34 (2004): 150-68. Print.
Trexler, Robert. "Dombey and Grandson: Parallels Between *At the Back of the North Wind* and *Dombey and Son*." *North Wind: A Journal of George MacDonald Studies* 29 (2010): 70-76. Print.
*Webb, Jean. "Realism, Fantasy and a Critique of Nineteenth Century Society in George MacDonald's *At the Back of the North Wind*." *A Noble Unrest: Contemporary Essays on the Work of George MacDonald*. Ed. Jean Webb. Newcastle, England: Cambridge Scholars, 2007. 15-32. Print.
*Wood, Naomi J.. "Suffer the Children: The Problem in *At the Back of the North Wind*" *Children's Literature Association Quarterly* 18.3 (1993): 112-19. Print.

Websites

The George MacDonald Collection
  Manuscripts of MacDonald's writings from Brander Library, Huntley, collection
www.aberdeenshire.gov.uk/libraries/information/georgemacdonald/index.asp

The Golden Key
Official Website of the George MacDonald Society
www.george-macdonald.com

North Wind: A Journal of George MacDonald Studies
  Full-text articles from *North Wind*: 1982-most current issue
www.snc.edu/english/northwind.html

Behind the Back of the North Wind

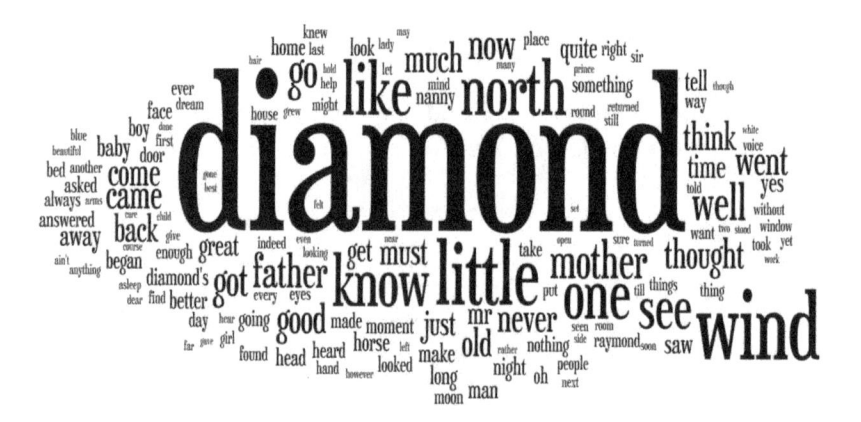

Wordle image of the most frequently used major words in
At the Back of the North Wind

Index

Aberdeenshire, 44, 46, 47.
  See also Huntly; Scotland
Adela Cathcart (MacDonald), vii, viii, 13, 93, 104
Aeolian harp, 46, 48, 188
aesthetics, x, 105
alcohol, 3, 117. *See also* drunken cabman; drunken nursemaid
Alec Forbes of Howglen (MacDonald), 26, 30, 63
Alice's Adventures in Wonderland (Carroll), vi, vii, xi, 6, 27, 52-60, 61, 92, 94-95, 102, 114, 175, 178, 180, 192
Alighieri, Dante, xi, 8, 18, 41, 42, 58, 87, 90-91, 125, 143
  Divine Comedy, The, xi
  See also Durante
allegory, 30, 34, 112, 145
Alter, Robert
  Partial Magic, 53, 61
anarchy, 54, 113
Andersen, Hans Christian, 54
androgyny, 48. *See also* gender
angel, 73, 101, 173
  boy-angels, 11, 100-101, 118
  Gabriel (the Archangel), 34, 36
  girl-angels, 11, 101-102
  horse angel, 35, 156, 158, 173 (*see also* Ruby)
  See also Diamond: as angel
apostles, 7, 83, 84, 85, 86-87, 154, 161, 164, 165
Arnold, Matthew, vii
asceticism, x, 23
Athenaeum, The, viii
At the Back of the North Wind (MacDonald), 13, 14, 19, 25, 32,
40, 51, 61, 80, 89, 108, 127
  audience and reception of, vi-ix, xii, 6, 11, 15-17, 26, 27, 28, 55, 65, 66, 83, 94, 115, 128, 143, 153
  biblical allusions in, 33-38, 129, 151 (*see also* Bible, the)
  Broadview critical edition of, v, vi
  characters in (*see specific names and descriptors*)
  dream narratives in (*see under* dream)
  fairy tale in (*see* "Little Daylight")
  genre of, v-xii, 6, 11, 15-17, 21, 22, 26-31, 41, 54, 77, 83-84, 128, 143, 148-49, 172, 175-90, 94, 128, 143, 148, 153, 175
  illustrations for, xii-xiii, 2, 36, 62, 92, 130, 132, 144 (*see also* Hughes, Arthur)
  as inspiration for other works, 1-5
  narrator of, ix, 7, 8, 22, 29, 31, 55, 56, 57, 58, 64, 68, 69, 70, 71-73, 76, 77, 84, 85-86, 94, 95, 96, 97, 98, 100, 104, 105, 106, 120-21, 125, 133, 134, 138, 142, 152, 157, 158, 165, 185, 186, 190
  popularity of, v-vi, vii, 6, 11, 26, 41, 54, 76
  publication of, v, 1, 11, 28, 72, 90, 92, 110, 122, 125, 148
  sources of inspiration for viii, 8, 15, 28, 30, 41-49, 92-94, 114, 128-143, 149
  structure of, 11-12, 30, 54, 57, 92, 99, 104, 161, 171, 177

uniqueness of, vii, x, 12, 15-17, 30, 41, 55, 114, 148, 152, 160, 164, 172
baby, 73, 74, 76, 117, 133, 156
   under care of drunken nursemaid, 9, 181 (*see also* North Wind: work of)
   as Christ figure, 9, 10, 73, 139, 172
   Diamond as, 9, 74, 113, 138-39, 146, 163, 181
   Diamond's brother, 7, 69, 72, 73, 94, 105, 118, 142, 156, 163, 188
   Diamond's sister (*see* Dulcimer)
   Diamond's songs for, 7, 56, 73, 118, 142, 163
   of drunken cabman, 3, 6, 10, 117
   God's (*see* Diamond: as "God's baby")
   land-baby, 149 (see also *Water-Babies, The*)
   water-baby, 149, 176 (see also *Water-Babies, The*)
ballad, 30, 43-48. See also *specific titles*; music
Barnardo, Thomas, 125-26
Barrie, Sir James, 114
   Little White Bird, The, 1
   Peter and Wendy, 1, 27, 121
Benjamin, Jessica
   Bonds of Love: Psychoanalysis, Feminism, and the Problem of Domination, The, 78, 80
Bettelheim, Bruno
   Uses of Enchantment: The Meaning and Importance of Fairy Tales, The, 44-45, 51
Bible, the, xi, 33, 34, 36-37, 39, 48, 136, 151. See also *At the Back of the North Wind*: biblical allusions in
Black Beauty (Sewell), x, 1-5
Blake, William, 24, 99
Bloomsbury, 33, 34, 36, 130, 141, 156, 167, 168
Boehme, Jacob, 24, 162
Bordighera, 49
Boreas, 129-30, 133, 134-35, 139, 140, 141, 142, 145, 146, 147. *See also* gods; horses; mythology: Greek
Borges, Jorge Luis, 54
Brontë, Charlotte
   Jane Eyre, ix
brownie, 41, 46
Bullock, J. M.
   "Bibliography of George MacDonald, A", 13, 14, 194
Burns, Robert, 45
Byron, Lord George Gordon, 45
cab-driving, vi, 1-5, 6, 7, 10, 15, 33, 35, 68-69, 71, 116-17, 120, 141, 148, 149, 154, 156, 160, 161, 162, 163, 167, 168, 182, 184, 188
Calvinism, 48, 64, 65, 66
cannibalism, 133, 140, 141
capitalism, 82, 87, 116, 179. *See also* consumerism; laissez-faire economics
"Carasoyn, The" (MacDonald), 46
Carpenter, Humphrey
   Secret Gardens: The Golden Age of Children's Literature, 59, 61, 78, 80
Carroll, Lewis (Charles Lutwidge Dodgson), vi, xi, xii, 52-60, 92-95, 101, 105, 106, 114, 127, 175, 178
   Alice's Adventures in Wonderland, vi, vii, xi, 6, 27, 52-60, 61, 92, 94-95, 102, 114, 175, 178, 180, 192
   "Jabberwocky", 97-98, 99
   Through the Looking-Glass, vi, vii, xi, 6, 52-60, 97-98, 187, 192

INDEX

Castle Warlock (MacDonald), 26
"Cat and the Fiddle, The", 58
changeling, 42, 46
Chaucer, Geoffrey
 Canterbury Tales, The, 104
Child, F. J.
 English and Scottish Ballads, 47, 51
childhood, ix
 MacDonald's view of, 30-31, 63-79, 109-26
 role of play in xi, 109-26
 Victorian attitude toward, xi, 48, 63-79, 86, 109-26
child labor, vi, xi, 10, 15, 109-11, 115-17, 118, 123-24, 125, 126, 148-49, 176. *See also* cab-driving; crossing-sweeper; Nanny
children's hospital, 6, 10, 11, 22, 69, 154, 156, 160, 162, 169, 170
children's literature, v-xii, 1, 11, 15-17, 21, 26-31, 41, 45-49, 52-60, 63-79, 101, 104-105, 109-26, 128, 148, 175. See also *At the Back of the North Wind*: genre of
Children's Literature Association Quarterly, 63, 109, 194, 195, 197
chimney sweep, 15, 121, 149, 176, 189
Christ. *See* Jesus
Christianity, ix, x, xii, 20, 23, 28, 33-38, 45, 55, 59, 65, 66, 82-88, 128-29, 136, 143, 146, 149-51. *See also* Calvinism; God; Jesus; MacDonald, George: theology of
Clark, Beverly Lyon
 "Carroll's Well-Versed Narrative: *Through the Looking-Glass*", 61
 Reflections of Fantasy: The Mirror-Worlds of Carroll, Nabokov, and Pynchon, 61
Coleman family, vii, 1, 6, 7, 8, 68, 71, 110, 115, 116, 117, 149, 155, 156, 158, 160, 168, 173, 179
Coleridge, Samuel Taylor, 45
colonization, xii, 87
consumerism, 82, 109, 118, 125. *See also* capitalism
Contemporary Review, the, viii, xiv
crossing-sweeper, vi, ix, 1, 6, 10, 11, 15, 69, 70, 114, 115, 116, 117, 119, 149, 159, 160, 182. *See also* Nanny
"Cross Purposes" (MacDonald), viii
cross-writing, viii, ix. See also *At the Back of the North Wind*: audience and reception of; *At the Back of the North Wind*: genre of
Cunningham, Hugh
 Children of the Poor: Representations of Childhood Since the Seventeenth Century, 125, 127
Dante. *See* Alighieri, Dante
Darwin, Charles, 150, 176
 Origin of the Species, 53, 150
Dealings with the Fairies (MacDonald), viii, 46, 148
death, vii, ix-x, 8-9, 15-17, 23, 28-30, 33-39, 41, 44, 48, 54-56, 57, 58-59, 74, 77, 86, 87, 90-91, 92, 96, 100, 105, 112, 119, 133, 152, 168, 170, 184
 of Diamond, vii, ix, xi, 1, 7, 8, 11, 15-17, 23, 28-29, 33, 36, 37, 41, 43, 56-58, 67-68, 74, 77, 86, 90, 92, 95, 105-106, 112, 121 23, 142-43, 152, 163, 168, 184, 189
 of Hyperboreans, 129 (*see also* Herodotus; Hyperboreans)
 justification of, x, 15-17, 30
 as "more life", 29, 58
 North Wind as symbol of, vi, 9, 16, 23, 29, 33, 41, 56, 74, 90, 111, 112, 119, 142-43, 149, 163-164
de la Mare, Walter

"Poor Old Horse", 2
Deleuze, Gilles, 63, 64, 66, 74, 76, 78, 80
devil, 3, 47, 64, 151, 159
Dewey, John
  Child Life, 112, 127
  "Froebel's Educational Principles", 112, 127
Diamond, vi, ix, xi, xii, xiii, 1-5, 6-12, 15-17, 21-23, 28-31, 33-38, 41-48, 55-58, 64-65, 67-69, 70, 71-74, 75-77, 79, 83-88, 90, 92, 93-106, 109-123, 125, 126, 130-43, 144-45, 146, 148-69, 171-73, 176-90
  as angel, 1, 33, 73, 100, 111, 117-18, 121, 146, 158, 167
  as babysitter, 7, 56, 74, 88, 92, 94, 105, 117-18, 142, 156, 163, 188
  as Christ figure, 10, 37, 39, 68, 106, 110-11, 114, 139, 146, 158-59, 171-72
  comparisons with other characters, ix, xi, 34-39, 41-48, 90, 92, 94, 97, 121-22, 189
  death of, vii, ix, xi, 1, 7, 8, 11, 15-17, 23, 28-29, 33, 36, 37, 41, 43, 56-58, 67-68, 74, 77, 86, 90, 92, 95, 105-106, 112, 121-23, 142-43, 149, 152, 156, 160, 163, 168, 184, 189
  as fairy child, 41-43
  as genius, 34, 73, 117
  as "God's baby", 1, 10, 73, 94, 139, 151, 162, 172
  good deeds of, vi, 3, 6-7, 10, 15, 22, 33, 41, 43, 69, 88, 94, 96-97, 99, 110-11, 114-17, 120, 155, 160, 162-63, 167, 168, 182, 189
  illness of, 7-8, 15-16, 21, 23, 29, 41, 67, 79, 112, 142, 163, 184, 187
  innocence of, 162, 163, 168, 172, 180, 189
  as prophet, 33-39
  as saint, 15, 41, 43, 70
Diamond's dream. *See* dream: Diamond's
Diamond's father. *See* Joseph
Diamond's mother. *See* Martha
Dickens, Charles, vi, ix, 55, 58, 74, 99, 121
  Bleak House, ix, 10, 58, 90, 94
  Dombey and Son, ix
  Old Curiosity Shop The, ix
  Oliver Twist, ix, 121, 127
didacticism, 44, 56, 75, 77, 114
Dish of Orts, A (MacDonald), 20, 46, 51, 84, 89, 156, 160, 169, 170, 171, 174
Disraeli, Benjamin, 176
  Sybil or The Two Nations, 175, 192
Donal Grant (MacDonald), 26
dream, viii, 6, 8, 42-43, 54, 57, 59, 66, 72, 76, 88, 99, 106, 114, 151-52, 156, 160-61, 168-69, 171-72, 179
  -child, 92, 95, 103, 105
  daydreams, 45
  Diamond's, 11, 41, 58, 72, 95, 98-102, 112, 118, 120, 154, 155-56, 165, 173, 180
  -fantasy, 30, 54, 154, 161, 169, 179
  interpretation of, 34
  -land/-world, viii, 6, 7, 57, 68, 111, 117, 160
  life as a, 42, 59
  Nanny's, 11-12, 34, 41, 72, 79, 99, 101, 104, 154, 156, 160, 162, 164-65, 170
  narratives, vi, 6, 11, 30, 41, 99, 148, 154, 161, 172
  North Wind as, 6-8, 57-58, 88, 98, 117, 151-52, 153, 160 (*see also* North Wind: reality of)

Index

truth of, 23, 34, 160, 169
drunken cabman, vi, 1, 3, 6, 10, 33, 88, 117, 160, 164. *See also* baby: of drunken cabman;
   Diamond: good deeds of
drunken nursemaid, 9, 181. *See also* North Wind: work of
Dulcimer, 7, 33, 94, 142, 146, 151
Durante, 8, 41, 42, 58, 90, 100, 125. *See also* Aligheiri, Dante
dwarf. *See* dream: Nanny's
Dyves, Mr., 10, 165
Eagleton, Terry
   Ideology of the Aesthetic, The, 82, 89
East Wind, the, 9, 73
Eliot, George (Mary Ann Evans)
   Mill on the Floss The, ix
   Silas Marner, ix
Eliot, T. S., 192
   The Wasteland, 185
empire, xii. *See also* colonization
Engels, Friedrich
   The Condition of the Working Class in England: From Personal Observation and Authentic Sources, 175, 191
eroticism, xi, 78, 84, 91, 101, 113, 145. *See also* sexuality
eucatastrophe, 58
Euripides
   Heracles Mad, 133, 145
Evans, Mr., 1
evil, x, 9, 16, 21, 35, 37, 47-48, 64, 66, 77, 106, 152, 167
Extrapolation, 52, 195
fabulation, 53, 54
faery. *See* fairy
fairy, vii, 12, 22, 27, 41-42, 46-49, 100, 103-104, 148, 153, 159, 165, 169
   -child, 41-42

Diamond as, 41-43
   -land/world, vii, viii, 22, 47, 148, 153
   tale/story, vi, vii-viii, ix, xi, 11-13, 17, 22, 26, 42, 44-46, 48-49, 52, 54, 57-58, 72, 78, 87, 92, 100-105, 122, 128, 148, 149, 152-54, 156, 161, 169-70, 171, 172, 176, 189 (*see also specific titles and authors*)
   queen of, 47
faith, xii, 45, 70, 82, 84, 99, 104, 149, 150-52, 159, 183
"Fantastic Imagination, The" (MacDonald), viii, xiv, 46, 49, 66, 80, 177, 179, 183, 184, 186, 187, 188, 192
fantasy, v, vi, vii, viii, ix, x, xi, xii, 4, 11, 12, 21, 22, 26, 27, 28, 30, 41, 43, 45, 52, 53, 54, 55, 56, 58, 60, 64, 66, 72, 76, 77, 79, 82, 83, 84, 85, 87, 90, 92, 94, 99, 101, 102, 104, 105, 106, 109, 111, 114, 119, 123, 135, 148, 149, 152, 154, 156, 158, 159, 161, 164, 168, 169, 171, 172, 175-79
fatherhood, xi, 35, 63-78, 115, 117, 119
femininity, 91, 93, 102, 103, 105, 112, 116, 188. *See also* gender; masculinity
fiction, viii, 12, 15-17, 22, 28, 43, 46, 47, 48, 53, 54, 55, 58, 68, 83, 85-86, 111, 114, 141, 156, 159, 161, 172
   children's, viii, xi, 15-17, 26-28, 46, 47, 48, 55, 114
   fantasy (*see* fantasy)
   metafiction, xi, 52-60
   realistic (*see* realism)
folk tale, xi, 41, 44, 45, 46, 47, 48
Freud, Sigmund, x, 44, 78
"Frog Prince, The", 104

garden, 23, 107, 173
  appearance of North Wind in, 7, 99, 155, 163
  in Diamond's dream 11, 99
  of Eden, 91
  in Nanny's dream, 11, 99
Gaskell, Elizabeth, xii, 175-76, 189
  Mary Barton, 175-76, 189, 192
gender, xi, xii, 66, 84, 93, 116, 123, 141-42. *See also* femininity; masculinity
German literature, 24, 42, 44, 48, 49
"Giant's Heart, The" (MacDonald), vii, 148
"Gifts of the Child Christ, The" (MacDonald), 75, 76, 80
goblin, 27, 46, 148, 152. See also *The Princess and the Goblin*
God (Christian), x, xi, xii, 15, 20-21, 24, 28, 34, 38, 43, 45, 52, 63, 64, 65, 66, 70, 73, 74, 75, 77, 85, 91, 121, 148, 149, 150-51, 152, 153, 154, 156, 157, 158, 159, 160, 165, 166, 168, 169, 171-72. *See also* Christianity; Diamond: as "God's baby"; Jesus; MacDonald, George: theology of
goddess, 63, 64, 66, 78, 93, 114
gods (non-Christian), 72, 129, 134-35, 139-40, 142, 146. *See also* Boreas
"Golden Key, The" (MacDonald), viii, 9, 18, 29, 42, 78, 148, 152
good, x, 1, 3, 4, 8, 9, 10, 12, 15, 21, 22, 23, 27, 29, 36, 41, 42-43, 47-48, 63,64, 67, 75, 77, 79, 82, 88, 95, 103, 110-11, 113, 120, 122, 142, 156, 158, 159, 162, 164-65, 167-68, 171, 172, 181, 189. *See also* Diamond: good deeds of
Good Words. See *Good Words for the Young*

Good Words for the Young, v, vii, 1, 2, 28, 92, 122, 125, 148. See also *At the Back of the North Wind*: publication of
grandmother figure, 9, 47, 64, 66, 159, 161, 167, 182
Graves, Robert
  The Greek Myths, 133, 134, 135, 140, 141, 145, 146
Grimm, Jacob and Wilhelm, vii, 54
Grylls, David
  Guardians and Angels: Parents and Children in Nineteenth-Century Literature, 65, 80
Guild Court (MacDonald), 15, 149
Haggard, Rider
  She, 102
Harriman, Lucas H.
  Lilith in a New Light: Essays on the George MacDonald Fantasy Novel, v, 194
Hearn, Michael Patrick
  Afterword to *At the Back of the North Wind*, v, 55, 58, 196
heaven, 11, 42, 43, 47, 54, 72, 76, 90, 114, 172
Hein, Rolland
  Harmony Within: The Spiritual Vision of George MacDonald, The, 20, 193
  "Outward Signs of Inward Grace", x, 20-25
Herodotus, 16, 18, 41-42, 87, 129, 134, 143, 157, 177. *See also* Hyperboreans
  Histories, the, 113, 125
Hesiod
  Catalogue, 125
"History of Photogen and Nycteris: A Day and Night Mährchen, The" (MacDonald), 12, 13
Hoffmann, E. T. A.

INDEX

Golden Pot, The, 6
Hogg, James, xi, 18, 41-49, 51, 87, 125
   Kilmeny, xi, 8, 41-49, 58, 100, 125
homeopathy, vii
Homer, 145
   Illiad, The, 144
   Odyssey, The, 142, 144, 147
Hope of the Gospel, The (MacDonald), 34, 150, 153
Horn, Pamela
   Children's Work and Welfare, 110
Horse Diamond. *See* Old Diamond
horses, vi, x, 1-5, 6-8, 15, 35-36, 47, 85, 87, 94, 129-30, 132, 134, 136-37, 139-41, 144, 145, 147, 157-58, 163, 173
   flesh-eating, 132-35, 140, 145
   nameless, 35, 140-41
   speaking, 2, 134-35, 145, 156, 164
   treatment of, 2-5, 69, 94
   See also Boreas; Old Diamond; Ruby
Hort, Sir John J.
   White Charger, The, 2
Horton, R. F., 65
hospital. *See* children's hospital
Howells, William Dean, vii, 55
Hughes, Arthur, xii-xiii, 2, 36, 92, 130, 132, 144
humanism, 82, 85, 87
humanitarianism, 1-5, 176
Huntly, 13, 30, 44, 47. *See also* Aberdeenshire; Scotland
Hutcheon, Linda
   Narcissistic Narrative, 53, 61
   Politics of Postmodernism, The, 87, 89
   Theory of Parody: The Teachings of Twentieth-Century Art Forms, A, 61
Hyperboreans, 16, 18, 41, 113, 125, 129, 130, 134, 144-45, 146. *See also* Herodotus
Imaginary, the, 65, 77, 78. *See also*

Lacan, Jacques
imagination, xi, 5, 6-13, 27, 41, 45, 47-49, 54, 56, 59, 63, 64, 82, 94, 99, 100, 104, 112, 118, 120, 124, 153-54, 158, 169-71, 176-81, 187, 188, 190. *See also* "Fantastic Imagination, The"
"Imagination: Its Functions and Culture, The" MacDonald), 169
industrialization, 118, 120, 123, 190
innocence, 77, 97, 99, 102, 103, 106, 120, 121, 151, 160, 176, 189
   Diamond's, 162, 163, 168, 172, 180, 189
irony, 53, 56, 58, 59, 66, 95, 104, 106, 141, 177
Jackson, Rosemary
   Fantasy: The Literature of Subversion, 61, 82, 89
Jauss, Hans Robert
   "Toward an Aesthetic of Reception", ix-x, xiv
Jesus (the Christ), 9, 37, 68, 85, 146, 150, 152, 158, 171-72, 183. *See also* Christianity; Diamond: as Christ figure; God
Jim (Nanny's friend), 1, 29, 34, 77, 79, 96, 102, 105, 119, 160, 167
John, Judith Gero
   "Searching for the Great-Great Grandmother: Powerful Women in George MacDonald's Fantasies", 78, 80, 196
Joseph (father of Diamond), vi, 1, 2, 3, 4, 6, 7, 10, 33, 35, 39, 55, 64, 68-70, 71, 72, 85, 91, 94, 98-99, 110, 115, 116, 117, 130, 132, 141, 148, 154, 155, 156, 157, 161, 163, 164, 167, 168, 182, 184, 188
Joyce, James, 58
   Finnegan's Wake, 58

Jung, Karl, 44, 45, 48
- *Archetypes and the Collective Unconscious, The*, 45, 51

justice, xii, 4, 67, 71, 76

Keats, John, 181

Kent, 1, 7, 29, 91, 155

Kilmeny, xi, 8, 41-49, 58, 100, 125.
- See also Hogg, James

Kincaid, James
- *Child-Loving: The Erotic Child and Victorian Literature*, 75, 78, 79, 80

King of the Golden River, The (Ruskin), 92, 93, 94, 189

Kingsley, Charles, xi, xii, 15, 17, 90-91, 114, 125, 149-50, 159, 175-76, 189-90
- *Water-Babies, The*, 15, 17, 90-91, 114, 121, 127, 149-50, 159, 175-76, 189-90

Knoepflmacher, U.C., viii, xi
- "Erasing Borders: MacDonald's *At the Back of the North Wind*", 92-108
- *Ventures into Childland: Victorians, Fairy Tales, and Femininity*, xi, 92, 195

Kristeva, Julia
- "Revolutions in Poetic Language", 98, 107

Lacan, Jacques, xi, 65, 78, 83

laissez-faire economics, 15.
- See also capitalism

language, 41, 46, 57, 68, 69, 71, 72, 73, 76, 84, 97, 114, 118, 125, 128-29, 136, 137, 138, 140, 143, 147, 186, 187, 188
- of Old Diamond and Ruby, 2, 134 (*see also* horses: speaking)
- "rough", 11, 120

law, xii, 1, 24, 37, 48, 71, 74, 110, 166, 168, 177, 179, 184, 186
- divine/moral, 90, 91, 168
- natural/physical, 24, 56, 115-16, 149, 150, 177
- of the Father, 64, 66, 68-69, 77, 78 (*see also* Lacan, Jacques)

Law, William, 24

Lear, Edward, vi

Leibnitz, Gottfried, 16

Lewis, C. S., vi, xii, xiv, 1, 27, 32, 53, 56, 63, 80
- *Allegory of Love, The*, vi, xiv, 61
- *George MacDonald: An Anthology*, 85, 89

liberalism, 82, 83, 85

"Light Princess, The" (MacDonald), vii, 54, 92, 93, 100-104, 148, 152

Lilith (MacDonald), vii, 1, 20, 31, 50, 51, 52, 59, 60, 61, 83, 85, 89, 148, 150, 152, 159, 169

linguistics. *See* language

"Little Boy Blue", 58, 99, 161, 173

"Little Daylight" (MacDonald), vi, 11-12, 22, 57, 87, 99, 101-102, 104-105, 148, 153, 156, 161, 169-70, 173

Little Diamond. *See* Diamond

"Little Lady and the Goblin Prince, The". *See The Princess and the Goblin*

"Little Red Riding Hood", 54

London, vi, 1, 3, 4, 6, 7, 15, 21, 22, 36, 41, 43, 49, 55, 68, 69, 90, 96, 99, 111, 113, 115-17, 125-26, 148, 149, 154, 155, 156, 158, 159, 161, 162, 165, 167, 172, 175, 181, 182, 184
- flight of Diamond and North Wind over, 7, 21, 56, 114, 117, 155, 159

love, vii, 9, 10, 22, 29-30, 33, 36-38, 42, 44, 55, 65-68, 71, 75-77, 79, 117, 124, 138, 139, 151-53, 155, 159, 163, 165-67, 170, 180, 185, 187, 188, 189

INDEX

God's and of God, xi, 33, 36, 64, 66-67, 75, 139, 153, 165-66, 168
romantic, 22-23, 101-104, 135, 145-46
Luke, Saint, 83, 84, 85
MacDonald, George, v-xiv, 1-5, 6-14, 15-19, 20-25, 26-32, 33-40, 41-50, 52-60, 63-79, 82-88, 90-91, 92-106, 107, 109-124, 125, 128-32, 134-43, 144, 145, 147, 148-66, 168-72, 173, 175-90
    childhood and life of, 30, 39, 44, 48, 65, 105, 141, 184
    theology of xii, ix, 15-17, 20, 33-38, 41, 49, 52, 54, 59, 64, 65-67, 72, 77, 82-83, 84, 87, 91,150-53, 156-60, 165-66, 171-72 (*see also* Calvinism; Christianity; God)
    works of (*see specific titles*)
MacDonald, Greville (son of George), vii, 28, 31, 52, 53, 55, 75, 78
    George MacDonald and His Wife, xiv, 24, 25, 52, 61, 193
    Reminiscences of a Specialist, 65, 80
MacDonald, Louisa (wife of George), 13, 39, 91
MacDonald, Maurice (son of George), 39
MacDonald, Ronald (son of George), 28
    From a Northern Window, 193
MacLeod, Norman, 28. See also *Good Words for the Young*
Macmillan, Hugh
    "Lump of Coal, A", 122-23, 127
Makman, Lisa Hermine
    "Child's Work is Child's Play: The Value of George MacDonald's Diamond", xi, 109-27
Malcolm (MacDonald), 26, 47

Manlove, Colin, xii, 83
    "MacDonald and Kingsley: A Victorian Contrast", 83, 89, 174
    "Reading of *At the Back of the North Wind*, A", 148-74
Marcus, Steven
    The Other Victorians: A Study of Sexuality and Pornography in Mid-Nineteenth-Century England, 80
Martha (mother of Diamond), 1, 6, 8, 10, 29, 34, 39, 57, 84, 93, 95-99, 106, 112, 113, 116, 119, 136, 138-40, 142, 146, 151, 157, 158, 166, 173, 184, 187
Marquis of Lossie, The (MacDonald), 4
Marvell, Andrew
    "The Garden", 163
masculinity, 64, 77, 88, 188. *See also* femininity; gender
masochism, xi, 64, 66, 74, 75, 77, 78. *See also* sadism; von Sacher-Masoch, Leopold
Matthew, Saint, 84
maturation, ix, 4, 22, 33, 36, 92, 94
Mayhew, Henry
    London Labour and the London Poor, 115, 127
McGillis, Roderick, xi, 39, 57, 74, 78, 128, 136, 138-40, 144, 146
    For the Childlike: George MacDonald's Fantasies for Children, v, xiv, 33, 41, 194
    George MacDonald: Literary Heritage and Heirs, v, xiv
    "Language and Secret Knowledge in *At the Back of the North Wind*", 39, 61, 80, 128, 135, 146, 195
    "Outworn Liberal Humanism: George MacDonald and 'The Right Relation to the Whole'",

82-89
McKendrick, Neil
  Birth of a Consumer Society: The Commercialization of Eighteenth Century England, The, 125, 127
metafiction, xi, 52-55, 58-59, 60, 196
metaphysics, 24, 48, 74, 77, 82-84, 171
Milbank, Alison, xi
  Dante and the Victorians, xi, 90, 195
  "Imagining the Afterlife: The Fantasies of Charles Kingsley and George MacDonald", 90-91
Mill, John Stuart, vii
Miller, Alice
  For Your Own Good: Hidden Cruelty in Child-Rearing and the Roots of Violence, 78, 80
Mills, Lauren A. (illustrations by) xv, 19, 51, 192, 214
mining
  for coal, 110, 123
  for stars (*see* dream: Diamond's)
Montessori, Maria
  Absorbent Mind, The, 123, 124, 127
moon, the, 11, 21, 42, 93, 100, 106, 168
  effect on Little Daylight, 12, 22, 102-103, 161, 169 (*see also* "Little Daylight")
  -lady (*see* dream: Nanny's)
morality, xi, xii, 3, 48, 52, 54, 59, 65, 71, 91, 110, 111, 113, 114, 115, 116-17, 118, 121, 122, 124, 149, 159, 160, 169, 175, 176, 181, 184, 190
  Diamond's, vi, 22, 112, 117, 126, 176
  MacDonald's, xii, 3, 30, 48, 49, 118, 175, 176, 181, 184, 190
Mound, The, 1, 34, 36, 37, 105, 119, 120, 167, 168, 173

Murray, E. R.
  "On Kindergarten Games", 111, 127
Murray Smith, George, 53
music, 8, 21, 23, 43, 46, 67, 71, 83, 97, 98, 103, 116, 118, 154, 156, 159, 170, 171, 173, 177, 187-88. *See also* Aeolian harp; baby: Diamond's songs for; ballad
mythology, 58, 84, 100, 113, 118, 128, 130, 140
  biblical, 34, 129, 136, 143 (*see also* Bible, the)
  Greek, xii, 128-30, 133-36, 140, 142-43, 144, 145, 146, 147 (*see also* Boreas; Herodotus; Hyperboreans)
  MacDonald's, x, 9, 122
  mythic grandmother (*see* grandmother figure)
  nature-myth, 12
  Roman, 143
Nanny, vi, xi, 1, 6, 7, 10, 11-12, 29, 34, 41, 56, 69, 72, 76, 77, 79, 88, 94, 96, 99-102, 104, 105-106, 110, 115-16, 117, 119, 123, 132, 151, 154, 156, 159-60, 161, 162, 163, 164, 165, 167, 168, 170, 171, 172, 182, 189
Nanny's dream. *See* dream: Nanny's
nature, 20, 23, 24, 28, 46, 57, 65, 118, 120, 146, 150, 154, 157, 159, 166, 178-80, 187-88
  laws of (*see* law: natural/physical)
  myth, 12
nests, 173, 187-88
  Diamond's nest in beech tree, 7, 9, 37, 73, 163, 167, 168
  Diamond's nest in North Wind's hair, 7, 21, 36, 37, 114, 131, 181, 182
  Diamond's nest in tower, 37

Index

New Testament, the. *See* Bible, the
Nicodemus, 83-84. *See also* apostles
Nietzsche, Friedrich, 63
nonsense, vi, 34, 56-57, 59, 60, 97-98, 101, 175, 187, 190
North Wind, vi, xii, 1, 6, 7, 8, 10, 23, 33-38, 39, 56, 57, 66, 67, 68, 69, 70, 72, 83, 85, 86, 87, 88, 90, 94, 95, 97, 99, 103, 105, 106, 116, 117, 118, 119, 125, 131, 133, 134, 136, 137, 138, 139, 141, 142, 148, 149, 150, 154, 156, 157, 164, 165, 166, 167, 168, 170, 172, 173, 177, 179, 184, 185, 186
 changing shape of, 1, 46, 57, 84, 162, 181
 changing size of, 7, 8, 56, 57, 94, 126, 162, 165, 180
 country/land at the back of, v, vi, ix, xi, xiii, 1, 7-8, 9, 15, 16, 21-22, 23, 33, 34, 38, 41-43, 55, 56, 57, 58, 59, 67, 68, 71, 73, 74, 77, 79, 83, 90, 95, 96, 98, 100, 110, 111, 112, 113, 114, 116, 117, 118, 119, 121, 125, 130, 132, 143, 145, 149, 150, 152, 154, 155, 157, 158, 160, 163, 168, 171, 173, 177, 180, 181-82, 184, 185-86, 187, 188, 189, 190 (*see also* Diamond: death of; Durante; Herodotus; Hyperboreans; Hogg, James; Kilmeny)
 hair of, 7, 8, 36, 37, 131, 132, 144, 157, 162, 166, 181, 184 (*see also* nest: Diamond's nest in North Wind's hair)
 as mother figure, 9, 28, 64, 66, 67, 74, 84, 93, 94, 105, 112, 113, 138-40, 141, 146, 147, 162
 names of, 9, 15, 28, 35
 reality of, 6, 68, 106, 112, 151-52, 153, 159-60, 161, 162, 164, 168, 169, 179
 relationship with Diamond, xii, 33, 111, 130, 151-52, 155, 157, 162, 163, 165, 177, 180, 181, 182-83, 184, 185
 symbolism of, 21, 28, 29, 30, 33, 41, 64, 66, 90, 111, 112, 118, 130-32, 146, 158-59, 164, 172, 177-78, 179, 181, 182, 185 (*see also* death: North Wind as symbol of)
 work of, 8, 9, 16, 21, 28, 29, 64, 66, 67, 68, 70-71, 73, 87, 90, 117, 119, 149, 155, 158-59, 160, 161, 165, 168, 181, 182 (*see also* baby: under care of drunken nursemaid; shipwreck)
 See also *At the Back of the North Wind*; Boreas
North Wind: A Journal of George MacDonald Studies, 195, 196, 197
Notes and Queries, 1, 195
noumenal, the, vii
Novalis, 59, 154, 173
nursery rhymes, 30, 37, 57, 58, 97, 156, 161. *See also specific titles*
Old Diamond, 1-5, 6, 8, 15, 33, 35-36, 68, 72, 87, 110, 118, 130-36, 138-41, 144, 145, 147, 153-55, 156, 157, 161, 164, 178-79164, 178, 179. *See also* horses
Old Sal, 10, 15, 102, 115, 158, 161, 164, 167, 182, 189
Old Testament. *See* Bible, the
Page, H. A., viii, xiv
parody, 53, 54, 60, 87
Parsons, Coleman, x, 195
 "Progenitors of Black Beauty in Humanitarian Literature, The", 1-5
Paul Faber, Surgeon (MacDonald), 45, 51

Pennington, John
 "Alice at the Back of the North Wind, Or the Metafictions of Lewis Carroll and George MacDonald", xi, 52-62, 195
Perrault, Charles, 54
Peter, Saint, 83, 84
Peter Pan. See Barrie, Sir James: *Peter and Wendy*
Phantastes (MacDonald), vii, 1, 6, 9, 22, 28, 52, 53, 59, 60, 61, 148, 152, 154, 169, 170, 173, 174
phenomenal, the, vii
philanthropy, 68, 69, 72, 101, 189,
philosophy, xii, 64, 78, 150, 173, 175, 183, 186. *See also specific names*; Platonism
"Photogen and Nycteris". *See* "History of Photogen and Nycteris: A Day and Night Mährchen, The"
Platonism, x, 23, 43, 54, 91, 168, 171
poetry, viii, 41, 42, 44, 45, 46, 48, 49, 60, 72, 74, 97-99, 120, 128, 136, 137-38, 143, 153, 168, 169, 172, 177, 187-88
 boat/poet discussion, 97, 137-38, 153, 165, 166
 Diamond's, 7, 56-57, 140, 177
 MacDonald's, vi, vii, viii, 43, 44, 46, 48, 52, 54, 57, 60, 91, 143, 148, 153, 156, 161, 166, 172, 177, 187-88
 North Wind as inspiration for, 28, 74, 188
 See also specific titles and authors; ballad; nursery rhymes; Raymond, Mr.
pornography, 75
Portent, The (MacDonald), 20
positivism, 53-54
post-colonial studies, xii. *See also* colonization
Postman, Neil
 Disappearance of Childhood, The, 126
Potter, Beatrix, 114
poverty, 11, 16, 22, 28, 57, 69, 106, 156, 158, 172, 176, 177, 190. *See also* social class
Powell family, 13
Princess and Curdie, The (MacDonald), vii, 30, 38, 40, 42, 46, 47, 50, 54, 63, 144, 148, 152, 159
Princess and the Goblin, The (MacDonald), vii, 15, 28, 30, 42, 46, 47, 57, 63, 72, 86, 105, 128, 144, 148, 152, 159
prophecy, xi, 33-38, 39
psychoanalysis, 64, 78, 84, . *See also* Freud, Sigmund; Lacan, Jacques
punishment, xi, 33, 64, 65-66, 67, 71, 74-76, 77, 117, 149, 167
Raeper, William, xi, 52, 72, 135, 173
 "Diamond and Kilmeny: MacDonald, Hogg, and the Scottish Folk Tradition", 41-51, 196
 George MacDonald, 61, 80, 174, 193
 Gold Thread: Essays on George MacDonald, The, v, xiv, 89, 145, 174, 194
Ranald Bannerman's Boyhood (MacDonald), 26, 27, 28, 30, 46, 63
"Rapunzel", 54
Raymond, Mr., 1, 2, 6, 7, 8, 10, 11, 12, 22, 29, 34, 36, 56, 68, 69, 70, 71, 72, 73, 76, 77, 86, 87, 94, 99, 101, 102, 103, 104-105, 106, 117, 118, 119, 120, 126, 149, 156, 158, 160, 165, 167, 168, 169, 173, 188, 189
 as stand-in for MacDonald, 57, 64, 72, 76, 86
realism, vi-vii, viii, ix, x, xii, 6, 10, 12,

15, 16, 21, 22, 26, 30, 48, 53-54, 55, 56, 59, 64, 65, 68, 77, 113, 114, 149, 153, 156, 158, 161, 168, 171, 172, 175-90. See also *At the Back of the North Wind*: genre of; fiction; North Wind: reality of
Reformation, the, 47, 48
Reis, Richard, x
   George MacDonald, 24, 25, 37, 40, 193
   George MacDonald's Fiction: A Twentieth-Century View, 15
   "Imaginative Fiction, The", 15-19
religion, 45, 47, 48, 54, 59, 63, 151. *See also* Calvinism; Christianity; God (Christian); goddess; gods; MacDonald, George: theology of
Ricks, Christopher
   New Oxford Book of Victorian Verse, The, 60, 61
riddles, 70, 71, 84
Robb, David, x-xi, xii
   "Fiction for the Child", 26-32
   George MacDonald, 50, 51, 193
*Robert Falcon*er (MacDonald), 26, 63, 149
Romanticism, 24, 42, 43, 44, 45-46, 48, 49, 87, 120, 180, 188
Rose, Jacqueline, viii, 32, 65, 78, 79
   Case of Peter Pan, or The Impossibility of Children's Fiction, The, 27, 32, 81
Rossetti, Christina, 179
   "Who has seen the wind?", 179
Ruby, 1, 2, 4, 7, 8, 35-36, 69-70, 87, 134, 145, 156, 158, 161, 162, 164, 167, 173. *See also* horses
Ruskin, John, 93, 94, 101, 105, 189
   King of the Golden River, The, 92, 93, 94, 189

sacrament, x, 20-21, 23
sadism, xi, 64, 68, 69-70, 76, 77. *See also* masochism; von Sacher-Masoch, Leopold
Sadler, Glenn Edward
   At the Back of the North Wind: George MacDonald, a Centennial Appreciation", 196
   Expression of Character: The Letters of George MacDonald, An, 87, 89, 147, 193
saints, 47, 84. *See also specific names*; apostles; Diamond: as saint
Sandwich, 29, 154, 173, 184
Scholes, Robert
   Fabulation and Metafiction, 53, 61
Scotland, 8, 42, 44, 45, 47, 48, 65, 136. *See also* Aberdeenshire; Huntly; Scottish literature
Scott, Sir Walter, 44
   Border Minstrelsy, 44
Scottish literature, xi, 4, 8, 26, 41-49, 50, 135. *See also specific titles and authors*
Selby, Thomas Gunn, 66
sentimentality, ix, 7, 12, 56, 58, 66, 68, 95, 103, 121
Sewell, Anna, x, 1-5
   Black Beauty, x, 1-5
sexuality, xii, 65, 66, 76, 79, 91, 93, 94, 100, 101, 112. *See also* eroticism
"Shadows, The" (MacDonald), vii, 8, 13
Shelley, Percy Bysshe, 84, 89
   Prometheus Unbound, 84
Sherwood, Mary Martha
   History of the Fairchild Family, The, 65, 81
shipwreck, 6, 7, 9, 16, 21, 28, 29, 67, 68, 83, 87, 90, 117, 149, 159, 160, 161, 165, 166, 168, 181, 182. *See*

also North Wind: work of
Sidney, Sir Philip, 49
Sir Gibbie (MacDonald), 15, 46
"Sketch of Individual Development" (MacDonald), 95, 107
"Sleeping Beauty", 54, 87, 104. *See also* "Little Daylight"
Smith, Lesley
  "Old Wine in New Bottles: Aspects of Prophecy in George MacDonald's *At the Back of the North Wind*", xi, 33-40, 128-30, 141, 147, 196
Smout, T.C.
  History of the Scottish People 1560-1830, A, 47, 51
social activism/criticism, vi, ix, 15, 30, 53, 76, 82, 84, 94, 99, 113, 115, 117, 121
social class, viii, 11, 15, 41, 68, 69, 70, 73, 76, 79, 94, 101, 102, 109, 110, 121, 163, 167, 175, 176, 184, 188, 189, 190. *See also* poverty
socialism, 79, 111
social problem novel, xii, 11, 175
Soto, Fernando J.
  "Two-World Consciousness of North Wind: Unity and Dichotomy in MacDonald's Fairy Tale, The", xi-xii, 128-47, 197
Southey, Robert, 61
  "Cataract of Lodore", 60
South Wind, the, 7
Spencer, Herbert
  "Comparative Psychology of Man, The", 115-16, 126, 127
Stevenson, Lionel, 1
Stevenson, Robert Louis
  Treasure Island, 27
street-sweeper. *See* crossing-sweeper
Stonecrop, John, 1, 35, 140, 141

Swedenborg, Emanuel, 24, 50
  Heaven and Hell, 24
symbolism, 20-21, 22, 34, 69, 71, 72,\ 97, 116, 122, 124
  alchemical, 158, 170, 172, 173
  algebraic, 24
  French, 24
  MacDonald's, vi, 9, 17, 24, 26, 30, 53, 149, 161, 163, 168, 169, 170, 189 (*see also* North Wind: symbolism of)
  mythic, 130
  Symbolic Order, 64, 65, 71, 73, 78. *See also* Lacan, Jacques
Tam Lin, 46. *See also* ballad
Thackeray, William Makepeace, 101, 104
  Rose and the Ring, The, 92
There and Back (MacDonald), 74, 80
Thomas, Saint, 84
"Thomas the Rhymer", 44, 47. *See also* ballad
Thomas Wingfold, Curate (MacDonald), 20-21, 24
Through the Looking-Glass (Carroll), vi, vii, xi, 6, 52-60, 97-98, 187, 192
Tolkien, J. R. R.
  "On Fairy-Stories", 58, 62
toys, xi, 109-11, 118-19, 120, 126, 137
toy shop, 6, 7, 118-19, 138, 184
Triggs, Kathy
  Stars and the Stillness: A Portrait of George MacDonald, The, 39, 193
Twain, Mark (Samuel Langhorne Clemens), vii, 55
Unspoken Sermons (MacDonald), 85, 89, 150-152, 156, 157, 165, 166, 168, 171, 174
victimization, 4, 21, 28, 33, 74, 75, 76, 77, 96, 117
Victorian era, xi, xii, 6, 11, 41, 49, 52,

Index

78, 79, 82, 94, 96, 101, 102, 113, 115, 120, 123, 137, 143, 148, 149, 154, 156, 158, 170, 175, 177, 179, 189
   literature of, v, vi, viii, ix, xii, 26, 41, 48, 52, 55, 58, 59, 68, 101, 102, 112, 121, 135 (*see also* specific titles and authors*)
   See also childhood: Victorian attitude toward
vivisection, 52
Voltaire (François-Marie Arouet)
   Candide, 16
von Krafft-Ebing, Richard, 78
von Sacher-Masoch, Leopold, 66, 78
   Sacher-Masoch, 80
   Venus in Furs, 78
   See also masochism; sadism
voyeurism, 76, 103, 105
Water-Babies, The (Kingsley), 15, 17, 90-91, 114, 121, 127, 149-50, 159, 175-76, 189-90
Waugh, Patricia
   Metafiction, 53, 55, 58, 61
Webb, Jean, xii
   Noble Unrest, A, v, 194
   "Realism, Fantasy, and a Critique of Nineteenth Century Society in George MacDonald's *At the Back of the North Wind*", 175-92, 197
Wilderness, The, 1, 33, 37, 130, 158
Willard, Nancy
   "Goddess in the Belfry: Grandmothers and Wise Women in George MacDonald's Books for Children, The", 78, 81, 128
   Wise Woman, or The Lost Princess: A Double Story, The (MacDonald), vii, 54, 152, 159
witches, 44, 47-48, 148
Within and Without (MacDonald), 43, 44
Wolff, Robert Lee, ix, x, 63, 64, 66, 68, 74, 78
   "Fancy and Imagination", 6-14
   Golden Key: A Study of the Fiction of George MacDonald, The, x, 6, 18, 39, 40, 81, 193
Wood, Naomi J., xi
   "Suffer the Children: The Problem of the Loving Father in *At the Back of the North Wind*", 63-81, 197
Wordsworth, William, vii, 45, 48, 60, 120, 158
   "Ode: Intimations of Immortality", 120
   Prelude, The, vii, xiv
   "Resolution and independence", 60
Young Diamond. See Diamond
Zelizer, Viviana
   Pricing the Priceless Child: The Changing Social Value of Children, 109, 127
Zipes, Jack, 66
   Fairy Tales and the Art of Subversion, 54, 62, 81

Behind the Back of the North Wind

Diamond got out the nose-bag again. Old Diamond should have his feed out now.

"Yes, he's a friend o' mine. One o' the best I ever had. It's a pity he ain't a friend 'o yourn. You'd be better for it, but it ain't no fault of hisn."

Illustration by Lauren A. Mills (© 1988)

About the Editors

John Pennington is a Professor of English at St. Norbert College, DePere, Wisconsin, where he teaches classes on the Victorian Fairy Tale, Science Fiction and Fantasy, and Charles Dickens. He is co-editor (with Fernando Soto) of *North Wind: A Journal of George MacDonald Studies* and co-editor (with Roderick McGillis) of MacDonald's *At the Back of the North Wind* (Broadview Press). He has also published on—besides MacDonald—Arthur Conan Doyle, J. M. Barrie, Beatrix Potter, Philip Pullman, J. K. Rowling, Richard Adams, and Ursula K. LeGuin. He is currently the director of the St. Norbert Collaborative: Center for Undergraduate Research.

Roderick McGillis is a professor of English (retired from the University of Calgary). His work on George MacDonald includes the two volumes of essays, *For the Childlike* (1992) and *George MacDonald: Literary Heritage and Heirs* (2007), and with John Pennington, a scholarly edition of *At the Back of the North Wind* (2011). Among awards he has received the Anne Devereux Jordan Award for distinguished service to Children's Literature studies and the Distinguished Scholarship Award of the Association for the Fantastic in the Arts.

Other Books of Interest

C. S. Lewis

C. S. Lewis: Views From Wake Forest - Essays on C. S. Lewis
Michael Travers, editor

Contains sixteen scholarly presentations from the international C. S. Lewis convention in Wake Forest, NC. Walter Hooper shares his important essay "Editing C. S. Lewis," a chronicle of publishing decisions after Lewis' death in 1963.

"*Scholars from a variety of disciplines address a wide range of issues. The happy result is a fresh and expansive view of an author who well deserves this kind of thoughtful attention.*"
Diana Pavlac Glyer, author of *The Company They Keep*

The Hidden Story of Narnia:
A Book-By-Book Guide to Lewis' Spiritual Themes
Will Vaus

A book of insightful commentary equally suited for teens or adults – Will Vaus points out connections between the *Narnia* books and spiritual/biblical themes, as well as between ideas in the *Narnia* books and C. S. Lewis' other books. Learn what Lewis himself said about the overarching and unifying thematic structure of the Narnia books. That is what this book explores; what C. S. Lewis called "the hidden story" of Narnia. Each chapter includes questions for individual use or small group discussion.

Why I Believe in Narnia:
33 Reviews and Essays on the Life and Work of C. S. Lewis
James Como

Chapters range from reviews of critical books, documentaries and movies to evaluations of Lewis' books to biographical analysis.
"*A valuable, wide-ranging collection of essays by one of the best informed and most accute commentators on Lewis' work and ideas.*"
Peter Schakel, author of *Imagination & the Arts in C.S. Lewis*

C. S. Lewis Goes to Heaven: A Reader's Guide to The Great Divorce
David G. Clark

This is the first book devoted solely to this often neglected book and the first to reveal several important secrets Lewis concealed within the story. Lewis felt his imaginary trip to Hell and Heaven was far better than his book *The Screwtape Letters*, which has become a classic. Clark is an ordained minister who has taught courses on Lewis for more than 30 years and is a New Testament and Greek scholar with a Doctor of Philosophy degree in Biblical Studies from the University of Notre Dame. Readers will discover the many literary and biblical influences Lewis utilized in writing his brilliant novel.

C. S. Lewis & Philosophy as a Way of Life: His Philosophical Thoughts
Adam Barkman

C. S. Lewis is rarely thought of as a "philosopher" per se despite having both studied and taught philosophy for several years at Oxford. Lewis's long journey to Christianity was essentially philosophical – passing through seven different stages. This 624 page book is an invaluable reference for C. S. Lewis scholars and fans alike

C. S. Lewis: His Literary Achievement
Colin Manlove

"*This is a positively brilliant book, written with splendor, elegance, profundity and evidencing an enormous amount of learning. This is probably not a book to give a first-time reader of Lewis. But for those who are more broadly read in the Lewis corpus this book is an absolute gold mine of information. The author gives us a magnificent overview of Lewis' many writings, tracing for us thoughts and ideas which recur throughout, and at the same time telling us how each book differs from the others. I think it is not extravagant to call C. S. Lewis: His Literary Achievement a tour de force.*"

Robert Merchant, *St. Austin Review*, Book Review Editor

Mythopoeic Narnia: Memory, Metaphore, and Metamorphoses in C. S. Lewis's The Chronicles of Narnia
Salwa Khoddam

Dr. Khoddam, the founder of the C. S. Lewis and Inklings Society (2004), has been teaching university courses using Lewis' books for over 25 years. Her book offers a fresh approach to the *Narnia* books based on an inquiry into Lewis' readings and use of classical and Christian symbols. She explores the literary and intellectual contexts of these stories, the traditional myths and motifs, and places them in the company of the greatest Christian mythopoeic works of Western Literature. In Lewis' imagination, memory and metaphor interact to advance his purpose – a Christian metamorphosis. *Mythopoeic Narnia* helps to open the door for readers into the magical world of the Western imagination.

Speaking of Jack: A C. S. Lewis Discussion Guide
Will Vaus

C. S. Lewis Societies have been forming around the world since the first one started in New York City in 1969. Will Vaus has started and led three groups himself. *Speaking of Jack* is the result of Vaus' experience in leading those Lewis Societies. Included here are introductions to most of Lewis' books as well as questions designed to stimulate discussion about Lewis' life and work. These materials have been "road-tested" with real groups made up of young and old, some very familiar with Lewis and some newcomers. *Speaking of Jack* may be used in an existing book discussion group, Sunday school class or small group, to start a C. S. Lewis Society, or as a guide to your own exploration of Lewis' books.

George MacDonald

Diary of an Old Soul & The White Page Poems
George MacDonald and Betty Aberlin

The first edition of George MacDonald's book of daily poems included a blank page opposite each page of poems. Readers were invited to write their own reflections on the "white page." MacDonald wrote: "Let your white page be ground, my print be seed, growing to golden ears, that faith and hope may feed." Betty Aberlin responded to MacDonald's invitation with daily poems of her own.

Betty Aberlin's close readings of George MacDonald's verses and her thoughtful responses to them speak clearly of her poetic gifts and spiritual intelligence.
    Luci Shaw, poet

George MacDonald: Literary Heritage and Heirs
Roderick McGillis, editor

This latest collection of 14 essays sets a new standard that will influence MacDonald studies for many more years. George MacDonald experts are increasingly evaluating his entire corpus within the nineteenth century context.

This comprehensive collection represents the best of contemporary scholarship on George MacDonald.
Rolland Hein, author of *George MacDonald: Victorian Mythmaker*

In the Near Loss of Everything: George MacDonald's Son in America
Dale Wayne Slusser

In the summer of 1887, George MacDonald's son Ronald, newly engaged to artist Louise Blandy, sailed from England to America to teach school. The next summer he returned to England to marry Louise and bring her back to America. On August 27, 1890, Louise died leaving him with an infant daughter. Ronald once described losing a beloved spouse as "the near loss of everything". Dale Wayne Slusser unfolds this poignant story with unpublished letters and photos that give readers a glimpse into the close-knit MacDonald family. Also included is Ronald's essay about his father, *George MacDonald: A Personal Note*, plus a selection from Ronald's 1922 fable, *The Laughing Elf*, about the necessity of both sorrow and joy in life.

A Novel Pulpit: Sermons From George MacDonald's Fiction
David L. Neuhouser

"In MacDonald's novels, the Christian teaching emerges out of the characters and story line, the narrator's comments, and inclusion of sermons given by the fictional preachers. The sermons in the novels are shorter than the ones in collections of MacDonald's sermons and so are perhaps more accessible for some. In any case, they are both stimulating and thought-provoking. This collection of sermons from ten novels serve to bring out the 'freshness and brilliance' of MacDonald's message."
    from the author's introduction

Pop Culture

To Love Another Person: A Spiritual Journey Through Les Miserables
John Morrison

The powerful story of Jean Valjean's redemption is beloved by readers and theater goers everywhere. In this companion and guide to Victor Hugo's masterpiece, author John Morrison unfolds the spiritual depth and breadth of this classic novel and broadway musical.

Through Common Things: Philosophical Reflections on Popular Culture
Adam Barkman

"Barkman presents us with an amazingly wide-ranging collection of philosophical reflections grounded in the everyday things of popular culture – past and present, eastern and western, factual and fictional. Throughout his encounters with often surprising subject-matter (the value of darkness?), he writes clearly and concisely, moving seamlessly between Aristotle and anime, Lord Buddha and Lord Voldemort.... This is an informative and entertaining book to read!"
    Doug Bloomberg, Professor of Philosophy, Institute for Christian Studies

Spotlight:
A Close-up Look at the Artistry and Meaning of Stephenie Meyer's Twilight Novels
John Granger

Stephenie Meyer's *Twilight* saga has taken the world by storm. But is there more to *Twilight* than a love story for teen girls crossed with a cheesy vampire-werewolf drama? *Spotlight* reveals the literary backdrop, themes, artistry, and meaning of the four Bella Swan adventures. *Spotlight* is the perfect gift for serious *Twilight* readers.

Virtuous Worlds: The Video Gamer's Guide to Spiritual Truth
John Stanifer

Popular titles like *Halo 3* and *The Legend of Zelda: Twilight Princess* fly off shelves at a mind-blowing rate. John Stanifer, an avid gamer, shows readers specific parallels between Christian faith and the content of their favorite games. Written with wry humor (including a heckler who frequently pokes fun at the author) this book will appeal to gamers and non-gamers alike. Those unfamiliar with video games may be pleasantly surprised to find that many elements in those "virtual worlds" also qualify them as "virtuous worlds."

Memoir

Called to Serve: Life as a Firefighter-Deacon
Deacon Anthony R. Surozenski

Called to Serve is the story of one man's dream to be a firefighter. But dreams have a way of taking detours – so Tony Soruzenski became a teacher and eventually a volunteer firefighter. And when God enters the picture, Tony is faced with a choice. Will he give up firefighting to follow another call? Afer many years, Tony's two callings are finally united – in service as a fire chaplain at Ground Zero after the 9-11 attacks and in other ways he could not have imagined. Tony is Chief Chaplain's aid for the Massachusettes Corp of Fire Chaplains and Director for the Office of the Diaconate of the Diocese of Worchester, Massachusettes.

Harry Potter

The Order of Harry Potter: The Literary Skill of the Hogwarts Epic
Colin Manlove

Colin Manlove, a popular conference speaker and author of over a dozen books, has earned an international reputation as an expert on fantasy and children's literature. His book, *From Alice to Harry Potter*, is a survey of 400 English fantasy books. In *The Order of Harry Potter*, he compares and contrasts *Harry Potter* with works by "Inklings" writers J.R.R. Tolkien, C.S. Lewis and Charles Williams; he also examines Rowling's treatment of the topic of imagination; her skill in organization and the use of language; and the book's underlying motifs and themes.

Harry Potter & Imagination: The Way Between Two Worlds
Travis Prinzi

Imaginative literature places a reader between two worlds: the story world and the world of daily life, and challenges the reader to imagine and to act for a better world. Starting with discussion of Harry Potter's more important themes, *Harry Potter & Imagination* takes readers on a journey through the transformative power of those themes for both the individual and for culture by placing Rowling's series in its literary, historical, and cultural contexts.

Repotting Harry Potter: A Professor's Guide for the Serious Re-Reader
Rowling Revisited: Return Trips to Harry, Fantastic Beasts, Quidditch, & Beedle the Bard
Dr. James W. Thomas

In *Repotting Harry Potter* and his sequel book *Rowling Revisited*, Dr. James W. Thomas points out the humor, puns, foreshadowing and literary parallels in the Potter books. In *Rowling Revisted*, readers will especially find useful three extensive appendixes – "Fantastic Beasts and the Pages Where You'll Find Them," "Quidditch Through the Pages," and "The Books in the Potter Books." Dr. Thomas makes re-reading the Potter books even more rewarding and enjoyable.

Deathly Hallows Lectures:
The Hogwarts Professor Explains Harry's Final Adventure
John Granger

In *The Deathly Hallows Lectures,* John Granger reveals the finale's brilliant details, themes, and meanings. *Harry Potter* fans will be surprised by and delighted with Granger's explanations of the three dimensions of meaning in *Deathly Hallows*. Ms. Rowling has said that alchemy sets the "parameters of magic" in the series; after reading the chapter-length explanation of *Deathly Hallows* as the final stage of the alchemical Great Work, the serious reader will understand how important literary alchemy is in understanding Rowling's artistry and accomplishment.

Hog's Head Conversations: Essays on Harry Potter
Travis Prinzi, Editor

Ten fascinating essays on Harry Potter by popular Potter writers and speakers including John Granger, James W. Thomas, Colin Manlove, and Travis Prinzi.

Poets and Poetry

Remembering Roy Campbell: The Memoirs of his Daughters, Anna and Tess
Introduction by Judith Lütge Coullie, Editor
Preface by Joseph Pearce

Anna and Teresa Campbell were the daughters of the handsome young South African poet and writer, Roy Campbell (1901-1957), and his beautiful English wife, Mary Garman. In their frank and moving memoirs, Anna and Tess recall the extraordinary, and often very difficult, lives they shared with their exceptional parents. Over 50 photos, 344 footnotes, timeline of Campbell's life, and complete index.

In the Eye of the Beholder: How to See the World Like a Romantic Poet
Louis Markos

Born out of the French Revolution and its radical faith that a nation could be shaped and altered by the dreams and visions of its people, British Romantic Poetry was founded on a belief that the objects and realities of our world, whether natural or human, are not fixed in stone but can be molded and transformed by the visionary eye of the poet. Unlike many of the books written on Romanticism, which devote many pages to the poets and few pages to their poetry, the focus here is firmly on the poems themselves. The author thereby draws the reader intimately into the life of these poems. A separate bibliographical essay is provided for readers listing accessible biographies of each poet and critical studies of their work.

The Cat on the Catamaran: A Christmas Tale
John Martin

Here is a modern-day parable of a modern-day cat with modern-day attitudes. Riverboat Dan is a "cool" cat on a perpetual vacation from responsibility. He's *The Cat on the Catamaran* – sailing down the river of life. Dan keeps his guilty conscience from interfering with his fun until he runs into trouble. But will he have the courage to believe that it's never too late to change course? (For ages 10 to adult)

"*Cat lovers and poetry lovers alike will enjoy this whimsical story about Riverboat Dan, a philosophical cat in search of meaning.*"
            Regina Doman, author of *Angel in the Water*

Fiction

The Iona Conspiracy (from The Remnant Chronicles book series)
Gary Gregg

Readers find themselves on a modern adventure through ancient Celtic myth and legend as thirteen year old Jacob uncovers his destiny within "the remnant" of the Sporrai Order. As the Iona Academy comes under the control of educational reformers and ideological scientists, Jacob finds himself on a dangerous mission to the sacred Scottish island of Iona and discovers how his life is wrapped up with the fate of the long lost cover of *The Book of Kells*. From its connections to Arthurian legend to references to real-life people, places, and historical mysteries, *Iona* is an adventure that speaks to eternal truths as well as the challenges of the modern world. A young adult novel, *Iona* can be enjoyed by the entire family.